BLIND FOCUS

Margie Vieira

Strategic Book Publishing and Rights Co.

Strategic Book Publishing and Rights Co., LLC
USA | Singapore
www.sbpra.net

For information about special discounts for bulk purchases, please
contact Strategic Book Publishing and Rights Co. Special Sales, at
bookorder@sbpra.net.

ISBN: 978-1-950015-91-7

Book Design: Suzanne Kelly

DEDICATION

For my loving husband and daughters—
your encouragement drove this story to reality.

"You always come home to family
even if it's just in your dreams."

ACKNOWLEDGEMENTS

A writer is lost without their left hand to keep their right hand in check.

A sincere thank you goes to my editor, J. Richard Jacobs. He kept me from falling off the tight rope.

Thank you, Richard Jones, for putting up with my craziness. Your insight hit the bull's eye.

June Fern, you are the earthbound angel that helped me see what Blind Focus could truly be, thank you.

Thank you SBPRA for working with me and guiding my dream to reality.

CHAPTER 1

THE PAST CATCHES UP

Run! Don't look back. You'll find a way to protect them.

I slumped against the ancient Oak tree and slid down the trunk. I thought ten minutes to catch my breath would do, but the mid-night chill intensified my exhaustion, smothering the last of my reserves. Too tired to go any farther, my mind drifted, and replayed the memory of the last twenty four hours.

* * *

My childish naivety blinded me to Theodore's misconstrued notion of love. I shouldn't have trusted him. The evening I disappeared was going to be our three year anniversary dinner. The table was set. I lit the candles and dimmed the lights. The only thing missing was a bottle of wine. I knew Theodore would enjoy a glass so I descended the stairs and stood in the damp corridor leading to the cellar and storage room. The door hung open, a sure sign to hightail out of there, but no, Mariana the nosy body had to see why it was ajar. Pushing the door inward, I heard grunts and froze.

"Mariana why are you here?" Theodore hissed.

"I came down to…to get a bottle of wine."

I stared at a Hercules of a man, hunching forward with his fist raised. He had stopped in mid-swing as I entered.

Before the interrogator moved into the shadows, he leaned his head to the side revealing a full beard. He was a stranger—a wolf from another pack. I then noticed Randolph next to Theodore, leering at me.

The only light in the room hovered over another man bound to a chair. Painter's plastic surrounded his feet. Of course Theodore couldn't have his immaculate cellar blemished by anyone's DNA. The man stared at me with one eye swollen shut. I felt as if I had met him before, but couldn't be certain. Lacerations and swelling distorted his features. My stomach roiled from the stench of blood and sweat. I had seen enough. I ran. Heavy footsteps followed me up the stairs to the kitchen.

"Mariana, wait. It's not what you think." Theodore grabbed my arm and twisted me around.

"I don't need to think. Just the thought of you watching that poor man being pummeled is enough."

"No, you don't know why. Listen to me before you assume the worst."

"You promised me you weren't a part of Randolph's games. Theo, you're made up of too many lies."

I yanked my arm free and ran up to the second floor hallway. Theodore followed closely. He took hold of my arm again. I halted in mid-stride.

"Don't. Touch. Me. Go back to your lackeys." I whispered, and clenched my jaw, in hopes of not waking Allison who was on the other side of her bedroom door asleep.

"Not until you listen to what I have to say." He opened the door to my bedroom and stepped forward to enter.

I pulled my arm from his grasp and remained placid. The last thing I wanted was for Theodore to lure me into my room and convince me once again that the life I was living was perfectly innocent and his family business was legit.

"Mariana, nothing has changed. I love you and…" Theodore lowered his head.

The stress was evident, but how could I feel sorry for him, when I had repeatedly asked him to run away with me and his sister Allison. We needed to leave this life of gun marketeering and money laundering.

I shook my head and placed distance between us. "You're not the same man I met three years ago."

"Mari, *please* don't be childish. We've talked about this before. I'm chained to this place for Allison's safety and yours. Do you think I haven't thought of leaving too? If we go, Randolph will hunt us down. Mariana, you're too important to his mission."

I tightened my lips and leered. "Coward. I'm dispensable. Randolph only wants my abilities. If not me, someone else will do the job. Go on fooling yourself that Randolph cares. Theodore, by staying in *this* house, you're committing an injustice to your sister. She needs a stable foundation, a life of peace away from an environment of thugs, gunmen and conniving individuals who only see dollar signs."

Theodore's parents had died in an airplane crash off the Catalina coast. Randolph became legal guardian of the Marino heirs, until Theodore was of age to run the family's business. But, Theodore's heart was not in the gun trafficking organization. He carried the family name and the pretense while Randolph controlled the operation behind the scenes.

"Don't run, Mariana. Randolph will find you and bring you back. Your freedom will diminish even more. And…I need you here by my side."

"Mari, why are you and Theodore angry?" I jerked when Allison's voice shot out behind me.

Allison the angelical blonde placed herself between us, rubbing her sleepy eyes and then she raised her chin higher and frowned. She was only a few years younger than Theo, but her autism gave her an eternal childlike appearance.

"Allie, Theo and I are not angry. We…" *How many times must I lie to her?* "We were just disagreeing about the dinner I had made for our third year anniversary."

"Oh, why?" She innocently stared back.

Theodore flinched when I mentioned our anniversary dinner which by now was cold.

"Mariana, I'm sorry. But, please, let's talk about this. I'll explain that what you saw was justified."

"No. There will never be justification."

3

"Mari?" Allison took hold of my hand. "Please, smile. You are angry with Theo."

"Allison, all is fine. Let's go back to your room. I'd like to hear the recording of your concerto, and tomorrow you can perform it for me. What do you say?"

"All right. Theo, you come too?" Allison's hopeful eyes held his gaze.

"Not tonight, Allie, but I'll see your performance tomorrow." He ran his hand lovingly down the side of her head. "I have a few business calls to make. Mariana, I'll be back in an hour to talk."

"No need, by then I'll be asleep." I gave him the cold shoulder with the full intention of blocking my sappy emotions and memories of the two of us.

Hand in hand, Allison and I walked into her room. I glanced back as I pushed the door closed.

I heard Theodore's hushed voice, "Mariana, we will talk," as the door clicked shut.

"Mari, you love Theo?" Allison hopped back into bed.

I faced her and hoped she had not seen the sadness in my expression. I joined her. We sat shoulder to shoulder. "Yes, Allie, I love Theodore and I love you too. Sometimes, people just disagree on what dinner entree is better, you know?"

"Yes. My favorite is fettuccine with olives, smothered in ranch dressing but…" Her giggle reminded me of when I was a child. "Theo says, every time I use the ranch, I'm destroying a culinary masterpiece."

"Not possible." I nudged her gently. "You enjoy the fettuccine the way you like. Got it?"

Allison cupped her mouth and yawned. "Mari, do you mind if we listen to my concerto, tomorrow?"

"Not at all."

My best friend, Allison Marino, was a violinist. The violin in her hand was like the paint brush in Monet's. The music sang out in shimmering perfection. We hugged and I stood to leave.

As Allison lay, her face lost all strain of worry. "Mari, you're my guardian angel."

I let out a soft chuckle and walked towards the door, "And you mine, Allie. You mine."

I wish there was another way. Someday, Allison, you will be free, or is it I who needs deliverance?

Swallowing back the tears I closed the door, not knowing when I would see Allison again.

* * *

The mansion's color faded in the distance, portraying a mountain shadow against the moonlit sky. I trudged through the woods, not looking back, but listening for footsteps other than mine. I had to leave and find a way to free a brother and sister born into a life not chosen by them. Staying another day in a dark, secretive house might have placed Theodore, Allison or me on Randolph's radar. He made it clear we were a family not to be broken.

I knew how Randolph felt when it came to loyalty. It would be best if I disappeared alone. I hoped that later I'd find a way to free Theodore and Allison. My nerves had passed the point of tattered. I didn't trust myself near him. The man seemed to have extra sensory perception, or maybe I was overly superstitious? There were times when I felt the strong urge to kill him and be done with my vexation. At every opportunity, I avoided Randolph's company, except at the evening meal. All family members were expected to dine together. One would have to be out-of-town or on their death bed to not attend dinner.

Randolph started out as Theodore's father's right hand man, but eventually he invested in the business and became his partner. He had sworn to protect the family, no matter what the cost. Outsiders wouldn't be tolerated if they didn't play the Marino game. Randolph's hawk like eyes never missed a beat in a conversation's connotation. The man made my skin crawl.

* * *

Digging my boots into the sodden soil, I inhaled deeply and gazed up at the oak leaves. For a few seconds I nurtured the thought of turning back toward the mansion, pretending that all I had seen and done was acceptable and that I wasn't evil. I looked back one last time at the home where I had lived for three years. It stood majestically with its chimneys standing guard, releasing smoke into the sky. I rubbed my arms, erasing my morbid thoughts. My family's words shouted in my head, forcing me to remember how I should've listened to them.

Teeth chattering, I wrapped my arms around my body and heard the words, *"Come on Mariana, you can do this. Remember Grandmother Mary's favorite saying, 'Everything happens for a reason.'" Great now I'm giving myself pep talks.*

The reason I agreed to live with Theodore was for my family's safety, but now I needed to get out from under his strong hold. If only I had listened to my grandmother. I had lost count of the many times she said, "Mariana, you must guard yourself, because some will take advantage of your clairvoyance. Not everyone you meet needs to know about your gift."

An acorn bounced off the tip of my boot interrupting my thoughts. I drew in a long breath and stood, adjusting the duffel bag on my shoulder.

"At least, one of us will be free. I'll find a way to unchain the three of us from the underworld's manipulation and illegal dealings."

Squirrels scurried for shelter as they heard me speak out to no one.

You need to disappear. Soon they'll forget about you.

I trekked the last five miles to the interstate, thinking of the good and bad choices I'd made.

Up until now, I had played the dutiful girlfriend, smiling and guarding Theodore from danger with my gift of clairvoyance. The word was that the next Warlord who took Theodore's place would hold more power than any man should have. But I knew Theodore. He didn't desire power. His misfortune was being born to a family of gun smugglers and control hungry humans. I came to live with Professor Theodore Marino because my past dictated the only path drawn out for me. This journey could not be ignored. I had to follow it for Theodore's and my family's safety. It was *always* for the family.

I wish I had never gone to the cellar. Sometimes ignorance is best.

CHAPTER 2

SIX MONTHS LATER: SHATTERED PLANS

You are my Bell' Angelo
I'm no one's beautiful angel. Those words haunt me.
Will I ever erase them from my mind?

"Mariana, pick up the pace." Chuck sniffed as he swiped the back of his hand across his sweaty forehead.

"Yeah, okay." I blew wisps of hair from my eyes and scrubbed the counter faster.

Here I am again, cleaning, serving food, and listening to Chuck, my boss. "Mariana this, Mariana that, Mariana get your head in gear!" Geez, I think he has more air in his head than in his lungs, but the guy sure can bellow.

I finished one task and shuffled to another. On opening the mini-blinds, the eastern horizon's pink blush reflected off the Formica tables.

New day, what will you bring?

I hung the thought in my mind's back closet and scrambled behind the counter. I started to replenish the sugar canisters, thinking of all the mistakes I had made in my life.

I believed fate should be nudged once in a while—sometimes pushed in another direction, but realization struck me faster than lightning. Running from what was meant to happen usually slapped me in the face. One might have said it was a wake-up call.

Numerous conversations with my dad ended in heated disagreement. "Clairvoyance is a part of me. Why should I hide it, Dad? I don't want to wear a mask."

My father would shake his head and say, "Mariana, many will take advantage of you, if you're not discreet."

I wanted to be me—to be free. Masking my ability made me feel like a fake. Not being who I am was like riding a horse bareback and facing backwards. There was no mane to hold onto and holding the tail was not advisable. I decided to push aside my elders' advice. From my defiance, I gained a rude awakening.

The sugar canisters were topped off. I inhaled a slow breath as I tightened the last lid. The diner's grease stuck to my nostrils. I blew into a napkin, hoping to rid myself of the smell then dropped it into the garbage-can behind the counter. Already tired, I sauntered toward the mug shelf to complete another chore.

One particular thought crossed my mind frequently. I should leave this dilapidated, out-in-the-boondocks town and disappear from California altogether. But then my common sense would step in and say, "No, he'll find you if you don't keep a low profile."

"Mariana, stop your day dreamin' and get over here!"

"Okay, I'm almost done with the coffee mugs."

The bell above the front door dinged. The first customer of the day entered.

"Sir, you can take any seat you like. Someone will be with you shortly." I said.

Good thing I laid out a few menus on the tables. Where's Carrie? She's always on some disappearing act. God knows I've done her job countless times.

While I shelved the mugs, I relived the last time I saw Theodore. I believed he truly loved me. He swore he was not involved in the family business. Our relationship should have remained as *just* friends, but Theodore convinced me to give us a try. He…promised. Throughout the day Theodore's pleading words visited me. "Mariana, please, wait…"

Distracted, I grabbed my mug off the counter. Coffee splattered everywhere. *Shoot!* I rushed to mop up the coffee before Chuck gave me another tongue lashing. Deep in thought, I rubbed the counter hard until it gleamed.

Geez, wake up Mariana. Pay attention to your work.

Flustered from the long hours, I dropped the soggy towel in a tray and dried my hands on my apron. Another wisp of hair came loose from my bun. I blew it away from my face and focused on the waitress dress hanging on my hips like a curtain. I hadn't always been a size four, but staying under the radar had made my appetite dwindle.

"Mariana, customers are awaitin'." Chuck clicked his tongue.

"I'm going as fast as I can."

While I submerged into my thoughts, more customers entered. An elderly couple and another man were seated in my station.

Thank God for miracles. Carrie is actually working. She took their orders.

I reached behind me to make certain the apron bow was secure. One hectic night, while I balanced four dinner plates, the apron fell to my feet. I took a dive toward four customers. They scooted closer to the window to escape the food shower. I hadn't been so lucky.

My dress had resembled a taco salad souped-up with all the fixings. That was an evening I didn't want to repeat and couldn't afford. Chuck made certain ruined meals came out of my paycheck.

Sighing, I glanced down at my white Nikes and wiggled my aching feet.

This God-forsaken speck on Earth has been the best hiding place so far, but I need to find a better job. I can't fill out a resume. If I do, they'll run a check on my credentials. Yeah, that would be a riot. My application would read: previous employment, body guard to Theodore Marino. I'd be back in Randolph's clutches faster than I could blink.

Offbeat jobs were my only chance to keep Theodore and Randolph from finding me. Today marked six months since I left Theodore. Maybe he had stopped looking for me?

"Mariana Molasses did you hear me? You got customers waitin' on you! Move your snail feet." Chuck shouted from the serving window.

"Yes, I heard you. I'm coming."

God, I hate that man. No, I don't hate. Mom always told me hate is what should be hated, nothing else. It hurts to think about her. I miss you, Mom.

"Mariana, move! Your order's up." Chuck laid a plate of burger and fries on the window shelf.

Carrie and I collided when I turned to grab the meal. We stepped back rubbing our foreheads.

"Girl, wake up! Good thing you weren't holdin' the customer's meal. If you don't move those cement feet, you're goin' to turn into a statue." She swiped a napkin off the counter and dried her brow, then stuffed it in her pocket.

Still dazed, I watched Carrie drag her swollen ankles as she swayed her round hips side-to-side. She grabbed three stainless steel canisters from the wall shelf and held them in the air. "Chuck, these are out of sugar. I'm goin' to the pantry to refill them."

He gave her a thumbs-up and continued cooking.

I shook my head. Those canisters didn't need more sugar. I faced the customers with plate in hand and paused to survey the place. The greasy walls needed a good scrubbing, maybe even a new coat of paint, but the black and white checkered floor was in good condition.

Hmm, if this diner were mine, I'd make it the place to be.

I served the customer his meal.

"Thank you, Ma'am."

"You're welcome." I returned to my safe zone behind the counter.

Often, I asked myself what brought people to this cold, desolate corner of the world? Was it their visit to the Humboldt Redwoods or just passing by to see the diner's old charm? I had decided that this twentieth century establishment's intrigue was its laid back ambiance.

Even though Chuck's place was an out-of-the-way stop, every day, like clockwork, I'd scope it out—couldn't be too careful.

Main entrance facing south clear? Check. The north exit good to go? Check.

11

I eyed my surroundings one last time before getting back to work.

My tables were in the middle of the diner. Carrie had the window booths, facing the early morn. The elderly couple waited patiently in my serving area. Their quiet manner captivated me. His hand brushed hers. She smiled in response, and their eyes secretly speaking to one another said it all. They were happy in each other's company. They fit in with this eatery. I wondered if I'd ever find such love.

The bell above the front door jingled. A biker entered and removed his helmet, jarring me from my non-existent love life. He was definitely easy on the eyes.

"Sir, you can choose any one of those booths." I pointed with my chin. "Your waitress will take your order shortly."

He gave a small nod and slumped into a booth seat looking out toward Highway One, just beyond the parking lot.

"That's fine. No hurry here." He smiled.

I maneuvered between the tables and topped off a customer's coffee cup. The gentleman was absorbed in a one-way conversation, or so it seemed. On closer inspection, he had a wireless ear bud pierced in his ear. At first glance a person might think it was an earring. He fitted his credit card cell phone into his shirt pocket. It was amazing how far technology had advanced. The bud ran on a battery, powered by body heat. He twisted the bud slightly to the right and continued the conversation.

"Is my voice still breaking up? No? Good. Yeah, I decided to take a sabbatical. I'm somewhere in the northern region of the state. I stopped for a bite. Boy this place is older than my grandparents."

I eavesdropped for a few seconds watching him and wondering where technology would take us next. He eyed me, and spoke into thin air. "Wait a sec." He twisted his bud to the left turning the volume down. "Ma'am was there something you wanted to ask me?"

Realizing I'd been staring, I shook my head. "No, sorry. I just find your cell phone intriguing."

"Oh, yeah, this is the latest CP on the market."

12

I gave him a wide smile.

"But, you must know about this right?" He eyed me up and down. "You're about my age?"

I came to my senses. "Uh, yeah…I'm just not very techy."

I escaped his world, my world. Humans are handcuffing themselves. Technology has become a cloud hovering over their heads. Theodore and I discussed this more than once. He believes it is the age of expanding one's intellect. I say technology will be humanity's demise. The question that remains unanswered is, will technology be the path to better man's life or is it to control our lives? In my estimation the era of robots and high tech communication is more intricate than a spider's web which can entangle a human's life without their realization.

"Mariana, the food's hot *now*."

"All right, I'm *coming*."

Chuck grunted loud enough for me to hear, "Dang, that girl. If only I didn't feel sorry for her." He shook his head and turned back to the grill.

The sizzling food and the greasy fumes invaded my senses.

The gentleman was still busy on the phone when I approached the table with his burger and fries, so I set the meal down quietly and said, "Is there anything else I can get for you?" in a subdued tone. I rubbed my sweaty palms on the apron.

"No, this is fine. Thank you." He returned to his phone call.

I flexed my fingers in and out, lowered my head, and double timed back to the serving window. The finger motion had become a nervous tic, one I picked up while on the run.

The doorbell jingled again. A dark figure stood under the threshold as California's northern chill rushed in. The man bumped the door closed, hunched forward, and unzipped his leather jacket. A hoodie drowned his face in shadow, giving the effect of a faceless man.

The small hairs on the nape of my neck stood up. I grabbed another meal, delivered it to a customer and scurried to my refuge. On impulse, like a rabbit in a field full of hungry hounds, I checked the exits—just in case. It was clear if escape became necessary.

The man glared at his surroundings, accentuating a ragged scar from his left temple down to his high cheekbone. His dark hand pulled the hood back from a thick, curly head of hair.

This frigging guy is at least six four. One of his hands could easily wrap around my neck.

On cue, as if he heard my thoughts, he jerked his head my way. I swallowed and turned my back on him.

"Mariana, there's a customer waitin' to be seated." Chuck hollered.

Jeez, that big mouth never lets up.

I twisted around. "Sir, is there anyone else in your party?"

"Just me, babe." He winked.

I grabbed a menu from its holder.

The man's smile revealed more than I cared to know.

"Follow me, please." I swiveled on my tip toes and headed for the booths.

The burly stranger sat facing the biker. I set his menu on the table. He stretched out a hand. I sidestepped to the left, avoiding a pat on the rump.

"Hmm, you're a quick one." He chuckled.

"Sir, in a few minutes your waitress will take your order."

"Sounds good." He rested his thick arms on the table and scanned the menu.

"Mariana, table one's breakfast is up. Hurry now. I'm goin' to the pantry for sliced bread." Chuck shuffled out of the kitchen.

Right. He has plenty of bread on the shelf. I stocked it this morning.

Alone with the customers, I balanced the elderly couple's breakfast plates on my arms.

"Here you go. Two orders of eggs over-medium, hash browns, and wheat toast with no bacon. Would you like more coffee?" I smiled for good measure, wishing the hours would stop dragging.

"No thank you, dear." The lady's vein-wrinkled hand rested on mine as she gently squeezed. For a few seconds, I heard my heartbeat drum in my ear. My head felt as if it were under water.

14

"Dear, there's no running. Face the demons head on." Her sweet smile and hypnotic voice kept me glued beside their table.

"Excuse me, Miss, may I get some coffee please?" The biker's voice broke the trance.

"Uh, yeah, be right there." I blew curly tendrils from my eyes. Rushing to the coffee station, I thought, *great another of Carrie's customers is waiting for me to do her job.*

I wanted to tell the biker his waitress would soon be at his table, but one quick look confirmed Carrie was still in the pantry. If Chuck saw me deny a customer service, I could bet my monthly wages, he'd have me sitting on the curb by the day's end. Carrie was always disappearing, leaving me to carry her orders and mine. The girl had more breaks than a body that has fallen out of a five story building.

She is SO sleeping with Chuck. Don't know why, all he owns is this decrepit diner. They must be in the pantry together right now. Sick.

On approaching the biker's booth, he held up his mug. I poured the coffee and stole a quick peek at his forearm. An eagle tattoo, wings spread artistically, was embedded on his muscular arm. Curious, I focused on his eyes. Sound and motion ceased. His sea-blue irises drowned me in thought.

Oh my God! It's him. Those eyes...I've seen them in my visions.

"Uh, Miss? Careful now, the coffee's hot." He steadied my arm.

I nearly dropped the carafe. "Sorry, I'll get this cleaned up right away. I'm really sorry." I pulled a bar towel from my apron and sopped the brown liquid, nearly knocking over his water glass.

"Hey, now, take it easy. Relax."

The biker in his fitted jeans and T-shirt scooted to the edge of the booth. He shoved his Harness boots into the aisle and towered over me in black. He grasped my left hand while I attempted to soak up coffee for the second time today.

"Christo! You're freezing. Miss, are you all right?" He wrinkled his brow.

"I'm fine." I withdrew from his grip. "Why are you calling me Miss? I could be married."

"Nah, there's no mark on your left ring finger and your hands are tanned in comparison to your legs. I'd say you've been doing a lot of driving before you hit this place." His smile revealed deep dimples.

I took hold of the coffee pot, and squared my shoulders. I turned to leave. He hooked a finger in my bow, stopping me in my tracks. I glared over my shoulder.

"Bright Eyes, why don't you sit here for a while? I'd say you need this coffee more than I do." He applied pressure on my arm. "Come, now. I promise not to bite, not even a nibble."

I held back the urge to roll my eyes but failed to hide a grin. Somehow, this man made me feel safe. It was not logical. But, his aura soothed me.

"Sorry, I can't. I'm on the clock." I pulled away.

"Mariana, Carrie's back from her break. She'll take care of her customers." Chuck said as he dragged the back of his hand across his mouth.

From the corner of my eye, I caught Carrie tucking in her blouse and smoothing out the crease in her skirt. Chuck smiled slyly and she puckered her lips.

"You're off the hook now. Will you join me for a cup of coffee? I'm buying. That is, if you don't pour the coffee on me first." He grinned, eyebrows raised.

"Okay, one cup. I guess. Chuck, I'm taking my break now."
Chuck nodded.

I sat across from the olive skinned Mr. Dreamboat. His eyes said, 'Don't get too close' but in the same instance they expressed sincerity. I planted the coffee pot on the table corner and dropped the towel on the seat.

It feels so good to sit.

Our legs brushed under the table. I drew mine back. Heat rushed to my cheeks.

"I'm sorry."

He smiled. "I'm not. Feel free to relax. I bet you've been here for quite a few hours?"

"Yes. It was my day to open."

"Ah, I see." He extended his hand. "Well, hello, I'm Cassius Russo. Friends call me Cas."

I wiped my sweaty palm on my blouse and we shook. "Hi. You must've guessed by now I'm Mariana with Mr. Big Mouth shouting out my name every fifteen seconds."

Cassius laughed and held my hand longer than necessary. His long fingers looked as if they'd never seen a hard day's work. He noticed me studying him. I jerked as if I'd been poked with a cattle prod. Pulling away from his grip, I sat stiff against the booth seat.

"So, it's just Mariana?"

"Yes." I lowered my chin and picked at a hang nail. I hadn't had a good manicure in ages.

"Huh, no last name." He settled back. "All right, I like Bright Eyes better anyhow. So, how did you end up in this place?"

"Don't you mean in this sorry excuse for an eatery? I stopped here for a while to earn some cash." His way of asking questions soon had me relaxing and crossing my legs on the seat. Slowly the stretched rubber band of tension in my shoulders eased.

"You said stopped?"

"Yeah, I'm the kind of girl who doesn't stay in one place too long."

"Ah, I see."

There's something about this guy. He's pleasant enough, but I feel darkness and pain surrounding him. That's it! Maybe I'm meant to help him, somehow?

I let out a long breath. "Soon, I'll be on my way again."

"To where?" He slouched and squinted. His dark, five o'clock shadow lightened in color as the sun's rays highlighted his profile.

I leaned toward the window and pulled on the mini-blind strings. A metallic crash sounded on the windowsill. I straightened my back against the seat and said, "I'm off to nowhere and everywhere."

"Huh, is that so?" He repositioned his lean, tall stature in the narrow booth.

"Yes." I wondered where he was going with this conversation.

"And where do you think you'll be going next?" He rested his hands on the table.

This guy is a knock-out, but nosy.

"Let me guess." I leaned in closer and linked my hands on the table. "You're the twenty questions guy?"

"Ha! Maybe." Cassius brushed my hand as he took hold of his coffee cup.

His touch made my hand tingle. I drew my hands back. His cheeks raised behind the mug as he sipped.

I moistened my dry lips. "Let's just say, I'm a follower." I gazed into his eyes.

"What do you follow exactly?" He downed the rest of his coffee.

I studied his countenance. No doubt he had Latin blood in him. *Is he a little cocky, or is it just me?*

"More coffee?" I held the pot up.

"Don't avoid the question, Bright Eyes."

"All right, since you asked. I follow the wind current."

"Hmm. Have you followed your doctor's orders and taken your meds today?" He tightened his lips and held back a smile.

"Yeah, right. I wish a dollar fell into my hand every time someone asked me that question." I sighed. "Cassius."

"Yes, Bright Eyes."

Oh, what the heck. This guy already thinks I'm crazy, so I'll tell him what I know. Then maybe he won't be so interested in what I have to say.

"I follow the flow of time. Sometimes, I see things happen before they occur."

"Now there's a refreshing story. I thought I'd heard them all." He grinned even more.

"It's true." My voice went an octave higher.

"Really? You see the future. Huh, but here you are in this place." He waved his hands in a flourish. "Why not play the lottery?"

"My talent doesn't work that way. It's not for personal gain." I narrowed my eyes all the while feeling my cheeks turning blotchy red. It was a genetic nuisance.

"You would think a person with your ability could take a peek in the pot of knowledge and splurge once in a while."

"Okay, Mr. Slick, know-it-all kinda guy. Listen up. You laugh now. But, you see Frankenstein sitting behind me?" I jerked my thumb over my shoulder. "In thirty seconds his breakfast will be all over your lap." I crossed my arms over my chest.

Cassius raised his brows skeptically.

"You'd better move." I stood and stepped toward the counter.

"Come, now." He winked. "I know you're not a crazy chick, but that's farfetched."

I stooped forward and in a low voice said, "You know the couple who walked in with their little boy and sat in the booth behind you?"

"Yeah."

"Well, that little boy is going to drop his Hot Wheels car in the aisle. Carrie will pass by with the doom and gloom guy's breakfast. She'll step on the toy car, lose her balance and deliver his food straight into your lap." I tilted my head to the side. "It's a shame really, 'cause you look hot in those jeans."

Cassius didn't budge. I stepped back. "Nine…eight…You better move. Seven…six…five…"

He leaned into the booth seat even more and smiled. A metal click was heard followed by a feminine gasp. Cassius jumped to his feet. Carrie screamed as they collided.

"Damn!" He hissed.

Dear Lord, even his grunt is sexy.

Cassius realized the truth three seconds too late. As he jumped out of the booth the food spattered across his T-shirt. I smirked, thinking for once it had not been me.

"Carrie, I guess Mariana's clumsiness is rubbin' off on ya." Chuck's laugh rang in the diner as he withdrew his head from the serving window.

"Shoot! I just bought this top yesterday." Carrie ran behind the counter to scrape egg yolk and country beans off her blouse.

I handed Cassius a bar towel. "Maybe I don't need the meds after all." This time, I winked.

"Maybe not." He dragged out a long breath and walked off to the bathroom.

Cassius's lilt echoed in my ears as he disappeared into the corridor. Still laughing to myself, I returned to work.

"Hey, sweet thang, more coffee here. It looks as if I'll be waiting a bit longer for my meal." The dark stranger held up his mug. I searched for Carrie. She was still rubbing food off her blouse.

This bites. I'm doing her job and she gets the tips.

Carafe in hand, I drew in a deep breath and walked over to his table. While I poured the coffee, five sausage fingers wrapped around my wrist. I froze. Nausea crept up.

"Sugar, don't make a scene. I don't want to hurt you or anyone else. But, you're comin' with me. Move to the side so I can stand and we be leavin'."

"Who are you?" I whispered.

"It's not who I am, but who you are. And you must be something special if Theodore Marino has placed a fifty K bounty on you."

"Mister, you have the wrong girl. I don't know anyone by the name of Marino."

He pulled a photo from his coat pocket. "Your hair is short and you're looking down in this picture but no mistakin' them legs. It's you all right." He stuffed the picture back into his pocket.

Memories gushed forth. The photo had been taken months after I moved into Theodore's home. I was standing next to him in a summer floral dress. Just before the moment was frozen in time, Theodore whispered in my ear. "A photo will never do you justice." I recall lowering my eyes, hoping the happiness I felt would never end.

Get over it. This is now! A voice shouted in my head.

"How did you get this photo?"

"Never mind how I have it. Now, be a good girl and play nice."

"If you let me go, I'll sweeten the prize with an extra five thou."

"Ha! And you have the cash on you?"

"No, but I can put my hands on it real quick."

"Now where do you get that much dough to raise the ante?"

I shrugged a shoulder. "My waitress tips."

"Huh, right. Darlin', you're somethin' sweet to look at, but I'd be signin' my death warrant if Marino found out I had ya and then let ya go. Play it smart and don't give me any trouble." He tightened his grip on my wrist. My finger tips tingled.

"All right, let me grab my duffle bag and we'll leave."

"You travel light, baby." He licked his lips.

"Yeah, I never know when I have to pick up and go."

Just when I'm comfortable and feel as if things might go right for a change, life goes upside down.

In neon lights, the words 'too good to be true' flashed before my eyes. I thought of Mrs. Carol, the kind-hearted widow who had rented me the apartment above her garage. She had been my one true friend out here in nowhere land. I hated leaving without saying goodbye. At least the rent was paid until next month. Chuck would tell her I had skipped town. I sauntered toward the breakfast bar in a drunken reverie.

Friends, I can live without them to protect the family. Many humans wear masks and drink lies as if it were their only life-line. Get a grip, Mariana! Think! How will I get away from him? He's big but I know I can outrun him if I get a head start. Remember your training.

From the corner of my eye, I caught Cassius sauntering back from the bathroom.

"Hey, Mariana, this was an unforgettable meeting. Maybe sometime we can go on a real dinner date?" Cassius cocked his head. "What's wrong?"

"Nothing. Have a good day. Take care." I turned. He laid a hand on my shoulder. I twisted halfway toward him.

"This is for you." Cassius shoved a twenty dollar bill in my hand. I gawked.

"Did you think I'd give the tip to the skank banging your boss? Plus, she never got around to taking my order. See you, Bright Eyes." He did a half salute and left.

The grim stare from the bounty hunter told me to keep my mouth shut. I noticed the bulge under his sweater as he stood, adjusting his jacket. No doubt he was packing a gun.

Once Cassius left, I placed the carafe on the counter and crouched to pull my bag from the bottom shelf. The bounty guy came up behind me. My chance had arrived. I rammed the end of the bag that held my shoes into his groin. He doubled over. I followed up with a kick to his knee cap and ran out the door. The doom and gloom guy hit the floor, curling into the fetal position.

As I rushed to my Mini Cooper, the sweetest voice called out to me. "Hop on, Bright Eyes." Turning on my heels, I saw a Harley roll up. Cassius shoved a helmet on my head, took hold of my bag, and bungeed it to the sissy bar. "Hop on."

I glanced at my car and back at the diner entrance. The bounty hunter staggered out grunting and cursing. He started to draw his revolver from its holster. I jumped onto the Harley.

Geez, that guy is tough.

"Hang on tight." Cassius peeled out of the parking lot.

The engine's roar deadened the hunter's shouts.

I wrapped my arms around Cassius for dear life. Every few seconds, I looked back to see if we were being followed.

Fifteen minutes later, Cassius pulled to the side of the road. I had caught my breath, but the buzz in my ears continued.

I was almost captured by Mr. Doom and taken back to Theodore.

"Mariana, you can loosen the grip. Not that I don't love your arms around me, but I need to breathe."

"Why did you stop? Keep moving. He must not find me."

"Breathe, Mariana." He rested his hands on his thighs and glanced over his shoulder.

"Who is this 'he' you don't want to find you?"

"Theodore. Theodore Marino."

"Marino. The Marino?"

"Yes. You know him?"

"No, but I've heard of him. Almost everyone in this state knows of him."

"I see."

I rested my forehead on Cassius's back and wept silently. My body betrayed me and I started to shiver. Cassius dismounted. He took off his leather jacket and wrapped it over my shoulders. That's when I noticed a bulge on his left side. He too wore a holster.

"Mariana, I won't hurt you. I want to help."

"Why? You don't even know me."

"I've seen enough and I think you could use some help."

I nodded, too exhausted to say anything. I sat like a blob on the Harley listening to his explanation.

"The ape back there won't be going anywhere too soon. His ride has two flat tires."

"But, how?"

"I noticed him when he got out of his Tahoe. Couldn't help it. A guy carrying a gun has a certain kind of walk. Then I noticed how he eyed you. That was like a huge bill board. When I came to say goodbye, the fear in your eyes and your cold shoulder said something was up. "

"Oh," was my weak response.

"Now, where to, Bright Eyes?"

"Anywhere and everywhere I guess?"

He tilted his chin up and gave me a broad smile. "Do you have pants in that bag?"

"Why?"

"It would be a good idea to put them on."

I hopped off the bike and slipped the pants on under my dress. Cassius took hold of his jacket when I pulled my coat from the bag. Once I put it on, he slid back on the Harley. I joined him and linked my hands near his heart. In one smooth motion, Cassius shoved the kickstand up, revved the engine, and drove off.

Hmm, his cologne is intoxicating. A girl could get used to this.

I had spent the last six months running, not knowing where I'd end up—constantly looking over my shoulder to be sure no one was behind me. The door to escape from Theodore's life was so small and I felt as if I were ten feet tall. But, I made it this far. My mind whirled as if it were on a Merry-go-round without a stop button. Then…Cassius appeared.

He wants to help you, girl—so let him.

For the first time in months, a flicker of hope lit in my heart. Holding onto my rescuer's warm body helped me to shed a layer of anxiety

Maybe…maybe there's a way to help Allison and Theodore.

Exhausted, I closed my eyes. We rode for hours.

CHAPTER 3

CONFESSIONS

What or who led you to Theodore Marino, Bright Eyes? More to the point, who clipped your pretty, little angel wings?

Alone in thought, I sat on the porch, a brewski in hand. The wicker chair creaked as I shifted my weight. I was doing the one thing I had avoided for years—thinking of a girl I had just met. I looked up at a starry sky. It reminded me of the nights I rode with Mariana. Cruising along cliff hugging roads, with her arms wrapped around me, got me to thinking of what I had missed. The warmth from her body, her lavender lotion filling the air, and her squeals when I cut the corners sharp reminded me of how alone I am.

God, this girl overrides my common sense.

Her melodic voice had me wanting to hear more. I didn't know why. It must've been those innocent-looking hazel eyes. But really, how innocent could they be?

Cassius, don't forget her father hired you to do this job, nothing more.

I was clueless as to how this one girl made me forget who I was the first time we made eye contact. But, I knew I was hired to protect her. She had dug her talons deeply into me. If my buds knew they'd laugh and say, "You're a goner, fool." Man, was I whipped.

I could hear Drake, my right hand bro, say, "Cas, innocent eyes have dumped you in hot water more than once."

* * *

25

Late last night we arrived at The Outskirts, my mother's bed and breakfast, Mariana plopped into the kitchen chair. She folded her hands on the table and lowered her head into her arms. I followed, depositing her duffle bag near the kitchen island.

"Mariana, I'll make us some sandwiches."

"Uh, huh," she murmured.

Within three minutes, I had slapped together some roast beef on rye. I carried the sandwiches and two glasses of lemonade to the table. Back aching, I sat beside her and stretched my legs.

I need to ride shorter stretches at a time.

Drake reminded me often, "Brother, you're not a twenty-year-old bronco anymore. You can't keep ridin' hard like you do."

I laughed under my breath. Old is a word that wasn't in my vocabulary, *yet.*

"Here you go." I shook her shoulder gently. No response. She was out for the count. I told Mariana we should stop to eat and take a snooze, but she insisted we keep on riding. I set the plates on the table and stood at her side, watching her sleep.

Even when she was dead serious, her eyes smiled. I hoped that someday I'd wipe the fear from her. No one should have to harbor constant wariness.

Footsteps caught my attention. I glanced over my shoulder. My mother had stepped into the kitchen. She gasped and nearly dropped the tray she was carrying when our eyes met.

A year had passed since I last saw my mother. Her beauty had matured. Silver strands mixed in with her ebony hair added more wisdom to a woman who faces adversity head on.

Instead of asking me anything, Mom jumped into action. She set the tray on the island and said, "Follow me."

I guessed Mariana's meal would keep. I sighed knowing later I'd have to answer to my mom. She has a way of getting to the truth. I shoved the two plates into the fridge, returned to the table, and I hunched over to cradle Mariana in my arms. I lifted her and headed to the hallway where Mom waited. I followed. Holding Mariana felt right—too right.

Don't go down that road. You're a fool always getting burned.
I had to remind myself to keep it simple
Mariana moaned. She opened one eye.
"Just me, Mariana."
She linked her arms around my neck and rested her head on my shoulder.

Her warm breath against my neck sent a shiver up my spine. I clenched my jaw and continued the climb to the second floor. On the top step, I realized I had not broken a sweat and feared if Mariana lost any more weight she might not be able to keep herself upright. Her survival instincts kept her going, but how long could she keep this up?

Mom's place would be perfect for Mariana to physically and emotionally regain her strength. The Outskirts is the place for her to heal.

* * *

After leaving Mariana in one of the guest bedrooms, Mom stayed with her. I shuffled my heavy feet to my old room. I thought I would sleep for a good ten hours. Yeah, that didn't happen. I slept four hours tops. Then as sure as a siren had blared, I lay wide awake looking up at the small cracks on the ceiling. Pondering on what needed fixing around the inn wouldn't get the job done, so I dragged my sore body out of bed and dressed.

I glanced at my watch. Six o'clock stared back. I took a quick look out the window. The night sky was fading away. What I needed was a double shot of espresso. Off to the kitchen I went with the weight of not enough sleep and the mindset of how to fix Mariana's problem.

* * *

Leaning back into the kitchen chair, I stared out the bay window. The sun was rising above the pine forest that sheltered the rolling hills. The scene triggered a memory of my father.

27

He smiled down at his ten-year-old son. We hid in the damp high-grass, hunting wild turkey. I watched a grey cloud cover the sun as the fog rolled in. How did my family's life take such a wrong turn?

This one memory reminded me why I avoided love. On our last turkey hunt my father tried to explain why he had to leave. "Cas, you'll be the man of the house now," he said. I fixed my eyes on him not grasping his meaning. "Cassius, it's for the family's protection."

Those were the last words he spoke to me before we entered the kitchen. The void branded in my mother's eyes hurt me down deep. Him saying goodbye to her like that was an unforgivable act. I vowed to never inflict such pain on another human. Not an easy promise to keep.

The man who fathered me made his choice and left his wife and children secluded in this hill country. As a young boy, I only understood that my father chose the job over the family. But here I was, in the same kitchen, where he changed our lives. I knew this would be the one place Mariana could be safe.

This early morn when I laid Mariana on the bed, I thought of running away with her. This girl was different from the rest, but I couldn't say how exactly. But then I thought, better not, because her father would find us. He had been the one who told me exactly where she was. I asked him how he knew. He said, "Son, I just know. And it's time she comes home."

Shoot. More than one person is looking for her. I don't believe it's just because she's a looker.

The kitchen door swung open, grating against the tiled floor.

Reminder, check the foundation.

Bianca strolled in humming. A small gasp escaped her as she halted near me. It felt as if I had returned to my teen years and my baby sister was trying to annoy me by lingering in my personal space.

I did not acknowledge her, instead I continued to peer out the window, watching the sun rays singe the hazy morning.

She straightened her posture, never the kind of girl to admit she'd been taken by surprise. "So, what are Cassius Russo's thoughts going for these days?"

"Huh, you couldn't afford 'em, Sis." I gave her a quick look.

"Good morning, big brother." Bianca leaned in and kissed my cheek. She joined me and picked at my croissant.

"Good morning. Here, help yourself." I shoved the plate her way.

"Aw, but food tastes better when you pick at it from someone else's plate." She smirked while spreading cream-cheese on what was left of the croissant.

"You were always too lazy to get your own food."

We smiled and sat in silence until she finished eating. Bianca took hold of her napkin, wiped her mouth, and turned halfway in her seat. She then rested her elbow on the table and leaned her head in the palm of her hand.

"You look good, Cas, even with a fuzzed face. We didn't expect to see you here so soon, not after the last time."

I scratched my chin. I was too tired last night to think about shaving.

"Bianca, what happened last time was a fluke. Those hunters were drunk. I'm positive they won't remember a thing about this place or how to get here again. My buddies and I made sure of it."

"How can you be so sure?" She sat straight.

"We drove them over hills and dirt roads for two hours before we came to the main road. Plus, they were completely wasted. They were in the back seat drooling on each other's shoulders."

"Cas, I worry about you. Mom does too and—"

"Sis, you know I'm good at what I do. No more talk about this. What happened is done and gone."

"Yeah, okay. So, what brought you back here?"

"I ran into a friend that needed help and we rode in this morning."

"So what's this girl's story?" She smiled.

I shook my head. "What makes you think it's a she?"

"Dear brother of mine. I heard the Harley last night and I don't imagine you riding with a guy so…, her voice trailed off. "Fess, up what's her deal?"

29

"Good question. All I know is that she needs help." I downed the rest of my coffee.

"You don't know *yet*, but soon, you will. It's what you do. Can you at least tell me her name?" Bianca pushed away from the table and went to the stove. She poured herself a cup of coffee, then turned toward me with the pot still in her hand.

"More coffee?"

"No thanks, Sis."

Bianca returned to the table stirring her coffee.

"Her name is Mariana, so she says."

"No last name?" Steam swirled close to her nose. She blew on her coffee then sipped.

"I'm sure she has a last name, but she hasn't shared that info yet."

"Hmm, Cassius is on a mission again."

"No, just helping out a friend."

"A friend, huh, must be a real good friend. You usually take in the strays and in a day or two, you send them packing. Mom said you'd been riding for hours with this one."

"And here I thought you were a psychic or something. You and Mom have nothing better to do than talk about me?"

"Hum, out here?" She lifted her chin and peered at me. "Nope, you be the best conversation piece, big brother." Her lips brushed the cup's rim. She grinned before taking another sip.

A shriek traveled down from the second floor. We jumped to our feet and nearly collided going through the swinging door to the hallway. Bianca followed, but I left her near the bottom of the stair case, taking two steps at a time.

Mariana's bedroom door hung open. I found my mother sitting on the edge of the bed cradling her like a child. Mom's eyes tore into me. My mother is a person of few words, but when she speaks it is direct.

Standing in the doorway, I watched her do what she does best, help a person feel whole again. The tension dissipated from Mariana's shoulders as my mother shushed her and whispered, "You're safe here."

Bianca pushed me aside and sauntered into the room.

"Hello, Mariana." Bianca's words sailed across the room as if they were a song.

My sister had my mother's talent to ease a person's mind. They kept the bed and breakfast running. The end of September was not their busiest month, but soon the holidays would keep them bustling. Fortunately, at this moment, there were no other guests in the house.

Mariana followed Bianca's voice, but then her eyes met mine. Mom fluffed the pillows and leaned Mariana against the headboard.

"Bianca, I need your help vacuuming and airing out the other rooms."

"Sure, Mom." Before Bianca followed my mother, she stopped near the doorway and twisted her body, facing the bed. "Mariana, if you need anything, we're just a holler away, okay?"

Mariana nodded slowly.

Darn, her eyes have the deer caught in the headlights gaze.

My sister eyed me. I knew that look. It said, "Don't hurt this girl." She then left.

One might say I had a knack for meeting the opposite sex when they needed help. There were times when I thought I had a beacon on the top of my head which only the neediest could see. Helping others was what I did best, but holding onto a romantic relationship was the same as walking on water. The girls I dated never stuck around long enough for me to tell them how I felt. My sister once told me I was messed up, afraid to love. She just might be right.

Whatever had made Mariana scream still had a hold on her. Cheeks flushed, eyes glazed, she stared at an invisible image.

"Cassius, denying your path delays destiny's arrival, but it will happen." Mariana clasped her shaky hands in her lap.

"What'll happen, Bright Eyes?"

She rested her head in her hands and inhaled deeply. The bed creaked as I sat on the edge.

"Mariana, talk to me." I waited, clenching my fists at my side, fighting the want to hold her.

She lowered her hands and scoped her surroundings like a professional marksmen.

31

"This room is very pretty. When I awoke…" She swallowed. "I thought I was back in Theodore's mansion. Then…I saw you, Cassius. Your face expressed so much pain. You were in so much pain, Cassius…" Mariana's voice broke.

I laid my hand on hers. "Mariana, what you saw was not real. I'm fine. I'll help you anyway I can, but first you need to tell me what's wrong."

"Why do you feel the need to help me?"

"I believe in paying forward."

"Oh." She examined her hands.

"Is something wrong with your hands?"

"No." She carried the last sound longer than necessary.

She still didn't appear fully awake.

"You mentioned a dream?" I said softly, trying not to spook her.

"Yes, there are always too many of them." She brushed a hand across her arm. The red satin pajamas were the perfect backdrop for her tanned complexion. "Who undressed me?"

"My mother helped you. Do you remember?"

"Yes, I remember, but some parts are fuzzy."

"I see. Do you want to talk about what made you scream?"

Her eyes went soft. "It was just a dream. I'll have to thank your sister for the loan."

I squinted.

Does this girl ever answer a direct question?

She smiled sweetly. "The pajamas I'm wearing belong to your sister."

"Who says they are hers?"

"Cassius, if these pajamas don't belong to your sister, then to whom? They're not your mother's."

"And how do you know that?"

"Your mother is petite. These pajamas are too big for her." Mariana crinkled her brow. "There have been times when I wished I was shorter."

This girl's mind is all over the board. She's jumping from one topic to another.

"Hey, now, your height is perfect. By the way, how tall are you?" A frown of inquiry spread across her face. "I'm just asking. It was a random thought I had last night when I carried you to the bedroom."

"Oh. I'm five eight. In junior high I was teased about my height. Sorry, you had to carry me."

"I'm not. By the way, you're pretty strong to stop that guy in the diner."

She shrugged. "I learned some self-defense. Theodore made certain I knew how to protect myself." She ran her fingers over the satin. "So, these pajamas belong to a girlfriend?" Mariana pursed her lips and eyed me slyly.

"You're a nosy gal."

She grinned and scooted to her left. I drew my legs up onto the bed and stretched them. My thigh brushed hers. I felt a slight shiver run up her body as she moved her legs away.

How do I convince her not to be afraid of me?

"Bright Eyes, you're safe here. Look at me." I gently pressed two fingers under her chin and turned her head my way. "Why was that guy after you?"

"Cassius, denying your path delays destiny's arrival, but it will happen."

"You said that to me earlier, but that doesn't answer my question. I'm not denying anything. It's you that won't talk to me."

Man someone messed with this girl's head real bad.

"You're very lucky to have your mother and sister close to you. I've had twenty years to accept my mother's absence. Amelia...she was beautiful." Mariana's eyes stared straight ahead. "I remember as a little girl wishing my hair had been the same as her long golden hair. Many times I'd spread red lipstick on my lips to mimic hers." Mariana peered at me enigmatically. "Her aura left everyone around her happy."

"Her aura?" I lifted a brow. I felt as if she was not in the room with me or at least her mind was somewhere else.

"Yes, we all have an aura. Only...not everyone sees it. You don't believe me. That's expected." She lowered her eyes. Then, in a flash, her glare took hold of me. She stared me down like a bull fixed on the red mark. "Cassius, life jumps from scene to scene. Do not dwell in the past."

"Woman, you need to speak plain English." I tried not to scowl.

"I'm sorry. Thoughts bombard my mind and I have to speak them. Cassius, I *need* to leave this place. Your family shouldn't be snared by my life's web."

"Now whoa there, no one knows you're here except the four of us. And you are safe here, trust me."

"I trusted once before, it didn't go well." She rolled and unrolled the embroidered sheets in her hand.

This beauty sitting next to me was sharing her deepest pain and opening to the fears rooted in her. I almost didn't want to make her tell me what happened, but in order to help her, I needed to know.

I tapped her hand. "Bright Eyes?" She glanced up at me. "You said, 'she was'. Does that mean your mother has passed on?"

A single tear streaked her rosy cheek. Mariana nodded and squeezed her eyelids shut. She inhaled then exhaled as if the oxygen had been sucked out of the room.

"How about we talk later? Maybe you should rest some more." I started to get off the bed. She grabbed my hand.

"No. I'm not sleepy." Her eyes pleaded.

"All right." I settled back against the headboard.

"I've never told this to anyone, not even to Aunt Samantha. It's my fault mom died."

"Your fault?"

"Uh huh." She linked her fingers. "When I was five my mother was a victim of a hit gone wrong—"

"Wait. How could it be your fault at the age of five?" I shifted my body to get a better look at her.

She turned away from my confused expression and ran a finger along the embroidery. "Cassius, I will try to keep this short. But please, let me finish. Then ask me all you want."

"All right."

"My family and I had just left the Gilroy Outlets. We were walking to the parking lot. Dad had bought me a red balloon and a red mini-sports car for my brother, Francisco. Mom held my hand as Dad told my brother about the mechanics of the car. I remember looking up at my mother and telling her, ' I love red, Mommy.' She laughed and said, 'Yes, you always have. It's the one color that has always captured your attention.' And then... somehow the balloon string unraveled from my wrist. 'Mommy, my balloon!' My mother jumped, stepping in front of my Dad. Just as her fingers wrapped around the string there was a popping sound and she fell into his arms. Screams. Running. Shouting. Dad pulled me into his arms and laid me on the concrete. He knelt over my brother and me. I peeked out from under my Dad's arm." Mariana paused and focused straight ahead.

I imagined seeing my mother as she had seen hers. My chest constricted.

Mariana tightened her eyelids nearly burying her eyelashes. She reflected. "Cassius, *her eyes,* my mother's eyes, were frozen. She was gone." Mariana opened her eyes again and fixed her glare on me. "One red dot appeared on the side of her forehead as a thin line of blood ran down her temple. Like the red balloon. Cassius, I'll *never* forget that look. Years later, Francisco told me the bullet that killed our mother was meant for my father."

"Your father? How does he play into this story?"

Man. And I thought my family had problems.

"My father, John Samuel Castillo." She scoffed. "He's a big farmer in the Linden community, who helps the local police with ongoing drug investigations." Mariana released a gush of air and continued. "Marijuana was being planted in orchards and cornfields then transported to an abandoned warehouse. He and the authorities confiscated four hundred pots of cannabis. Have I mentioned that my Dad is clairvoyant?" She stole a glance my way. "They say my father's gift has destroyed a great deal of money. Obviously, someone was not happy with his actions. He's had to lay low at certain intervals in his life just to stay off the Cartel's radar."

"But what does your father's clairvoyance have to do with you?"

She inhaled as if she were taking in her very first breath. "Cassius, when a secret is revealed it leads people to believe that superman's offspring will have the same talents. And I was too stupid to listen to my family."

"How's that?" I knew I was pushing it, but at this point there was no turning back, her pain needed an outlet. I was there for her.

"I'm just stupid, Cassius, and I'm nothing like my father. I wish I was." She buried her face in her hands.

"Don't put yourself down. I'm sorry about your mother. But in no way was it your fault. C'mere." I enveloped Mariana's shivering body. She rested her head on my chest.

God, she smells good.

I held her for a while. She then raised her head. More silent tears streaked her cheeks.

"You're like my Aunt Samantha, Cassius. Anyone you touch or talk to feels safe." She sniffled and sucked in another quick breath.

"Well, I've been called bull headed and compared to some others things I'll leave unmentioned, but never to a lady."

A flicker of a smile appeared on her lips. "No you definitely are not girly. What I meant is that you remind me of my aunt. You have a way of making me feel safe as she does." Mariana placed her hand near my heart. I felt it skip a beat.

Mariana must have sensed it too. She retracted her hand.

"I don't know much about making any girl feel safe, but I'm here to help any way I can."

A soft laugh escaped her lips. "You and my aunt are also too modest. Cassius, you're both lonely too."

I swung my legs over the side of the bed. She grabbed my forearm. I glanced back at her. "I'm living my life the way I know how."

"True, but hear me out. When Aunt Samantha was engaged, her fiancée died in a car accident. After that, she never married. I asked her why. She said marriage was not for everyone. She came to live on the farm with us and step into mom's shoes. Aunt Samantha is clairvoyant too. She showed me how to be discreet with my gift and explained that only the people who need help should know of my ability. You should listen to your mother, Cassius. The past is not your fault. I should have listened to my family."

"My past is my past. Don't worry about me."

Mariana let go of my arm. Her heat lingered on my skin and triggered memories I had buried long ago.

Dang it, this girl. I need to keep my feelings in check.

"You said should have?" I asked on a long drawn out breath.

Mariana's manner hardened. One moment she was this little girl in her father's house then she sat before me cold and distant—almost as if a light had been switched off and the real Mariana was yanked into a dark room. She sat back straight, stiff, glaring at her reflection in the mirror across from the bed.

"Yes, I should've listened to Dad and Aunt Samantha, but I was naive and full of myself. When I went off to college, I felt as if the world was my playground to explore. I wanted to be me and not hide behind a mask. I didn't care if other people knew of my gift. I led a life of parties, palm readings, and just plain stupid adventures with girlfriends. One evening, during my senior year, I was walking back to my dorm when a gloved hand covered my mouth and dragged me into the bushes. His minty breath trailed down my neck. He sniffed me like a dog. I at first fought him, but then a cold blade pressed against my throat and halted my resistance. A ski mask hid his face. He raped me." Mariana paused.

I clenched my teeth, causing my jaw to ache.

I don't want to hear this, but the sooner she faces her demons the sooner they'll release their hold on her.

"Bright Eyes, I'm sorry." I dug my fingers into the palm of my hand.

Mariana dried her cheeks. Her eyes held a cold leer as she spoke. "Shivering under the bushes, I remember him, saying, 'My Bell' Angelo'. I think he had a cold because his voice was nasally. My assailant then stood. I heard him zipping his pants. With all my visions, not one warning came to me of my predicament. I don't know how long I remained hidden in the bushes. I remember a chill veiling my senses. Eventually, I dragged myself out from under the ever-green shrubbery and stood. My legs, arms and hands were caked in soil. A voice called out to me. 'Mariana, what happened to you?' I recall moving my lips, but there was no sound. Professor Theodore Marino looked me over and his eyes widened. He took hold of my hand and found my door card next to my purse. I had taken it out to unlock the door before I was attacked. Theodore collected my book bag and helped me to my dorm."

"He didn't take you to the Urgent Care?"

"Theodore wanted to, but I pleaded with him to help me to my room. I know I was not thinking straight, but I insisted. He didn't want to cause me more distress and did as I asked. Two days later, Theodore convinced me to go to the hospital, but by then all evidence had been washed away."

Slowly, an exasperated breath escaped between my teeth. "He should've taken you to the hospital, or called a nurse or doctor to your dorm to examine you. Damn him."

Mariana lowered her head. She unraveled my fingers from the grooves in my palms.

"No, don't blame Theodore."

"Why do you defend him?"

She continued to stare at my hands. "Because, Cassius, I believe that two innocent children, born into a world of corruption, gun dealing, hitmen, money laundering, and having everything at their disposal can still maintain morality and innocence to someday escape the invisible shackles." Her eyes sought my understanding. "Theodore was my guardian angel. After the assault, I couldn't concentrate on my studies. I wanted to go home. Theodore offered to drive me to my father's farm. That was one of the hardest days of my life. Looking into my Dad's eyes and telling him I'd been raped. I felt as if I had taken a dagger to his heart. I felt so dirty. Theodore showed me the way. He convinced me that it was not my fault. I lived under my Dad's roof for a year, but the guilt I felt for not heeding his warning of discretion was too much for me. Theodore invited me to live in his mansion."

A heavy sigh escaped me. Mariana paused and tilted her head.

"Don't judge me, Cassius. I had nowhere to go."

"You had your family."

"Yes, I did. But...every day seeing the pain in my father's eyes was too much. Theodore convinced me to finish my last year of college. He paid my tuition. The first year living with Theodore was bliss. He was like a big brother to me. But, life's pressures intervened. Theodore's parents died in a plane crash and he had to take over the family business. The Theodore I loved was slipping away. Life's demands turned him cold. Cassius, Theodore's family business is real estate, but I found out a year ago he's involved in other businesses. Deep down, I must've known, but I didn't want to know. I heard the noises, the bumps in the night, down in the basement. Theodore has a self-defense training room, equipped with all the necessary devices to train hitmen. These men are employed to hurt others. Like the one that killed my mother."

"The bastard. He should've never taken you to that house."

"Cassius, you know where he lives?" Mariana's soulful eyes dug into me.

"Yeah, I've heard of the place. What Marino should've done was convince you to stay home with your family. Not live with him."

"It was my choice, Cassius. Only, when I found out about Theodore's second business, I left, but within two months he found me—more like his henchmen found me. *Randolph*. Weeks later, I escaped again with only the clothes on my back. Six months I've been free from Theodore's life. I can't go back there, Cassius. Not with what I know."

"Did you confront Marino with what you saw?"

"Yes, and he told me it was all perfectly legal. His men do freelance work, some for the government. He runs a private bounty company too. But, I've seen some of his men. I've felt and seen things in their minds that have kept me awake during the night. Cassius, he must not find me again."

"Sh, don't worry. You're safe now." I smoothed Mariana's curls on her back. She calmed down. "Mariana, I promise, when I find the scum that attacked you, he will pay."

Actually, when I wrap my hands around the low-life's throat, he'll pay with his life.

"You mentioned with only the clothes on your back, how have you supported yourself? Living off restaurant tips is not much. And the Nikes and jacket you have are not cheap."

"Before I left Theodore, I transferred my monthly paychecks to a secret account under an alias name. I then cashed it when needed."

"Hmm, you're a thrifty gal. But wait. You worked for him?" I breathed in her scent.

"Yes. Let's say, I kept Theo healthy."

"How?"

"No, Cassius. There were no sexual favors. I kept his… itinerary in order."

I opened my mouth to ask what the heck she meant, but Mariana raised her head and looked up at me. Without a word, she unraveled her arms from around me, kicked the comforter aside, and slid off the bed. She stepped methodically toward the open window and stood between the shear curtains waving beside her. Her hair flowed back in the morning breeze. Sunlight streaked her bare feet. She reminded me of a fallen goddess, trying to find her way back up to the heavens. I decided not to push the subject any further since she had already cut deep into her memories of her mother and herself.

I joined her. Mariana intertwined her fingers with mine and viewed the front yard.

"Cassius, do you believe Theodore will not find me here?"

"Out here, surrounded by five thousand acres of rolling hills, there's not much to fear. Plus my mother goes by her maiden name. Anyone who tries to connect her to me won't have much luck."

"I see. And your sister as well?"

"Yes."

"But, what about the road?" She pointed. "Couldn't someone follow it to this place?"

"That graveled road leading to this house is a maze. All guests are trusted repeats and newcomers are recommended by close friends. When it's time to leave, they're shuttled back to the main road where their vehicles are parked in a commercial garage. It's the appeal of seclusion that brings the guests here. No. He will not find you."

Mariana squeezed my hand. "You have barriers. I sense your pain. You've placed strong shields, blocking your true essence. Why, Cassius?"

I lowered my chin to see her better. She did not shy away from my gaze. "Mariana, you mind explaining what the heck you're talking about?" The angel next to me beamed. Her thumb slowly rubbed the back of my hand.

"Cassius, did you forget what happened in the diner? I sense pieces of people's thoughts and sometimes see what's going to happen. The events are not always clear. You, Cassius, you…at a young age trained yourself to hide your emotions. Darkness surrounds you."

"Ahh. Now I'm beginning to understand. This is why Theodore Marino wants you back. You're a human lie detector."

"I guess you could say that. But, Theodore isn't all bad. He does have heart, but it's been buried."

My cell phone buzzed severing our link. She let go of my hand and continued to gaze out the window. I stepped back and headed toward the hallway.

I spoke in a hushed voice, "Hello, this is Cassius. Yes, I'm fine thank you. In a few days the package will arrive. These things take time. I'll call you when it's close. Thank you, good-bye." I stepped back into the room.

Mariana's curls fanned across her shoulders. She leaned her head to the side in a ghostly stance while the sunlight crowned her head. Then she turned and locked eyes with mine. Her lips curved up. I wasn't certain, but it looked as if she were happy.

"Cassius, does your father live here?"

"No, he's gone. Look, I have to take care of some details with the foreman. My family not only owns the B&B, but we also manage two thousand head of beef cattle here on these hills. I run the cattle business. My mom and sister are the masterminds of the B&B."

"What's this place called?"

"The Outskirts."

"I like that. Clever." She angled her head upward and drew her eyes to the ceiling. "But, Cassius, you haven't seen your family in over a year, why?"

"Did my mother tell you that?"

"No." Mariana lowered her eyes. A smile played across her face.

"Like I said, I run the cattle business. I'm not into playing house. I'll see you downstairs for breakfast."

Mariana stayed near the window. In a distant tone she said, "Don't fear love, Cassius."

I was about to tell her to stay the hell out of my business, well not in so many words, but something kept my mouth shut. Who was this girl? She glanced over her shoulder with a faraway look. I had seen that stare before in my mother's eyes when my father had left us.

"Did you hear me? I'll meet you for breakfast."

"Yes, that'll be fine." Mariana twined an ebony ringlet around her index finger. She had done the same thing in the diner, just before I handed her the twenty dollar bill. Something was messing with her mind.

"Mariana, you're safe here." On those words, I left.

I need to be more on the alert when it comes to Mariana. She definitely has some kind of gift. I've worked too hard for her to breakdown my barriers. Distance is probably best.

CHAPTER 4

SCORCHED MEMORIES

Cassius's probing dredged memories I had struggled to drown in the trenches of my mind, but reliving the day I was attacked gave me a sense of liberty. The memory still invaded my dreams although now, I could face it and talk about it.

Cassius, on the other hand, hid his feelings behind a barricaded wall of darkened thoughts.

He needs to admit the truth to himself. The one million dollar question is how will he do it?

I sat in bed, elbows propped on my knees, writing in my journal. I hummed a tune I heard last night on Bianca's iPod. The device was a mini robot, hovering near me, resembling a humming bird near nectar. The soft music had me dancing in my head. I felt as if I were not alone because the iPod followed my every move. I returned to my writing.

Journal Entry:

It has been months since I've felt this free or safe, although I do miss Allison. She's such an angelic being. I wonder how she's doing. I hope she hasn't locked herself in her room. I tried to figure out a way to take her with me, but her autism, and the rocking back and forth when she's out of her comfort zone would be too much to handle. Plus, I didn't want her to go through the possibility of being caught by one of Randolph's goons. That would push her into her don't touch me zone. She can go days without speaking when she travels there. Theodore, he's crossed my mind a few times too. I know he hasn't lost his good side. I see it when he's around his sister. I'll find a way to free them.

Mariana Castillo

43

I closed the journal and placed it on the night table. Sighing, I stretched out on the bed and folded my arms behind my head. My train of thought traveled to other distant memories.

Grandmother Mary, my dad's mom, passed away when I turned eight. That year taught me about loneliness. I lived in a big farm house surrounded by male figures. Frank and Dad taught me survival skills and I felt their love, but I also felt the pull from the darkness, until my Aunt Samantha came to live with us. She became my mother, grandmother and mentor. My aunt on more than one occasion told me I should bury the sad memories. She didn't say to forget them completely, but to tuck them away where I could recall them when necessary.

Often my aunt and I sat sipping our tea and she'd say, "Mariana, your heart is willing to move forward, but you must exercise the will to let go. Forgiveness is key. Also, remember, negative occurrences hold a bigger impact. The lesson taught is not forgotten."

As a little girl, those words were simple. When someone called me a freak in school, I'd smile, say thank you, and move on. Sometimes the ignoring worked. Other times, I knew if I told the bullies what was going to happen to them on the play-ground or in the cafeteria they'd leave me alone. I realized that incomprehensible fear can be beneficial. Once kids saw what I told them came to pass they left me in peace with my thoughts and books. I cherished the solitude, no one to tease me, no one to judge me.

Adversity had brought me to Cassius. Had I not been me, had I not shown the people I met who I am, and what I know, would I have reached The Outskirts?

I stretched and yawned, lingering in bed longer than I should. Six months of looking over my shoulder, before I arrived at this Inn, gave me a sense of it's okay if you pamper yourself a little. I hummed a tune I'd heard earlier on the radio. My mom loved music too and our home had been alive with it. Music always played in my head when she was with me.

Carla's and Bianca's auras surround the Outskirts with such warmth and love. My family's home was once like this place. I wish I could hide here forever. Bianca would make a great sister and her mother, well, she's just calming to the soul.

Drifting back to family thoughts, I saw Dad, who played the tough man, but his heart was in the right place. He loved to tell me, "Mariana, stop the wishing and do things cautiously." He was my biggest fan, but life's circumstances change an individual's beliefs. I felt I had lost my Dad the night I came home from college and told him what had happened to me.

Running from Theodore had kept my mind on high alert, but when I relaxed the visions manifested, insisting that I pay attention to them. I had yet to choose which was better, being exhausted to the point of no thought or relaxed which allowed the mind open passage to bridges between this world's reality and beyond death's realm.

My concentration wasn't always erratic. Friends and family more than once said, "We can count on Mariana to deal with the situation at hand and apply a solution on the spot." Count on me to see what might happen, count on me to tell them how they should perceive life, not anymore. From age twenty-two, when my attacker decided my fate was his to abuse, to my present age of twenty-five, my reality changed drastically.

Maybe I can pretend that I'm not me, maybe Carla will give me a job, maybe, just maybe, I might disappear from Theodore's radar forever.

One consistency remained. Every night, for a year, I dreamt of a man. Whom I now recognized was Cassius. I didn't realize it was him, until we met in the diner, but I knew our paths were destined to cross. The eyes in my dream pleaded for me to see the truth of how much my family truly loved me, but in turn they deepened my fears. How would I protect them?

Okay, no more moping. Go see if Carla and Bianca need help. You must do something to pay for your room and board.

I tucked the journal under my arm, and went in search of my new lady friends.

Earlier this morning, I found them in the kitchen preparing the ingredients to bake fresh bread. I offered to help, but they said the process would go faster if they did it on their own. Their system of one mixed the dough and the other kneaded it was fascinating to watch. These two women's self-sufficiency had me wanting to learn all that they knew. Funny though, they sent me to the laundry room where the linens hung drying. When the weather threatened to pour buckets of water, they were prepared. Their indoor drying room allowed the laundry to be undisturbed by the weather and save on electricity bills. After I finished folding the sheets, they said I could go relax. I caught the hint. They needed their space.

I stepped into the kitchen right when they were wiping the last remnants of flour from their hands. The marble island was spotless and all the baking trays were drying on the counter. I lifted a brow high as they smiled. A sweet smell, mixed with cinnamon had me wanting to inhale even deeper.

Mmmm. Mom used to bake every Sunday.

"Hey there, sleepy head, you have perfect timing. We're all done with the baking."

I gave Bianca a quizzical frown. She laughed.

"I'm just kidding. Don't worry your curly head. We actually finished baking the bread early and decided to bake some apple pies." She displayed a toothy grin.

Carla nodded, "And now it's time for a nap. The sitting room is warm. Cassius brought in the firewood and lit a fire. It should be cozy in there."

I glanced at my feet. *I don't feel like talking to him right now. I know he'll want more answers as to how I could leave my family.*

"Ah, don't you sweat it, Mariana. He's in the shop fixing our old tractor. He should be there a while." Bianca dried her hands on her apron.

I felt my cheeks redden. A small laugh escaped me. Bianca was fabulous at reading facial expressions. I felt as if her empathy was like no other person's I had met before.

"Okay, well thanks. You two enjoy your siesta and I'll do some reading."

"Sounds like a grand plan. Enjoy your read, Mariana." Carla folded her apron on the island and kissed my cheek. "If you need anything, don't hesitate to call."

Bianca gave me a quick hug and followed her mother.

Here at The Outskirts these women were up with dawn's light. They were made from the same cloth as pioneer women. If Bianca asked 'Mom can we do it?' Carla would say, 'Yes, let's.' If Bianca responded, 'But Mom, what if it doesn't work?' Carla would shrug and pragmatically say, 'At least we'll know what not to do next time.'

These women played the cards they had been dealt and manipulated life's game to their advantage. There was no woe is me. When the inn called for more efficient devices Bianca and Carla were the first to climb to the roof-top and install the solar panels. They cultivated their own organic garden, and milked their cow Milly for the best fresh milk. On winter days when they were closed in, they crocheted intricate throw blankets. There seemed to be no stopping these two ladies. Their motto, carved on a block of wood, hanging above the stove-top read, "Take adversity by the horns and steer it to positivity." Their 'we can handle this' attitude gave me hope.

I stood alone in the middle of the kitchen and massaged my temples. I told myself that I would find a way to be free from society's corrupted beliefs. Money, power, being on the peak of the mountain is not what life's about. My self-pep talk encouraged me to move on, not dwell on the past.

I pressed the journal close to my heart and entered the spacious sitting room. I indulged in the warmth. Reading chairs with matching round tables faced the crackling and hissing fireplace. I delved back into my thoughts and watched the flame's shadows wave back and forth on the wall. Fascinated by the flickering fire, I imagined a freed woman dancing. A long sigh escaped me. I sat down and read. A strange thought arose. I retrieved a pencil from the side table and scribbled the words in the journal.

Lies create gashes that bleed you dry. For the lucky those gashes might clot, but will leave irrevocable scars.

I was lost for what seemed like hours, until a distant noise, a scuffle or shuffle jarred me from my writing. I lifted my head.

Cassius stood in the doorway and smiled. "Here you are. Sorry I didn't join you for lunch, but I had a lot more details to clear up than I expected. You know, you really need to eat, Mariana. Mom told me you hardly touched your breakfast and just picked at your lunch."

I glanced at him but said nothing.

As he approached me, I placed the laced book mark in the journal and drew the cover over my thoughts. I rested the Standford-Castillo journal on the side table—a family tradition handed down from five generations. Family members who had the gift of clairvoyance kept a diary, recording their fears, disappointments, happiness, and revelations. I held on to this tradition because my sanity relied on the written word.

"Sorry to interrupt your writing, but I thought we could talk." Cassius sauntered confidently as if cupid had fired an arrow and it had hit its mark.

I attempted to figure out if he was happy to see me or just determined to make me smile.

Distracted, I watched the firewood crackle in the hearth. Little sparks floated and disappeared in the air. It was unusually nippy for the first day of October. Cassius sat across from me in a twin Victorian chair. I withdrew my legs from under me and slipped my feet into the new Hearthside slippers. Bianca had said they were a gift to the guests of The Outskirts. I stared at my feet cushioned in the red wooly comfort. I knew Cassius wanted to talk, but I wanted to sit in silence.

I continued to admire the room's decor. The deep-evergreen sofas, the amber curtains, and various tones of brown comforted my erratic thoughts. Here in this place, I felt the yoke of fear crack slowly day by day.

When will I drown all my fears?

"Mariana, what's the going price for your thoughts?" Cassius moved to the edge of his chair and laid a hand on mine.

I offered him a meek smile.

"You're probably thinking I can't afford your thoughts, right?" He smiled back.

"Cassius," I let out a soft exhale. "The price I've paid for my thoughts has no dollar value." I wrung my hands together.

He scooted off his chair and squatted in front of me. "Hey now, Bright Eyes, talk to me."

"How will talking help? You can't turn all the wrongs into a right. I've prayed, hoping for a vision that would show me how to turn the negative happenings to positive again. But, you see, Cassius, the gift doesn't work that way. I'm here to help others not myself."

"That's where I come in. I'm here to help you."

Cassius gently kneaded my hands. His gorgeous dimples distracted me.

I wish I could bury myself in your arms forever, Cassius.

"Listen. If there is only one thing I know, it's that expressing your thoughts out loud unravels the confusion." Cassius stood and pulled his chair closer to me. We sat face to face. "I'm here for you."

"You want to know how weird I am? As a child I used to ponder on the word extraordinary. To me the word seems like such an oxymoron. When someone says to me, 'you're extraordinary, Mariana.' I wonder. Does that mean I am less than ordinary, or beyond ordinary? The definition of ordinary is usual, regular, common, and normal. Oh, how I want to be normal and common like others. Yet, people have said that I'm to the point of extra ordinary. Now, Cassius, do you see how my mind is distorted?"

"Look, right now, I can't even categorize you, and I'm usually pretty damn good at placing a person's character in the right slot."

"I bet that drives you nuts, Mr. Control Freak kinda guy."

"You'll never know how much. But know this, I want to know who you are, here." Cassius placed his hand over my heart.

I nodded and swallowed the lump in my throat. Our eyes met. We remained silent for seconds, absorbing one another's presence.

I giggled as a thought popped into my head. He tilted his head to the side.

"Care to share?" His eyes smiled.

"I've come to the conclusion that I like the male smell."

Sheesh! You are the definition of weird, Mariana. Why would you tell him such a thing?

My teeth caught my bottom lip. He slowly lifted a finger and freed my lip.

"So, you've concluded that males smell good?" He sat back in his chair and crossed his ankles. "This should be good. Let's hear it." A roguish smile crossed his face.

"Well after my attacker, the male scent was repulsive. In the mansion, during self-defense lessons, the stench of sweat, sometimes drunkenness, and arrogance filled my nostrils to the point of puking." I crinkled my nose. "But...now one male in particular smells nice. You know?" I asked demurely.

"Hmm...I see, and who might this lucky guy be?" He folded his hands over his chest.

Cassius was definitely not going to make this easy for me. I felt like punching him.

"Mariana, you mentioned arrogance with all the other smells. I didn't know arrogance had a smell." He baited me.

That's right. Ask me Cassius.

"Arrogance does have a smell and it's a turn off." I lifted my slipper feet and crossed my legs in the chair.

Cassius burst out laughing.

"I'm serious. Why are you laughing?" The heat rushed to my cheeks.

Cassius lifted his fisted hand, feigning a cough. "Bright Eyes, I know you are." He choked back another spasm of laughter. "But the way you express yourself, it's..."

"It's what?" I demanded.

"Endearing. Yeah that's it, it's endearing." He chuckled silently.

"At least I express my true feelings." I glared at him.

He cleared his throat and lowered his chin, trying to look serious. "And who does *not* express themselves?"

"You. You arrogant rooster. You don't know how to express your true feelings." I stared back, with my arms crossed over my chest.

Cassius composed himself, but then his laughter burst out and bounced off the walls and ceiling.

Annoyed, I jumped to my feet. I swayed in my new slippers. His appreciation did not go unnoticed, but I was too fired up to care. I faced the window and watched the setting sun, then I turned back around and pointed a finger at him.

"Just now, you were thinking that you're falling for me, but..."

Cassius's condescending grin made me stumble in thought.

"Go on. Don't stop now." He tightened his lips, showing off his dimples.

"Oooh, you make me so angry. But remember this, your denial, your arrogance, will leave you on the side of the road hitch hiking."

"Umm, not likely. I have plenty of rides."

I lifted my arms in the air and let them drop at my sides.

"Fine play pretend or whatever it is you do best, Cassius. I've enjoyed your family's hospitality. This past week has been heavenly, but it's time I leave."

"Whoa, Mariana, I was playing with you. You don't have to go, because of it."

"I'm not leaving because of you. Oh brother. See? Arrogant."

"Then why? You're safe here."

"No, Cassius, I have to go. Last night's dream held me frozen in a room surrounded by a blinding light. The word 'leave' was constant in my psyche. It kept saying, 'Leave, Mariana, it's time to leave.' If I don't go now, soon Theodore will find this sanctuary and that can't happen. Please, will you take me to the nearest bus station, today?"

"Today? But it's close to dinner time."

"I know. Traveling in the dark hours is best."

"Fine, but what about your Mini Cooper? Don't you want to go back and get it?"

"I loved driving that car, but it's just a worldly object. Besides, it was bought with Theodore's money, blood money. I'd just as well travel by bus. I have enough cash so there won't be a paper trail."

"Fine, if this is what you want, I'll take you. Can you be ready in an hour?"

"Sooner. All I have is a duffel bag, remember?"

"Right, then I'll meet you in the kitchen in an hour." Cassius stood, repositioned his chair and left.

I stayed a moment longer, internalizing the conversation that had materialized between him and me. He wants to know me?

I'd love to know you better too, Cassius, but it's too dangerous. And you still have to admit to yourself that you can love and not fight it.

I feared what Theodore would do if he knew another man might love me. Releasing a long breath, I stood, clutched the journal to my chest, and went upstairs.

I wrote a quick note to Carla and Bianca, thanking them for their hospitality. I then started tidying up the room. After changing the sheets, I walked out to the hallway and pushed the used ones down a laundry chute. On returning to the room, I washed up and prepared myself for a long ride to nowhere. Before closing the bedroom door, I glanced back and recalled how peaceful this week had been.

* * *

I stepped into the kitchen. On hearing my cowboy boots thud against the kitchen floor, Bianca rushed forward and drew me into a hug. She held onto me as if I was about to jump off a cliff.

"Mariana, do you have to go tonight?" Tears trailed down her perfect complexion.

"Yes, but remember we'll see each other again. I promise." I swiped at my tears too.

Carla waited silently near the stove. Bianca released me and stepped aside. Carla stretched out her arms and I was drawn into her motherly embrace.

"Mariana, my son can be difficult, but remember his heart is in the right place. Even when you believe he's wrong, promise me you'll consider listening to what he has to say?"

Still in an embrace, I whispered, "Yes, I will. But, he's just driving me to the bus station."

Carla pushed me gently to arm's length and frowned. She then met Bianca's stare. Carla lowered her eyes, said nothing else, and turned to her cooking.

Cassius popped his head through the kitchen doorway. "Ready, Bright Eyes?"

"Yes." Both women faced me without a word. "Carla, Bianca, you're my sisters in heart. Staying here at the inn, getting to know you both was a blessing. Thank you for your kindness."

"Mariana, you're right. We're sisters now, so don't let big brother bully you, okay?" Bianca smirked.

A half-hearted giggle escaped me. "Bianca, you must know this. Soon, your heart's desire will arrive. Your wish for a mate will come true. And Carla, Cassius's heart will thaw. I'm not certain how long it will take, but the Cassius you raised is not gone."

Bianca and Carla gaped at him with identical frowns.

Cassius lifted his hands in the air. "Hey, now, you know I'm not that kind of guy. It's not like me to tell anyone that sappy stuff. That's all her." He pointed at me. "I told you, ladies, Mariana's weird like that." Cassius gave me a crooked smile and took hold of my bag.

I hugged Carla and Bianca one last time and turned towards the door.

My first steps, taking me away from peace, made my stomach churn. I reached the stairs to the front yard, and gawked. Bianca and Carla remained behind me on the veranda. Cassius stood at my side.

"How and when, Cassius?" Before me, in the driveway, my Mini Cooper awaited.

"Early this morn. I have a buddy who owns a tow truck company and he owed me a favor. You still want the bus station?"

"Uh, yeah, I mean no, I don't want the bus. Thank you, Cassius." I gave him a quick hug.

"You're welcome. Now let's go."

I had already descended the porch stairs when I stopped in mid-step and looked over my shoulder. Let's? What's this let's thing?"

"Well, you and I, of course."

Mouth open, I stayed rooted to the cement. Cassius took hold of my hand.

"Mariana, I'm not taking any chances. You're going back to your family, your home where you belong."

I stiffened and lifted my chin. "And…what if I don't want to go back?"

Cassius shifted his weight to one hip and cocked his head to the side. "Come now. Is that what you really want, to not go back home to your family?"

"Cassius, have you forgotten about Theodore? He'll find out."

"Nah, I've sent word through the grapevine that a certain drop dead brunette has been seen crossing the California border into Oregon." Cassius's dimples deepened.

"Hmm, you know, I think you have some of the gift yourself, Cassius. And you're being hush, hush about it." I snatched the duffel bag from his hand and left him standing in the middle of the walkway. I threw the bag in the trunk and ambled to the driver's side.

"Hey, mind if I drive?" Cassius held out his hand.

"What about your Harley?" I dropped the keys in his palm.

"It's parked in a safe place. I'll come back for it later." Cassius sent his mother and sister a wave above the Mini Cooper's roof top. I went around to the passengers' side and shouted towards them, "I know we'll see each other again, just don't know when." While I opened the car door, Bianca, Carla, and the foreman waved goodbye. I sat, fastened my seatbelt, and closed my eyes. Cassius closed his door.

"Relax, Mariana, I won't cut the curves so sharply this time around."

Snapping my eyelids open, Cassius laughed. The engine came to life and we drove on to the dirt road. Another unknown journey lay ahead of me, but this time I had the company of Cassius Russo.

* * *

We drove until early morning, then stopped to rest. I felt as if I could sleep for days, but no such luck. I awoke after sleeping for five consecutive hours. I stretched and sat in bed. To my surprise, Cassius was not in the other full bed. I scooted off mine and noticed the bathroom door was ajar. *Where did he go?* I peeked through the vertical blinds and saw the Mini parked. Still groggy, I decided to shower.

Refreshed and ready to leave, I stepped back into the bedroom and found Cassius sitting at a round table with takeout cartons.

Breakfast and coffee, yes!

"I see you couldn't sleep either." I finished brushing my hair.

"No, not with all the snoring you do." He divided the food.

"You must be confused. You heard yourself snore and thought it was me."

"Aah, that must be it." He smirked and continued to chew.

While I finished my breakfast, Cassius showered. I packed the little items we had and then we were off again.

CHAPTER 5

FALLING FOR HIM-HER

This girl makes my heart skip a beat every time she speaks.

"Cassius, if you want me to keep my breakfast in its rightful place, slow down on the curves, *please*." Mariana brought her hand up to her mouth and I eased up on the gas.

"Sure thing. I got carried away. This car hugs the road just right."

"Well, I'm glad you approve of my car choice, but less pedal to the metal, okay?"

"Understood." For good measure, I took one more curve faster than the speed sign suggested. Mariana tightened her lips and gave me one of her awesome scowls. "Sorry, I couldn't resist. You're eyes get as big as Bambi's when you're irritated."

"I've never understood that. So, a guy purposely angers a girl because it turns him on?"

"Sometimes, yeah." I chuckled and reduced the speed even more. I knew a lot of the cops in the county, but it didn't make any sense getting stopped. Marino probably wouldn't go to the cops, but one could never be too sure.

The view was breathtaking, but nothing was more captivating than Mariana. I could've put her on a bus with a buddy of mine, unknown to her, to make sure she got back home, but the thought of being with her another few days was heaven.

I glanced her way. "So, what do you think of dyeing your hair blonde?"

Mariana stroked her hair and said, "Blonde is okay. I never really thought about changing my hair color."

"I was thinkin' a red head to go with your fiery spirit, but blonde's more on the other side of the color spectrum. You think you could handle being blonde?" I eyed her while taking another curve.

"Eyes on the road, Cassius." Mariana crinkled her brow. "I guess I could. Sure, why not?"

"Good. When we reach San Joaquin valley, we'll get your hair done. Marino believes you're out of the state and changing your hair color will add to our insurance policy."

"And you know this because?" Mariana readjusted herself in the seat.

Shoot, it *would be good to have those legs—stop it, Cas. Focus, man.*

"I've got connections that keep me in touch. There's this new thing called texting. You must've heard about it by now?"

"You're such a twerp, Cassius. You know I'm disconnected from my contacts. No cell phones, no phone calls to family, nada. So…you can say for the last six months, texting has been foreign to me." She pouted.

"Yeah, sorry about that, I hope to help you out if I can, at least by taking you home to see your family."

Mariana slumped in the passenger seat and kept quiet. Something brewed in that sweet head of hers. I decided not to ask since going home was a touchy subject for her.

We drove on in silence. Hills, trees, blue sky, passed by in a blur, but I was in no hurry. I was driven to make our time last as long as possible. Mariana continued to brood. Her eyes took on a darker shade of green.

Man, I'd love to pull this car to the shoulder and just hold her right now. And somehow make her worries disappear.

"Bright Eyes?" I kept my voice close to a whisper.

She swiveled her head. Her eyes softened as they questioned me.

"I've been thinking. You never did tell me your last name. Do you have one?" I gave her a quick glance.

"Thinking can be dangerous." She held a straight face. "Umm, last time I heard, my father gave me a last name." She allowed herself to smile.

"And?" The road was straight with nothing in our way. I swerved.

Her fingers instinctively dug into the dash panel. "All right!" She giggled. "I give."

"Right, so, what's your last name?" Mariana went serious on me again. One car passed us in the opposite direction then the road was completely clear. "So, you're going to play with me? Okay, I'm game." I did a three-sixty leaving tread marks and rubber smoke trailing in the distance.

"Cassius! It's…my last name is Castillo." She choked on the last syllable.

Christo! She's an aphrodisiac. Seriously.

"You do that again and I swear the first chance I get, I'll disappear."

My eyes widened.

"I promise," she added.

"I've no doubt that you would. But I had to do something. You looked as if you were staring down the Grim Reaper."

"No. I was thinking of how I'm a nuisance. My family will accept me merely out of obligation."

"I don't believe that. Hey, you said Castillo. Are we talking Castillo Farms?" I decreased the speed and cruised down the hill into a canvassed valley.

"Yes." Mariana clammed up.

Oak trees peppered the roadside while a light breeze danced through a wheat field. Distracted by nature's painting, Mariana nodded and continued to look out the side window.

"This valley is so beautiful and pristine." She spied me trying not to smile. "What? Why are you grinning like that, Cassius?"

"To me, the countryside is the back drop to what I'm seeing. You're beautiful." I kept my eyes on the road, stunned at what I'd said.

Don't get all sappy. Stick to your guns.

Mariana shifted in her seat and whispered in my ear. "If the countryside is the background then let's stop and give it more color."

Brows lifted, I jerked my head to the side to get a better look at her expression. She giggled and sat squarely in her seat again.

"That's one suggestion I'm up for." I did a U-turn and parked the Mini Cooper in the protective shade of an ancient oak tree. The keys dangled from my finger. "Ready?"

"You took me seriously?" She goggled.

"Yup. Is there a problem with this?"

Small pearls of sweat formed on her upper lip. I loved every second of this game.

With long delicate fingers she rubbed her lip. "Uh, no, but I'm hungry." On cue, Mariana's stomach gurgled.

"Ah, your second wish of the day will be my pleasure to accommodate, along with your first request." I winked.

She pushed back into her seat.

"Relax, Bright Eyes." I brought her hand to my lips and kissed it. "Next time choose your words carefully." I slanted my head to have a better view of her.

She crinkled her eyebrows, catching on to my tease. "So, what's on the menu? I mean...what are we going to eat? I don't see a restaurant anywhere near here. Are we going to forage in the meadow for berries and maybe suck on wheat stalks?"

"Yup, we can, after we've eaten the food my mother packed for us." I pointed my thumb toward the back seat.

Mariana twisted to get a better look. "There's a basket under my blankets?"

"Right again."

"Thank God. I'm starved." She sat back in her seat and the tension fell off her shoulders.

"Yesterday, when you told me you had to leave, I asked my mom to pack a basket, but by the time we stopped at a hotel you crashed. I think you were asleep before your head hit the pillow. I then figured, since the nights have been cold, the food would be fine for the night, by the way, why all the blankets?"

Mariana let out a quick breath. "Sometimes, my bed was the back seat."

"Oh, I see." I stretched an arm over the seat, grabbed the picnic basket, and opened the door.

Mariana took hold of a flannel-checkered blanket and followed my lead. She stepped out and with her hip bumped the door closed. I waited for her to come around to my side. We climbed over a run-down rock wall.

The waving sea of wild high grass interspersed with orange-poppies was a perfect camouflage. A passerby wouldn't see us in the middle of the meadow.

Mariana spread the blanket. We sat side by side. I opened the picnic basket, and we laughed at the abundance of food. Four meatloaf sandwiches, bottled lemonade, homemade apple pie, and fresh carrots, chopped into sticks, stacked in a zip lock bag lay between the napkins and paper plates.

"Your mother knows how to lay out a spread." Mariana unraveled the plastic from the sandwiches and put them on the plates.

"No doubt, my mother is the picnic queen. She used to take my sister and me on the best picnics. After we were stuffed, she'd have us lie on our backs, looking up at the sky and tell us a story. The best one was about the prince coming home to his family."

What the hell am I doing? Why am I telling her this?

Mariana laid her hand on mine. "Cassius, I see you as a prince." She gave me a wide smile.

"Huh, yeah right." I pulled out the lemonade bottles and napkins from the wicker basket.

This luncheon was perfect. Being with Mariana was perfect. We talked about our childhood, adolescent years, and the awkward moments when we both thought we had found "the one" and later discovered they only wanted to hook up with our friends.

As Mariana ate, I concentrated on her lips and how she spoke between bites with her flushed chipmunk cheeks. Normally her cheeks were sunken, but here in this meadow, she stuffed her face more than any other time I had seen her eat. Perhaps the fresh air was the right remedy to bring her appetite back.

Mariana's eyes smiled. A constant breeze caused her curls to brush her face. She kept pushing them back with her free hand.

"Cassius, I know you told me you own beef cattle, but what exactly do you do?"

"I do odd jobs, here and there. I like fixing things that seem impossible." I took a bite of my meatloaf.

"So, you're a fix-it-man?" She said.

"Yeah, something like that."

About ten minutes later, between talking, I washed down my last bite with a swig of lemonade and dragged the napkin across my mouth.

"Hey, you weren't kidding when you said you were hungry." I handed her another napkin. The first one sat balled up next to her leg.

"It must be you who brings my appetite to the surface. And your Mom's excellent cooking." Mariana said, between bites. She then swallowed the last piece of her sandwich and settled back on the blanket, looking up at the sky.

The mixture of the breeze rustling through the grass, and Mariana's presence invited me to lie on my back too and lose myself in the moment. I retrieved my gun from the holster and set it on the blanket to my left. She followed my every move.

"Don't worry. I have a permit."

Mariana gave a small nod, sat up, and cleaned the picnic area. She then joined me and pillowed her head on my chest.

"Cassius, how old are you?"

"Old enough, why?" I crossed my arms under my head.

"I was just thinking. You're not much older than me. I'm twenty-five, and I'd say you're around thirty-two?"

"Yeah, minus two." I shifted my hips to avoid a dirt clod under the blanket. When I moved, I bumped her hip with mine.

She raised her head and fixed her eyes on me. I lowered mine to meet hers.

"Cassius, what's your favorite color?"

"Hum. I'd say blue." I lifted one brow questioning.

"That fits. But sometimes, I see the blue surrounding you outlined by bright yellow."

"You're seeing colors? Is the sun's heat getting to you?"

"No." Mariana tee-heed.

God I love that laugh.

"Then what?"

"There are many levels of the gift. My Aunt Samantha senses things, or spontaneously a word will pop into her mind and she focuses on it. For others it's visions. My Grammy Mary had many visions. I…I'm a mixture of both. Sometimes I have visions. Other times I see words and colors. But I don't control the events, no one does. They appear on their own accord."

"Uh huh, I see. And what does blue tell you?" I knew Mariana saw my skepticism.

"Blue tells me you're intuitive, and you love helping all living creatures. You strive to make things right. Yellow is your playful spirit, when you're in a goofy mood, but you act on your thoughts responsibly. You've been scarred emotionally. Cassius, don't hide from the truth." Mariana's right hand rested near my heart.

"What truth, Mariana." A shiver ran down my spine. I tensed up on feeling the electrical jolt that came from her warm hand.

"Never mind." Her countenance gleamed with what looked like a pinch of mischief.

Does she really not know how my nerves are going haywire?

Her fingers did a walk down to my stomach and stopped. My abdomen muscles coiled.

Shoot!

"Cassius?"

"Yeah?"

"I love how the sunlight falls on the Earth, signaling a new season. My favorite is winter. I see it as a time to reflect on the year that is near its end and more time to snuggle." She laughed again.

Is this girl serious? She's talking about the seasons now. Okay, I'll play.

"Hmm, winter just might become my favorite season too."

"Too? What's your favorite time of year, Cassius?" Mariana drummed her fingers against my chest. She had no idea she was playing piano on my fired-up nerves.

Electrical prickles ran from my scalp to my toes. I let out a slow hiss. "Spring is my favorite. It reminds me of Earth awakening from a long nap, time for a rebirth."

"That's really good. I didn't know you were poetic." Mariana stilled her hand and stiffened. Without warning she slid off me and knelt at my side.

"Cassius?" Mariana called out an octave higher.

"What?" My hand went straight to my gun as I sat up.

"Have you no control, man?" Dreamy eyed, Mariana studied my demeanor, head to toe. She gulped. "I forgot how men have two brains and one mind."

"Are you serious, girl?" Her goggle-eyed expression told me she was. I doubled over in laughter. Mariana's child-like innocence amused me to no end. I inhaled hard and let out the air in a rush.

"So, we men have two brains and one mind, is that right?"

She nodded in a quick short motion.

"Bright Eyes, it was your fault."

"Mine?"

"Girl, you really don't know, do you? Your voice, your warm touch, makes my southern brain override the northern one." I laughed some more. Not certain as to what else I should say, I controlled my laughter and grinned. Mariana's cheeks reached fuchsia status. She lowered her eyes and smoothed out the blanket to keep her hands busy. In the same instance, she froze. Her hands shook uncontrollably, and she turned pallid. I thought she was about to faint.

"What's wrong? Mariana, talk to me." I grasped her hand. An arctic chill trailed up mine.

"They are near, Cassius."

I applied pressure on Mariana's back. "Get down. Stay on your belly. Try to breathe slowly. Don't move, until I tell you to move. Understood?"

"Yes."

I shoved my boots back on, secured my gun in the holster, and went around toward Mariana's feet. She was completely hidden by the grass and poppies. I faced the outlining hills with my back to the road. The rumble of at least three bikes came to a halt near the Mini Cooper. I positioned my hands to waist level and shimmied my thighs. I motioned as if I were zipping up my pants, then turned and headed toward the car. Three burly men sat on their hogs. One smoking, another pulling on his beard, and the other had a cell phone to his ear. I heard him say, "No, the numbers don't match."

I laughed inwardly, because the day after Mariana and I had arrived at The Outskirts, I made a call to a friend in the San Joaquin DMV. The license plates on the Mini Cooper were new.

"Hey, how's it goin' man?" The older guy smoking jutted his chin.

"It's goin'. But you know how it is, one too many beers and nature calls."

"Is this Mini yours?" The younger guy on the cell phone asked.

"Yup, safe travels. Gotta go."

They nodded and revved their engines. I slid into the driver's seat, shoved the keys into the ignition and started up the engine.

Damn, they're waiting to see what I do next.

I had no choice and sped onto the road southbound. I eyed them in the rear view mirror, heading north. It killed me to leave her alone, but there was no other option. I cruised for ten minutes, then turned around, and returned to the oak tree. From the road side there was no sign of Mariana.

God did she get up and leave?

Dust and pebbles flew as I brought the car to a halt. I scrambled out of the car, cleared the rock wall at a brisk run, and nearly tripped over Mariana's feet. Her body shook, but not a sound was heard. I knelt.

"Mariana…? Bright Eyes, it's me." She pushed up to her knees and flew into my arms. "Hey now, relax. It was just some riders bein' nosy."

"You left me, Cassius. They came back. One of their cell phones rang. I heard them talking, but couldn't make out the words. Then they spun back out toward the north. Those were Theodore's thugs."

"How do you know?" I rubbed her back.

"The first man who spoke to you was he an older man? Say in his late sixties?"

"Yes."

"That was Randolph. He's Theodore's right hand man. I'd know his voice anywhere."

"Listen, they're gone. And like I said, they're going on a wild hog hunt. Your car plates have been changed, you're supposedly well into Oregon country, and soon you're going to be a blonde. Most importantly, you're with me now."

I held Mariana in my arms until her shivers stopped. When she calmed down, we packed the picnic basket and headed back to the car.

CHAPTER 6

A NEW START

Theodore Marino, the name dug deep under my skin. Dear God, there were times when I wanted to take out the garbage with my bare hands. I wanted to feel and see the life seep out of the scum who makes other lives a living hell.

It's difficult to erase the fear from Mariana's eyes when she believes she'll be taken back to Marino.

* * *

Mariana's head lolled on my shoulder. Her curls brushed my neck and her scent overrode my senses. I thought this is how my life should be, driving through the countryside with this woman. What would it take to feel every inch of her skin against mine?

Man, am I really falling for this girl? Don't forget. This is a job.

When I returned to the meadow and saw the terror in Mariana's eyes my gut turned inside out. I hoped to never see such turmoil in her again, but I'm not a super hero. I can't promise her happiness forever.

God knows I have much to account for and some of my mistakes include Mariana in the equation, but I'll do what I can to keep her safe.

Mariana stirred, rubbing her eyes. Once she realized she had laid her head on my shoulder she sat upright, and ran her hand across her mouth.

"How long have I been sleeping?" She yawned.

"Not long. You've been a sleepyhead lately."

"I guess my body is trying to catch up on lost sleep. You've made this possible. I haven't felt safe in a very long time." Mariana curled her left arm around mine, leaned in, and kissed my cheek. "Thanks for caring, Cassius."

"Mariana, there's no way I wouldn't help."

"I know. That's what I love about you, Mr. Fix-It-Man."

Mariana unraveled her arm from mine. I held her hand in my lap. We traveled in silence enjoying one another's company. An hour later, we were in the San Joaquin valley. Our second stop of the day was in a small town off of Highway Ninety-Nine. I parked and silenced the engine.

"So, are you ready to be a Blondie?"

"Yep. I think it'll be fun. Plus the look in my father's eyes will be worth the sitting in a salon for an hour or so." Mariana held a faraway stare. "My mom was blonde, but I inherited Dad's complexion and his hair color. I miss her so much." Her eyes glistened with unshed tears. She shook her head and said, "Let's do this. Soon, Mr. Russo, you'll be looking at a new Mariana Castillo."

"All right then, let's go. I made an appointment for you at Sensuous Salon."

"Sensuous?"

"Uh, humm." Tongue in cheek, I eyed her. "I know. The name says it all for me. Mariana, before we go in will you tell me your family's address?"

Mariana shot back a questioning look.

"I want to call a few buddies of mine to check out the place before we get there. If they don't give me the okay, we might stay the night here in a hotel."

Her brow lifted higher.

"Oh, come now. This isn't the first night we've stayed in the same room."

"After you insisted. I'm not used to sharing a room." She lowered her eyes.

"But, you have no problem sharing a picnic blanket?"

Mariana twirled a curl around her finger and started to hum.

"Relax, we can get a room with two beds again, but that's the only option. I won't leave you alone in a room where I can't keep an eye on you."

"Why, Mr. Russo? Do you believe the Humming bird will take flight?"

"One can never tell." I held my phone in hand, waiting to punch in her address.

"Fair enough." She gave me the information.

I logged it. "Thanks, for trusting me. My guys will check for anything suspicious."

"Your guys?"

"Yes. My long time buds from high school."

"Okay…" With her eyes downcast she said, "I've never met someone with so many friends. Theodore has acquaintances, but I would not call them friends."

"I thought we agreed not to mention his name again?"

"Yes, you're right. Cassius…" She eyed me. "Do you trust me?"

Mariana's question lingered. I took longer than expected to answer her. She deciphered my silence as a no. She opened the car door and swung her legs out.

"Mariana, wait." I gripped her arm.

She looked back over her shoulder. In a monotone voice, she asked, "How much, Cassius, do you believe the human mind can endure, before it overloads and shuts down completely?"

The void in Mariana's eyes was the same glare I had seen in the meadow before the bikers showed up. I squeezed her hand.

Mariana shook her head. "Sorry," she said.

"Bright Eyes, I trust you."

Mariana shared her knock-out smile and left me sitting in the car thinking how am I not going to hurt this girl? Knowing my track record it would be the greatest challenge in my life. She was not like other girls I had dated. Lies were not a part of her thinking process. She says what she feels and acts on it. I scrambled out of the car and met her near the entrance. We linked hands. As we walked in, heads turned.

"Hello, how can I help you?" A slender, middle-aged woman said as she approached us.

"Hi, I have an appointment to dye my hair."

"Okay, name please."

Fortunately, the woman was looking down at the appointment book when I whispered in Mariana's ear.

"The name is Cassie Russo." Mariana said.

"Yes, here it is. If you'll take a seat, Linda will call you in a few minutes to get started."

"Thank you." Mariana sat down near the windows, facing the main street.

I sat close to her. "Bright Eyes, I need to make some phone calls and text the information we talked about. I'll be across the street in that bar and grill. I can see the salon from there."

"Sure, no worries. See if you can spot me in an hour or so." Mariana smiled shyly.

An hour later, I returned to the salon and sat, pretending not to feel out of place. A few winks and smiles came my way, but I feigned unawareness. The owner told me Mariana had gone to the restroom. I drummed a tune on my leg, hoping she wouldn't be long. The door to the bathroom opened. A blonde with an hour-glass body emerged. She approached me and remained silent. I cleared my throat and lowered my eyes.

"You are a silly man."

I jerked, lifted my head, and dropped the magazine on the table. Those eyes were unmistakable.

"Ready to go?" Mariana let out a small chuckle.

I stood and started to pull my wallet out of my back pocket. She stopped me.

"I paid her cash. Ready to go dance?" Mariana twirled once and bit down on her bottom lip. "So, what do you think, Cas?"

"Did you call me Cas?"

"Well, yeah. You told me at the diner friends call you Cas."

"Yes, they do." Mariana thawed right before my eyes. She transformed from the doom and gloom girl to the happy-go-lucky woman.

Mariana latched onto my arm and turned toward the woman that had dyed her hair. "Linda, you're a miracle worker. I love your purple aura. You're a true visionary. This shade of blonde you chose for me is fabulous, thank you. But, remember to treat yourself to fun, okay?"

"You bet, sweetie. Be sure to come by and say hello." Linda turned back to another customer.

Mariana waved bye to everyone in the salon and held my hand, leading the way. "Let's go, too many eyes on you. I don't want to share." She tightened her grip.

We strolled to the car. I felt there was no hurry to get to where we were going.

"This feels right…" Mariana halted. Keeping it on the down low, she exhaled. "Cassius, the MINI, it's been stolen." She cupped her mouth.

"Relax." I rested my hands on her shoulders. "Hey now, look at me. I had a friend park your car in a storage facility. This is my Wrangler."

She lowered her hand. "Oh, you're full of surprises. And you seem to have friends everywhere." She leaned toward the Jeep and peered in.

"I'm sorry I didn't tell you sooner. I actually forgot when I saw you."

Mariana let out a long slow breath. "It's a slick Sports S." She ran a finger over the metallic-blue hood.

"Yeah, I call it my fun ride."

"Your fun ride? Sounds like you're at an amusement park."

"With you, I am." I opened the passenger door. "Hop in."

Mariana sat gracefully. Her golden curls fanned the black leather seat. She folded her hands in her lap. I couldn't help but stand there and watch her every move. She frowned. "What's wrong, Mariana?"

"I'm just wondering. How many vehicles do you own?"

"Three tops. I have my Harley, this Jeep, and my business car."

"Wow, you sure like your toys."

"I guess I do." I closed her door, pulled the keys out from my pants pocket, and crossed to the driver's side. One good thing about Mariana, she was not the type of girl to ask many questions, but that also made it harder for me to read her.

I settled behind the wheel wondering how I was going to keep my job separate from my personal life.

Mariana twisted a lock of hair around her finger again and looked down at it. "This will take some getting used to. Blonde is so out there. What do you truly think, Cassius?"

"I don't have to think. Any hair color on you wouldn't change your beauty. You'll always be my Bright Eyes."

"Thanks, Romeo." She lowered her chin and scoped the Jeep's interior. "I see you didn't forget the picnic basket and my duffel bag." She smiled.

"That's right, now where to?"

"Well, in the salon I thought about our unfinished picnic. We didn't get to the dessert."

"True. It would be a crime to not enjoy the dessert. I know of a small lake just outside of town. It's quiet. We can finish our picnic there." I shifted into drive and pulled out of the park.

"Sounds like a plan." Mariana stared ahead.

I felt as if Mariana was taken away from me by her thoughts again. It was just as well. I needed to figure out what the next step would be to keep her safe.

We drove through the main street straight to the outer limits of town. The auburn panorama held my attention. The mulberry trees stretched their semi-bare limbs in welcome while the squirrels ran along worn paths from the oak trees, carrying off their winter stash. I turned onto a remote road leading to the lake's north shore and parked in a paved area. Mariana unbuckled her seat belt and faced the backseat. Doubling over, she unzipped her bag and pulled a sweater out.

"Hmm, nice view."

"Hey, were you just checking out my behind?" She settled back in her seat.

"Now what kind of question is that? You move like a swan and stretch over the seat console to grab a sweater, all the while my face is a foot away from your *behind,* and I'm not supposed to enjoy the view?"

"Umm, yeah. I guess I wasn't thinking about that." Mariana blushed as she slipped on her sweater.

"Believe me, I didn't mind."

"Good to know, now onto another subject. Cassius, while you assumed I was lost in thought, I was appreciating your humming. You're a fan of George Ezra's song, Budapest."

"Yeah, it's one of my favorites. It's like the song says, if you own me, all doubt will go away."

"Cassius, are you, saying...?"

We sat in silence for a few seconds. Mariana eyes brightened.

"I love you too, Cassius. Let's go have that dessert." Mariana hooked the basket's handles in her hand and got out.

I grabbed a blanket and followed content to watch her, to smell her, to hear her laughter, to *just* be near her.

Mariana chose a spot under an oak tree close to the shore line. I spread out the blanket and sat. I drew my gun from its holster, and set it next to my thigh. Oblivious to her beauty, Mariana casually put the basket in the middle of the blanket. She then settled next to me and let out a content sigh.

I have to snuff out these feelings I'm having.

I felt as if I'd been waiting for this day for years. This one moment when I sat next to the woman with whom I could share the rest of my life.

Mariana is clueless— to her beauty, to her grace, to her everything.

A hunger came over me, to absorb her every move, her every mannerism, her self in a mental photo to log away for future's sake.

"Do you carry your Glock everywhere?" She asked out of the blue.

"Huh, now where did you learn about guns?"

"Theodore is well stocked. You carry a Glock 17. It's popular with the police because of its interchangeable parts with the Glock 19."

"And, you know this because?"

"Funny, you want more info." Mariana laughed. "Okay, the Glock is a popular invention because it's lighter than its counterpart the Smith & Wesson. For a person on their feet eight to ten hours a day the benefits are crucial. Plus rate of fire is greater, no safety latch and the Glock doesn't need as much maintenance as other guns do. Also, Theodore taught me how to shoot." Mariana brushed the curls from her cheeks and turned toward the picnic basket.

I shook my head.

Who is this girl? She's definitely not just some farmer's daughter.

"Thanks for the heads up. So, is you're aim any good?" I settled back on my elbows and crossed my ankles.

"Umm, you can say that." She laid out the plates and cut into the apple pie. "You must be famished. We ate like six hours ago."

"I see. No more talk about firearms?"

"Nope, the topic bores me. Shall we dig in?" Mariana handed me a piece of pie big enough for the two of us. And she did the same for herself.

We ate, listening to the water lapping on the shore, the squirrels bickering over acorns, and the hawk hunting its next prey.

A small burp escaped Mariana's perfect lips. "Oh, excuse me. Your mother's pies are divine."

"Yup."

I helped with the cleanup and then lay on my back studying the clouds. Soon it would rain. I could feel it in my muscles. It was something I had felt since I was a kid.

Mariana joined me. Side by side we held hands. A smile played across her face.

I'm not one to worry much, however at that moment I felt the prick of fear jabbing at a constant question. Is this girl real? Is it safe to hope?

"Cas?"

I swiveled my head to meet her eyes. Our lips were inches apart.

"I'm real." She kissed me.

Sound ceased. Life around us continued, but I only felt the soft touch of her lips. It was as if she took me to some other dimension. Mariana slowly severed the link. I didn't dare move, for fear I might take her right then and there. She gave me a rueful smile.

"Are you sorry that you kissed me, Bright Eyes?"

"No. It's just...so much will happen before we can truly be together."

"You've seen the future?" I propped my elbow up, and held my head in the palm of my hand.

"Not the future, Cassius, but small...oh how do I explain this? Words, little patches of scenes in my dreams and vibes bombard me every day. I see the obstacles."

"Mariana, that's all they are, obstacles. I'll help you break through them." I tucked a strand of hair behind her ear.

"Hmm, yeah, together." She nuzzled.

I drew her in closer and we enjoyed the afternoon solace.

"Cassius, have you heard of the song, My Immortal?" She whispered as if she were half asleep.

"No, can't say I have."

"Someday, you should listen to it."

"How about right now?" I searched the song on my cell phone.

Mariana watched me type in the song's name. A small shiver ran through her body. I slid the picnic basket to the dry grass and folded the blanket's end over her. Our body heat soon stopped her shivering.

The song played. The lyrics led me to see more of Mariana. As the melody ended, I kissed the top of her head.

"There's always hidden truths in the underlining of such songs." She muttered with one side of her face buried in my chest.

"You amaze me, Mariana."

"How so?"

"I have memories from my childhood that take me to a dark place, but when I'm with you none of it matters. It's as if it never existed."

"Cassius, it's important to remember the past. Certain life lessons we must not forget. Others should stay in the past. Remember, memories are life's album."

"Life's album? *Only* you, Mariana, would say such a thing."

"Ahem." She replied.

We dozed off. Twenty minutes later my phone buzzed. Still half asleep, I grabbed it. The phone slid through my hand and fell on Mariana's back.

Her body jounced.

"Sorry, about that."

"Uh-huh." She remained still.

I caught the call on the last ring. "Hello. Yeah, this is Cassius. All clear? Right. Thanks. Talk to you later." I checked the time on the screen, four p. m.

"Hmm, that was a delicious nap." Mariana flipped onto her back and stretched.

"Yes it was. You ready to go home?" I stuffed the phone in my back pocket.

"I'm ready, if you are." She lay still. A spark of uncertainty shone in her eyes.

"Yeah, it's time. Let's go." I squeezed her hand. "I'm here for you."

"But, for how long?" She smiled meekly.

"Don't you ever live in the present? Mariana, enjoy the moment. The other days will fall into place."

"Do you write for 'Hallmark' on the side?" She plucked an oak leaf out of my hair.

"Nah, that stuff is too sappy. You, somehow, bring it out of me." I fitted my gun in the holster.

She giggled like a teenager and stood. We packed the picnic basket again, on a happier note, and headed to the Wrangler.

CHAPTER 7

HOT-COLD HOMECOMING

Life granted Cassius and me a few more hours together. The drive through the countryside soothed my nerves, but for how long?

When I see the look of desire in Cassius's eyes, my stomach churns, remembering the night I was attacked. I feel as if my lungs are water logged and there is no escape.

"Mariana." Cassius squeezed my hand gently.

I jerked, making him question my reaction. "Sorry, I…was thinking…"

"Don't be afraid of my touch." He drew his brows together.

"Cas, I love holding your hand, kissing you, it's just…will I ever be able to physically love someone?"

"You mean…?" He kept his eyes on the road.

"Yes, I'm saying I never slept with Theodore or anyone else. That one night haunts me."

"Well, you've slept with me." He tried to keep a straight face.

I punched his arm. "Ow, is your bicep made of rocks? You know what I meant." I cradled my hand.

"Don't stress. When it's right, you'll feel it in here." Cassius laid his fisted hand over his heart.

My head fell against the headrest, and I closed my eyes. I heard the engine rev as Cassius sped up. The Wrangler's new car smell, mingled with Cassius's words, gave me a new sense of hope. Something new, going back home. Something new, might it be possible? Home, a word I cherished and avoided. The family's safety shouldn't be jeopardized by my wants, yet here I was heading home. Maybe, Theodore wouldn't know. Maybe, I could stay for a few days to absorb my family's love again. Then, I would leave. Thorns had been lodged in my heart by my own hands. I felt Dad's distance, but the years showed me it was not him who led us to this crossroad. I was to blame.

Riding in the Jeep allowed me time to place my thoughts in order. I thought of how Cassius's barriers had crumbled some. He recounted the day his father left his family. Listening to his explanation divulged the pain, disappointment, and anger. There were moments I wanted to hug him and say, "You have all the right to be angry, but try to see your father's side."

The problem was that Cassius didn't know why his father, in his words, abandoned the family. The irony— I understood why his father withdrew from his wife and children. There had to be a grave reason for a man with such love to leave. I had done the same. And there was absolutely no doubt in my mind if the situation had fallen in my dad's or Cassius's lap, they would've taken the same measures.

"Hey, you're in that zone again. What's bugging you?" Cassius smiled as he drove down the road I had grown to love— the road leading home.

"I'm just thinking of the homecoming." I twisted a strand of hair on my index finger and hummed.

Cassius caressed my cheek. "I'm here, Mariana. I'm here."

I lifted my eyes to meet his and smiled for his sake. "I know, Cassius. And...I'm grateful for all that you have done for me."

"But?" Cassius said. His eyes fixed on the road.

"There's no but, I'm just wary of the future." I folded my hands in my lap.

Sometimes his seriousness scared me. I didn't want to cause him pain, but how could I hang on to a love I feared would bring him and me heartache? How could I be intimate with him?

"Mariana, have you ever thought that maybe it's you that's helping me?"

"Hmm, maybe." I wrung another curl around my finger and returned to defragmenting my thoughts. I hummed a tune in my head to relax my erratic thinking.

The hours Cassius and I shared instilled the tiny seed of hope in me again, but I knew I must yank it out before it took root.

Cassius believes family and home is where I belong. There's nothing in this life that I would love more, other than Cassius at my side. Enough thinking about what I wish.

I shifted my body in the seat and watched him drive.

He's really handsome when he's brooding.

He looked my way and winked then continued to drive in silence. I was content to just watch him. His sculptured Roman nose caught my attention.

"Cassius, did you at one time break your nose?"

"Yeah, in a brawl. Some drunk guy mistook me for his girl-friend's ex." When he frowned a distinct line appeared across the bridge of his nose.

"And how did you get this scar?" I traced a finger above his right brow.

"One might say I was the guy who blindly jumped in when his buddies were being bullied or needed their backs covered."

"Oh, you're Superman's sidekick." I held back a laugh.

"No, I'm my own man."

"That you are." I closed my eyes and saw him perfectly. His features were well rooted in my mind.

Cassius is the man in my vision. The vision I pushed away and said it wouldn't and couldn't happen. But...it has. How fool-ish am I to play hide-and-seek with fate?

"In a quarter mile, turn left." The GPS voice interrupted my train of thought.

Cassius had logged the directions to the farm in his cell. He said, "In case you dose off, sleepy head."

"Castillo Farms, in five hundred feet turn left."

Cassius turned into the driveway.

"You've arrived at Castillo Farms." The sultry voice confirmed.

I realized I'd been holding my breath when air gushed between my teeth.

Cassius drove five miles an hour. I reluctantly eyed the entrance. Italian Cypresses guarded the long driveway. On pass-ing them, buried memories came back like a rushing river.

A scene of me running down the driveway to a taxi reappeared. I recalled not saying goodbye to my family, knowing that if I did they would stop me. A lone letter awaited them in the library. My written word explained I was leaving not because I didn't love them or because I wanted to, but because I *had* to.

The pain in my father's eyes left an irremovable dagger in my heart. I should've known better. I shouldn't have told him I was going to live with Theodore, but he kept asking me what was wrong. We were alone in the library. He directed me to the leather sofa. His strong, callused hands held mine.

"Mariana, don't leave us. We love you. Tell me what's wrong."

I wanted to live with my family forever, but I knew what had happened to me wouldn't end here. My rapist had impregnated me. The thought of terminating the pregnancy was never in question. A dream revealed my attacker coming back and taking my child. I knew then I had to leave once the baby was born.

Twice in my lifetime, I witnessed tears stream down Dad's cheeks, the day my mother died, and the night when I explained to him why I must leave the family.

Dad sank back into the sofa and his head fell into his hands. He shook his head and said, "Mariana, this is a one way ticket. You trust Theodore, but he's up to no good."

"Daddy, please understand I must go. I love you so much, but I have to go."

"Mariana, why do you insist on telling everyone of your gift? Don't you know what's at stake? It's because of your indiscretions that you were attacked."

"I know Daddy. I won't make that mistake again. And you know as well as I do, the reason I'm leaving is because family comes first. They must never find this child. I *will* protect my family."

"You will *not* go. I forbid it!" My father pounded his fist on his thigh. "We'll find a way to protect the innocent and keep harmony under our roof."

I knelt beside him and placed my hands on his face. His weary eyes stared back. "Daddy, this is the only way I know how to protect us all. I feel that the person who attacked me did it to get back at you. I'll die before they know of my son. Please trust me, Daddy." My father said nothing after I gave him my reasons. He sauntered toward the window and stood rigid.

"Daddy, I'll stay here until the baby is born. Frank has agreed to give him his name and be his father. I'll never be able to repay my selfless brother or you Daddy, but know I'll go down protecting this family." I held my head high and swallowed the ache in my throat.

I heard my father sigh roughly. "You're my daughter and now you're carrying *my* grandchild. Mariana, don't leave…" His voice broke as he bowed his head. The pain on his face made me determined to never put my family in danger again. But, we do not control fate.

A year later, when my freewill overrode my common sense, I packed my bags, and wrote the letter which guided me onto a path I knew had to be taken.

Three months passed when I realized I needed to go back home. I *had* to see my baby. When Dad was informed I had returned he rushed into the house. His stature filled the library's doorway. He drew his eyes downward and I sensed his painful shame.

"Daddy, please look at me! I'm your daughter not some stranger who just stopped by to say hello."

"Why did you come back, Mariana? I told you if you walked out the door you'd only meet pain. You chose. What makes you think you have the right to come back?" He ended our short conversation by leaving.

I don't know why I had expected him to run up to me and gather me in his arms. Stunned, my emotions rammed my psyche and tears streaked my face. From that day on, distance was wedged between us. During the time I was home, I kept in touch with Theodore. He continued to say his door was open should I decide to go live with him. Through many phone calls Theodore listened to me rant about my father's cold indifference. Aunt

Samantha would say, "Mariana, give your father time. He loves you. You must know that the knowledge of someone hurting you in such a manner has left a deep scar in your father's heart. He blames himself." Blame? How could it have been my father's fault? I confronted him with this knowledge. He simply said, "A child shouldn't suffer because of their father's errors." He then hunched forward and walked out of the room. I felt the subject was not to be approached again. Aunt Samantha, once said, "…a moment in time to create errors, a lifetime to correct them."

My interpretation of her words was that my stubbornness led the family to suffer. I would make it right again for the family. Aunt Samantha's love kept me sane all these years, but Theodore was the one who found me under the bushes. I believed there was a distinct connection between us.

A wall erected and distance became my companion. I left my family's home at the age of twenty-three and sheltered them from my mistakes.

"Mariana, that's some deep thinking you're doing there." Cassius gently squeezed my shoulder. "You think any harder and you'll have a permanent unibrow. What's going on?"

"Cassius, this is a mistake." I rubbed my clammy palms on my jeans and noticed my surroundings. "Please, turn around. Drive me out of here."

"Mariana, this is a good thing. Don't worry."

I bit down on my bottom lip, holding back the tears.

"Cassius."

"Yeah?"

"Look at the lights. They're not on." I straightened in my seat.

Between every other cypress, a black candy-cane lamp post usually lit the driveway to the farm house, but instead we rode forward under a moonless night. Usually by dusk the lights turned on.

Thoughts of what might've happened painted scenarios in my head. My first thought was Theodore could be in the house waiting for me, or Dad's involvement with the authorities had finally caught up with him.

Stop speculating. Anything could've happened.

Cassius parked near the iron fence, dividing the house's front landscape from the farm yard. He killed the car lights and the engine.

"Cassius, there aren't any lights on in the house either." This was unusual because Aunt Samantha was not one to go out much anymore. Just thinking about my aunt spread goose bumps along my arms.

I miss her so much.

"Mariana, stay in the jeep. I'm going to check the perimeter." Cassius closed the car door without making a sound.

I fixed my attention on the orange-red horizon faintly visible now. I shook my head. "No way, I'm not waiting here." I unbuckled my seat belt and jumped out of the Wrangler.

Cassius halted when he heard footsteps behind him. He glared.

"I'm going with you." I whispered.

In one clean sweep, Cassius's leg met the back of mine. The ground greeted my buttocks in a distinct thud.

"What the hell!" I gritted my teeth.

"Stay there or I'll drop you again." He scrunched his brow, shadowing his eyes.

"You Neanderthal." I hissed and drew myself to a crouch.

Cassius grabbed my arm, tightening his grip. "You in danger won't happen on my watch. Let me do my job."

I yanked my arm away from him. "Your job? You're a cattle rancher and this is *my* family." I jumped to my feet. "I can help, Cassius."

He, again, swept the ground with me.

Air gushed out of my lungs. I wanted to floor him as well, but fighting Cassius wouldn't have helped my family.

"Fine, go. *Mr. Machismo.*"

He gaped. "Are we really going to do this?"

"And whose fault is it?" I leered.

He tapped my nose with his index finger. "You need to know when to bow down, just as much as when to help someone. I can't let you go in there without knowing what's on the other side. I'll go see if the power has been cut off to the house."

I started to stand. His hand came down firmly on my shoulder. "I promise I'll come back, Mariana."

I crossed my arms and stared at my feet.

God I want to put him in his place.

"Mariana, look at me."

I lifted just my eyes to meet his smirk.

"You're such a child."

"Me?" I scoffed.

"Mariana, I promise you this, if you're not here, in this spot, when I return—"

"What? You're going to spank me? Cassius this is ridiculous. We're wasting time."

"Yes, because you're too damn stubborn. And speaking of spanking, believe me, it'll be my pleasure."

"In your dreams, Mr. Control Freak. Go see what's wrong."

Cassius started to leave. On impulse, he stopped and looked over his shoulder. I stood, rubbing my rump. He lifted a brow.

"Go. Stop staring." I ran my fingers through my hair to keep them busy. The urge to punch him was close at hand.

He shook his head and said, "You're somethin' else," and then sprinted behind the house.

I sat, and rocked back and forth while rubbing my arms.

I'll give him exactly three minutes. If he doesn't show up, I'm running to the garden shed to find some sort of weapon. If anything, I can hoe down the intruder. What's taking him so long? One more minute and I'm out of here.

I glanced at my watch. No sound and no sign of Cassius returning cast me into Mariana mode. I scrambled to my feet and went straight to the garden shed off the south side of the house. The door was unlocked.

Thank goodness for small miracles.

I turned the knob and waited a few seconds, listening for sounds. All was quiet. I stepped inside and felt my way through the darkness, shuffling to the far left corner where the gardening tools were usually hung. Knowing that my dad was meticulous in where his tools belonged, my hand fell upon the weapon of choice.

"Gotcha. Now let's see what I can do with this." I left the shed hoping I didn't take a false step. It had been some time since I walked these grounds.

"Mariana, where are you? I told her to stay put." Cassius's voice traveled my way.

Another sound, sweet laughter which I had longed to hear also greeted my senses.

"Now Cassius, you've been with Mariana long enough to know she's not a follower. She leads."

Before the shadows took form, I saw a camping lantern that looked as if it were floating in my direction. I waited, holding the hoe in attack stance. I met the lantern and the Glock head on.

"Girl, what do you plan on doing with that hoe?" Cassius chuckled. He holstered his gun.

I thought, *perfect.* One calculated swipe and the hoe caught Cassius's mid-calf. A grunt was heard. He fell onto a mulberry leaf pile. I hadn't been as fortunate. My buttocks stilled smarted.

"I thought I'd hoe down the weeds." I lifted a brow, dishing out my best cocky smile.

"Mariana, my dear, you certainly have not changed." Aunt Samantha set the lantern near her feet and spread her arms wide.

I dropped the hoe. "Auntie." I bent down to meet her hug, and buried my face in her shoulder. Her familiar scent made me feel safe. "Auntie, I've missed you so much."

"Sweet Mari, I've missed you too." She tightened the hug.

Cassius brushed off the leaves and dry grass from his jeans. His cocky grin told me he'd get me later.

I chuckled. "You can try, Cassius. But I owed you, remember?"

His smile grew wider.

I released Aunt Samantha from our bear hug. "Auntie, why are all the lights out?"

"There was an accident down the road. A drunk driver slammed into an electric pole. The poor soul didn't survive the impact and he left this whole community in the dark."

"That explains the spooky Halloween night." I twisted my body to get a good view of Cassius. His head was down as if he were deliberately avoiding eye contact. "Cassius, are you all right?"

He let out a small cough and lifted his head. "Yeah, I'm good, even though I was attacked by a hoe."

A small snigger escaped me. "Sorry, you think you'll be able to sit, or do you need an ice pack? I know I need one." I added the last sentence to emphasize payback was a complete B.

He snorted, but didn't retort.

"Oh, where are my blasted manners? Come inside you two." Aunt Samantha took hold of my hand. "Mariana, your father will be thrilled to see you."

Aunt Samantha was not oblivious to our parley, but she opted to stay out. Her sense of recognition didn't deal with little talk. She had a sense of humor, boy did she ever, but when it came to clairvoyance and sticking to the matter at hand she wasn't distracted by chit-chat. Aunt Samantha once told me, "Mariana, choose your battles carefully and fix your mind on the bull's eye. When the target is near, take aim." It was obvious our childish conversation was not the target she was aiming for.

I tugged on her hand. "Aunt Samantha, the last time I saw Dad, he—"

"Don't worry." She brushed a hand over my hair. "I love the new look, Mari."

"Thanks, but Auntie—"

"Remember, your father was upset because he believed you chose Theodore over the family."

"Auntie, you know he's wrong. The family has always been first. That's why I left."

"Yes, Mari, you and I understand the circumstances, but your father believes differently. Let's not worry about this now. Frank and your father are in the library. I know they love you very much and they'll be happy to see you."

"They're in the library and..." I swallowed back the last part of my sentence. I had nearly forgotten that Cassius stood behind us.

85

"Mari, trust this old lady. I might not be able to see very well anymore, but... " Aunt Samantha pointed to her head, "...this old noggin still sees quite well what needs to be seen. You can take that promise to your afterlife." A smile spread across her face. "Now, follow me and watch your step. The moon decided not to visit tonight."

The moon not visiting tonight had been a childhood joke that Aunt Samantha and I shared. I swallowed the knot in my throat. She still remembered.

In a strange quiet manner, Cassius followed us into the kitchen. We crossed to the open French doors and entered the library.

Aunt Samantha linked her hand with mine and steered me to the sitting area on the south end of the room.

"Gentlemen, we have visitors."

Cassius stood off to the left. Aunt Samantha and I approached my dad and brother.

She whispered in my ear, "I'll be back shortly," and left the room.

Frank and Dad occupied two reading chairs near the hearth. They had been in a deep conversation when we entered. I watched them and listened to the wood crackle in the fire place. Their shadows danced on the far wall. With Aunt Samantha's announcement, Frank jumped to his feet and in three quick strides embraced me. He then unraveled his arms and stood back. Dad kept his gaze on the papers in hand. I felt him fighting with his own emotions, reining in his negative comments. On seeing my dad, a memory flooded my mind. My thoughts traveled to a childhood memory.

"Please, John. I can't keep up with her. I need to finish correcting these school reports."

My beautiful mother was sitting in a reading chair. Dad came up to me.

"C'mon, Mariana. Let's go for a walk." He knelt on one knee, arms wide open. I ran to him.

"All wight, Daddy. Where go?"

"We're going for a walk out on the ranch. Is that okay with you?"

"Yes." I hopped on one foot. My head bobbed up and down. I held onto his pinky while we walked out through the kitchen door. I must've been three. I remembered Aunt Samantha more than once telling me I did not pronounce my R's until the age of six.

"Look, Daddy, C'wane."

"Where? All I see is a yellow Crane." He smiled.

"No, Daddy. White C'wane." I giggled.

"Are you sure it's a white crane?" He dragged the two letter blend so I could hear the 'R'.

"Uh huh, C'wane."

Dad laughed and swept me up into his arms. I remember thinking how much I could see sitting on his shoulder. He then brought me down into a hug. I placed my little chubby hands on his chest. I lowered my brow and pouted.

"No be sad, Daddy."

He raised his eyebrows. "I'm happy, Mariana."

I don't know why, but my next words were said in a whisper. "Daddy, no play with guns. Be happy, Daddy." I pointed to his heart.

Dad's stunned appearance made me giggle.

Someone cleared their throat. I stood in the middle of the room staring into my brother's eyes.

Why did life become complicated? I loved talking to my Dad.

"How are you, Sis?"

I blinked and shook my head to erase the past.

"I'm fine. It's good to see you, Frankie."

Frank rested his hands on my shoulders and studied me at arm's length. "Huh, not bad, I never imagined you as a blonde, but it looks good. Yeah, not bad."

On hearing Frank's words, Dad glanced up. He laid a folder on top of the Victorian table and scattered papers fell to the floor. His eyes bore straight through me.

"Daddy?"

He stood.

"Daddy, it's me, Mari."

"Mariana, you look so much like her."

Dad's words made my heart skip a beat. My mother had been a natural blonde.

I ran a hand through my ratty curls. "Yeah, I dyed my hair. I'm sorry. If it upsets you, tomorrow, I'll have it changed back to brown."

"No, no. You caught me by surprise, that's all." Dad opened his arms and I settled into his embrace. He sighed. "Mari, it's good to see you."

"Daddy, I've missed you too."

Shuffling of feet, coming down the hallway, ended our conversation.

"Mariana, someone was busy in his room, drawing a picture. But he's ready to see you." Aunt Samantha returned to the awkward reunion.

A little chubby porcelain hand curled around Aunt Samantha's thigh.

"Auntie, don't move and don't freak out, but I think you're growing a hand on your leg." Sweet giggles filled the room. I walked behind Aunt Samantha.

"Oh, no! It's worse than I thought, Auntie. You have a whole little boy growing from your back side."

A puffy cheeked toddler stared at me in his Cars pajamas. His brown curls crowned his rosy face and his perfect round eyes smiled back.

"Mariana, this little gentleman is Michael John Castillo." Aunt Samantha stepped aside.

Michael smiled shyly.

"It's very nice to meet you, Michael." I squatted and held out a hand.

Michael placed his hand in mine. I studied it for a few seconds. His warmth ran through me. I coughed to clear the lump forming in my throat.

"Hello, Auntie Mari."

"You know me?" I stole a quick look at Aunt Samantha. She nodded.

"You pretty, but your hair is yellow. In the pictures your hair is brown." Michael kept his eyes on me.

"Yes, that's correct. I had it dyed blonde for a different look. What do you think?"

"I like the old pictures of you, but you still pretty."

"Thank you, Michael. You've grown so much. You were a baby the last time I saw you. How old are you now."

"I'm three." He held up three chubby fingers. "You know me too?" Michael's button nose wrinkled, as if there was a foul smell in the air.

"Yes." I choked. I couldn't resist the urge any longer. I pressed his little body against mine.

He returned the hug and said, "You smell nice like Auntie Samantha. Daddy tells me stories about you."

"He does? I hope they're all good?" I glanced at my brother. Michael's childish laughter lightened my heart.

"Uh huh, they are good and some funny."

"Ah, yes. Well, wait until I share some funny stories about your daddy, Frank. Would you like that?"

Michael laughed more and nodded yes. He hugged me again. For three years I dreamed of holding my son. And now, here he was with his sweet, soft arms around my neck.

"Yeah, well, those stories will have to wait 'til tomorrow. It's your bedtime, little man." Frank scooped Michael into his arms and carried him off to bed.

"Bye, bye, Auntie Mari. No be sad, Auntie. Be happy."

My jaw dropped. I stood and stared at Frank's back as Michael waved goodbye. I then faced Aunt Samantha. She nodded, confirming what I thought. Michael had the gift too.

"Cassius." I turned towards him. "I'm so sorry. I forgot to introduce you."

A soft pitter-patter sounded in the hallway, coming back into the library.

"Cas, me forgot to say hello. Sorry, goodnight." Michael said in a huff.

Frank stumbled into the room. "Mikey, what have I told you about interrupting adult conversations?"

"Sorry, Daddy, but I no say hello to, Cas." Michael pouted.

"It's all right little buddie. Goodnight. I'll see you later, okay?" Cassius waved goodbye. His eyes met mine briefly, before he lowered his head.

Frank threw Michael over his shoulder and played drums on his padded bottom. Michael's giggles echoed down the hallway.

Within seconds the air around me thickened and my lungs couldn't get enough oxygen. The innocent words rang in my head. Michael. Cas. Buddie. What? How? A deafening buzz sounded in my ears.

"Mariana, my dear, do you hear me?" Aunt Samantha clutched my hand. A shock wave shot through my nervous system.

"Cassius, help me sit her down." They led me to the leather loveseat.

Aunt Samantha knelt beside me. She was quite agile for her age. Cassius sat on the edge of the sofa.

"Mariana, listen to me. I can explain."

"Cassius, tell me you told Mariana you're a private investigator." My father's voice boomed in my head.

"No, Mr. Castillo. There was never a right time, because I was avoiding this. Do you believe she would've come willingly had she known?"

Dad returned to his overstuffed, reading chair next to the loveseat. He ran a hand through his thick peppered curls. "Cassius, you're the best at what you do. And you know lies lead to more lies." Dad blew out a long breath and sat back.

"Mariana—"

"Don't talk to me." I tightened my jaw to the point of aching. "Cassius. Get. Away. From. Me."

"Mariana, listen to me, please."

"My dad is right, lies lead to lies. You, me, we are a lie. This was planned. My father hired you?" I held my ground and refused to shed tears on his behalf. I bit my lip. The pain was better than feeling his betrayal.

"No. I've known your father for nearly six months. We met at a town meeting. Then I met your family. They told me about

90

your predicament. I wanted to help. Your father wanted to hire me, but I said no because…" Cassius halted his explanation as my cold stare fell on Aunt Samantha.

"You asked me for the farm's address and…and I foolishly gave it to you." I swallowed attempting to find reason for his pretense, and the answers behind his affections for me. The invisible blindfold faded and my mind's eye saw. "Auntie, you taught Cassius how to block his emotions. That's why I couldn't read him, so much deception." I flexed my fingers.

All lies. Every single day I was with him I lived a lie.

Dad jumped to his feet. "Young lady, don't you blame your Aunt Samantha. She's been the one person who has defended you throughout your escapades." He returned to his chair.

"Dad, I had to go."

"No. You *chose* to go. I told you we'd find a way to keep you safe from your attacker, but instead you went into a lion's den." He fell silent, squared his shoulders, and rested his head on the chair's back.

I had witnessed Dad's cold demeanor more times than I cared to recall.

Cassius tightened his lips and scrubbed his hands over his face. He strode in the direction of the windows did an about face and gave me the most pitiful gaze. "Mariana, you *are* the most real part of my life. Until I met you, my days were just occurrences mixing into the past. You're not a lie. You're my one truth."

"The *package* is delivered. You can go now, Mr. Private Eye." I stood and held my fisted hands at my sides. "Aunt Samantha, is my room still the same one?"

"Yes, Mariana, but please listen to me."

"Nothing needs to be said, Auntie. I'm tired. I need to sleep." I headed for the hallway.

"Mariana, please?" Cassius's voice choked.

I paused and turned half way. "There's *nothing* more to talk about. Cassius, stay clear of my family, especially from my… nephew. Forget me, Mr. Russo. Forget me."

Distance is imperative. I'm a fool for hoping.

I headed to my bedroom, shut the door, and slumped against it. Rubbing my temples, I thought of the last twenty-four hours.

Why didn't I see this coming? Cassius, the fix-it-man, all the mysterious calls, I'm blind when it comes to men.

I kicked off my shoes, fell into bed, and cocooned myself in the blankets. That night, sleep wrapped me in multiple dreams. Cassius and Michael were in every one of them. My warm homecoming froze over.

CHAPTER 8

THE TRUTH LIES DORMANT

The past three weeks were a hell. Mariana refused to see me or take my calls. Every time I phoned, Mr. Castillo would say, "Be patient, Cassius."

Darn that woman. Thoughts of Mariana burrowed under my skin to the point where I dreamt of her. Alcohol didn't do any good, either, when I drank, I felt as if she was standing before me, grinning that all knowing smile. Mariana's words about family and for the family's safety were on replay.

When Mariana found out I was a private investigator, she stormed out of the library, and left me staring at her back. Her father said, "Son, give her time. My daughter is as stubborn as a mother possum protecting her young." Huh, give her time? Who needs a drama princess? Pretty soon I'll brush her off my skin and not look back.

Lounging in my desk chair, I wondered why I gave this girl more thought than necessary.

This is a job. After this assignment, I'm out of here.

I had a temporary living arrangement above the office. It was a comfortable bachelor's pad with a one bath, two bedroom apartment equipped with a chef's kitchen, and living room. This set-up became home away from home, too much so. The private eye company was our front.

For two years, my FBI partners and I infiltrated and befriended the underworld of organized crime. We were close to sending Randolph and his scum affiliates to their permanent residence, behind bars. A few more details needed to be worked out, but I anticipated that by the end of next month, I'd be drinking a brewski somewhere on a beach and just kicking back, not thinking about some girl. A crazy one, at that.

I leaned into my chair and rolled a pencil between my fingers, thinking of my family. Visiting my mother and sister unburied old memories. I hadn't realized how much I missed them and The Outskirts.

I had lucked out on having my office below my living quarters. Convenience was a plus when it came to my line of work. I laughed inwardly when I recalled Bianca's words, "Your middle name is convenience, big brother. You're scared to leave us and go off to college."

I said, "No, I'm practical." *Huh, practical. I don't know about that anymore.*

Then Mom would jump into the conversation, "Cassius, don't push away spontaneity. You've been the man of the house long enough. It's time for you to live."

Their positive attitudes kept me going all these years. And one other fact, I was close to finding my father.

I pushed back in my desk chair and gulped down a cup of water. My eyes strained to stay open under the weight of a hangover. Last night a few of my buds and I went out for drinks. Man that was a forgettable night, literally.

A few minutes of shut-eye won't hurt.

What seemed like seconds later, the sound of a hand slap on wood jarred me out of my siesta. I heard a low snore escape me as I sucked in air. Chin against my chest, I drew my eyes up to meet Drake. He stood across from me, palms flat on my desk.

"Hey, bud." He held a smile of satisfaction. "Time to work."

I sat up straight. A kink in my neck shot pain down my spine. I stretched my neck side to side. "Drake, you're here earlier than norm." I gathered the scattered papers on the desk, avoiding my partner's piteous expression.

"Did you sleep all night in that chair?" Drake waited for a response. When none came he chuckled and said, "Man, she's gotcha roped, tied and branded."

Laughter came from the third desk in the office where Tracy my other partner sat. We worked long hours together, laughing, arguing, and sometimes just kicking back. Our desks faced each other in a U-shape.

"What's so funny, Tracy." I gathered the client files into a pile and rolled the chair away from the desk. I stood, but then sank back into the leather seat.

Man. My head feels like it's going to split open like a melon.

Feminine heels sounded on the wood floor, adding more pain to the hammering in my head. Tracy stepped around the coffee table and sofa in the middle of the room. She set a mug of green tea in front of me with a couple of aspirin. Her expression said, "You're a damn fool."

"Here, take this." She said.

"When did the two of you come in?" I scratched my chin.

"Exactly. When did we come in? You were so conked out. A thief could've waltzed in, pulled your pants down to your ankles, run off with your wallet, and you'd still be snoring. Now, take these pills."

"I wasn't sleepin', I was thinkin'." I scratched my head.

"Well, that's the first time I've heard you snoring while you think. Go on, Cas, take them."

"Tracy, I don't need—"

"Now, no backtalk. It's your fault your head feels like it's been thrown into the middle of a stampede." Tracy didn't budge until I swallowed the pills and drank the tea.

"Uh-hem," Drake agreed and smirked behind his coffee mug. He then said, "Last night, that one chick, what's her name?" He sat on the corner of the desk.

"Jennifer." I pushed my fingers through my hair.

"Yeah that's her. That hot piece of art was into you, but all you saw was your beer. Bro, you need to wake up. Used to be, no one could keep you from a good party. Yesterday, you were a complete hobo, sittin' on the stool, leanin' into the bar to keep your balance. No doubt, this Mariana girl has messed you up."

I eyed him, trying not to move my head. "Nah, that's not it. I'm just distracted by this latest client. I couldn't sleep last night, so I came back to the office and tracked down Ms. Espinosa's mother, only to find that the woman is dead."

I leaned back in the chair and scrubbed my face.

I'll kiss a donkey on the lips before I admit these two are right.

"Tracy, here's the phone number and cemetery address. Be a sweetheart and call Ms. Espinosa to inform her of her dearly departed mother."

"And what are you going to do?" Tracy arched one brow as she took hold of the paper.

"I'll be out of town. I found a lead on my father. This time it looks like the real deal."

"Sweet baby Jesus, Cassius Russo, this is your what, one hundreth attempt to locate your father? Cheeky boy, the news article says there was no trace of his body. That anonymous note you received last month doesn't prove he's alive. Cas, I can't stand to see you heartbroken again when you don't find him." She grabbed the files lying on my desk and stuck the note on top of them. "What you need to do is snap out of your funk and open your eyes."

"What are you talking about, Tracy?"

Drake shook his head and returned to his desk. Tracy sat in one of the chairs facing me with the files in her lap.

"All right, it's like this." She smoothed out the paper I had handed her. "Ever since you returned to the office from your so called trip to the north, which I had been led to believe was a visit to your mother and sister's place…" She glanced at Drake from the corner of her eye, and he looked down."…later to find out you were on a savior mission for some girl. Obviously she knew the right numbers to punch in and mess with your head. You poor baby, you're lost."

I shook my head, but stopped immediately. Wrong move. The painkillers hadn't kicked in yet.

"Oh, yes, Cas. You gots what we call, sweetheart hangover and the only way to take care of it, is to confront it head on." Tracy paused, but I knew she was not finished. "Cas, you're walking blind. You need to call this girl, Mariana, or bury her name in the back yard and move on." She grabbed a post-it off my desk and scribbled something on it. "Here." She stuck it to my forehead and then sat.

I pulled it off and read. One word stared back at me, *Mariana*. I glanced at Drake. He nodded solemnly.

"Fine, I hear you loud and clear. When I get back I'll call her." I stuck the note on my calendar. "But, I can't ignore this lead."

My partners stared back.

"What? Is that not good enough?" I slouched in the chair.

"It's a start. But remember, Mariana has lost faith in you. You need to come clean and tell her everything." Tracy shook her index finger at me.

"Everything? Tracy, I can't tell her everything I know about her so called friend, Marino. And—"

"Shoot. You sure can be thick headed when you choose to be. Cas, I'll type out an outline if you need me to, but first try to listen. We women need to know that our man is going to be there for us. Our man will need to dance along with us during the monthly drama song and keep tempo when we need him to. We women need a man that won't give up when he knows deep down, he loves us and nothin' in this world, not even booze, keeps his girl off his mind." Tracy gave me a know-it-all stare.

"Yeah, okay, Tracy, but what if this so called woman, pushes the man that loves her away and wants nothing to do with him, then what?"

"The great Russo is afraid of female rejection? Ha! Where's the Cassius I met three years ago? This here, Mr. Russo..." Tracy pointed to the post-it with Mariana's name, "...is the real deal." Tracy stood, placed the files back on my desk, and laid her hands flat on top of them.

She leaned forward and stared me down. Her caramel irises grew bigger. "You love that girl and you're afraid to admit it, out loud no less. Push your ego aside and tell her that you love her. It's as simple as that." Tracy straightened her posture and opened her arms wide expressing how she saw it to be an easy task.

"You weren't in her father's house the night she told me to stay away. It's like she locked herself in a room and a robotic Mariana took her place."

"It's called self-preservation." Drake stepped forward.

"Uh-huh." Tracy agreed.

"Pfft, yeah right. Or she's a crazy girl carrying some deep psycho garbage." I pushed up against the chair and sniffed. The aspirin was starting to do its job. The look in their eyes gave me the feeling I was getting nowhere. I knew I was outnumbered by three. Tracy's persuasiveness was two people in one and Drake was along for the ride.

"Cassius, from what you've told us, Mariana has felt and seen things that not too many people could handle and still remain sane. She pushed the cold and distant button on and shoved you to the curb. You, my friend, need to disassemble that button." Drake sat in the other chair and crossed his arms over his chest.

I snorted. "She's one stubborn chick. I don't need the drama."

"Ha! Sorry, Bro, you're in it neck deep." Drake let out another hardy laugh.

"Did you think she'd fall into your arms after finding out you had brought her home under false pretense? I mean, come now, Dimple Boy, you had to know she believed in you and then *bam,* she's punched in the gut. Heck! I would've literally *punched* you." Tracy sat back in her chair, giving me her puppy eyed face.

How could I not listen or take their advice? These two had covered my back more times than I could count. Drake, a farm boy, had enrolled in the police academy with me. After four years on the force, he and I joined the Federal Bureau of Investigation. Tracy's family emigrated from Jamaica to Chicago. She was born and bred in the U.S. I met her on official business in the windy city. Tracy had been between jobs and assisted me on a case unofficially. She relocated to California and after her credentials cleared, she came on board as our third partner.

We are clock work. The sensible Jamaican beauty keeps the two men in check while Drake and I protect Tracy like a sister, even though she can hold her own against a thug.

"All right, I give." I bowed my head and raised my hands. "What you've said has been heard and understood. I promise when I get back it'll be the first thing I do. I'll have a serious talk with Mariana." I got to my feet, grabbed a backpack from under the desk, and hung the straps over my shoulder.

"Whoa! And where do you think you're going? You look like the living dead and your head is doing its own dance. Have you even eaten anything?" Tracy blocked my way.

"I got coffee in the thermos, and I'll get something to eat when I'm on the road."

"Males, straight forward creatures and too tough for their own good, here take this bag."

I squinted. "What's in here?"

"Dear Dimples, food! I know you almost as well as your dear mother. You'll ride with only coffee in you for hours. Cas, we need you back in one piece, you hear?" Tracy huffed.

"Yes, Mommy." I kissed her on the cheek.

"Don't forget to keep us in the loop." She waved her manicured finger at me.

"Godspeed, Bro. You takin' your Harley?"

"Yes, it's out back."

"Which way will you be goin'?" Tracy picked up the folders from my desk and started to file them in the cabinet.

We logged electronic files, but a paper trail was inevitable. The client info was kept locked in a cabinet.

"I'll be riding south. The destination borders Mexico."

Tracy glared over her shoulder. "Men." She said.

I gave her another quick peck on the cheek.

"Promise me, Tracy, you'll keep Drake in line?"

She laughed and turned back to work.

"Oh, I'll keep her as close as possible." Drake grinned.

I knew Drake and Tracy had a thing for each other, just couldn't figure out why they had not taken the final step to the I do's. They were probably waiting on me so I wouldn't be the third wheel when we went out together.

"I'll be gone three days, tops. Tracy, inform Mr. Castillo, if he needs to contact me, he can call the private number. I have the second cell in my bag, and I'll check it periodically."

"Will do. Cassius, stay out of trouble."

With a nod and a wave, I walked out the back door.

* * *

I rode for eight hours only stopping for gas, bathroom, and extra food. It was mid-afternoon when I passed through high wrought-iron gates onto a winding road between rows of magnolias. In the distance, a Spanish hacienda awaited with a welcoming landscape.

Two days ago, I researched this place on behalf of a client. The client's mother was here, but I also found a whisper in the wind. This whisper hit me in the gut. It was a lead I could not ignore.

I parked near the front doors, took off my helmet, and slid it onto the handle bar. I dismounted and my boots clanked on the sidewalk. I stretched my back and focused on the building's stucco arches that shaded the walkway to the double oak doors.

This house once belonged to a Mr. and Mrs. Cruz, who were vintners. The surrounding land held acres upon acres of vineyards. Their daughter, a neurologist, Doctor Marissa Cruz inherited the place including all the land when her parents died in a car crash. She later turned the home into an assisted living facility. My research led me to a news article which stated that at the time of the renovation the doctor generously offered her parent's home for ten live-in patients dealing with head traumas or fatal neurological impairments. The upscale living accommodations were like a five-star hotel. Couldn't ask for more, pool, gym, gourmet chef, gardens, benches facing the mountains— the perfect package.

"Not a bad place to live out your days." I said to no one as I opened the front door.

A girl with short bangs and heavy eyeliner sitting behind the front desk glanced up.

"Hello Sir. How may I help you?"

"Hi, I'm here to visit a Jacob Russo."

"I'm sorry sir there is no one here by that name."

"Oh right, he probably goes by the name Jacks Russo." I gave her my best smile.

"I apologize, but there is no one by that name living here either." The receptionist frowned. "Sir, who exactly are you looking for?"

"Well, uh…my father. I was told he was living here." I snapped my fingers. "I know. He's most likely under the name of Jacks Stephano."

I watched as her hand went under the desk top. Undoubtedly, she had buzzed for back up, a sign that I either was bugging her, or I had finally found my father. Two, mammoth, body builders dressed in white uniforms appeared from the left wing of the house. Needless to say they were not smiling.

The younger of the two came forward. "Karen, is there a problem here?"

"This gentleman has asked to see his father, but I've told him there's no one living here by the names he mentioned. I thought maybe you might know, Larry."

I stepped back three paces. "Perhaps, I could speak to Dr. Cruz?" They closed the gap. "You know what, how about I leave my name and phone number with you, Ms. Karen, is it?"

The two guys crossed their arms over their chests. "The doctor is not here and all information is confidential." Larry lowered his brow.

I nodded and took another step back. "I understand." I handed Karen my private eye card.

She glanced at the card and smiled. "Thank you, Mr. Russo. When the doctor arrives I'll give her the information. I'm sorry I couldn't help you more."

"No worries." I turned to leave. Head lowered, I opened the door to exit, but instead held it open for a woman dressed to stun. She crossed the threshold in knee-high boots, a navy blue dress fitted over a body with all the right curves. The dress matched her eyes. She tucked her brunette hair behind her ear.

"Thank you." She said.

"You're welcome." I crossed the threshold.

"Mr. Russo? Cassius Russo?" The woman asked.

I halted, and held the door open, facing the Latin beauty. "Yes, ma'am. I'm Cassius Russo."

Karen stood. "Dr. Cruz, this gentleman came by looking for a Mr. Jacks Russo, but then he mentioned a Jacks Stephano."

"I see. Mr. Russo, do you have identification?"

"Yes, doctor." I entered the building again and shoved my hand in my jacket's inside pocket. The two males made a move my way when they saw my holster. I held my hands in the air. "Easy guys. I'm getting my I.D."

I pulled out my wallet with two fingers and handed it to the doctor. She stared at my photo for few seconds before she looked up at me. "I can't believe it. He told me you'd be the one to find him." She handed me the wallet and rubbed her goosed bumped arms.

"I'm sorry, Doctor, he?"

"Your father, of course, but how did you find him?"

"Doctor, are you saying my father is here?"

The doctor kept her eyes on mine as she gave me a careful nod.

"I was on a case for a client, and I happened to see the name Jacks and Stephano. The name Jacks is my father's nickname and Stephano is his mother's maiden name. It seemed too much of a coincidence so here I am."

"You saw the name?" The doctor leaned her head to the side.

"Huh, let's say I have a partner that's a genius when it comes to uh…deciphering codes on the computer." I grinned broadly.

The two men kept the circle tight. They didn't look pleased with my explanation.

"I'm a private investigator." I lifted my chin and gave them the 'what now' look.

"Ah, very well." She faced the receptionist. "Karen, call Phil. Tell him we need to update our passwords, as of two days ago."

"Doctor, how did you know I was Cassius Russo?"

She faced me again. "Please, follow me. You need to see this, Mr. Russo."

The two guys stepped aside as the doctor and I walked by. We ambled down a carpeted hallway, passed two doors, and at the third halted. The doctor knocked, but there was no answer.

"Oh, that's right. Your father is most likely wading in the pool. He loves the water, you know?"

I shrugged. "No, I can't say I do."

"Oh. Sorry for the assumption. It's been many years since you've seen him, correct?"

"Many years? Yeah, that's about right." I scoffed.

"Right." The doctor lowered her eyes and retrieved a ring with keys from her purse. She unlocked the door and looked back at me. "I normally don't do this, but there are exceptions. It's important you see before you meet your father." She stepped into the room. I followed.

A well lit room with a panoramic window faced the mountain range. It was a comfortable living space with a bookshelf covering one whole wall. I remembered how my father loved to read. I was drawn to the matching night stands on either side of the king sized bed. I stared at what rested on top of them. Picture frames with photos of…my family. I got closer and saw picture after picture of us. Frozen in time were photos of Bianca, from one year old till now and me with my mother. One picture was of my father with his arm around my shoulders. The photo had been taken around the time he left us.

I held the frame that lodged my sister's photo, taken last New Year's Eve.

"How's this possible?"

"Your mother knows about your father. She sent him all these photos."

"My mother?" I must've had a disgusted look on my face because the doctor stepped back.

"Mr. Russo, shall we sit?" Dr. Cruz pointed to the chairs.

I set the picture back on the nightstand and followed suit.

"Mr. Russo—"

"Cassius is fine."

103

She smiled. "Cassius, your mother has corresponded with your father for years only she doesn't know where he lives, because all his mail is delivered to a P.O. Box."

"Huh." I grunted.

"Please, don't be angry with your mother. Your father made her promise not to tell you or your sister that he was alive. It was for the family's safety and after his diagnosis he didn't want the family to suffer by watching him fade away."

"Didn't want us to suffer? Too late for that." I blew out a long breath to keep my anger in check.

Doctor Cruz held her hands in front of her in a protective manner. She was no fool to the tension in the room.

"Look, I'm sorry, but my father has a lot of explaining to do. You said, fade away, how?" I propped my elbows on my knees and rubbed my forehead.

"Your father suffers from FTD, frontotemporal dementia." Dr. Cruz relaxed and laid her hands in her lap. "He left his family to keep all of you safe. When he suspected his condition he wrote to me for a diagnosis. Once it was confirmed that he definitely had FTD, he checked himself in here to live out the rest of his days."

"What do you know about keeping our family safe?" I exhaled loudly.

"Your father and I have had many talks. He loves you very much."

"Ha! Now that's a joke." I jumped to my feet and paced around the room. "You're telling me, *Doctor*, that my father checked himself in here instead of being with his family? Who's paying for all of this?"

She crossed her legs, all the while holding onto her calm professional posture. "Cassius, your father generously donated two million dollars to the FTD research foundation. He has also deposited in a private account a generous amount for you and your family. I'm to hand over the will once he has deceased. This way no one can come after you to get to him."

"But why did he leave? And don't tell me for the safety of the family." My anger became a challenge to harness.

104

"Please, Cassius will you sit? You're making me nervous."

"Sure no problem, Doc, don't want to make you nervous." I returned to my chair.

Holding her breath and then releasing it, she uncrossed her legs and said, "You first must understand what FTD is exactly. Your father's condition has no cure and it's progressive. He's losing day by day more neurons in his frontal and temporal lobes."

"How much time does he have?"

"There's no exact date. Every patient differs. Your father might have a year or more."

"How is he now? Does he still recognize people?"

"Yes, his recognition is still intact. But the semantic dementia is noticeable."

I lifted my brow.

"Your father's verbal domain is impaired. At times, some patient's speech slur. They are able to articulate words but produce frequent near misses, for example they might say sitter instead of sister. Your father comprehends sentences, but following a full conversation is difficult for him, especially if too many speakers are in the room. Communicating by phone is not easy either. His speech slurs excessively now."

"Fine. I hear what you're telling me, but what about the years before the onset of FTD? Where in the hell did my father go and why? Sorry doctor. I know you had nothing to do with him flaking out on his family." I stood, shoved my hands in my pants pockets and strode to the window. I could see why my father had chosen this place near the Mexican border. The view was spectacular and seclusion had always been a priority for his family or for him.

"What eventually will happen to my father?" I continued to admire the vista.

"The speed of decline is different from person to person. FTD causes muscle weakness. Problems swallowing, chewing, moving and controlling bladder or bowels can occur. Eventually patients with FTD degeneration die from the physical changes that can cause skin, urinary tract or lung infections." Dr. Cruz sniffed.

I faced her. She wiped her eyes and forced a smile.

"Cassius the one important fact is that you're here. Your father will be very happy to see you. I know because he talks frequently about you. Every single day, he dusts his picture frames. No one is allowed to touch them."

I shook my head and headed for the door. The doctor rose and followed.

"Please, Cassius, talk to your father. At least let him see you." Dr. Cruz placed a hand on my arm. "His language abilities have declined, but his right temporal lobe has not been affected as of yet. Your father recognizes family and friends."

"All these years I've been living a lie. Believing my father had...died."

I crossed the bedroom and opened the door to leave. Before me stood a man I hadn't seen in decades. Had it not been for the eyes, I wouldn't have recognized my father. His hair was silver and he hunched over slightly. My father, the strong man who taught me how to hunt, live off the land, and treat everyone with respect stared back through fifty-six year old eyes, but his facial features belied his age.

"Dad."

"Ka...sss...us."

Words could not exactly explain the emotions firing through my head. Before me stood the man who had been my hero. He wound his arms around me. My father then released his embrace and moved towards the sofa. He motioned for me to do the same. My first gut feeling was to walk out, but curiosity and his glare kept me from leaving. The three of us sat in silence until my father attempted to speak.

"Ka...sss...us. Gud son. So...so m u u ch tulk about."

"Dad, what happened? Why did you leave Mom? Why leave us?"

He grimaced.

"Jacks are you in pain?" The doctor scooted to the edge of her chair.

My father shook his head. He lifted his hands, shoving them forward in the air, as if he wanted the doctor to wait. Dr. Cruz sat back and folded her hands in her lap.

My father looked me in the eye. "Girrl...rred...b u ll uun. M u ussst le eeve." He exhaled as if he were in pain. His bitter beer face churned my gut. A simple sentence was torture for him. But, his eyes reflected the urgency he felt. Wide hand movements expressed his need for us to listen.

"What is he saying? Girl red balloon?" I stared at the doctor for affirmation.

She nodded. "Be patient, Cassius. This is difficult for him."

My father squeezed his head between his hands, then stood, and shuffled over to his dresser. He opened the top drawer and pulled three envelopes from under a sweater. He then returned to the sofa.

"F...fo r you." He handed me one of the envelopes.

I exhaled a quick blast of air and settled back in my chair. My name was written in bold letters. A date in the left hand corner confirmed the letter had been written six months ago.

"Ka...sss...us, ree ad." My father grinned. He scooted back into the sofa, leaned his head against the wall, and closed his eyes.

I looked at the doctor questioning this letter in silence. She tightened her lips and stared at her folded hands. I tore one end of the envelope and pulled the letter out. Unfolding the paper revealed the same bold lettering. I blew out another frustrated breath and read.

Cassius, my son, if you are reading this letter it confirms that my speech function has declined considerably. I love you, Cassius. I've thought of you and the family every single day. And I've imagined sitting across from you explaining my sudden disappearance. Your childhood and juvenile years didn't go unnoticed. I've kept tabs on your good and bad times. A father couldn't be prouder of his children. Cassius, do you remember the last morning we went hunting? You were ten. A piece of my sanity left me that day as I looked into your eyes and told you I had to leave for the family's safety. I knew you were too young to understand and I knew your hatred towards me would fester. I hope with this explanation you will agree that family always takes precedence. The U.S. government hired me to clean the disorder created by man's greed. Yes, I was a hitman for hire. Before I met your mother, my life existed from one mission to another. Once we married, the jobs lessened, but I was never completely free. The first time my sanity suffered a blow was when I witnessed and heard a child's cry after her mother fell onto the sidewalk, dead. I was hired to protect John Castillo and in turn this was my last contracted job. John assisted the local government on taking down organized crime. His exceptional gift of clairvoyance enabled him to inform the authorities when contraband was crossing the Mexican border into California. The Cartel had placed a bounty on his head—their number one priority. John didn't scare easily and so he continued to assist the feds as I became his shadow. A day out with the family turned into my nightmare. I walked ahead of them to check their car. When I turned around all four were on the sidewalk. Behind them I caught the sun's reflection off a rifle's scope. Sitting on a nearby bench, a man in black aimed his short barreled rifle at John's family. The hunter in me took over. I took aim and fired. The hit was dead on, but Mariana's red balloon flew away. Her mother jumped forward to catch it. My one and only time, I fired two rounds on a marked hit. As soon as the first bullet didn't meet its mark, I fired another shot. Amelia Castillo and the man, hired to kill John Castillo, were dead. The red balloon haunts my sleepless nights along with Mariana's voice calling out to her mother. Soon after, word came through the grapevine that my family or I must pay. Word traveled to the Cartel that my plane had been bombed. My demise was over the Pacific Ocean. The other blow to my sanity was saying goodbye to my children and wife. Cassius, my actions have been solely for the family's safety. Choosing not to be with my wife and children was a sacrifice I had to make. Your mother knew I lived, but she never knew where I was. Don't ever blame her.

Jacks Stephano.

I stared at the letter.

I don't know when my father opened his eyes, but he stooped towards me.

"Ka…sss…us." He squeezed my hand. "I l l ove uuu. Not m u th r f u l t." He squeezed my hand again and shook his head.

"Yes, I know it's not mother's fault. I understand Dad, family comes first." I sucked in a tired breath and exhaled through my nose. "Damn, Mariana's mother was killed by your gun."

"Y e sss." He sat back, looking as deflated as I felt.

"Does Mom know about Mariana's mother?"

"No." My father shook his head. "O n nly fa a m i ly s a f f e ty." Beads of perspiration spotted his forehead.

"So Mom knows you left to keep the family safe?"

My father nodded yes as he blew out a long breath.

"Dad, years later Mariana was attacked and raped in her senior year of college."

My father wrinkled his brow and ran a hand over his upper lip. "Mari, lit-t-le, Mari."

"Now, I don't know if the attack is connected to the Cartel, but she's deep in with Marino. He found her the night she was raped. I vowed to her father that when I find the S.O.B who did that to her, he'll pay, even if it's with his life."

The doctor cleared her throat.

I glanced over at her. "Well, I won't kill him, but he'll be sorry he hurt her."

My father grunted. It was obvious this conversation had drained him.

"Cassius, perhaps we should go now so your father can rest." The doctor stood and waited for me to do the same.

I stepped around the coffee table and hugged my father. His eyes brightened.

I whispered in his ear. "I'll be back, Dad, promise. I love you too."

My father handed me the other two letters. One was for my mother the other for Bianca. I tucked all three inside my jacket pocket and left. The doctor met me at the front door.

"Cassius, thank you for making your father happy."

"Doctor, don't thank me. Thank your poor computer firewalls."

I left the hacienda, slid onto my Harley and rode off.

* * *

Hours later, tired, but renewed in hope, I sat behind my office desk. Tracy was the first to see me.

"Well, 'tis one good day when a woman walks into a room and sees Mr. Cassius Russo working." Tracy rested her hands on her hips and gave a short clipped laugh.

"Hey, Tracy, it's good to see you too."

"Cassius, did Drake tell you what his plans were for today? I mean did you send him out on a job?" Tracy swallowed. It looked as if she were holding back tears.

"Sorry, I arrived early this morning and…come to think of it I haven't received any messages from Drake. What's going on, Tracy?"

"Drake received a call this morning as we were having breakfast. He told me he had to go meet a client, but I didn't have a chance to ask him who or where. As I picked up the dishes from the table, I turned to ask, but he had already slipped out of the apartment without even a hug."

"Huh. Well, I wouldn't worry. Drake knows how to take care of himself."

"Yes, that he does, but it was strange how he left without a word. I've called his cell, but it goes straight to his voice mail. Wherever he is mustn't have good service." Tracy wrinkled her brow.

"Hey gorgeous, don't frown, you'll get permanent wrinkles." I gave her one of my best smiles. Tracy forced one back.

"Drake is most likely following a lead on Marino's dealings. He'll fill us in. Hey, would you mind mailing these two letters for me?" I handed them across the desk to her.

Tracy glanced at the names. "And do tell why you can't deliver them yourself? Your mother and sister don't see enough of you." She waited for an answer, head cocked to the side.

"I would go, but tomorrow I'm having a talk with Mariana. What I need right now is a hot shower and that king size bed waiting for me upstairs."

"Hmm, good. More than about time you go talk to that girl." Tracy lifted the mail bag and shoved the two letters inside. "I'll be back shortly. You want anything from the deli?"

"Uh, yeah, that'll be great. If I don't answer, use the spare key and leave the food on the counter. Thanks."

"No thanks needed. I'll order your usual sandwich and soup. But, if you don't talk to that girl tomorrow you'll be in hot soup with me."

"Yeah, I hear ya." A headache had kept me company on the ride home. I squeezed the bridge of my nose to alleviate the pain.

"Cas, you all right?"

"Yes, just tired."

"All right, if you say so. I'll be back in a few." Tracy closed the back door with her free hand.

Hot soup, huh, the info I had received was a jumble of alphabet soup. How was I going to approach Mariana with what I knew?

Man, she's had enough pain in her life.

CHAPTER 9

A FATHER'S SECRET

The Harley cruised through Castillo Farm's main driveway. I encountered Mariana's father under the shop's awning. I parked the bike and hung my helmet on the bars. John Castillo pulled off his work gloves, tossed them onto the metal table, and met me halfway. We shook hands. I sucked in air as an electric shock ran up my arm.

What was that?

I examined my hand. My fingertips still tingled.

"Young man, she must never know." Mr. Castillo held a stern frown.

I lifted my head and met his eyes. "Sir, what must she never know?"

"You found your father and you know how Mariana's mother died, correct?"

"Yes, sir." I nodded.

"Then you know not all truths are meant to be told or known." Mr. Castillo stepped back and leaned his left hip against the worktable. He studied me longer than I cared for.

"Mr. Castillo—"

"Cassius, we've known each other long enough, it's John. Let's keep this simple."

"All right. My father wrote me a letter. He mentioned how he helped your family."

"Yes. That's correct."

"He was your family's bodyguard."

A distant, weary expression came over him. He resembled a man standing on a stockade wall looking out onto the plains, the sun beating down on him with no hope to grasp.

"John?"

112

"I told Jacks enough was enough and to report back to his superiors that I demanded he not guard my family anymore. I forced him to leave at gunpoint but…" He flexed his hands as if trying to get circulation back in them. "After my wife died, your father, Cassius, felt duty-bound. He saw you and your sister in my children. Jack's sense of family is strong. In his mind, he did not leave his family, he saved them."

"Yeah, right, family. John, my father also mentioned that you're clairvoyant."

"I am." John wiped his brow with the back of his hand.

"And Mariana and Ms. Samantha are too. Anyone else I should know about?" I sat on my Harley.

"Well now, that's not my place to say. If others do have the gift and they choose to reveal it to you, it'll be their choice." John lifted a callused hand to his chin and rubbed it.

"John, how do I keep this information from Mariana? If she ever finds out, she'll hate me for life."

"Why would Mariana hate you? You were ten when her mother died. Cassius, every truth shouldn't be told. There is a place and time for all circumstances. Right now telling my daughter what you know won't help her."

I shook my head. "I don't know about that. You saw how Mariana reacted when she found out about me being a P.I. She doesn't handle lies well."

"No, it's for her safety and peace of mind. My daughter loves you, Cassius. With time she'll see the truth. But now, if you tell her, all she'll see is the son of the man who killed her mother."

I dragged out a long breath and raked my fingers through my hair. "Even, if it was an accident?"

"Exactly, so you know nothing and the past stays in the past." John stood up straight.

"Yeah, until, the past bites me in the butt." I kicked Mikey's abandoned soccer ball under the table.

"We'll rebuild that bridge if necessary. For now Mariana must not know." John came forward and patted me on the back. "Let's go inside and have a drink."

Ms. Samantha joined us on the tail-end of our conversation. She held a purse in hand. Her usual flower print apron over blouse and jeans was gone. In its place was a navy blue suit fitted to a slender waist line. This woman exuded beauty and an elegance that commanded attention. I knew she was close to eighty, but she certainly didn't look her age.

"Cassius, what a surprise. I was just going to ask John to drive me to your office. You must've read my thoughts." Ms. Samantha's eyes beamed as she finished her sentence.

"Glad I saved you the trouble. You look real pretty, Ms. Samantha. It would be a shame to not take advantage of your fancy suit there. How about I buy the family dinner tonight?"

"Thank you, Cassius." Her cheeks gained a little more blush. "Going to dinner is an excellent idea. But…the one you must convince is our dear, Mariana." Her smile broadened.

"Speaking of Mariana, is she inside?" I jutted my chin toward the house.

"No. She went to pick up Mikey from day care. He loves interacting with the other children. We old farts don't have the magic like children do." Ms. Samantha shared an inaudible expression with John.

"Huh, that's funny. Ms. Samantha, I believe you have more magic in that delicate pinky of yours than you care to share." I kissed her on the cheek. "John invited me for a drink. Will you accompany us? We can come up with a plan to convince Mariana to join us for dinner tonight."

"That's the best idea I've heard in the last two weeks. I actually wanted to talk to you about her." Ms. Samantha hooked her arm around mine. "Cassius, my name is simply Samantha."

I smiled. The three of us strolled to the house. I left my Harley under the shop's awning where Mariana wouldn't see it when she arrived.

On entering the library, booted footsteps from an adjoining room sounded on the wood floor. Frank peeked around the doorframe.

"I thought I heard a familiar voice. How's it going, Cassius?" Frank shook my hand.

Another tingle ran up my arm, but not as strong as John's. I frowned, but said nothing. Frank smirked.

"You know about my mother. It's going to be tricky keeping Mariana in the dark." Frank held an unworried air about him. You might say he appeared amused.

"Frank, would you mind fixing us a drink?"

"Sure thing, Dad."

Frank went to the mini-bar set up in the dining area. He placed four glasses on a tray and poured brandy into each glass. I followed his moves, not quite certain how to respond to what he had said. He offered me a drink first.

"Thanks." I raised the crystal tumbler in salute and downed a swig.

Frank handed John and Samantha their drinks and then placed the tray on the coffee table. He sat with his ankles crossed and took a swig from his own. A satisfied grin spread across his face. I tried to pull off the same look. Samantha and John sat in twin chairs, facing us. I wondered if it was just me that felt uncomfortable even though this was not my first time talking to them.

This family held a strong resemblance. Samantha was not related to the Castillos, but in every other sense she was family. She and Mary Castillo, John's mother, had grown up together. I glanced at John. He set his glass on a side table and then rested his hands, palms together, against his mouth. A deep crease etched between his brows. He then looked up at me and fanned his hands on his knees.

"Well, we don't have much time before Mariana returns. Cassius, in your thoughts you need to see your father and only your father, nothing else about that fateful day. Think about when you were a child hunting with him. Mariana's mind is clouded by Marino's words and her fears. Ironic really, we want Mariana to face her fears and abolish them, but right now they'll be helpful, because fear blocks the process of foresight."

"John, are you saying that if I only think of my father and me, Mariana won't see what I know about her mother?"

"That's exactly what I'm sayin'."

Frank rose from his seat. He went around the sofa, tapped me on the shoulder and said, "It's good that you're back, Cassius. I'll be in the kitchen keeping an eye out for Mariana." He sauntered on out as if we'd had a chat about the ball game on T.V.

Samantha let out a tired sigh and joined me on the sofa. She took my tumbler, placed it on the coffee table and then rested her freckled hands on mine. Her bronzed skin housed few wrinkles, except for the laugh lines near the corners of her eyes. She stared at me as if she could see directly into my soul.

"Cassius, Mariana will need you to be strong for her sake. When you believe she's gone and she no longer wants to see you *that* will be the moment she'll need to hear these words, 'heart of my heart, together we be for eternity'." A single tear rolled down Samantha's cheek.

What is this woman talkin' about? I see where Mariana gets it from.

"Trust me, Cassius. Say, 'heart of my heart, together we be for eternity.' Memorize those words."

I guess it can't hurt. I nodded and repeated the words under my breath.

"Samantha, why do you want me to memorize that? Did you see some kind of bleak future of me with Mariana?"

Sad eyes stared back at me. She nodded, "Do *not* believe in Mariana's granite heart. When you see her frigid demeanor remember it's a façade. Her heart cries for companionship. You, Cassius, are the one. Don't forget what I've told you. Heart of my heart, together we be for eternity. Do *not* forget."

"But I don't understand." I felt a small pang on my left temple.

"You will when the correct moment reveals itself." She tightened her lips and nodded once.

John scooted back into his chair and closed his eyes. I had a weird feeling he was sensing what Samantha felt, but I was not certain.

Samantha eyed John. Her smile faded as she said, "John and I have talked about telling Mariana who truly killed her mother, but you see, your father was like an uncle to her. When she was five he read her Stella Luna practically every night before bedtime, played go-fish, and talked to her as if she were his daughter. She loved him very much. I see the pain in your eyes, Cassius. Bianca and you were unjustly robbed of your father's love, but know that every night Jacob wept and prayed for your safety. Your father would rather have died than place his family's life in jeopardy. For Jacob Russo, leaving his family and faking his death was the one way he knew how to keep you safe."

I shook my head and drew my hands into fists. "I have one question for John," I said above a whisper, holding my frustration in check.

John opened his eyes.

"After my father went into hiatus, who protected you from the hitmen?"

"Samantha and I took matters into our own hands. We tapped into our abilities. Sometimes we were told by the gift when it was not safe to go out to help the authorities. You might say we were hermits. I told the local government I didn't want a bodyguard, but they wouldn't listen. After that incident, they listened."

"But if my father hadn't been there you wouldn't be alive."

"Exactly!" John balled his hands and leaned forward in his seat. "And my sweet Amelia would be with her daughter and son. I told them no. They wouldn't listen. Cassius, always listen to what is revealed. Or at least try to understand. I told them no." He looked at Samantha. "Samantha, I told them no." John's eyes pleaded for understanding. He then relaxed his shoulders, and flexed his fingers. Mariana had inherited her father's nervous twitch.

"I know you did, John. I know." Samantha then turned towards me. "Cassius, for the safety of the family, a father, mother, daughter, or son will go to extreme measures. At times the actions do not seem logical, but...it is the ultimate sacrifice." Samantha dried her eyes. "Our dear, Mariana, has always been too free spirited. My niece believed she could be herself and not have to hide her gift. She's paid a hefty price." Samantha moved her head side to side and clicked her tongue.

I coughed to clear my throat and drew my eyes away from her. I then said, "John, don't you worry about Mariana discovering who killed your wife? Your daughter might break all ties with you and the family." My gut told me this would be a hard truth to juggle.

"Yes, Cassius, I've thought of the consequences. Many times I've wanted to tell her the truth, or at least explain how and why her mother died, but Mariana sees life on a black and white screen. To her there is good and evil, but no in between. The day…" John bowed his head and rubbed his eyes. He then returned his gaze towards me. "The day my daughter told me she had been raped, I wanted to lock her in her room and never let her out of this house again. But, tell me, how does a human have the right to clip the wings of a free spirit? Mariana accepted her fate and faced her reality head on. Her example set me thinking. What happened to her mother was in the past, and…" John slammed a fist against the chair's arm. "After Amelia died, your father refused to leave. Perhaps it was guilt or a sense of duty that kept him from leaving and with me gone on business from time to time, Jacob shadowed our family. Mariana loves Jacob and the memories she holds onto will be destroyed if I tell her who shot the fatal bullet."

"You underestimate your daughter, John. She's stronger than most men I've met. God only knows what Mariana saw when she was living under Marino's roof. But, I'll respect your wishes. I won't tell her."

"Thank you." John massaged his knees. The horizontal creases on his forehead faded.

"Cassius, remember what John told you to guard your psyche from Mariana." Samantha linked her hands.

"Yes, I will." I sat with my back straight against the sofa. The thought of knowing such a truth and withholding it from Mariana weighed heavily on my mind. But then, I thought, what would Mariana gain with such a truth?

"Cassius, the truth will be revealed when fate chooses the day. Now, we don't have much time. This is going to be a twenty minute crash course on blocking your thoughts even more." Samantha retrieved my hands and squeezed them. "Look at me, Cassius."

I followed her command. An electric buzz surged through my ears. John left his chair and stood behind Samantha. Paranormal psyche class part B had begun.

CHAPTER 10

CAN'T RELAX TOO MUCH

As soon as I entered the day care class Mikey ran up to me. "Auntie Mari, see my picture?"

I knelt before my sweet son, kissed him on the forehead, and ruffled his hair. We hugged. I loved the scent of his little boy sweat mixed with Johnson shampoo.

I've missed so much of his first years of life.

"Auntie be careful. No bend paper." Mikey stepped back.

"Sorry about that. Wow, did you draw this all by yourself?"

"Uh huh." His proud stance made me smile.

"Super. I see an apple tree, clouds, and…who are these people?"

Mikey held the drawing to the side and pointed. "This is Daddy. He's happy you're back. In the middle, it's you with your gold curls. Will you make your curls brown again, Auntie?" He wrinkled his brow.

"Someday, I will, I promise. Mikey, who's this other person?" I touched the drawing.

"This is Cassius. See how he holds your hand. He likes you, Auntie." Mikey smiled innocently and hopped on one foot.

"Well, you've been very busy today, little Rembrandt." I ruffled his hair again. He shuffled to his right. I scooped him into my arms and tickled his belly.

Mikey squirmed, but then he kissed me on the cheek and said, "The teacher showed us pictures of old people who draw."

"You mean famous painters."

"Yes." Mikey rolled the paper into a cylinder.

"Well, Mikey-O, let's sign you out." I signed the in-and-out sheet while Mikey wrapped his arms around my neck. His warmth held me in a safe zone. A zone where I wished I could remain forever with him.

Shake it off girl. You're dreaming again.

"Bye, Miss Sara. See you tomorrow." Mikey waved and took hold of my hand.

We left the daycare and sat on a bench facing the building. The trees behind us had shed their leaves. Sun rays peeked through the clouds and crowned Mikey's head. He sat sideways in my lap as an angel in disguise, holding his drawing.

I watched his happy expression fade as his brow furrowed.

"What's wrong, Mikey?"

In a serious manner he gazed up at me. "Auntie Mari, how much do you love me?"

"Well, what a question." I pulled on his shirt collar. "I, little guy, love you to the ends of heaven."

His demeanor brightened. "Auntie, you funny. Heaven has no end." He held his adamant stare, daring me to challenge him.

"Exactly, and my love has no end." I waited.

Mikey's eyes smiled as a small laugh escaped him.

"You squirt, you were testing me." I pulled gently on his nose.

He moved to the side to avoid any more nose prodding. His happy hazel eyes gazed up at me.

"Mikey, why did you draw a picture of Cassius? Why not one of Grandpa or Auntie Samantha?"

"Cuz, Daddy is daddy. And you can be my mommy and—"

"But, Mikey your daddy is my brother we can't marry."

"I know." He stuck out his lower lip. "But, I can have two daddies and one mommy."

"Do you mean Cassius and I marry?"

Mikey's smile stretched from ear to ear. He bounced in my lap. "Yes."

"Aww, Sweetie, I don't know about that. Cassius might not want to marry and…"

I was at a loss for words. I *just* held Mikey close to my heart, rubbing his back.

121

Mikey withdrew from my embrace with his eyes wide open and said, "Auntie, Cassius loves you. I know."

"Well, Mr. Smarty, only in a blue moon will I ever know if Cassius loves me, right?"

"I guess so." He shrugged.

One corner of Mikey's shirt collar had rolled up. As I straightened it, he leaned towards me and kissed my cheek again. He then folded his arms around my neck and gave a little squeeze. His curls brushing against the side of my face unraveled my reserve.

How did I ever walk away from him? What kind of mother am I?

Mikey whispered in my ear. "Auntie, stay with family. I protect you."

On a short intake of breath, I nearly choked. Biting down on my bottom lip, I thought of what I should say, but my mind was a clean slate. Instead, I glanced at my watch.

"We better go. Auntie Samantha prepared your favorite for lunch, chicken soup. I bet she's wondering where we are."

"Mmm." Mikey rubbed his stomach and licked his lips. "I love chicken soup."

"Down you go, Mikey-O."

Mikey held the drawing under his arm. He took hold of my hand and looked up at me.

I can't have this sweet boy worrying about me. He's too young. What made him think of such a thing? Frank and I need to talk.

I shuddered. A tingle filled me from head to toe. Mikey attempted to tap into my thoughts. "I see that Auntie Samantha has taught you some new tricks." I stared down at him.

He cupped his mouth and giggled. "Grandpa, Daddy, and Auntie Samantha are different like us, Auntie."

"Yes, but it's a secret. Right? You must never tell your friends or anyone else. Okay, Mikey?"

"Auntie Samantha tells me that too." Mikey lowered his head. It was obvious he wasn't happy about masking his ability.

I knew all too well what it felt like to wear masks and how not wearing them led to trouble.

We stopped off to the side of the walkway and I knelt before him. "Mikey, believe me. It's better to not tell your friends about your gift. When you're older, you'll help many people, but now enjoy being a little boy. Do you understand?"

"I think so. You telling me to have fun and not listen to the voices." He brooded.

"If you hear a voice or have questions you go to Grandpa, your Daddy, Auntie Samantha or me, okay?" The thought of saying goodbye to him again muddied my happiness.

As if on cue, a Blue Jay landed two feet from us, pecking on a discarded cracker. Mikey followed its movements. He hopped, mimicking the bird. "Okay, Auntie. Look I hop like the birdie."

"Yeah, silly guy, time to go."

We strolled hand in hand toward the Wrangler. Cassius's friend loaned him a Harley. He had left the Jeep on the farm for my use. I hadn't spoken to Cassius in over three weeks, but the message had come via my brother about Cassius loaning me his car. When I showed indifference, Frank shook his head and said, "Girls are the hardest creatures to figure out. Sis, I know you're into him, but you insist on pretending you're not." I shrugged and walked off to my room. Secretly, I was glad that Cassius had forgotten his Polo sweater in the back seat. His cologne lingered. I wondered if he would miss it. Weird, I was not the kind of girl to hang onto mementos, but there I was thinking of stealing a man's sweater.

I opened the passenger door and was about to give Mikey a boost up into the seat when a voice literally stopped me in mid-motion.

"Well hello sweet e v e r y t h i n g. You new around here?"

I gulped hard, keeping down a gasp and kept my back to the voice. Mikey clung to my pant leg. I felt his body tremble. He peeked then hid his face behind my leg.

Shoot! I forgot my farmer's cap.

As fortune would have it, my sunglasses sat on my head. I pulled them down over my eyes and turned to face the man.

"Uh, hello." I swallowed again hoping my heart wouldn't jump out of my mouth.

Dear Lord it's Randolph!

"Hmm, you're a kind sight for my sore eyes. Where've you been hiding?"

"Hiding? Not really." My voice quivered. *Get a hold of yourself, Mariana.* "I'm new to these parts." *Think. Quick. Or he'll know you're not telling the truth.* "I'm the nanny. This little boy here is my charge. And he's late for lunch. Bye." I turned to help Mikey onto the seat.

"Now hold on there, baby." Randolph placed a hand on my forearm.

Oh, God, please help me keep it together. "Yes." I said coldly. *Don't turn Ice-Queen. He'll know it's you.* I gave him my best sweet smile.

"How 'bout you and I go out sometime for a drink? I can show you the sights."

"That's kind of you, really. But…I have a boyfriend overseas and well, you know?"

"Ah, come now, what the lion doesn't see, he can't eat." Randolph grinned.

"Thank you, Sir. But just the same, I better go now."

I swiveled around and nearly pushed Mikey into the passenger seat. Poor little guy kept looking down at his feet. If he cried, I think I might have also. I took a quick peek, as I seat-belted him. Mikey's eyes shot back a burning fire. Dear Lord, I believed if he'd been Cassius's size he would've taken that man down. I shook my head no. Mikey understood and kept quiet. I shut the door and scurried to the driver's side.

I shoved the key into the ignition while Randolph ambled around to my side. I choked the steering wheel with a white-knuckled grip. As he approached, I eased the tension in my hands, hoping he hadn't noticed, then stole a quick glance at the glove compartment. Cassius had told me there was a gun stashed in there, just in case I needed it.

Keep it together, girl. This is no time for the Ice-queen.

Randolph reached up and shoved a card through the half open window. "If you ever get lonely, baby, here's my number."

I took hold of the card and forced a smile. He held a satisfied smirk as he sauntered back onto the sidewalk. His egotistical aura reeked of self-righteousness. I started up the engine and drove off.

Breathe in, breathe out. He's gone. You did it girl. I felt as if I might hurl.

"Auntie Mari, you okay?" Mikey's voice released me from my panic attack.

Air gushed out of my lungs. Short breaths kept my chest rising painfully.

Randolph. God! Did he recognize me? I'm so stupid for leaving my cap at home.

I inhaled a long breath, held it for five seconds, and then let it out slowly through my nose. "Yes, I'm okay. How about you, Mikey?"

"That man bad. I want to punch him." Mikey curled his fingers into little fists.

I watched him amazed. Even at such a young age, his male instincts were highly defined. "Mickey, hitting another person doesn't resolve a problem. Do you understand?"

"Uh, huh. But sometimes it makes Daddy feel better." He pouted.

"Mikey, are you saying you've seen your Daddy hit someone?" I kept my eyes on the road.

"One time. A man in black came to the house. I peeked through the door crack of Daddy's office."

"What were they talking about?" I licked my lips and swallowed, attempting to moisten my dry throat.

"I don't know, but the man said he would come back. That's when Daddy punched him in the stomach." Mikey demonstrated, shoving his little fist into the air. "Daddy strong!" Mikey stared at me, wide-eyed. "Someday, Auntie, I be strong like Daddy and protect you." He lifted both fists into the air. His drawing rolled off his legs and fell to the floor.

"Oh, Mikey." I caressed his rosy cheek. "You grow up to be a leader of humanity."

"Auntie, what huwaty?" His hands fell flat on his lap.

"Humanity. You, Mikey, will show the leaders of this world what it's like to be a real human. Always be kind and love. You know love?"

"Uh, huh. I love Grandpa, Auntie Samantha, you, Daddy, oh and Cassius and Mr. Curly."

"Mr. Curly?" I'd forgotten about the toy sheep. It once belonged to my grandmother Mary. "You, little man, are my hero." I gave his hand a little squeeze. "Thanks for being my protector. But for now, Mikey, when you see a stranger or a bad person you stay close to whomever is with you and do *not* try to be a big man, okay?"

"Yes." Mikey held a stern expression.

"Mikey, what's wrong?" I lifted his chin with my forefinger.

"The man in black will call someday." Mikey tightened his lips as if he wanted to cry.

"Hey, sweetheart, don't worry. This man in black will *not* hurt you. Daddy and your family won't let that happen. Do you hear me?" I swallowed a lump in my throat.

Mikey is too young to be worrying about a man in black.

Frank had some explaining to do, big time.

"Cassius, protect too." Mikey lifted his head.

From the corner of my eye, I saw hope spread over his countenance.

Darn Cassius for giving Mikey hope.

"Mikey, I know if you were in danger, Cassius would protect you. But always remember family comes first, okay?" Mikey kept his eyes drawn down. I brushed his curls away from his forehead, making him look at me. He nodded yes, but said nothing. "Well, here we are." We cruised up the driveway. I parked and killed the engine.

Mikey unbuckled himself, grabbed his drawing, hopped out, and came running to my side of the jeep. He took hold of my hand.

"I love you, Auntie."

"Ditto, my hero."

We followed the pathway adorned with evergreen bushes to the back yard. I opened the kitchen door. Frank turned from the sink on hearing us.

"Daddy." Mikey ran to him.

"Hey, Mikey, how was your morning?"

"Good, I painted today. See?" Mikey unrolled the paper.

"Wow, you were busy. Nice colors." Frank tousled Mikey's hair and kissed the crown of his head.

"I be an artist like you, Daddy."

Frank, ever since childhood, loved to draw. He even went to art classes during his teen years, but farm life kept him from following his dream. He once told me there wasn't time to be all he was meant to be. I admired my baby brother. He and I were only a year apart, but at times, he acted as the elder.

"Look Daddy, I drew you, Auntie Mari, and Cassius. See?"

"Yeah, excellent depiction of your Auntie, only you made her nose small, I think it's longer and a little wider." Frank gave me a crooked smirk.

"It seems to me, someone else's nose is getting a little longer, too." I gave him a side-long look.

Frank eyed me. A confused expression spread over his face.

I walked over to the stove and ladled two scoops of chicken soup into a bowl.

"Mariana, what happened?" Frank caught me off guard.

"Nothing, it can wait." I glanced back at Mikey.

I checked the temperature of the soup. It was fine.

Frank lowered Mikey into the chair, as I set the bowl on the table.

"Mariana, what's bugging you."

"Who's the man in black? I heard he had the honor of meeting your fist." I rested my hands on my hips.

"How, did you…" Frank looked briefly to where Mikey sat.

The smarty lowered his head and spooned his soup faster.

"Ahh, I see. Yeah, well Sis, we'll talk later. Just know that episode has been taken care of. No more men in black will be knocking at this farm door."

127

I sighed.

Mikey sensed the tension in the kitchen and stopped eating. "Auntie Mari, will you keep my picture in your room?" He held the slightly wrinkled paper in his outstretched hand. I took the drawing.

"Sure thing. I'll go and put it in my room right now, okay?"

"Okay." Mikey slurped a spoonful of soup.

I stood in awe for a moment. Mikey's white aura glowed gold. He drew his eyes up and smiled. A shiver ran down my spine.

Frank joined Mikey. He sat back in his chair with his own bowl of soup. I turned and went toward the door leading to the hallway.

"Mariana, I just sprayed wood oil in that section of the hallway. Do you mind going to your room through the library?"

"Okay. Is Dad in there?"

"Yup." Frank stuffed a piece of bread in his mouth.

I shuffled to the French doors and pushed them inward. The urgency I felt to talk to my dad about the encounter with Randolph filled my mind. Dad was sitting in his favorite reading chair near the fireplace. On my entrance he straightened in his seat.

"Dad, you won't believe who I ran into today." I stole a quick look to my right. Aunt Samantha sat in the twin reading chair. "I…"

A clearing of throat halted my explanation. I remained near the French doors. The sound came from the office. I turned in place to see Cassius enter the library.

I stepped back ready to scram when I ran into a hard fleshy wall.

"Uh-hem. Excuse me, were you planning on going somewhere, Sis?" Frank's six foot three frame blocked my exit.

"I…umm…was going to take Mikey to his room for his afternoon nap." I kept my nerves in check. Holding Mikey's drawing reminded me why I had rushed to see my dad.

"No worries, Sis, I just came from his room."

"The hallway was not oiled?" I drew my brow together and caught a slight smirk play over Cassius's lips.

Frank took hold of my arm and directed me to the sofa. "Sis, you look a little piqued. I think you should sit for a minute. Did I hear you right, you ran into Randolph?"

"I never said. Someone interrupted me. But yes, it was Randolph." I eyed everyone in the room. This was an obvious ambush. I felt the blood rush up my neck and redden my cheeks.

"Your complexion is looking better. Cassius, I do believe you're the best medicine when it comes to bringing color back to my sister's cheeks."

I attempted to stand, but Frank laid a heavy hand on my shoulder. "Now, fiery Sis, tell us what happened."

Cassius sat on the other end of the sofa.

"Why are you here, Cassius?" I snapped.

"We need to talk." He leaned back and stretched his legs under the coffee table.

"No, *we* don't." I refused to look at him.

"Dear Mariana, the moon hides tonight—"

"But the dreams remain bright." I finished Aunt Samantha's sentence. When I was a child she'd comfort me with a word game. *I'm not a child anymore.* I sunk my fingers into the cool leather.

"You have a good memory." Now, Mariana, relax. Don't block the messages that have been sent to you. See Cassius for who he really is. I know you've dreamt of him. But you doubt." Aunt Samantha held her hands in prayer position. "Please, Mariana, listen to what will be said here today." Aunt Samantha returned to her common sitting position. She loved to sit crossed-legged with a good read. Only today, she didn't hold a book, instead she folded her hands in her lap.

"I can't allow myself to see Cassius, or any of my dreams. The path I must take doesn't grant me this luxury." I clasped my shaky hands between my legs.

Cassius scooted forward. He opened his mouth to speak, but Aunt Samantha held her hand up. Cassius bit his tongue and sat back.

"Mariana, Mikey told me a man approached the jeep. Are you sure it was Randolph?" Frank fetched a chair from the dining table and sat near me.

"As sure as the day I heard him speak near the meadow." From the corner of my eye, I studied Cassius. His face had thinned and he was in desperate need of a shave. "Is that a new look you're going for, Cassius?"

God even from this distance I could feel his pulsating aura and smell him. Why did he come back?

Cassius rubbed his chin. "I've been busy. Some things have to wait."

"Some things? You're quite selective on what should be told or known. Playing God will get you in the quicksand sooner than you think." I leered.

"Mariana, I—" Cassius repositioned his legs.

"Mariana, what did Randolph want?" Dad lit a cheroot and puffed.

I flexed my fingers, releasing pent up energy and then swiveled in my seat to face my dad.

"At first, I thought Randolph had recognized me. I was so afraid he might take Mikey. The fear kept me from reading him. I'm sorry."

"That's all right, but what did you say to him?" Dad scooted to the edge of his chair.

"I told him I was the nanny. He offered to take me out for drinks, but I explained how I had a boyfriend overseas." I met Cassius eyes. He lowered his. "Dad, this can't be good. I need to go." I stood a little too quickly and lost my balance.

Cassius lunged forward and kept me from falling into the coffee table. His touch was a hot iron scorching my psyche. I gasped. "You found your father, Cassius." A void drew me in. A lonely man stood in a meadow staring back at me.

Cassius withdrew his hand as if it had been burned. Frank stood and lowered his hands onto my shoulders. He drew me back down onto the sofa.

"Mariana, we're family. We want to help you. You don't need to run." Dad stood and snuffed the cigar in the brass ashtray. He swayed as he said, "We'll work this out."

"Dad, are you feeling sick?" I jumped to my feet and grasped his arm.

He stepped back. "I'm fine. I didn't sleep much last night. It's time for an afternoon siesta." Dad rested a hand on my cheek. "Mariana, we're family. I'll be in my room if anyone needs me." He turned to leave, then stopped and said over his shoulder, "Mariana, listen to Cassius. Listen, my little bear." Dad shuffled out of the library.

Tears filled my eyes on hearing the words little bear. After my mother died, I dreamt of her death every night. I'd cry out in the middle of the night. Dad would rush into my room and hold me close. I called him my Papa Grizzly and he in turn said I was his little bear. I sniffed and dragged the back of my hand across my nose.

"Mariana?" Cassius called out.

I met his soulful eyes and said, "Cassius, I'm glad you spoke to your father, but there's nothing more to talk about."

"Yes, there is." He scooted closer to me.

I shook my head no and then noticed Aunt Samantha's and Frank's eyes bulge, "What's wrong Frank, Auntie?"

"Nothing, dear, I know you were remembering how your father called you little bear, and I believe Frank felt it too." Aunt Samantha replied.

Frank nodded and shoved his hands in his jeans pockets. He sat in Dad's reading chair.

Cassius's hand covered mine. I withdrew from his warm touch, pretending to brush a curl from my face.

"Cassius, why did you keep the truth from me?" I scooted closer to my end of the sofa.

His cheeks filled with air. Silence reigned as we watched him exhale slowly. I sensed he was placing his thoughts in order.

Cassius bent forward. He propped his elbows on his thighs and looked down at his biker boots. "Mariana, usually when my head hits the pillow, I'm out for the night. I sleep as if someone has hit me over the head with a log. This last month everything's changed. I see *you* in my dreams." He paused, lifting his head. "We're in a house. I don't recognize the surroundings, but you hold out your hand to me. I take hold of it. Then you begin to fade. Mariana, don't push me away." He focused on us again.

I sensed Cassius's loneliness. His declaration was too close to my visions. Part of my dream was coming true. "Is that what you had to tell me besides finding your father?"

"Yeah. After talking to my father, I understood family comes first. The people we love come first. You come first, Mariana." Cassius moved closer to me and held his hand out palm up. My throat constricted. I lay my hand in his. His thumb traced circles on the backside of my hand.

"I'm sorry, Marianna."

"Cassius…you need to trust me."

"Yes, I know. But the door swings both ways."

"Okay." I blinked, holding back tears.

Frank and Aunt Samantha made themselves scarce. Cassius and I talked for an hour. He told me how he had found his father, suffering from Frontotemporal Dementia. My heart hurt seeing the pain in his eyes. Yet Cassius's visit brought us closer.

"Mariana, I have to go to the office to tie up a few loose ends on a case. I'll call you tonight, if that's okay?" He stood.

"You better call." I smiled.

"Actually, before you came home with Mikey, I had invited your family to dinner tonight. Would that work for you?" Cassius shifted his weight to one foot.

"Um, do you think that's a good idea since Randolph ran into me today? Maybe I should lay low for few days?"

"You have a point. Let's plan the dinner date for another day. Say, tomorrow?" His grin defined his dimples.

"Right, Randolph should've forgotten about me by tomorrow." I chuckled.

"No, not possible, but the nanny will be accompanied by three capable men who make some darn good knuckle sandwiches if necessary." Cassius winked.

"Uh, huh. And Aunt Samantha and I, the two delicate flowers, will be forever grateful." I flexed my fingers. The action didn't go unnoticed by Cassius, but he said nothing.

Someday Cassius you'll know just how deceiving a flower can be.

I was the first to stand. He followed suit. The heat between us felt as if it could weld our bodies.

"Until tomorrow." Cassius kissed me.

"Yep." I muttered.

He then cupped my face between his hands and our foreheads met. "Mariana, we'll find a way to leave Marino in the past."

"I know." I said under my breath. "What I fear is the barrier that must fall. When it does, which way do we run, to the left, right, or straight ahead?"

"I don't know, but I'm here to help." Cassius linked his hands with mine. He stood back. "Mariana, I know you're scared. Trust me. You're no longer alone." Cassius lifted my hand to his lips. He brushed butterfly kisses on my knuckles.

I closed my eyes for a few seconds. "Cassius, a baby has his parents' support and guidance, but the first step must be taken by him."

"Is that your way of telling me that slowly you'll begin to trust me?"

"Maybe." I shrugged and smiled.

Cassius pressed one more kiss on my forehead and left. The tingle from his bristly beard lingered.

The Harley roared, piercing the quiet afternoon. I pictured Cassius in his black attire racing down the driveway.

What am I getting into? I guess I can't keep playing hide-and-seek with fate.

* * *

The afternoon slipped by somberly while the evening brought in its wake a pleasant ambiance. Dad lit a fire and sat in his well-fitted chair. Mikey sat in my lap while Aunt Samantha attempted to teach Frank some dance moves.

"One, two, back step, three, four. One, two, side step, three, four." Aunt Samantha kept the tempo to Jazz Suite number two that played lively from Frank's phone.

133

Drawn forth by determination, Frank blew out air as frustration blemished his features. His feet stomped on the wood floor like a baby elephant.

Poor Frank, his two left feet had him stumbling more than dancing. Mikey swayed in my lap, giggling at Frank's awkwardness. My brother's concentration on every step and his lack of rhythm kept us entertained.

"Daddy, no worry. Someday you dance very good with your wife."

Dad's baritone laugh filled the library.

"Mikey, the word is well not good. Someday you will dance very well."

"Uh-huh, that's right, Auntie Mari."

Frank froze with his arms hovering in the air. Aunt Samantha doubled over laughing. She breathed in deeply and straightened her posture.

"Oh this child, he says the most unexpected things at the best moments. Frank, I need a break. We can take up where we left off tomorrow." Aunt Samantha joined Mikey and me on the sofa. She folded her hands near her heart. "Perhaps tomorrow we can dance to a more modern song." Aunt Samantha wheezed, "I'm an old woman. What makes me think I can still dance?"

"You best dancer, Auntie Samantha. Daddy, will be too with future auntie." Mikey bobbed his head up and down.

For a second, I thought Frank was going to roll his eyes, but instead he leaned his head back and stared at the ceiling. His patient nature inspired me to work harder on mine. Frank went around to the back of the sofa and lifted Mikey into his arms.

"I hope you're right, Mikey. A good woman at my side would be nice. Time for bed little man." Frank dive-bombed Mikey toward the three of us. One by one, he kissed our cheeks.

"Goodnight, Grandpa, goodnight Auntie Samantha, goodnight Mama Auntie." He waved his chubby hand.

The family stared at me. I shrugged. Mikey giggled as Frank disappeared with him to his bedroom.

"That little boy is an earthbound angel." Aunt Samantha exhaled and lifted her legs onto the sofa.

"I've thought the same thing often." I stared into the fire.

"Mariana." Dad called me to attention. "He deserves to know his mother."

"Dad, he's safer not knowing."

"It seems he already knows, but needs confirmation." Dad lit another cheroot. The smoke swirled around him.

"Frank is a wonderful father." I sunk my teeth into my bottom lip.

"I know Frank loves Michael as if he was his son, but it's not right to ask your brother to keep up this farce. You were furious with Cassius for not telling you the truth. How do you justify your silence? By the way, when do you plan to tell Cassius you have a son?"

"When Mikey is no longer in danger." I hopped to my feet, arms pressed tightly against my sides. "It kills me when he calls me Auntie, but I live with the pain to keep him safe."

"Mari, why did Mikey call you, Mama Auntie?" Aunt Samantha's eyes glistened in the firelight.

I waved my hands in the air and let them fall to my hips. "Mikey drew a picture of Frank, Cassius, and me at daycare today. He thinks he can have two fathers and me as his mother."

"Ha! That boy." Dad grunted. He then mumbled under his breath.

"Dad? Care to share?"

"I might, but will you listen?"

I bit my tongue and gave a small nod.

"Mikey has your spirit, Mariana. You need to guide him. Don't follow your father's mistakes. Talk to my grandson and show him it's fine to be yourself, but it's important to be careful with the gift."

"Daddy, you were right. And...what happened to me was in no way your fault. There's a reason why it happened."

"What reason would that be?" Dad took a slow drag from his cheroot.

"Your grandson, Daddy. He *is* the good from an evil deed."

I curled my lips inward, holding back a sob. Dad smiled. It had been a long time since I saw him smile as he did.

"I can't argue with that. But, Michael's gift is strong, very strong. I don't think you'll be fooling him much longer. Mariana, if you don't want your son to fester animosity toward you, don't smother the truth. Tell him all of it. There was a time, when I thought that not telling you about your clairvoyance was the best thing to do, but your grandmother Mary, told me otherwise. She was right all along." Dad snuffed out his smoke and left it on the ash stray. He grunted as he lifted his tired body from the chair. "Time to rest. You ladies have a peaceful night." Dad brushed his hand against my head. "Little Bear, push the darkness away, bring the light forward. Reveal the truth to Michael, if not tomorrow, soon."

"Daddy, I can't. Not yet."

"Michael deserves to know his mother." Dad gently squeezed my shoulder. "Good night, Mariana. Good night, Samantha."

Dad ambled toward his room. My father loved farming life, but unfortunately five years ago, hc had broken his right femur in a tractor accident. When Jack Frost visited the northern hemisphere, Dad's limp became more distinct.

I wondered if our family would ever be allowed a normal life like other families that did not have to deal with clairvoyance.

Aunt Samantha turned off the sconce lights beside the book shelves. I waited for her. We walked side by side down the hallway to our bedrooms. Aunt Samantha lingered near my door.

"Mariana, remember, denying your path delays destiny's arrival." My aunt gave me her I gotcha smile. "You told Cassius the same thing, right?" She patted my hand. "Good night, dear." She then turned, crossed the corridor, and entered her room.

"Good night, Aunt Samantha." I chuckled lightly and closed my door. Mikey's drawing lay on my bed. The sky had been changed from blue to black. Little yellow stars severed the darkness. In the right hand corner where the sun had been, a blue moon now hovered above the landscape. The words I'd spoken earlier today came to mind, "Only in a blue moon, Mikey, will we know if Cassius loves me." I held the drawing close to my heart.

Oh, you clever boy. I love you.

136

I laid his painting on my vanity desk and drew the bedcovers back. The adrenaline rush from the day's encounter in town, and Cassius's visit had left me drained. I kicked off my shoes and dropped onto the bed belly down. Exhaustion steered my conscious into a fitful slumber.

CHAPTER 11

THE HEART CRIES

Some dreams you hope to never forget. Other dreams, no matter how much you try to bury them, are the glowing red-eyed monster stalking you through the night.

"Get off me!" I rolled my hips side to side on the garden soil. *He's too heavy. I can't shake him off.*

Earlier in the day, sprinklers had watered the university gardens. The night and mud hid my flailing legs behind the manicured hedge. I had been wearing one of my favorite outfits, a gift from Aunt Samantha. The lacey white blouse and baby blue cardigan were caked with mud and the spring floral skirt was pushed up to my stomach.

The moonless night gave my attacker ample camouflage and courage to roam freely over my body. He adjusted himself, lodging my hands behind my back. His weight trapped my legs. He said, "Shh, this won't take long." His warm breath, trailed down my goose-fleshed skin. I wanted to fight, to…scream, but what ensured my silence was the cold blade pressed against my throat.

This nightmare would have ended quickly had I pushed up against the blade, but my family's faces filled my mind and knowing the pain I would cause them, if I chose to end my life, kept me from acting on impulse. So, I lay in the mud, closing off all thought to what was happening to my body until his words broke through my mind's barriers. That night the Ice-queen was born in the depths of my existence.

"My Bell' Angelo. You're mine." He brushed a hand across my cheek.

"You're demented." I turned my face and focused on the darkness, thinking it would be over soon. Little did I know this was just the first chapter of my ongoing horror.

Cackling surrounded me as he whispered, "Bell' Angelo."

"Nooo!" My chest ached. Breathing became a chore.

Another small voice joined my attacker's—a disjointed whimper from the future distracting me from my terror.

"Mama, I'm here."

"Mikey? Run! Don't let him see you."

I then realized it was my son calling out to me. Why was my son calling out to me? This was the first time I'd ever heard his voice in my dreams.

"Auntie Mari, I'm here. Open your eyes." Mikey's cool fingers tapped my cheeks.

"Mikey?" I forced my heavy eyelids open, and felt my little boy's chubby hands cupping my face.

"Yes, me, Auntie. You safe with me." Mikey knelt on the bed. He laid his head on my chest. "I keep you safe, Auntie."

The moon swathed the bedroom in a somber light. I swallowed a sob and said, "Mikey, why are you in my room? What time is it?" I glanced at the glowing clock face on the desk. "It's two thirty. You should be asleep." I reached toward the stained glass lamp on the Victorian table and pulled on the chain. A soft light filled the room. I ran my hand through Mikey's silky curls. His hurried breaths set me to thinking. What if the dream was real and Mikey is in danger?

It was a dream. You're stronger than this wimpy Mariana. Get with it girl.

"Auntie?" Mikey's soft voice called me back. "I woke up. I was alone. Daddy working in the office." He yawned.

"What woke you up?" I lowered my head and stared into his eyes.

"Dream told me to help you, Auntie."

"Oh, sweet baby, it was just a dream. I'm fine." I smiled, hoping it would erase his frown.

"Auntie, I sleep with you today. Okay?" Mikey lifted his head from my chest. In two swift movements, his little body dressed in Star Wars pajamas disappeared under the covers.

"Okay, my hero." I scooted my chilled body under the blankets too and hugged Mikey close to me.

"Auntie." Mikey's round eyes stared into mine. "The moon is blue."

"Yes, it is. Thank you, Mikey."

My little boy planted a kiss above my brow then snuggled. I decided to leave the light on. We fell asleep with our foreheads glued to one another.

* * *

"Mariana. Mariana wake up." A whisper badgered my subconscious.

"Bright Eyes. Wake up." Cassius's bass voice filled my mind.

I opened my eyes and found myself sitting in bed. Mikey continued sleeping.

Oh God, Mikey, he heard me calling out last night.

"Mariana, are you awake?"

On instinct my arm swung out. It met a firm resistance.

"Woman, what's your problem?" Cassius hissed. He grabbed my arms and drew me to my feet.

I stifled a yelp.

"Who taught you to do that?" Cassius rubbed his right thigh. "Three more inches to the left and I'd be me on my knees."

"It would've been well earned. Why are you in my bedroom?" I whispered through gritted teeth.

"Follow me." Cassius jerked his head to the left as he walked toward the door.

I looked back at the angel in my bed. Mikey's lashes fanned his cheeks. I kissed him. He stirred, but continued sleeping. I followed the one man I couldn't erase from my dreams.

In the corridor Cassius took me by the hand and led me to the kitchen. Frank and Dad were seated at the table. They were drinking coffee and whispering fervently. The look on their faces told me they weren't talking about farm business.

"What's going on?" I muffled a yawn.

"Mariana, sit." Dad pulled the chair from the table.

I obeyed. "Is Aunt Samantha, okay?"

"Shh, she's fine. Listen and don't worry." Frank commanded.

"What do you mean don't worry? Look, Dopey comes into my room, like the boogeyman in the night, and orders me to follow him. Then I see Grumpy and Bashful in the kitchen and you want me to be calm?"

"Sis, shut up. Listen."

"Little brother this better be good, or—

"Frank, get on with it, quick. Your sister has a rude right hook." Cassius puffed. He sat next to Frank. They faced my father and me.

I sat, shoulders squared, hands resting in my lap.

"Huh, I see you've been introduced to my ninja warrior sister." Frank's smirk unleashed memories of our teenage years. All the wrestling matches we had. He was a good teacher.

"Yeah, thanks for the warning." Cassius crinkled his brow. "Is she always so rough?"

"My friend, as a sibling she could dish out a good punch, now as a girlfriend—"

"If you kiddies don't mind, I need my beauty sleep. Why am I in the kitchen listening to you two juveniles?" I glimpsed at the kitchen clock. It was five thirty. Through the window I watched the sun outlining the horizon creep slowly upward.

One of these days, I hope to sleep a full eight hours.

"Hey, Cas, you think you need an ice-pack?" Frank let out a deep chuckle. "My Sis has always been quick on delivery, she once—

"Frank, do *not* reminisce." I stared him down.

"Yeah, all right. You're the biggest story spoiler, Sis." My jokester brother smiled, but I sensed his unease. He was buying time, but for what?

"I'm out of here." I pushed my chair back.

My father's hand pressed down on my forearm. "Get on with it, Frank."

Frank filled his cheeks with air and exhaled slowly. "I was in the office paying some bills when I heard the door-bell. The grandfather clock chimed five times. I thought it strange for someone to be at the front door so early. I grabbed the shotgun, went to the living room, and pulled the curtains aside. There was no one on the front porch or near the door. Then I went into the foyer and noticed an envelope on the floor. Someone shoved this note under the door, rang the bell twice and left. They must've come up the driveway on foot, because I would've heard or seen a car leave." Frank opened the envelope and laid a monogrammed stationery on the table. I gagged, swallowed quickly, and pressed my hands flat on the table's surface.

"Oh, God." I controlled my short breaths. "I recognize the stationery."

My father took hold of my hand. I looked up at him. I sensed a father's pain when he knows there's not much he can do.

"No, Mariana, we can do something and we will. Cassius is here to take you somewhere safe." Dad affirmed.

I rested my elbows on the table and leaned my forehead against the palms of my hands. "What does the note say?" I stared at the table's wood grain. Silence answered me. "Tell me what he wrote." I lifted my head.

Frank tucked the note back into the envelope. No one volunteered to read.

"Cassius, tell me."

He leaned back into his chair. "Aw hell." Cassius jammed his hands into his jeans pockets and let out a deep breath. "It says, bring her back. The family's fate lies on Mr. Russo's conscience."

"What? But they sent the note to our house. Why mention you, Cassius?"

Cassius shrugged, "Marino's thugs might have seen me with you and put two and two together? Either way, we'll deal with it."

"No! I'll deal with it. This family will not pay for my mistakes. Right? Dad, Frank?" I waited longer than expected for an answer. None came. I shoved the chair back and bolted down the hallway.

I heard another chair scraping the kitchen floor. Cassius grabbed me by the waist and pulled me into him.

Burying my face in his chest, I sputtered, heaving. "I have to say goodbye. I have to…to um, kiss Mikey one more time. Cassius, please, let me go. And don't follow me. Don't look for me."

"Mariana, this is not goodbye. You'll see Mikey again. I have a plan. But you need to listen and not fight my every move. Do you understand?"

I sniffed and wiped my nose on my sleeve. "Okay."

"Marino knows you'll never place your family in danger. That's why he sent the note. Samantha and Mikey will leave today to The Outskirts. They'll stay there as long as necessary. Your Aunt is packing while we speak. You'll come with me. I'm going to give these dogs a scent they can't refuse. And then you'll disappear into the hills too."

"Theodore must've had a head hunter watching the farm." I swallowed a moan, squeezing my eyes shut.

"No. Mariana, I have my own people watching the farm. He found out some other way. Marino plays with words, I deal with action. One thing he's not is stupid. He won't act on his threat just yet. There's no way he'll take the chance of losing you."

I drew my head back to see his eyes clearly. "How do you know this, Cassius?" I rubbed my hands against my thighs, flexing my fingers.

Cassius stopped my nervous fidgeting. "Christo! Your hands are icebergs. Look, I've dealt with men like Marino. We'll stage your death."

I stared at him wild-eyed. My chest tightened. The thump of my heart echoed in my ear.

"Don't worry. Your family will know the truth. Only for now, they won't know where you are. Mariana you asked me to trust you. Now trust me."

"You said my aunt and Mikey are going to the inn. What about my Dad and Frank?"

"They refuse to leave. I know your father and brother can take care of themselves."

"They're not leaving? What if Theodore's men come after them?"

"Look, there's a plan and I got your back, Mariana." Cassius glanced over his shoulder. He ended the conversation as Mikey rushed out into the hallway. Aunt Samantha followed him.

"Auntie!" He ran up to me. "This for you, Auntie."

Mikey handed me his recent drawing. As I stared at the picture, he wrapped his arms around my legs. "Auntie, I dream with pretty lady. She told me to tell you, 'Heart of my heart together we be for eternity. Auntie, no be sad."

I bit down hard on my lip almost cutting into it. The pain kept me from crying out.

Aunt Samantha gasped. "Those are your Grandmother Mary's words. He dreamt with Mary, John." Aunt Samantha cupped her mouth.

Frank and Dad stood behind me.

I turned and stared at them.

"Yes, it was her." Dad ran a hand across his unshaven face.

I knelt and drew my son close to me. "I love you, Mikey, beyond the universe."

"That's far, Auntie."

"Yes." I chuckled, drying my eyes.

"Mikey, you're going on a little vacation with Auntie Samantha."

"You come too, Auntie? I protect you." Mikey's chin quivered.

"Michael, listen to your elders, all right?" Aunt Samantha spoke softly as she helped Mikey put on his robe.

I straightened his collar. "Mikey…" I whispered. "When I can, I'll come to you, okay."

"Come with me, Auntie, please. The man in black…" His voice choked. He draped his body around my legs and hid his face.

"Mikey, your Auntie Mariana has a very important meeting to go to. In a few days…" Aunt Samantha looked at me. "She'll come to see us. All right? Now my brave young man, hold my hand." Aunt Samantha stretched her hand out. Mikey looked up and kept his eyes on me as his hand fell into hers.

This is harder than when I left him as a babe-in-my-arms.

I ran my fingers through Mikey's curls, logging his features in my mind's eye. Cassius rested his hand on my shoulder and gave it a little squeeze.

A knock sounded on the back door. Frank went to see who it was. On hearing a friendly hello, we stepped into the kitchen. A man I'd never met shook hands with Dad and Cassius. "Ladies." He touched the brim of his cap.

Cassius sat Mikey on the kitchen counter. "Hey, Buddy, I'll be with your Auntie Mari. Okay? I can't protect her like you can, but I'll do my best, deal?" Cassius held out his pinky. Mikey hooked his little finger with Cassius's.

"I, Cassius Russo, pinky swear to do my best."

"To protect, Auntie Mari." Mikey eyed him, long faced.

"To protect, Mariana. I love you buddy." Cassius hugged him. "You ready?"

Mikey tightened his trembling lips. He glanced at everyone in turn. I felt the fight within him not to cry. My three-year-old son was doing his best to be brave for *me*. I wanted to forget Cassius's plan and run with my son to the other side of the world.

Frank intercepted my thoughts. "Mariana? Hey, Sis. This is all good. Look at me."

I drew hesitantly away from Mikey's sad eyes and saw my brother. His red-rimmed eyes told me he too was crying inside, but we needed to be strong.

Cassius distracted my little boy. "Mikey, you'll go with this nice man. He's a good guy and he'll take you and Aunt Samantha to a place with a pond, swimming pool, go-cart track, and guess what, you'll see wild turkey."

"Oh, I be their friend." A small smile fell upon his serious expression.

"You bet." Cassius ruffled his hair.

Sometimes I forgot that Mikey was just a little boy.

While we were in the kitchen listening to Cassius's oath to Mikey, Frank brought the suitcases from the bedroom. The gentleman took hold of the bags and walked outside.

There was too much at stake. I could *never* allow Theodore to dream I had a son or anyone else for that matter. The underworld knew of my talent and I'd die before they knew of my son. They'd use him as a pawn also. With Mikey's drawing in hand, I kissed my little boy, hugged Aunt Samantha and ran to my room. My heart felt as if it was too big for my chest. Numb, I sat on my bed and I focused on my surroundings through bleary eyes.

Fate, you are so cruel.

The bedroom door remained open. I heard Mikey cry out, "I love you, Grandpa, Daddy, Cassius. I love you Auntie Mari!" My heart skipped a beat as the kitchen door closed.

Will I see my baby again?

Cassius stood just inside my bedroom door. "You packed?"

I did not respond.

In five long strides, he approached me, took hold of my free hand and drew me to my feet.

"Bright Eyes, you can do this. Where's your bag?"

"Over there next to the armoire."

He followed my pointed finger. "You, never unpacked."

"I thought…" I sniffed, bringing down my teeth on my tongue.

You can do this. You did it 'til a month ago.

I pulled the hem of my blouse down and straightened my back. "I thought I'd only be here a week. Cassius, I had a month with my family. Now I have to leave them again."

Cassius cupped my head between his hands. "Mariana, you *are* strong. We'll make this work. Let's go." He grabbed my duffel bag.

I laid Mikey's blue moon drawing on the dresser and studied it one more time. The moon mocked me. Cassius loves me, but I can't allow myself to feel the same emotion. Fate plays many games. I rolled up the portrait and leaned it against the mirror where Mikey could find it later. I had thought of hiding the drawing in my bag, but I didn't want to take the chance of Theodore seeing it or the hired help, who periodically reported to him of my doings. Yes, I knew what must be done.

I'm going back to Theodore, only Cassius can't know.

On zombie mode, I followed Cassius out to the kitchen. Dad and Frank waited near the back door. They took turns hugging me. I then turned to leave.

"Little Bear, I love you."

Cassius kept me from walking down the stairs.

"I know you did everything for the family's safety. Now we do this for you." Dad waited for me to respond.

I swiveled around. "Daddy." I hugged him as if I were three again. "I'm sorry for all the pain I've caused you, starting with the red balloon." I coughed and choked on my saliva.

My dad lowered his head and shook it side to side. "Mariana, you've been blaming yourself all these years. I'm the one to blame. I'm your father and I didn't protect my family the way I should have. But now…this will be corrected."

"Daddy, what do you mean?" I searched for the truth, but he was stronger than me when it came to camouflaging our gift.

Frank leaned against the veranda rail and scrubbed his face.

"Frankie? Talk to me." My darn voice quivered. "I'm not leaving. Not until you talk to me." I shook Frank's arm. He didn't budge.

Cassius hooked his long fingers around my arm and pulled me out the door. "Cassius, stop. What's my dad going to do?"

"What your father is saying is that the authorities will know what's going on and we'll stop Marino from threatening this family."

"You don't know Theodore Marino like I do. When he becomes infatuated with something, he's…he's like a little child who won't let go of his toy. What do you think you can do, Cassius? Because, I know what Marino is capable of." My eyes darted from his face to the kitchen stoop where Frank and Dad stood listening.

"Sis, we're all here for you. Remember, family is the stronghold."

I said nothing to Frank, but I knew he felt my love. Instead, I glanced up at the sky and said, "Memories are life's album. I love you guys."

"Mari." Frank called out to me.

I didn't look back at my brother. I feared if I did, I'd lose my nerve to go through with the plans drawn out for me. Instead, I followed the biker that had taken me from refuge.

Maybe that had been a mistake, like this right now.

"Frank, John, she'll be safe." Cassius assured them.

I yanked my arm from his grasp and rounded the house to the front yard. He was close behind. Beyond the iron gates, a black BMW 7 series with tinted windows occupied a parking space. I expected to see Cassius's Harley or Jeep. I froze in mid-step.

Who is Cassius Russo?

"Mariana, why look so surprised? I told you I owned more than one ride." He pulled the keys out of his blazer pocket. The car beeped. He then opened the back door, dropped my bag on the seat, and opened the front door for me.

I slid in and on auto-pilot secured the seat belt as Cassius closed the door. I lay my head on the headrest. The cool leather soothed my uneasiness.

Where do I go from here? I must keep my family safe. I can't lead Cassius to danger. I'll find a way. There must be way to run from the life I'm in.

Cassius sat in the driver's seat. The BMW purred to life.

I wish my heart beat as smoothly. Right now it's running on a double shot of adrenaline.

Cassius laid his hand over mine. He said nothing, but I sensed he truly thought he was doing the right thing by hiding me. My heart ached, because I knew what must be done and the man I loved would not be part of my plans. Fatigue veiled my predicament. I closed my eyes and Cassius drove us away.

* * *

I awoke from a light squeeze on my arm. "Mariana, we're here."

My eyelids fluttered. I twisted my head against the headrest and met Cassius's smile just like the first day I met him in the diner.

The minute I saw Cassius that day, I should've ran.

I studied my surroundings. Cassius had parked in an alley. Garbage cans separated the adjacent buildings. More edifices stood as sentries along the street. Before us a door opened, showering light onto the pavement. A gorgeous female stood under the lighted door frame. Her corn row hair accentuated her heart shaped face.

"Where are we?" I asked groggily.

"I'll explain once we're inside." Cassius pushed down on my seatbelt button then his. He opened his door and stepped out.

"Hey, Tracy. Thanks for meeting us here. Will you take this duffel bag to the spare bedroom?"

The magazine model approached him. They talked for a few seconds in a whisper. Her aura emanated strength.

I jumped into the driver's seat. This was a new model. *Dang!* I wasn't a stranger to hot wiring older cars. I sat deflated. Tracy nodded in my direction. Cassius looked over his shoulder. God, I wanted to wipe the smirk off his face.

I need to get out of here.

Tracy chuckled as she took hold of my bag and went back into the building.

I choked the steering wheel until my knuckles ached.

Cassius bowed towards me. "How far do you think you'd get in a stolen car?"

"You know so little about me Mr. Russo. I could easily pawn this car for another."

Cassius wrapped his fingers around my left forearm in a careful loving manner and said, "Let's go, Bright Eyes."

Defeated and tired I followed Cassius. He stepped aside for me to walk into the building then locked the door behind us. The foyer wall supported my weight as I waited for him to lead the way. We walked into an office. One desk lamp illuminated the room. I stood near a sofa facing a window with closed vertical blinds. Three desks were positioned in a horseshoe fashion.

"Where are we?" I balled my hands.

"Relax, Mariana. This is my office. C'mon, we're going upstairs."

I didn't move. Life teetered on Fate's see-saw. One word, a smile, a nod, a simple acknowledgement set me on a course I couldn't steer. Fate, led by multiple possibilities, had brought me to Cassius.

Will the door that constantly appears in my dreams open? Will my fears come true?

"Mariana the threat on your family won't see the light of day. Not if I have a hand in it. Please, let me help."

The word threat dragged me back from my reverie. I leered. He slowly caressed my hand.

"Trust me. I'm here, Mariana. You no longer have to protect the family on your own."

Bleary eyed, and tired, I clenched my jaw then released. "I had to say goodbye. He didn't look away, Cassius. His innocent eyes begged me to go with him. I had to say goodbye to my family and my ss...to Mikey..." I nearly told Cassius Mikey was my son, but for some reason I stopped.

"C'mere." He bathed me in his warmth. "I will help you. That's a promise. What the outcome will be, I can't say. But, I'll be at your side, Mariana." He smoothed my hair down and held me until I broke the embrace. We headed for the foyer and climbed the stairs.

"The second floor is my apartment." Cassius spoke in a hushed voice. He took hold of my hand and opened a frosted glass door. He entered and I followed like a little child who's too tired to do anything but sleep.

The woman I'd seen earlier stood in the middle of the apartment.

"Cassius, there's fresh coffee. Drake sent word. The message is on the kitchen counter. If you need anything else just call." The woman smiled, shaking her head. "Dimples, I told you to talk to her, but when you talk things get complicated don't they?" She frowned.

Cassius grunted. "No drama free chapters in my life. Tracy, thanks, you're the best."

"At six-thirty in the morning, you bet I am." She walked over to me. "Hello, Mariana. I'm very happy to meet you.

I'm one of Cassius's business partners." Tracy drew herself close to my ear. We were the same height. "Cas, pretends to be a hard ass, but he's actually a kitten. Remember he does everything with the best intentions." She gave me a quick hug. "Mariana my number is on the fridge. Call me if you need anything. There's a burner phone in the spare bedroom on the nightstand." Tracy snatched her keys from the sofa table and left.

Cassius strolled to the kitchen. His black dress boots thumped on the marble floor. It was obvious Frank's call to Cassius had interrupted his plans. The man before me was not dressed in his usual jeans and black T-shirt. His muscular shoulders fit perfectly into a straight cut, navy-blue tailored blazer. He removed his coat, rolling his immaculate white sleeves up to his elbows.

The open area housed a black granite breakfast bar dividing the sitting room from the kitchen. Stainless steel appliances were shelved above the stove, and white cupboards brightened the apartment.

Cassius went to a kitchen cupboard. He pulled out a mug and held it up in the air. "Coffee?"

I shook my head. "No thanks." I sat on the black sofa, sinking into the soft leather. Sleep weighted my eyelids down. "I'm sorry if I ruined your plans for the day. She's really pretty."

Cassius joined me. "Mariana." He set the mug on the coffee table.

"Hmm?" I kept my eyes closed.

"She, being Tracy, is my other partner's girlfriend. And today I was going to meet a potential client in Woodbridge. But no worries, Tracy will take my place."

"You dressed quite early." I continued to rest my eyes.

"Yeah, I couldn't sleep. So, went to the office to finish some paper work, until our meeting. The client I was to meet is up with the roosters. He's a vintner."

"Yes, farmers do start the day early." I opened my eyes.

"Mariana, we'll make this work." Cassius rubbed the back of his neck.

I swiveled my head to look him in the eye, but was distracted by the window panorama. Bright yellow-orange spread across the skyline. The morning globe peeked through a thin cloud layer. Sun rays stretched across the apartment floor warming my feet, but the chill I felt from within couldn't be comforted by the solar heat.

"Mariana, we'll get through this. Did you hear me?" Cassius rested his hand on my knee.

"Cassius, you say we, but you've done enough. I *need* to figure this out on my own."

"You're one stubborn chick. You don't have to be Wonder Woman."

I studied his manicured hand. The contrast of his work hands to my Dad's and brother's made me smile.

"Why are you smiling?" He gave my knee a little squeeze.

Cassius's touch drew me in to a scene of his past, lifting my eyes to meet his sympathetic smile teleported me to a second vision.

I saw Cassius's father holding his ten-year-old son's hand in the meadow, it then faded into a scene of me holding Theodore's hand as he helped me from under the bushes. If only, I had listened to Dad, if I had been smart, if I had not ignored my family's advice, I shook my head, too many ifs.

"Bright Eyes?" Cassius repositioned his body to face me. His hands rested on my shoulders. "Mariana, look at me."

I stared into his ocean blue eyes and wished I could hide in them forever. "Cassius, my reality has become a lie." I sniffed, rubbing my nose.

Pain stabbed the middle of my cranium. My head fell onto his shoulder. He encased me in his arms as I blurted out. "My fears have resurfaced. Theodore is back and the demons have to be slain. Don't assume all that appears before your eyes is reality. Cassius, love, pure emotion without a single notion of deceit, is my heartbeat."

The look in Cassius's eyes told me he thought I had gone crazy. But, he took my rambling in stride and massaged my shoulders.

"Mariana, I don't know exactly what you're talking about, but you can take this to the bank, when I find your attacker, he'll pay."

I lifted my head and exhaled a shuddered breath. Cassius's scent was a mental blanket, one I didn't want to leave behind. There was no choice. Soon, the life I had lived for a month would vanish. As Cassius continued to hold me, he pushed back into the sofa. I lifted my legs onto the soft cushion and rested my head in his lap. He spread a crocheted blanket over me and I fell asleep to Cassius humming the Budapest song. Life gave me one more day to record his warm embrace in my mind's album.

CHAPTER 12

LIFE IS NOT WHAT IT SEEMS

I had a long talk with Drake about Mariana, before my heart overrode my common sense.

"Drake, this is our job, to serve and protect this country. And that's what I'm doing, right? I will help this girl and her family and then move on."

"Cas, going to bed with doubts is worse than going to bed with no supper. Your hunger to help others can't always go the way you like. You know what you have to do. Don't forget, Cas, sometimes the safest place is sleeping in the bear's den."

"Yeah, she might be safe with Marino, but the hell hole is goin' to be buried, and I want her nowhere near it when it does."

"I hear ya. But, plans change?"

"Yes, they do, and I aim to keep our mission as tight as possible."

"Ha! Good luck, Bro. Mariana might tug on that rope of yours harder than you expect."

Truer words had not been spoken. It's as if Drake had seen the future.

There were many tracks a man could follow, but the more practical choice wouldn't resolve the inevitable dilemmas. My first plan was to take Mariana far from this town, even if it was across the Atlantic Ocean, but Marino has Grand Canyon pockets. When that type of man sinks his claws into a prize, there's no cost to hold him back. No, the game would be played on the home front. Drake was right when he said the one alternative was to return the jewel for the family's safety.

How do I look into those bright eyes and tell her this? There has to be another way.

* * *

154

I watched and listened to her breathing softly as she lay on the couch.

"Don't touch me! Get off me!" Mariana spluttered and kicked her legs in the air.

I jumped off the bar stool in time to keep her head from hitting the coffee table. She'd slept peacefully for three hours.

Whoever did this to her will go to hell. That's a promise.

"Bright Eyes, you're safe." I held her close to me.

"Cassius." Mariana buried her face in my chest.

"Shh, I'm here." I shifted my weight, sat, and stretched out my legs. She wrapped her arms around me.

Mariana held on until her shivers stilled. Her body next to mine was paradise. No other girl made my emotions go haywire as she did.

"Cassius….it's so real. I hear my attacker's whisper, Bell' Angelo and feel his hot breath against my neck." She stifled a cry.

"Mariana, let go of the past. Focus on us."

"I've tried, but…I can't control my dreams."

"Maybe you can't control what you dream about, but you can change the *now*. I'll help you." I held her closer.

We continued to sit between the coffee table and sofa. She then stood, bent down and kissed me. I was about to kiss her back, but she withdrew, and sat in the love seat.

Mariana's hand went to her stomach as it gurgled. "Excuse me. Sorry about that." She blushed.

"You're sorry your stomach rumbled? I'm a guy. It takes more than that to offend me." I stood and stared at her perfect bare feet on the shag rug. "Hey, how about some breakfast?"

The clock chimed nine gongs.

"It's nine already? What time did we get here?" Mariana crinkled her brow.

"A little after six, why?"

"I'm just wondering how much longer before Aunt Samantha and Mikey reach The Outskirts."

She started twisting her hair around her finger again. I wanted to run my whole hand through her hair, drag her onto my lap, and hold her until Marino had been taken care of.

"They left the farm a little after five-thirty. It's a ten hour drive. They should be there around three thirty this afternoon."

"Oh." Mariana twisted her hair tighter.

"Hey. My man will call. I've spoken to him and all is clear at this point. Plus, some biker friends of mine are tagging along." I unraveled the hair from her finger. "You keep that up and you're going to get bald spots." I smiled for her sake, but I hoped the plan would go down smoothly, also.

"Okay." She shuffled to her feet. "You'll tell me as soon as they arrive?"

"Of course. Why are you so worried?" I went to the oven.

Mariana shrugged. She hopped onto a stool. "It smells chocolaty in here."

"Yeah, I baked your favorite, chocolate muffins. I was having mine when you decided to dive off the sofa." I opened the oven door and pulled out a covered plate with three over-sized muffins.

I set a plate with a muffin and a cold glass of milk in front of her. She closed her eyes and inhaled.

"Mmmm, thanks. I love these. "

I chuckled. "That's right. You're one sweet-tooth breakfast girl."

"Woo, that's a mouth full." Mariana spoke between bites. "Your mom brought you up right. Your baking is almost as good as hers." She smiled.

"Ha! I haven't had any complaints so far about my baking." I winked.

Mariana blushed. She gulped and puckered her lips. "I bet. You have a fancy bachelor pad."

"Uh, no. I have a nice town house which is convenient considering my office is down stairs. But this is *not* an entertaining facility if that's what you're insinuating." I settled in the stool next to her. Half of my muffin waited for me.

"So, you have another sweet, hot place for the ladies?" Mariana finished her last bite and grabbed her second muffin.

It amazed me how she turned off the wary Mariana and the playful one came out. I guessed it was her way of dealing with the situation at hand.

156

"No, there's no other place. You have the wrong idea about me." I leaned into the counter, facing her.

"Maybe I do, and maybe I don't." She smirked. "Mmm. These chocolate chips are delectable. They literally melt on tongue contact." She chewed slowly.

I huffed. I knew it was pointless to explain to her I didn't have a love life. Sure there had been girls and on occasion a nightly distraction, but no love. "Yeah, the chocolate is imported from Switzerland." I sat back wondering what it was about this girl that had me wanting to know more about her.

"Whoa. This is an expensive muffin."

"Nah, I have a client who deals in chocolate."

"How many clients do you have? More like, how much detective work can there be in this one small town?" Mariana sucked on her chocolate covered thumb.

God, I want to be the one licking the chocolate off her fingers.

"Cassius, are you okay?" Mariana rested the back of her hand on my forehead. I jerked back.

"I'm fine, why?"

"You spaced out on me. Cassius, do you have other businesses?"

"I'm in real-estate also."

Darn her touch.

"Oh that explains the Bimmer." Mariana used her forefinger like a magnet and picked up the crumbs. She then slipped them into her mouth.

She had no clue how seductive she looked right then. I scooted off my stool, took the dishes to the sink, and soaked them in the soapy water.

"Cas?"

Mariana's tone had me turning around abruptly.

"I'm tired. When I close my eyes, I see my attacker and other shadows. I can't stop them from invading my mind." She squeezed her head between her hands. "But, I can't let the shadows find my family."

I hurried over to her and embraced her trembling body. Her weight fell against my chest.

"I miss them and it's only been three hours. Mikey has grown so much. I've missed *so* much."

"Mariana, I've been meaning to ask you this. Uh…never mind."

She lifted her head. "Just ask me, Cassius."

"Is… Mikey's mom around?"

"If you're asking if she's alive, yes she is, but she's not in his life as much as she'd like."

"I see."

"Cassius, life sometimes deals cards that are hard to pawn off, you know? His mother loves him very much, but she needs to get part of her life in order."

"But—" She cut me off.

"Mikey is surrounded by love. Frank is the best father ever and you saw him, don't you think he's a well adjusted little boy?"

"Well, yeah, but how does a mother walk away from her son?"

Mariana glared at me and in the same instance lowered her head, picking at a hangnail. "Mikey loves you too, Cassius."

"The feeling is mutual. He's an exceptional young boy. But you didn't answer my question."

"Yes…" Her eyes stared past me.

There's something she's not telling me. Something big.

"Yes, what? Mariana, what are you thinking?"

"I…um…I know when Mikey's mother can, she'll come back to him. I *even* wish I could be more in his life."

"And you will." I took hold of her frigid hands. "But, Mariana, you're his aunt."

"Yeah, so?"

"You're not Mikey's mom. How does his mother not do everything to have her son in her life?"

Mariana slid her hands out of mine. She shrugged. "You know, life's bad judgments, mistakes that bite you in the butt, circumstances which keep you from living the way you wish. It doesn't mean you don't love your son or daughter less. Your father is a perfect example, right?" Mariana's eyes begged me to drop the subject.

"You're telling me Mikey's mother skipped out on him, because her problems were more important than raising her son?"

Mariana jumped off the stool. "Cassius, don't judge." The sharp edge to her voice told me I was on thin ice. "I know Mikey's mom loves him very much. She needs to get her life in order, before she can be the best mother Mikey deserves. She didn't abandon him. She loved him enough to leave him with his family and get herself straightened out." On that note Mariana turned her back on me. Her shoulders slumped forward and she cried into her hands.

I hopped off the stool and stood behind her. "Hey, I'm sorry. I know Mikey is with his family, I just thought that his mother—"

Teary eyed she spat, "Well, stop thinking about it. I know his mother's story. Her unconditional love to let go of him, to keep him safe from her mistakes was her best option." She leaned into me.

"All right, I hear ya. I'll back off. But I have a feeling if you were Mikey's mother, you'd find a way to be with him." I stood my ground staring at her. Mariana's eyes took on a deep green. I could almost feel an inner turmoil within her mind near eruption. I knew I had crossed the line, but there was no taking back my words.

She focused on a painting behind me. "*His* mother will come back. You, Cassius have no idea what she's given up." Mariana hissed through her clenched jaw. She then rubbed her eyes.

"You're right. Sorry. You need to sleep. Let's get you to bed."

Mariana didn't argue. She followed me to the guest bedroom.

How do I stop her pain? The gut wrenching feeling that I couldn't end Mariana's fear ignited my instinct to kill the bastard responsible for her nightmares. The bright eyes I loved were fading. I could literally see Mariana withdrawing from me.

I can't stand seeing this girl turn into a robot.

I pulled back the comforter and faced her. She waited droopy-eyed. I led her to the edge of the bed. She sat. I slipped off her tennies and lifted the end of her hooded sweater.

"I can do this." She pulled the sweater up over her head and it brushed her hair, making it stand on end.

Smiling, I peered down at her, as if she were a three-year-old, and slowly ran my fingers through her hair. Mariana lifted her sweet eyes to meet mine.

"Will you stay with me until I fall asleep?" She lay, crossing her arms over her T-shirt.

I nodded.

The angel before me settled into bed staring at the ceiling. I went around to the other side, joined her, and I slipped my left arm under her shoulders. She curled into fetal position with her head on my chest.

Within seconds, her breathing became faint. I plotted revenge, which might or might not happen, but one way or another, I was Mariana's official protector.

"No! Cassius, run!" Mariana shot up in bed, staring at the north wall. She heaved. "Run!"

"Mariana, I'm here. It's Cassius, Bright Eyes." I took hold of her shoulders.

A white film faded from her eyes. Tears replaced the empty glare. She wound her arms around my waist and pulled me towards her.

"Caaa… ss…sius!" Mariana cried. "It will never end, if I don't end it."

"Shh, you're safe. It's just a dream." I rubbed her back.

She pushed away from me, sniffled and ran her fingers across her upper lip.

"What must you end?" I said.

Mariana drew in a slow breath and exhaled just as slowly. "Cassius, I shouldn't be here. I'm placing you in danger."

"Shh, I'm a big boy. And yes, you should be here. Marino won't hurt you ever again. Mariana look at me, do you understand? You don't need to fear him."

She sniffed again, inhaling a stuttered breath.

"You've only been asleep for an hour. Try to rest some more."

Mariana laid and curled her knees to her chest. I drew the comforter over her.

"I'll be in the kitchen. Mariana, you *will* be free." I waited until she closed her eyes and then left, shutting the door behind me. I needed to work out some details.

The man who did this to her will wish he never met her.

A couple of hours later, I sat on the sofa in a daze. Sleep crept up on me. I ran my hands up and down my face. I heard the bathroom door close. I glanced at my watch. Mariana had slept another two hours. That was good. It was time for some lunch. I went to the kitchen and made us tuna sub-sandwiches with green peppers. I chuckled. That girl loved anything that was edible. She made me feel as if I could be the next chef Ramsey.

From the time I started lunch, prepared the homemade lemonade, and set the table, fifteen minutes had gone by.

I knocked on the bathroom door. I could hear the water pelting the shower curtain.

"Mariana, lunch is ready." I leaned my forehead against the door. The water continued to pitter-patter. "Did, ya hear me? A yes will do."

There was no answer. "Mariana?" Two good kicks and the door slammed against the tiled wall. A towel sat on the bathtub edge. "Mariana, you okay? Answer me, ah, to hell with it." I nearly ripped the shower curtain off the hooks as I pushed it aside. No Mariana. Instead, I found two bed sheets tied to the tub faucet leading to the open window.

The crazy girl climbed out the window. Shit!

I shoved the shower knob in and ran downstairs to the back of the building. I caught a glimpse of a white cab leaving the premises, blonde curls bobbing in the back seat.

"Stop!" I waved my hands in the air to get the driver's attention, but he kept going.

Dammit, Mariana.

I pulled my phone from my back pocket and called Drake.

"Bro, she split." I raked my fingers through my scalp. "Yeah, I saw her leaving in a white cab. The plate number is alpha, two, bravo, nine, eight, six, five. Call the company and find out where she's going. Drake, when you can, meet me in the office." I hung up and headed back to the apartment.

161

I went to the guest bedroom. Mariana left a book opened in the middle of the bed. At a closer look I guessed it to be her journal. I sat and read the page staring back at me.

Escaping

Memory— freight train crashing through my thoughts. I can't stop it!

I run. I hope I have spun the web of illusion to evade the intrusion.

Running, hoping, the lie remains at a distance.

My heart chooses to believe until the lies make it bleed.

I run to be taken and awaken

Seeing and believing

The lies before me

I run to be free.

Below the poem she had left me a note.

Cassius, don't be angry or hate me. I don't know what caused your father to run, but I understand why he might have done it—his family's safety. Cassius, I love my family. Marino won't hurt them, if I go back. I know I have no right to ask you but...please, Cassius, watch over Mikey when you can. I know he loves you very much.

You once asked me who had stolen my heart. Michael John Castillo has half of it. Cassius, Mikey is my son. You see, good can manifest from evil. There must be a balance. Mikey is the good. The other half of my heart belongs to the blue-eyed man in my dreams named Cassius Russo. I knew the day I met you at the diner you were the other half of my heart. I have never felt a man's physical love. I hope the knowledge that I love you will be a comfort. Know this was the only path to take. My family will be safe now.

"Stupid, stupid woman!" I threw the book against the far wall. It tumbled to the floor. "What a dumb move, Mariana." I stomped out of the room.

Out of breath, hot air rushing out from my nostrils, I entered the office.

Tracy stopped in her tracks, files in hand. "What in the good Lord's name happened to you?"

"You women are impossible. Foreign creatures I'll *never* figure out."

I rammed my hand into my jeans pocket, pulled out my cell, and dialed Drake's number. "Drake, plan B is in effect. You were right. She's going back to Marino. I thought for sure I could convince her." I paused to take in a deep breath. "I don't know how, but she called a cab." I paced between the sofa and coffee table, turned and stopped by my desk. "No, she used the bed sheets. Tied them to the tub faucet and climbed out the window. Yeah, she's a regular cat woman. *God!* She's going back to the lion's den. Drake, I know we talked about the same thing, but not like this. There was a plan, but the hot headed diva decided to change it. You called it, Drake. She pulled on the rope. Now all we can do is redirect the route of action. Keep me posted from your end."

Tracy pulled on my sleeve, questioning what Drake and I were talking about. I hit the speaker button so she could hear both sides.

"Let me know when you've reached your destination." I blew out a long breath.

"I will, but she's gonna be pissed." Drake said.

"Yeah, well, that's her problem. She chose to change the rules of the game."

When I get my hands on her— God, how can one woman drive me nuts like this?

"Cassius." Tracy laid a hand on my shoulder. She jumped back as I slapped her hand away.

"Drake, just a minute. Yes, Tracy?" I asked more sharply than intended.

Tracy returned to her desk. "I'm sorry, it's my fault. I left a paid phone on her nightstand in case she needed to talk. I never thought she'd run." Tracy twisted her fingers together. I kept quiet. "I know you're upset, Cas, but you need to focus on what's to be done now."

"It's not your fault, Tracy. This is all on Mariana."

Tracy sighed and shook her head. "But, I should've known better."

"No, I should've kept a closer I eye on her, Tracey."

"Cas, this is goin' to be one crazy ride. But we can do it." Drake said.

"Yup, there's no gettin' off this roller coaster until it stops. Drake, do what needs to be done on your end." I sucked in a long hard breath and sat behind my desk. "Look, I'm not happy about this plan B, but it's all we have for the time being. Drake don't be a hero, got it. You know I'd do it, but she might bolt again. Report in when you can. I'll work on the other semantics of Mariana's bull headed idea."

"I got this, Cas." Drake then called out to Tracy. "Eh, sweet lips, you keep thinkin' of me. Soon, I'll keep your nights warm again." Drake let out a deep laugh.

There were no guarantees of returns when it came to playing house in the Marino Estate.

"You heard what Cassius said, Drake, no heroics. And you're darn straight you'll come back to me, or I'll hunt you down." Tracy sniffled as she turned her back on me.

"Drake, when you see her, tell her, 'Bright Eyes, the moon is blue'."

Mikey had told me to say that to Mariana someday. I hoped it would help Drake when he met her face to face.

"The moon is blue. Got it, Bro. I'll call when plan B is in motion."

"All right. I have some other phone calls to make." I ended the conversation and rested my elbows on the desk. "Tracy, please do me a favor. Upstairs in the guest bedroom, there's a book on the floor near the armoire. Will you get it and stuff it in my traveling bag?"

"Sure, no problem. What do you plan to do with it?" Tracy stood.

"I plan to use it as a spanking paddle."

Tracy smirked and shook her head as she went upstairs.

I sat back in my desk chair and cleared my throat. I felt the urge to punch something or someone. Instead, I grabbed the stress ball off my desk and threw it across the room. It hit Tracy's computer screen. Good thing it was soft.

Mariana, you're doing this for the family's safety. What about my sanity?

CHAPTER 13

THE HOT BOX

Dusk powdered the Earth with a purplish-blue across the horizon. Soon sunlight would visit the other side of the world. How I wished I was going that way too, following it with my son.

The taxi driver agreed to drive me to the mansion. He was hesitant until I told him it was a life and death situation. Three hundred dollars in my hand also helped him to decide. I gave him back road directions. I knew Cassius would have the authorities searching for this cab. We drove all day and had reached a first name basis. The driver's nickname was Chubs. He did most of the talking as I listened and nodded, smiling when necessary.

Just when I thought I couldn't take any more of his chatter, he stopped the taxi cab half-way up the driveway. Pine trees shaded the drive from both sides. A gentle breeze pushed through the evergreen branches. I leaned my head toward the open window and inhaled the fresh pine scent.

Chubs adjusted his rear view mirror. He eyed me. I pressed down on the automatic button and the window glided up. Chubs seemed to be a nice guy, but a girl could never be too cautious.

I unzipped my duffle bag and slipped my hand inside. I wiggled my fingers under a blouse and felt the smooth surface of my unforgotten partner. I curled my thumb and index finger around the Glock. I hadn't touched a gun in months. Now, here I was in a taxi cab, going back to old habits.

"Mariana, are you sure a nice girl like you should be coming to a place like this? I hear the owner of this place is…scum." His reflection stared at me from the mirror.

I loosened the grip on my piece. "Chubs, maybe I'm not as nice as you think I am." I lowered my eyes, so I wouldn't see the surprised emotion on his face. My heart pounded and my lungs heaved painfully.

God, I'm back.

"Mariana, but…is this what you really want? It's not too late to leave. No one would know."

I stared straight ahead and said, "I would know."

Chubs pressed down on the meter button. The time stopped ticking. He twisted his body and faced me. "I have a daughter about your age. This isn't a place I'd send my enemy's daughter. Please, let me take you anywhere else but here. That guy that ran out of the building earlier today looked worried. I'm sure you and your boyfriend—"

"Chubs, he's not my boyfriend and I'm exactly where I should be. Here's the money we agreed on, plus a little extra for the fatherly advice." I opened the door seconds before he tried to lock me in. I stepped out and kept my distance from the cab.

Chubs killed the engine and also stepped out. He held his hands in the air. "I mean you no harm, young lady." He adjusted his baseball cap on his receding hairline and pulled his pants over his belly.

"Even though you tried to lock me in?" I eyed him.

"I…wanted to give you more time to think about what you're doing." He wiped his brow with the back of his hand.

I held out my hand. "Chubs, thanks for caring. I'll be alright, don't worry."

We shook hands. Chubs's firm handshake lasted longer than expected. I gasped.

"Chubs, your daughter, Tasha, is alive. She made her own bed. It's not your fault."

He pulled his hand away and stepped back, squinting. "Who are you?"

I withdrew two paces. "I'm no one and everyone, some-times. Believe me. Your daughter lives." I gave Chubs a quick nod and hefted my still open duffle bag over my shoulder. I headed west toward the mansion in the distance.

"Be safe, young lady." Chubs's voice trailed off.

I halted with my back to him.

"Thank you, for the tip on my daughter. Tonight you'll be in my prayers."

I twisted my head to the right and rested my chin on my shoulder. I gave him a weak smile. "And you, Chubs, are in mine."

We parted ways. I heard the taxi-cab start up and back out of the drive.

I closed my eyes and patted the front pocket of my sweat shirt. The Tomcat was still there. Before leaving Cassius's apartment, I had stuffed it safely inside the pocket. Lucky for me, Cassius didn't check my bag. The duffle had a false bottom where I had hid both guns.

I drew in a deep breath, and took my first step back into a world I had longed to escape since the day I set foot in it.

"Here we go. No walking away now. You can do this, Mariana." My weak pep talk did not convince my erratic heartbeat that I was doing the right thing. Even so, I kept my pace steady.

A crisp autumn wind ruffled my hair. The sunny twilight stood in juxtaposition to the darkness smothering my insides. I reached the six by five stucco building where one man guarded the Marino Estates front gate. It wasn't a bad set up. Inside the small structure there was a counter with a microwave and a mini-fridge. He could heat coffee, warm his lunch, and not interfere with his duties.

The security guy had a clear view of the driveway down to the road. He no doubt saw me coming. As I neared the gate, a young man, no older than me, blocked my way.

"Ma'am, please stop." He held out a hand.

"Wow. Marino is teaching his lackeys manners, kudos to him." I halted ten feet from him. "No babe, or how's it goin' girl?" I mimicked his stance ready for anything.

"Ma'am, please state the reason for your visit. This is private property."

"Okay. Please, be so kind as to radio Mr. Theodore Marino and tell him Russo's package has arrived."

"Ma'am, your first name please."

I sized up the guy before me. He was about an inch shorter and not all muscular so I figured I could take him, but then I was too tired and not in the mood. Besides, I didn't want to ruin my already botched manicure.

A sore sight approached the gate from the other side. It was Randolph, leering. I pulled the hood over my head and stared at my feet.

"Thomson, what's the problem here?"

Randolph's pinky rings clanked against the wrought-iron as he wrapped his hands around the gate. "I see you have some sweet thang keepin' you company. You know the rules Thomson, no distractions on the clock."

"Yes, sir, I know the rules. She's not keeping me company. I've asked her name and the purpose of her visit. Ma'am?" The young man said.

I lifted my chin, stared into Randolph's eyes and said, "The nanny is here."

"Well now, Babe, you could've called. Did you walk all this way just to see me?" Randolph's smile showed off his gold tooth.

"Yeah, something like that." I tightened my jaw.

"What happened to your nanny job?"

"I got bored and decided to move on. Plus, my boyfriend dumped me."

"His loss, Honey, but how did ya find this place?"

"I asked around about you. I didn't call because I wanted to surprise you. Surprise." I gave Randolph my good girl smile even though what I really wanted to do was wipe the smirk off his face. "I also heard Mr. Marino has odd jobs for girls who might be interested."

"Huh. Did ya now? And what odd jobs are you talkin' about?" His lecherous eyes traveled up and down my body.

"The kind of jobs that keep some male population happy." I stuffed my hands in my sweatshirt pocket.

"Thomson, unlock the side gate." Randolph bellowed.

"Sir, I haven't checked her bag or patted her down." The guard studied me suspiciously.

Shoot, Theodore finally hired a guy with brains.

"No need. I've met this girl in town. She's all right. Unlock the gate. Now." Randolph's tone had Thomson scurrying to open it.

My arm brushed against Thomson's shoulder as I passed through to the other side of the grounds. I smiled sweetly. He lowered his head and went back to his post.

Randolph looked me over again. I kept smiling, hoping he wouldn't recognize me as of yet.

"Follow me, Darlin'. Mr. Marino is in the pool house."

We walked side by side in silence until we reached the entry to the pool.

Randolph opened the door. "Ladies first." He gave a small bow.

Hmm, Theodore must've given all his men etiquette classes while I was away.

When we entered, all poolside activity stopped. This was a common reaction when an unknown visitor came onto the premises. Some men assessed the situation with their hands close to their guns, others eyed me with curiosity, and a few gawked lasciviously while the women froze, not knowing what to expect.

"Look what the mailman left in the yard." Randolph gripped my arm. He repressed a laugh.

Randolph's voice clanged against my mind. His words had motivated me into the lie. I thought I could run from fate, but I was obviously wrong.

Only the foolish believe they can change destiny. Human nature enables them to trust their own instincts. Many times they bury the voice that speaks to them and trust only what they can see and touch. I knew better, but hoped I could escape. Yet here I was, back in the one place I wanted to never see again.

Theodore Marino sat in a cushioned reclining chair a few feet from a pool bar. He turned his head when Randolph roared his announcement. A red head clung onto his arm. She gave me a mental third degree. Her aura screamed for help, but her body stance told me she was the lady of the moment and she wasn't modest to say the least. A spaghetti-string bikini bottom, accompanied a triangular top, barely covering her. This girl had no problem exploiting herself before so many men.

"Don't be shy, sweet thang. Come now, let's talk to Mr. Marino." Randolph pulled me forward. But not before he patted my buttocks.

Surprisingly, I didn't retaliate.

Theodore stood. His fresh clean shaven cologne stung my senses. I knew the scent all too well. "Randolph, do introduce us to your friend." He took hold of my hand and drew it to his lips. "Hello, I am Theodore Marino."

I nodded while staring at my tennies.

"Theodore, this is the nanny I told you about." Randolph let out a small chuckle.

"Ah, I see. It is my pleasure, Miss…" He leaned in and lifted my chin with his forefinger.

Our eyes met. He was no longer the Marino, the business man, but the Theodore I remembered. His smile froze as his eyes widened. In the same instant, Randolph laid his hand on my bum for another squeeze. I was never a girl for much tolerance. One step back gave me the distance I needed. My right hand pulled the Glock from the duffle bag and the other grabbed the Beretta.

My hands flew out like a bird in flight. Theodore, sure of himself, didn't flinch as the Beretta met him face to face. Randolph on the other hand jumped a few inches back, but obviously he wasn't about to make a move with the Glock pointed at his manhood. The shuffle of other guns clicking to attention echoed in the pool house. A few girls screamed.

"You squeeze any part of my body again, I'll squeeze the trigger." I glared between the two men.

"Sweet Thang, why didn't you say you wanted to play. I'm all in." Randolph's repulsive voice sang out.

I pressed the Glock in further. Randolph smirked. But I sensed the fury within him. One small bead of perspiration rolled down his nose. Oh how I wanted to pull the trigger.

"Young lady, we are a peaceful group of business men enjoy-ing the evening. Why such a heated introduction, Miss...?" Theodore came to Randolph's rescue.

"Baby, since we haven't formally met, I'll let this one time slide. But the next time, you point a roscoe at any part of my body, you better shoot." Randolph called my bluff and stepped back two paces. He grabbed my hood from behind and pulled it off. I kept my Beretta pointed at Theodore.

As the hood fell to my shoulders, a loud gasp sounded from the corner of the room.

"Mari!" Allison ran up to me and hugged me. She nearly knocked me into Theodore.

I stuffed my guns in my pockets.

"Allison, sweetheart, you see Mariana? I see a blonde bombshell." Randolph smirked. "I'd hoped the ice queen had melted away. I see she hasn't." Randolph sniffed and drew his hands behind his back. The man stood strong with a body builder's stance. Randolph was faithful to his morning ritual of lifting weights.

God the man was infuriating. I could see now. He knew it was me the day we met in town. His smile couldn't be mis-taken. No doubt he had been under orders to follow, but not apprehend. I must admit the man was a true loyalist. Randolph had been Theodore's father's business partner and he promised the Marino family to protect their son, if the occasion should arise. I stood before the man who convinced Theodore to leave his safe life. Theodore, the professor, had been placed on a high shelf covered with hard core memories of his father's dealings in underground gun smuggling and corrupted negotiations with government officials.

Like an eagle searching prey in a field, Randolph missed nothing. "Miss Nanny, did ya really believe I wouldn't know that ass? Hmm?" Randolph tsked.

"Ha!! Allie, you are correct. Who can deny those bright hazel eyes unlike any others? It is *our* Mari." Theodore laughed and returned to his seat. "And...how many women do you know who are ambidextrous? Did you see how *my* Mari pulled out her firearms?" Theodore stuck a tooth pick in his mouth and rolled it around.

His Mari? Not any more— not for a long time now.

The tooth pick had become a habit when I told Theodore how smoking stunk and it repulsed me. Theodore in his own way did care about me.

I had no intention of shooting, but I needed my message to come across loudly. These men would *not* bully me.

"Heck, she looks good as a blonde. Boys, our cougar is back." Randolph strolled to the other bar stationed near the north wall, leaned against it, and pulled a cigarette from his shirt pocket. The girl behind the bar lit it for him. "I'm just sorry I didn't get a hand full of that ass." Randolph winked.

Guns were holstered. Bodyguards returned to their post near the pool doors. The other men in the room jumped back into the pool or returned to their poker game.

"You're so full of it, Randolph. I feel like puking. Keep on dreaming. You'll *never* see or have any part of me." I stuffed the armor into my bag.

"Ah honey, seein' ya in those jeans is enough to know you have a good bare ass." Randolph smacked his lips, turned around and took hold of a drink waiting for him.

He's such a pompous turd.

I inhaled ready to retort, but Theodore cut me off. "Randolph, how did Mari come in armed?"

Randolph cleared his throat. "You know how she is. She's like a witch. One minute she's clean, the next she's packin'." Randolph sniggered and went back to his drink.

I wish I was a witch. Then I'd make you disappear without a trace.

"Mari, I missed you." Allison clung onto me like a child. Her head rested below my chin.

"I've missed you too, Allie." I returned the hug.

Allison had been under Theodore's parental care since the age of twenty five, when their parents died in a plane crash off the coast of Carmel. I had my suspicions it had been an attack on the family. Theodore and Allie had gone sightseeing that day. The death of their parents rewrote their life's path.

Allie was thirty now. Theodore was her senior by five years. He could have placed his sister with autism in a group home, but she was his only living relative. Theodore didn't dwell on morality, but strangely enough family came first.

I caressed Allison's blonde hair as it fanned her back. The resemblance between the two siblings couldn't be mistaken, only Allison portrayed all the good roaming in this world, while Theodore did what he thought was best for his sister and him.

"Allie, I told you not to worry. Our Mari has returned." Theodore leaned into his chair, exposing a triumphant smile.

I tightened my lips and held back a snide remark. I wanted to tell him I could easily wipe his gloating smirk from his face, but instead I decided to stab his ego. "I came back because of Allison. She deserves to have one sane friend."

"Yes, my tenacious Mariana, you're always on the ready to belie your true feelings." Theodore hissed. "Tasha, will you be so kind as to retrieve the other chair from across the pool.

"Yes, Professor." Tasha obeyed like a well trained puppy.

I lifted my brow. "Professor? You goin' for the kiddies now, Theo?" I scoffed.

"Dear, Mariana, Tasha is an ex-student of mine. You know quite well it has been three years since I set foot in a university room. My duties here surpass my wishes." Theodore rolled his tooth pick to the left corner of his mouth and blew out a long breath. "Professor is a friendly way of showing me respect. Perhaps you could learn from Tasha." He lifted his brow, taunting me.

"Me? Keep on holding your breath, Theo." I hid my hands under my sweatshirt.

"Mari, when you go on vacation." Allison pulled on my chin so I'd focus on her. I lowered my eyes to meet hers. "Take me with you. I like to travel." Allison lifted her head for a few seconds so I could see her smile. She then returned to the bear hug.

"I'm sorry, Allie. The next time I go on vacation…" I lifted my eyes and made certain Theodore was looking at me, "I promise to take you with me." I wrapped my arms around Allison's petite body.

Theodore squinted, but remained silent. Tasha positioned the chair next to him.

"Please, Mari, sit for a while. You must be tired from your travels." Theodore waved his hand at the empty chair. Tasha sat in the other.

"Mari, did you bring me a present?" Allison released me and clapped her hands together.

I stared back, stumped.

"Of course, our Mari brought you a gift, Allie." He snapped his fingers and Allison's day care provider, Sara, pulled from her front pocket a small velvet bag. She handed it to Allison. Obviously, Theodore was sure of himself. He had planned this reunion or at least prepared in case I did return.

"Oooh, for me?" Allison squealed. She opened the gift, pulled its contents out and discarded the bag. In her hand, she held a mother of pearl bracelet adorned with small gold beads between each pearl."

"Allie, Mari brought this gift back from the Caribbean islands. Do you like it?" Theodore asked.

"Yes, Theo. It's very pretty. Thank you, Mari." Allison hugged me again. She then pulled away and frowned. "Mari, you're hair color is like mine." Allie ran her fingers through my hair. "I like your brown hair." She then turned and headed toward Sara.

Sara held out her hand. They went toward the kitchen. The U-shaped mansion housed the pool room in the middle. Two other doors led to the library, and the grand room.

"Thank you, Mari, time for my music lesson. Bye!" Allison waved. She then yanked her hand from Sara's hand and ran back to me. "Mari, don't leave again, okay?"

Shocked by Allison's sudden anxiety, I opened my mouth, but the words stuck in my throat.

"Allie, Mari is like your sister. She loves you. Mari did not leave. She went on vacation. Now go practice your music. Tonight you can give Mari a welcome back recital." Theodore said.

Nodding her head vigorously, Allison said, "Yes, okay. And I can wear the white-pink dress that Mari bought for me last year for Christmas with my new bracelet." Allison held her wrist up high for all to see. She quickly hugged me and ran to Sara. They disappeared into the kitchen.

I sat and not too soon. My legs were starting to feel like rubber. The words, 'I'm back' kept playing over in my head.

Theodore didn't hesitate. He wound his fingers around my hand. Hiding mine in the process. He squeezed more than expected. I squinted, but didn't shy away from his grip.

"Dear Mariana, it's so good to see you again. Ah, but look at your hands. You need a new manicure. And…" Theodore clucked his tongue. "Your hair definitely needs a trim and to be treated once again with love. Wouldn't you say, my dear?" He smiled his well known command, the smile that no one said no to.

I didn't respond. Theodore knew my silence was not defiance, but compliance.

He swiveled in his seat and faced the red head. "Dear Tasha, will you accompany our Mariana to Angela. She'll take care of you, Mari."

I drew my brow together.

"Ah, you haven't met Angela. She's our new in-house cosmetologist. She's a miracle worker. Soon your hands will be back to the delicate flower they once were." Theodore squeezed my hand again. Harder than the first time. "Dinner, Mariana, is as usual, seven o'clock." With a short bow, he kissed my hand and then went to the bar, to where the loathsome Randolph awaited him. They conversed in hushed voices.

Tasha, who'd remained seated during the welcome home, sized me up. Her stare could've frozen over the heated pool, had someone pushed her in. The thought had crossed my mind, but because she was clueless of where she was, I decided not to make her take a dip.

"Follow me." Her tone could've driven a nail into the wall.

From her accent, I guessed her to be from South America.

I had definitely stepped on her toes. This place brought out the worst in me. Without a care of how it would affect her, I blurted out. "Tasha, you should call your father. Let him know you're alive. If you don't, I'll do it for you." I forgot to hold my tongue. My gift and personality clashed once again. I knew I had blown it, but it was...too late to cover my tracks.

Tasha halted with one foot ahead of the other. She twisted in place and shot a deadly glare my way. "Don't tell me what to do." She stared me down.

I let out a small laugh. "I'm not telling you what to do, but if you want your father to be safe and not come here with the police, you'll call him. Trust me, I know these things." I stood and followed her.

"How do you know my father?" Tasha asked in a hushed voice.

"He was my taxi driver." I whispered back.

"My father wouldn't have told you about me."

"No, he didn't, but I told him you were alive. He thanked me." I smiled. "Tasha, I'm not the enemy. You still have time. Leave while you can."

Tasha stole a quick look at Theodore and decided to hold her tongue.

Theodore rested his elbows against the edge of the bar and grinned. His smugness reeked. I wanted to punch his perfect Finnish features and erase any satisfaction he may have felt.

Randolph winked and blew me a kiss. His chuckle bounced off the walls.

God that man is revolting.

Tasha took hold of my elbow and said, "C'mon let's go."

"Yeah, let's. It's dank in here."

I missed a step as a vision hit me. I saw Tasha, weeks later, leaving this place. I did not know why, but relief swept over me. At least one of us would make it out of this house.

I caught up to Tasha. Theodore noticed my quick glance over the shoulder and said, "It's good to have you back, Mariana." He resumed his conversation as we walked away.

CHAPTER 14

THE BODYGUARD

Theodore shared his satisfied grin with me as we sat in the grand room listening to Allison's recital. He slipped away shortly after she started to perform her newest masterpiece. It was a rare occurrence to see Theodore sit for even as long as he did.

I concentrated on Allison. When she united the violin to her arm and fingers, they melded into one. The gift of music graced her and emotion poured forth from her essence through the strings. I wished I could lose myself in such a way. Allison was the fortunate soul in that room, because she couldn't see all that was going on around her. Gun running, prostitution, government pay offs, money laundering, endless lies to satisfy the greedy people who were not content with the life they had, always wanting more.

Allison and Mikey are surrounded by the white light. Their innocence remains intact when many others lose theirs to the dictates of society.

Applause resounded as Allison ended her performance. I clapped along with the other guests, but I thought of something else.

Someday, Mikey, we'll be happy together and Allison will be a part of our lives.

"Mariana, did you like the song? Mariana?" Allison shook my arm.

Still in a fog of thought, I glanced up at her. She stood there in her white lace dress, embroidered with pink roses. The three-quarter sleeves laced her delicate arms as the rest of the dress fell just above her ankles. She stared at her pearl ballerina shoes that completed her angelic presence. I stood and ran a hand along the golden locks that caressed her shoulders.

"The music was ethereal. Allie, did you compose this piece?" I brushed her hair away from her porcelain face.

Allison's eyes gleamed as she nodded yes. She then lowered her chin and refused to look at me.

"Allison?" I tried to get her to focus on me again.

A shadow fell over us. Someone had come and stood behind me. Allison was not one to shy away from family so I knew it was not Theodore, Sara, or even Randolph who had been with them since their childhood. I turned. The double chandelier light, hanging from the vaulted ceiling, was obscured. A man no less than six foot four stood, but a foot from me.

On meeting his eyes, I nearly choked. Bile crept up to my throat burning my esophagus. I swallowed repeatedly and grasped at the black beaded shawl around my shoulders.

Theodore joined our little group. "Ah, Mariana, I see you and Drake have met."

Allison continued to peer at her shoes, swaying and jiggling her bracelet on her wrist. Theodore attuned to his sister's needs signaled Sara.

"Yes, Mr. Marino." Sara said.

"I believe Allison has had enough excitement for the day. Will you be so kind as to accompany her to her room? Allison?"

Allison continued her swaying and didn't meet her brother's eyes.

Theodore rested a gentle hand on her forearm. "Sweetheart, your performance was magnificent. I should like an encore soon. Would you like that?"

Anyone listening to him at that moment would have seen and heard the true Theodore Marino. A compassionate man, a man with heart, soul, yet I had seen the cold, ruthless Theodore Marino, the man who gets the job done no matter the cost.

Allison's delicate features relaxed. She didn't look at Theodore, but she nodded and took hold of Sara's hand. As an afterthought, Allison turned and hugged me.

"Good night, Mari," she whispered.

"Sweet dreams, Allie."

Allison turned to Theodore and kissed his cheek. She then hurried away with Sara in tow.

I rubbed and twisted the double-heart locket resting near my heart. It had been years since the locket had seen light. My grandmother Mary had given it to me before she died. The only reason I wore it this night was because the dress I paraded in didn't require much jewelry. I had decided on no ear rings or bracelet, only a simple necklace and so the locket was released from its velvet casing. Somehow, rubbing the family heirloom between my fingers gave me comfort.

"That's an unusual necklace, Mariana. I haven't seen it before." Theodore brushed his fingers over mine.

I released the locket and my hands fell to my side. I could definitely sense the jealously arise within him. He wondered if another man had gifted me the necklace.

"It belonged to my grandmother. I haven't had a reason to wear it until tonight." I stole a peek at the man still standing near us.

"Forgive me. Mariana as I said before, this is Drake. He'll be your…guardian shall we say?" Theodore's smile widened.

Theodore's words didn't register. Thoughts of Mikey and Aunt Samantha possibly hurt or locked in some dark forsaken place filled my mind.

"Mariana." Theodore laid a hand on my shoulder. I jumped a step back.

A vertical crease appeared between Theodore's brows. He cocked his head to the side.

I shook off as best as possible my morbid thoughts and held my hand out. "Hello, it's very nice to meet you."

"The pleasure is mine." Drake shook my hand and then lowered his eyes. His warmth shot through my rigid, arctic palm.

My shawl slipped off my shoulders. Guest's eyes followed my motion as I attempted to take hold of the shawl before it fell to the marble floor. A chill ran down my spine.

The gown Theodore had graciously bought from a local seamstress was designed to my measurements. The black v-neck front housed the locket while the backless dress revealed the curve of my spine down to my waistline. The fabric swayed over my closed toed slip on shoes.

"Here you go, Mariana." Theodore's breath brushed my neck as he draped the shawl over my shoulders. My newly dyed brunette hair was in a chignon and thin ringlets feathered my cheeks. A small shudder escaped me.

"Mariana, are you not feeling well?" Theodore took hold of my arm.

"I'm fine. Did you say this gentleman is to be my... guardian?"

"Yes, for the time being."

"Why? You know I can take care of myself." I sidestepped to my right. Theodore's hand fell from my elbow.

"Mariana, certain matters have arisen. I'm taking precautions to protect my family." Theodore gave me the eye. His look said we'd talk later.

"Sir, there is a phone call for you from Italy." One of Theodore's henchmen informed him.

"Thank you. Please excuse me. I must attend to this call." Theodore left me alone with this man. My...guardian.

Unbelievable! I wanted to hit him. Stay calm, Mariana.

I studied this Drake fellow's countenance to give my heart-beat time to regulate. He wore a penguin suit like all the other men in the room. Theodore's dinners were always a suit and tie affair. On special occasions like this a tux was expected. Drake's eyes bore into me. I wanted to run, jump into one of Theodore's cars and go to my father to find out about Mikey and Aunt Samantha. The man who stood before me was the man who had supposedly driven Aunt Samantha and Mikey to the inn. I held the ends of my shawl and folded my arms around my waist.

Drake smiled, attempting to pillow the tension his sudden appearance in my life had caused. I returned a scowl. No way would I warm up to this man.

The morning he had walked into the kitchen his features were obscured by his cap and beard, but his grayish-blue eyes couldn't be mistaken. He now stood before me clean shaven with a full head of slicked back wavy hair. I wanted to grab him by his necktie and choke the truth out of him. Although, Cassius had said he was a good friend of his. What game was this?

"Ah, Drake, buddy." Randolph came up behind him and gave him a manly slap on the back. "I see you've met the cheetah. She's not bad eye candy, but watch out for this one. She's a bit tricky at times."

"Thanks for the heads up." Drake's bass voice rang in my ears. The same voice I had heard in the kitchen the last time I saw my son.

"Eh, has she told you about her witchy ability? She claims she can see things. What she actually does is she scopes out her victim and then lays out her plan." Randolph slurred. "Ain't that right, babe." He attempted to pat me on the rear.

I took hold of his pinky and bent it in toward the palm of his hand. "You never learn do you?" I stepped away from him and wiped my hands on my shawl.

"Ha! She's feisty. And she's a bit..." Randolph twirled a finger near his head.

"Then I guess she and I will get along just fine." Drake lifted one corner of his mouth and chuckled silently.

I must admit I enjoyed seeing Drake toy with Randolph's attempts to derail my credibility.

"Randolph, you might see me as a biological mistake, or witchy, but this crazy girl has saved Theo on more than one occasion. And we know Theo runs the show here, so, why don't you do yourself a favor and go drown your sorrows in Dom Perignon. I'm certain Theodore won't miss a bottle or two."

"You're such a cold hearted witch. Good luck with her." Randolph set his mouth in a grim line and walked off to the bar at the far end of the grand room.

I was once again alone with Drake. A vision of a shattering mirror appeared before me. I shielded my face as if it were directly in front of me.

"Hey, are you all right?" Drake supported my weight as I swayed to the side.

"Yes." My head fell into my hand. "I'll be fine. It's been a long day. Excuse me." I withdrew from his hold and started toward the door leading to the staircase.

As I reached the stairs, I felt Drake's presence behind me. I turned and glared. I couldn't believe this man was here and not too long before had been with my aunt and son. Exhausted, I forced my legs to do their expected function. Every step taken in the direction of the second floor was a thought of my family. Were they all right? What happened once I left my father's home? Does Cassius know his so-called friend is here with me now?

Drake climbed the stairs two at a time. He grasped my arm. "Mariana."

I yanked it from his grip. "Don't touch me."

"My apologies, but I saw the dread in your eyes when we met." Drake sighed. "I'm not here to hurt you. I'm here to protect you." He whispered.

"What happened to my family? Where's Aunt Samantha and Mikey?"

"They're exactly where you were told they would be." Drake lowered his voice even more. "Mariana, I have a message for you. I hope it'll convince you I'm on your side. Bright Eyes, the moon is blue." Drake held my stare as his eyes bore into me.

I nodded, but did not speak. My dried tear ducts irritated my vision. I rubbed my eyes, "Thank you," and continued ascending the stairs.

Once I reached the second floor, I spun to my right facing the north wing. My bedroom was at the end of the corridor. Drake followed breathing heavily. I wasn't convinced that he was out of breath, because his athletic body dictated otherwise. I believed he was in a rush to explain his presence before anyone witnessed our conversation. I came to an abrupt stop and faced him.

The mirror that had shattered before me earlier came back piece by piece. I saw a reflection of Tracy.

Drake stood before me with his hands folded in front of his waistline gathering his composer. I placed a hand on his.

"Drake you shouldn't be here. Tracy loves you very much. Please, leave. I'll be fine."

"Mariana, it's been about ten years since Cassius and I met at the police academy. He's family to me. Being here with you is what I do for a brother. He wanted to be the one here, but Randolph would've recognized him."

"Recognize him? I thought Cassius never met Theodore or Randolph." I lowered my voice, hoping Allison would not hear us. Her room was across from mine.

Drake followed suit. "Mariana, we are private eyes. And I guess, Cas didn't mention that he's had a run-in or two with Randolph. He didn't think it wise to mess with the beehive. So, here I am." Drake lifted his hands in the air.

Another lie. Cassius has met Randolph.

"Yes, here you are. Dear Lord! I don't need a body guard. That's what I do for a living. You, here, is my fault. Tomorrow you leave, Drake." I left him in the middle of the corridor and opened my bedroom door.

Drake placed a hand on my shoulder. I glanced back at him as he said, "Look, if I leave. The next guy in line is Frank and if not him then Cassius is coming in disguise. I'm your best bet. Trust me."

"Frank?" I balled my hands. You men make me furious. I'm in no danger here. Theodore won't hurt me."

"No, but what he's involved in is dangerous. That's why he hired me to watch you."

"Ha! Theodore hired you so I wouldn't run again." I stepped into my room.

Drake didn't enter. He stayed in the hallway. "Mariana, I'm next door. Who's in the room across from you?" Drake pointed a thumb over his shoulder to the door behind him.

"That's Allison's room. The room next to Allison's is Sara's. What a lucky guy you are. You're surrounded by women."

"And Theodore?"

"His room is in the south wing." I swung the door closed.

I heard Drake wish me a good night as he opened and closed his door.

The light in the suite remained off. I knew my way around the room better than the back of my hand. I kicked off my shoes and unzipped my dress. It slithered to the carpeted floor. I slipped on the nightgown already laid out on a settee and fell into bed. I smothered my sorrow in the down pillow. Now I had one more worry added to my list of people. Why did Drake have to come here?

Hatred of all greedy people filtered through my reasoning and fed my anger. I slept fitfully. The sheets were crumpled and pushed to the foot of the bed.

"No! Don't touch me. I'll kill you." I sat up abruptly. Catching my breath, I stared into the dark space between my bed and the walls of the suite that barricaded my freedom.

I swung my legs off the oversized queen bed and walked toward the bedroom door.

"You plan to leave me again, Mariana?"

With a start, I sucked in air and swirled around, switching on the light in the same motion. There was Theodore sitting in a Victorian chair that matched the other furniture.

"No. I don't travel in my nightgown. I…was going to the kitchen for a glass of warm milk." I swallowed to moisten my dry throat.

"Here allow me. I'll have it brought up to you." Theodore pulled his cell from his tuxedo pocket.

"No. Don't wake anyone. I'm perfectly capable of getting my own glass of milk." I wound my arms around my stomach. The Ansonia porcelain clock chimed three a.m. I watched its pendulum sway faithfully.

"Mariana, please, join me." Theodore waved his hand in the chair's direction.

"What are you doing in my room, Theo?"

"I was pacing the hallways and thought to come see you, but you were already asleep. So, I sat here to be near you."

"Don't make it a habit."

I must've forgotten to lock the door.

The bright overhead light hurt my eyes, so I turned it off while turning on the hurricane lamp on the table by the door. A soft illumination lighted Theodore's features. I retrieved my robe from the settee and swiveled back around to see a gratified smile on his face. He was a handsome man. It was not difficult to see how women were attracted to him if they were only acquainted with his youthful appearance and charming manners, but I knew both sides to Theodore. The professor I met at the age of twenty-two was in the room with me, but the Theodore I came to know during these three years filled me with an anxious tremor I couldn't ignore.

Theodore grasped my hand. Unguarded, I stepped back a pace, but he held on. "Mariana, did you know yesterday was the first time Allison played the violin since you left? She needs you, as I do."

I patted Theodore's hand and unraveled his fingers from mine. I sat in the matching chair.

"I've missed her soulful music. Allison looks well." I focused on his baby blue eyes.

"She's well now, because you have returned, but when you left she floundered. No one, not even her beloved Shih Tzu could make her smile. And believe me. Buddy has enough love and energy to fill this house two times over."

I breathed in a full lung of air and slowly let it escape.

"Theo, don't worry. I'm here."

"For how long?" His question drilled into me.

I didn't know the answer. But, it was certain my hard feelings toward Theo started to soften. I had returned to protect my family, but somehow I had to save Theo from his own destruction, and dragging his sister along with him.

The words spoken to me by the elderly woman in the diner danced in my head.

Dear, there's no running. Face the demons head on.

"Theo, there's no running. I must face my demons." I smiled for his sake.

"Mariana, I was not the one who ran. And I'm not one of the demons."

Can I truly trust this man?

Even though I disapproved of Theodore's business ventures, he was the man who shared my darkest fears. He knew the robotic Mariana who lived within me. The woman who wouldn't blink if the occasion arose to shoot, kill, and then ponder on the repercussions. Theodore had seen me at my lowest. To me he was my older brother. Somehow, I had to convince Theodore the love I felt for him was a sibling's love.

"Mari, together we'll fight the demons." Theodore lifted his hand offering to hold mine.

Tired, I nodded yes and ignored his gesture. I stood, and returned to bed.

Theodore exhaled a long sigh. He approached my bed side, stooped, and kissed my cheek.

"It's good to have you back, Mari." He ran a finger down the side of my face. "I love you and always will."

"Theo?"

"Yes?"

"I see you in my dreams. The three of us must leave this house."

"What exactly have you seen in your dreams?" He brushed a curl back from my face.

"My attacker returns to kill us."

"Mari, I've told you before, your attacker was most likely a drunk student. You are safe here."

I closed my eyes. The man who stood next to my bed was Theo, not Theodore Marino the cold hearted monster who did what he must do to always remain on top.

"Theo, I love this side of you. Don't ever lose it." I turned my back on him.

Theodore breathed heavily. "I'll try my best, Mari." He ran his hand through my curls once, then he switched the light off and left.

How was I to destroy the beast and unchain Theodore's gentle heart? I drifted to sleep imagining the possibilities of saving Theodore from his own demise, yet every scenario had me seeing the good Theo for the last time, before he was taken from this life.

CHAPTER 15

LONG AWAITED REUNION

The last time I drove the Bimmer, Mariana had left her sweater in the front seat. I hung it in my bedroom closet, and every morning when I opened it her scent left me feeling like a love sick puppy. I always thought that kind of love to be weak, but I guess I'm not as strong as I thought I was.

* * *

The orange-red dusk fanned the sky. I focused on it and thought of Mariana as I cruised north bound on Interstate 80, obeying the speed limit. That wasn't the norm for me, because I was usually the one speeding to nowhere.

I had finally figured it out. I had to slow down and enjoy life, but somehow there was always some pressing matter that needed attention. I should've thought of another way to keep Mariana away from Marino. My father's words came to mind, "It's best to be the hunter than the hunted".

She'll be all right. Shoot, she better be all right, or I'll hunt Marino down.

My cell phone buzzed. Hands on the steering wheel, I eyed the number on the GPS screen and hit the call button.

"It took you long enough. What's going on, Drake?" Agitated, I spoke louder than expected and brought the chorus of my snoring passengers to an abrupt halt. The men coming along for the ride awoke. My father straightened and took in his surroundings. John and Frank rubbed their eyes, grumbled something unintelligible, and squirmed for comfort.

"Good morning to you too, Cas. Hey, was that snorin' I heard?" Drake said.

"Yeah, I'm on my way to the hills to surprise my mom and sister. I'm takin' my father home. John and Frank are along for the ride. Guess Mikey has them wrapped around his pinky." A glimpse in the review mirror confirmed what I had said.

John nodded, while Frank whispered, "Damn straight."

"How's she doin'?" I sensed the others tense up.

"Mariana's holding her own. Her shootin' average is close to yours." Drake clicked his tongue. "She's a regular Robin Hood."

"Yeah, I bet. How's Marino dealing with her return?"

"Marino is playing it cool, although his trust issues have veered with Mariana's disappearing act. He has her bedroom door wired to a silent alarm. Every time Mariana leaves her room, Marino's cell phone and mine ding."

"He's a snake. I wish it were me there."

"Hey Bro, no worries, yours truly is Mariana's bodyguard." Drake laughed.

"Huh, and how did my daughter react when she saw you, Drake?" John said.

"Let's say that if your daughter's glare was a weapon, I'd be dead right now."

Short grunts resounded.

Drake continued. "Mariana, at first sent me packin'. She wanted nothin' to do with me. But, she's comin' around and beginnin' to see I'm on her side."

"Yeah, that's her," Frank said. "Hey, Drake, what's the weather like there?"

"Huh, the atmosphere is thick. Last night Marino had a welcome back celebration for his Mariana. While he introduced me to her, the butler informed him of an international call. He said it was from Italy, but the *word* is the call came from Russia."

I choked the steering wheel when I heard Drake say, *his* Mariana. Dad patted my forearm. I gave him a side-ways glance.

Frank interjected. "Sounds like more arms dealings. I'll dig deeper into Marino's latest business transactions. Give me two days, Drake. I should have somethin' by then." Frank grabbed his laptop.

"Will do," Drake said. "Guy's time's runnin' out on this call. I'm in a guest bathroom sittin' on the john. Eh, no offense, John. It's the only place I can get five minutes without looking suspicious."

"None taken, but where's my daughter right now?"

"She's out back in the shooting range. The girl gets up before the rooster and goes for a run, then for another thirty minutes she works on her marksmanship. I stand clear when she's packin'. Word is she has saved Marino more than once from a hit."

John exhaled loudly and shook his head. "Now I know how my intel to the Feds has been scrambled. Mariana is Marino's human satellite."

"Yep, he lost the last two hardware shipments when Mariana disappeared. She wasn't there to give him the heads up. It might be tricky since she's in the bear's den again." Drake explained.

"My sister is a softhearted fool. She thinks the good Marino will come out and bury the cold hearted bastard selling guns to the extremists, before this country gets better Marino needs to be out of the picture." Frank pounded the keyboard.

"Huh." My father let out a guttural huff.

"Others will slither in to take Marino's throne, Frank. But, it's a start, considerin' Marino's family is the alpha in this country." I said.

"Eh, the target practice has stopped. Time to get off this toilet seat. Cas, don't give up. I know she thinks of you. Later, guys." Drake ended the call.

The last four hours of our drive was John calling his local fed connections, Frank on his cell with some of his buddies in the deep web, and my father dosing off and on. I drove buried in my thoughts.

* * *

A low fog skirted the tree trunks in the distance. The rolling hills shadowed the sky, amplifying nature's canvas. Two wild turkeys crossed the dirt road, five hundred feet from our desti-

189

nation. They scuttled in unison then took a short flight into the meadow. The sun burned through the cloud cover and sent rays down on The Outskirts. It made the house look as if the hand of God had reached down to shield it from the outside world. Maybe it was.

I drove up to the white picket fence and parked. I stepped out of the car and inhaled the cool scent of pine. The guys joined me. Two heads popped into view from the side of the house.

"Bianca, people. Daddy, Grandpa!" Mikey ran to Frank. He crouched and they hugged. "I missed you, Daddy." Mikey swung his arms around Frank's neck.

Frank laid his hand on Mikey's head. "I've missed you, buddy."

John stepped forward. "What? No hug for me?"

"Yes, Grandpa." Mikey opened his arms wide.

John held his grandson and closed his eyes. He kissed Mikey on the crown of his head and then lowered him to the ground. "Boy, you're getting big. What are these ladies feeding you?"

"Fresh bread and wild pheasant and..." Mikey heard me snigger. "Cassius!" Mikey's legs pushed him forward as quickly as they could. He rushed me like a linebacker and I drew him into my embrace.

"Hey, little man. So, have you made friends with our turkey neighbors?"

"Uh-huh. Bianca crumbles the old bread and we spray it on the grass."

"You spray or spread?" I smiled at his enthusiasm.

"Yes we spray, like this." Mikey opened his chubby hands, imitating fans and wiggled his fingers.

His warmth felt right. I had dreamt of him being my son. I gave him another quick hug and planted his feet back on the ground.

He took hold of my hand. "Auntie Samantha wants to see you, Cas." Mikey drew his brows together.

"Okay, but first I want you to meet my father." I stepped aside. "This is Jacob Russo, the man who built this place. I swung my right arm out.

"Oh." Mikey held his mouth open in an O shape.

Bianca came up behind Mikey and placed her hand under his chin, closing his mouth. She then froze, staring at the father she had last seen at the age of eight. Tears welled up in her eyes. She stood her ground and didn't shy from our father's fixed wide-open eyes.

"Li-tt-lle Bee," he said, as he spread his arms wide for her.

Bianca fell into them and wept. Dad lifted his chin, leaned his head back, and stared at the sky as if he were praying. He then closed his eyes. Seconds passed in silence, before a gasp traveled from the wrap-around porch. Everyone glanced toward the double front doors. I let go of Mikey's hand and ran up the steps.

"Mom?" I wound my arms around her to steady her. "I'm sorry, Mom. I thought of calling first, but I wanted to surprise you."

My mother gently pushed me aside and stood fast. She dried her eyes on her apron and squared her shoulders. Bianca linked her hand with my father's, and they walked toward the porch.

My father, Bianca, and mother continued their reunion in the den. I was led by Mikey to the sitting room where Samantha awaited us. Frank and John followed.

"Auntie, he's here." Mikey pulled me by the hand.

Samantha lifted her eyes from the book she had been reading. She was wrapped in a wool shawl near the fireplace. We grabbed chairs and joined her. Mikey sat in Frank's lap.

"Samantha, are you feeling all right?" John folded his hand over hers.

She didn't answer right away. Dullness fell over her pupils.

"What's going on?" I turned my attention to John.

"She was in her own world, before we walked in. She'll be fine in a few seconds." John sat back into a chair.

Samantha lifted her eyes to meet mine and said, "The day will come when I will be the one to leave. My tears will flow, but I will smile and walk the mile. I cherish time and am not blind."

The other two men grinned and nodded their heads.

"Well, I'm glad you two know what she's talkin' about." I sat back in the reading chair and rested my hands flat on my legs.

Mariana definitely gets her weird talk from Samantha.

"Dear Cassius, it's so good to see you." A sheen returned to Samantha's eyes.

"Good to see you too, Samantha. What's botherin' you?"

She giggled like a teenage school girl. "Life, Cassius, leads a person on many paths, but family will lure them back home, even if it's only in their memories."

"Are you telling me Mariana is not coming back?"

"No, she'll return. Cassius, Mariana told you about her… nephew." She eyed Mikey.

"How did you know?"

She laughed freely.

"Right, of course you'd know. Mariana didn't tell me. She left me a note in her journal before she ditched me."

"And now, you must find a way to tell her about her connection to your father."

I eyed her skeptically. *You're her family, why do I have to do it?*

"Yes, Cassius, of course, we could tell her, but hearing it from you will show how much you care."

I shook my head. "Samantha, how?"

"Dear Cassius, she knows her family loves her, but to have you tell her will confirm your love for her."

I rubbed my unshaven face. *How the heck am I goin' tell her?*

Mikey jumped off Frank's lap and hustled up to me. His hands enveloped mine and I felt as if I had stuck my finger in an electric outlet. A wave of nausea hit me. Variables of truth, possibilities, surged through my mind. I sucked in air. Frank pulled Mikey away from me. The room came back into focus.

"What the hell was that?" I jumped to my feet and plowed a hand through my hair. I then faced the window looking out to the garden.

192

"That was a small taste of our weird world." Frank explained. "Only Mikey still needs to work on finesse."

I faced them. John quirked the corners of his mouth up, amused.

"Care to share why you're smiling, John?"

"Not everyone can feel or see when we touch them. You, Cassius, saw possible scenarios of Mariana's fate. Am I right?" John waited with the others for an answer. This family had a high level of patience or they were freakin' aliens.

"Yes, I saw Mariana briefly."

"Cassius," Frank said. "We're not aliens. We're human enough. But, to others, we're freaks, frauds, crazy, certified nut jobs, you name it, we've heard it." Frank stood and walked around the room. "The look on your face, Cas, was the same expression I've seen throughout my life and now Mikey knows it too."

Mikey stood near Samantha. She smoothed down his curls. He stared at me as if he was parsing my every word. He then came up to me, but was careful not to touch me. His little boy pout worried me.

"Hey little buddy, I'm sorry if I scared you." I knelt on one knee next to him.

Mikey lowered his eyes. I misunderstood his reaction. He shook his head.

"I not scared, Cas, I sad. You promised to protect, Auntie Mari, but you here." His eyes, like his mother's, held my gaze.

"Ahh, now I understand. You're talkin' about the pinky promise in the kitchen, right?"

"Uh-huh." Mikey returned to Frank's lap.

I stood. The Castillo family watched me as if they were wired to my every move.

"Mikey, your Auntie Mari is safe. Drake is with her, and we'll find a way to bring her back home, even if I have to storm the mansion and bring her back hog-tied and squirming."

Mikey giggled. "That funny to see Auntie Mari dancing like piggy."

Frank and the others laughed. I missed the humor in what Mikey had said, because I was too wrapped up in my thoughts about how I would convince Mariana to leave the mansion.

Putting that girl over my knee and giving her a spankin' *until she shouts uncle would be therapeutic. There's never been* *a girl who scrambles my nerves like she does.*

My parents and Bianca joined us. Samantha's eyes glistened. As my father approached her, unshed tears rolled down her cheeks.

"Jacob. You're home." Samantha pulled a tissue from her sweater pocket.

My father knelt beside her and they hugged. The silence between these two individuals spoke volumes. He then stood and stretched out his hand.

"I knew you would return, but I didn't know the day." Samantha sniffed, dabbed the tissue under her nose and took hold of my father's hand. She slowly stood from her chair. "Winter is coming early this year. My old bones slow me down when it's near."

My mother joined them. "Dear Carla, he's home." Samantha let out a teary laugh.

"Yes." My mother sniffled.

"Hey you weepy babes, lunch is served. Let's go into the dining room." Bianca said as she clapped her hands.

Frank was the first to follow and one by one the others did the same. I stayed behind to ponder Mariana's situation. An incoming call from my cell phone interrupted my thoughts.

I wandered toward the window facing the gardens and hit the call button.

"Drake, how're things goin'?"

"Hey, Bro. It's goin', but there's a storm brewin'. Within the next three weeks, I'd say somethin' big will go down."

"There's always something goin' down at that place. Tell me somethin' new." I moved away from the window and took a few steps in the direction of a sofa table. I noticed yesterday's newspaper opened to page five.

"Cas, I've tried to convince Mariana to leave. She insists she'll find a way to get Marino to leave with his sister."

"Sister?" The word distracted me from the newspaper.

"Yeah. Theo's sister Allison. Mariana won't leave this time without her."

"Well, what made her leave the first time?" I glanced at the newspaper once more. I picked it up and read the headline. *"Guns Sitting On Our Doorstep"*

"I'm not sure, but Mariana has planned to leave and find a place where she later can take Allison and disappear. Bro, I might need some help convincin' her to leave with us."

"Okay, I'll work somethin' out."

"Cas, work what out?"

Drake's voice droned on the other side of the line as I read the first line of the article, *"Mr. Theodore Marino has confirmed that he will do what he can to assist homeland security capture the guilty party."*

What the hell is this guy up to?

"Cas? You know, Mariana is great in bed. She's soft like baby skin."

"Hey now! What do you mean she's soft?"

"Where the hell were you?" Drake grunted. "Cas, you're usually at the top of your game. What's goin' on?"

"Sorry, man. I haven't slept much, but I'm here. Drake, I just read about the arms dealing in the U.S. It's escalated within the last three weeks. Marino told a reporter he'd help find the guilty. Has he said anything to you about helping us?"

"No, that's Theodore playin' with words."

"I know he's behind the arms sales." I said, as I dropped the newspaper on the table.

"That's right, Drake said. "And he's hired extra watch dogs. The underground word is that the Russians are not happy with their cut on the hardware. Marino has been buyin' from some other distributor. They wanted exclusive rights. But, the in house intel says an inside job is goin' down, only I haven't been able to pinpoint who is after Marino's head. We need this guy alive. He has enough info to implicate a truck load of dealers."

"First we need to find a way to get Mariana and everyone else that's not involved out of the picture."

"That'll not be easy, Cas. Marino has kept Mariana close. And when it's not him, it's me, or Randolph." Drake cleared his throat. "That man rubs me the wrong way. Randolph was partners with Marino's father until he died, or more like was removed, then Theodore jumped into his father's shoes. Signs are pointin' to Randolph wantin' full control."

"Is that right?" I moved closer to the window. The fog had lifted.

"The truth, that man doesn't have one good bone in his body. I've seen how he looks at Mariana." Drake breathed heavily.

"Drake, watch her, she's—"

"I know, Bro. She's one of a kind. How's Tracy? I haven't called, because you never know who might be listenin' and I want her name as far from here as possible."

"Tracy, huh, she's like Mariana. Tough and doesn't know the definition of vacation. She'll be joining us here tomorrow for Thanksgiving dinner."

"Good. Tell her to take some time off."

"Right. Telling her and making her do it, is day and night."

"I hear you brother. We pick the most bullheaded women. But gotta love them."

"Drake, watch yourself. If anything seems out of place, call for backup."

"Will do. Cas, my five minutes are up. Later." Drake ended the call.

I watched the turkeys cross the yard and hoard the hen's feed.

Another world war is boiling beneath the surface. How does anyone communicate with humans who only see dollar signs?

"Cas, you help Auntie Mari?" Mikey tugged on my pant leg. I nearly jumped out of my boots on hearing his voice.

"Hey buddy." I drew Mikey into my arms. His brow looked as if it would stay crinkled permanently. "Look, your auntie is fine. Don't worry, all right?"

Mikey placed his hand on my chest. "She need you. Auntie lost in here." Mikey pointed down at my heart.

"What are you saying, Mikey." I sat with him in my lap.

Mikey turned to face me. "Auntie helps other people, but she need you. Her heart hurt."

"Got it, Little Buddy. I'll do all I can to help your auntie, you understand?" I lowered my chin to look into his eyes.

Mikey's intellect blew me away.

He nodded. "Yes, you help. Cas, no forget, when Auntie tell you to leave, you not listen to her. You stay, Cas. She *need* you. She not safe. She not." Mikey's chest heaved.

"Hey, Mikey, look at me." He raised his eyes. "By next year, your Auntie will be celebrating Thanksgiving here with us, okay?"

"Cas, Auntie push away. You no listen to her."

The knowledge this kid shared floored me. I believed if he were a grown man he wouldn't be here in this house, but in the mansion somehow getting *his* mother out of there.

A smile played on the corners of his mouth. He nodded slowly.

"Mikey, what you say, we go have some lunch, and after we'll go find us a fat turkey? The day after tomorrow, I'll go help your Auntie. Sound good to you?"

"Uh-huh." Mikey jumped off my lap and ran to the archway leading to the dining room. He then stopped and swirled around. "Cas, we no kill my friends in the forest. Only one you hunt."

"Now which one would that be, Little Man?"

"The one that is boss of other turkeys, he can leave." Mikey took hold of my hand.

"Ah, gotcha. We'll find that bully with your help. Sound good?"

"Yes, good." Mikey gave me a quick hug then ran ahead of me. We joined the family.

CHAPTER 16

CAMOUFLAGED TRUTH

On Thanksgiving Day I sat alone in my room, looking out at the mansion's panoramic landscape and thinking about my mistakes. There was no one to blame, but myself.

I miss you Mikey.

The thought sent an ache through my body. I could hear Grammy Amanda say, "Everything happens for a reason." Those five words dug a permanent crevice in my brain, a groove that couldn't be filled with other thoughts.

Does everything happen the way it should?

At least one speck of guilt was removed from my conscience. *Cassius knows about my most cherished secret—Mikey...my little boy.* How I feared I would never see him again. *What would Grammy do?* I recalled the happy times we spent together and other times when Grammy caught me in a fib. She'd shake her finger and say, "Mariana, do not run from the truth, embrace it and let it guide you." As a child, I had pushed my gift into the unknown regions of my psyche. I was afraid what I might see. I didn't want to dream of my mother anymore and hear her voice. Grammy showed me that listening to my mother's words would heal me and guide me through my childhood, but it also kindled the guilt I felt because of my mother's death.

I let go of the red balloon. No one else, but me.

I grabbed the crocheted pillow in my lap squeezed it and then held it to my mouth, suffocating a cry.

"Grammy, I miss you so much. Why did you and Mom leave me? I was a little girl, why?"

Grammy's words resonated, "Don't fear the lion, Mariana. You will conquer him."

That's what she said to me every single time I awoke from a nightmare. She'd hold me in her arms and repeat them. The pain in her eyes told me I would travel a dark journey, but I would survive. And as long as she remained near me, I believed her, but when I sat in her lap on my eighth birthday that fearless Mariana left with Grammy. My father didn't want me to know that I was like him. But, Grammy told me I was clairvoyant like so many of my ancestors because secrets will lead to lies and bury the truth even though it always finds its way to the surface. I decided to tell Cassius about Michael, because I had to return to the mansion to hide my son from this destructive life I was living. Cassius would help even if we would never be together.

I saw bits and pieces of reality, but it did not guarantee my freedom from Theodore or Randolph and that could never be Mikey's fate. My mistakes were mine alone to harbor.

I swiped the sleeve of my sweater across my tear-stained face and continued to stare out the window.

The fog is rolling in. Wish I could hide or create a world in which I make all my happy dreams reality.

I glanced over my shoulder as I heard a knock on my bedroom door.

"Mariana, are you planning to sit there all day?" Theodore entered and sat next to me on the bench below the bay window.

I did not answer him but returned to the scene outside. Allison played catch with the two German Shepherds. Theodore watched too.

Mikey would like Allison. They're surrounded by the same auras—a white light outlined by silver illuminates their path.

The thought of seeing them together made me smile.

"Mari?" Theodore traced a finger over my hand.

I stared at him. His aura scared me sometimes. It was red, the color of blood that could hold a positive or negative charge. I'd seen both.

I wrapped my arms around my body. He grabbed the throw blanket from the windowsill and covered my shoulders.

"Mari, please talk to me. You've shut yourself in your room for hours. What's going on?" He slowly tucked a strand of hair behind my ear. "Let me help you. You look lonely." His soft spoken words sent a tingle down my arms.

I scooted away from his touch. "I'm not lonely. Allison makes me happy, and I'm grateful for your hospitality."

"Hospitality!" Theodore stood abruptly. He balled his hands at his side and leaned his head back, exhaling through his teeth. He then knelt next to me and enveloped my hands. "This is your home, Mari. Why do you still see yourself as a guest?"

"I'm sorry, Theo. I know this can be my home." I lowered my eyes to avoid the hurt my words incurred.

"Not can be, *is* your home. You have no idea. Mariana—"

I placed two fingers over his lips. "Don't say it. I know you love me, as I love you. But…mine is brotherly love. Theo, you know where our relationship stands. Why make it more?"

He rose and sat next to me again.

"Theo, you've asked me before what color aura I see surrounding you."

"Yes, I have."

"Well, it's a vibrant red." I waited for him to ask me what it meant, but instead he stood back up and started to stroll about the room. He studied my books, brushed a hand over my hairbrush, and then across my robe that laid on the back of the vanity chair. When he didn't answer, I continued. "Theo, you're enthusiastic and always ready for an adventure. I love that about you, but your competitive nature scares me."

He halted in mid-stride and gave me a sideways glance.

"Theo, your motto, 'I'll try anything once,' can be destructive. I've seen what happens to anyone who betrays you. Your business deals consist of two options, your way or six feet under." I wrung the hem of my blouse. Some of the stitches snapped. He had to understand that we could never be more than friends while we still lived in this house or this life.

Theodore settled in one of the Victorian chairs. He placed his hands against his lips in a prayer manner. He lowered his eyes and frowned. Then he lifted his eyes and met mine. His glare prickled my senses.

"You're wrong, Mariana. I'm not a killer."

"Have you forgotten the night I found you in the cellar? Whatever happened to that man?"

The creases on his forehead deepened. "That man, who you assumed I had killed, was a child pornographer. He wouldn't tell us who his partners were so we had to persuade him. Mari, I'm not a saint, but I do value life."

"Was?" I pressed my lips tight and wrung my hands in my lap.

"I did *not* kill him, Mariana."

"But, you know who did?"

Theodore looked away.

"Theo, this is not the way to live. Don't you see?"

"Mariana, please trust me. The day will come…" Theodore stopped and looked back at the door. We both heard a noise out in the hall. He drew a finger to his lips and headed to the door. He opened it, but if anyone had been there, they were gone. Theodore closed the door.

"Mariana," he whispered. "I'm on your side."

I want to believe him so much.

"Then why do you deal in illegal arms?"

"My dealings are with the government. But, this is not what's really bothering you. I know you, Mariana. Who is he?"

I stared back, hoping I had not expressed shock.

How do I answer him truthfully without mentioning Cassius's name?

"Your heart is pure, Mari, and I know the only thing keeping you from me, is someone else. I've been patient during these *long* three years. Now…I need to hear it from you. I need the truth."

"And what if the truth is not what you want to hear, then what?" I avoided eye contact.

"If you're asking, will I harm the man you love, the answer is…no." Theodore's bottom lip twitched. "I'll learn to accept your decision."

I left the bench and sat in one of the twin chairs.

I know my being in love with another person bothers Theodore.

201

"Theo, how can you sit there and say you'll accept my decision? I'm not yours to let go. You've had so many women in your bed. It's obvious you don't need me. And for your information, there's no other man."

"Ha! You the woman who sees the future can't see the truth right in front of you."

"What truth, Theo?"

"I'm a man. I laugh. I cry. I have needs like every other. The one woman I truly love doesn't want to warm my bed and keep me company, so I look for the next quick fix which has no meaning, just a distraction." Theodore exhaled loudly. "The day you stepped into my discussion hall, I lost the free-will to love whomever I wanted. You, Mari, have my heart." Theo leaned forward, rested his arms on his legs, and balled his hands together.

"Theo, you know I would die to protect you. I love you, but not in the way you want me to." I held back the tears, refusing to give in to my feelings for him. Desperation within me wanted Theo to change, but how could I expect him to be the professor again when I wasn't willing to give us a chance? I stood to gain distance. He jumped to his feet and took hold of my arms.

Theodore tenderly traced my face. At that moment, it was the professor who stood before me, but for how long?

"Mariana, I respect you too much to ever go against your wishes. But, promise me you won't run off again. Allison was beside herself, and I imagined the worst when you disappeared. We're family." He caressed my cheek and kissed my forehead. He then stooped forward. Our foreheads met. "Family comes first, correct?" He whispered.

"Yes." I stepped back.

Two familiar knocks halted our conversation. We glanced at the door.

"Drake, come in." Theodore said.

I returned to the bench and scrunched my legs up to my chest as Drake entered. His expression led me to believe what he had to say was not for my ears. Before Theodore excused himself, he turned towards me.

"Mariana, Thanksgiving dinner is at six this evening." The cold Theodore had returned.

"Why one hour earlier?"

"I have a business meeting I must attend. Think about our discussion." He left, head lowered.

Drake stayed back. His eyes questioned what he had interrupted. Drake had become my confidant. He was my only connection to Cassius, but I feared what Theodore might do, so our talks were always brief.

"Mariana, when Marino is in his meeting, I'll find a way for us to talk."

"Drake, that won't be necessary. There's nothing more to talk about. My life as I've known it and hoped for is over. Go now before he catches us talking."

"Mariana, there *is* more to talk about? Don't give up."

"I'm not giving up. I'm accepting the cards that have been dealt. Now, go."

"I'll get out of the meeting early. Then we'll talk." Drake assured me.

"Since when have you been a part of his business meetings?" I lifted a brow.

"Since Marino found out there's a contract on his life." Drake announced coldly.

I gaped.

"Mariana, don't look so surprised. With Marino out of the picture you'd be free to live the life you deserve."

"No, Theodore does *not* deserve to die because of his father and Randolph. They were the ones who brought him into all this. He tried to leave with Allison, but Randolph found him and forced him into this crime-laden world. I have to help him."

I turned my back on Drake and peered out the window. A group of rabbits hopped to their warren. This landscape held such carefree life.

If only my life could be as free as those rabbits'.

Drake rested a hand on my shoulder. In a hushed voice he said, "Mariana, Cassius calls every night for an update. He'll find a way to get you out of this house."

"Drake, have you watched the rabbits hop around in the yard?"

"What?" Drake's tone sounded just like Cassius's when he thought I was crazy.

I twisted my body to see his expression. He shrugged his shoulders.

A chuckle escaped me as I said, "The rabbits, they hop, eat, play, then they run back to their safe place underground. How awesome would it be to run and hide below ground forever, knowing the people you love are safe?"

Drake's complexion paled. I sensed the word delusional cross his mind. His cell phone dinged. He checked the text.

"It's Marino. I gotta go." He started to walk toward the door and then he paused, twisted his body to face me, and pointed his finger my way, "Mariana don't be foolish. You're not alone." He then closed the door behind him.

I had three hours before dinner to submerge into my lonely thoughts.

The peaceful hours drove my thinking to a plan, but pot holes in the road still needed to be patched. Somehow, I would find a way to leave this house with Allison and Theodore.

* * *

I decided to treat myself to a bubble bath. I usually took a shower because I was in a hurry to guard Theodore's back or be with Allison. Sweet Allison was rehearsing for her recital. She'd be lost in her mind's melodies for the next few hours. Theodore didn't want me at this meeting. I figured it was one of his gun deals. He knew where I stood on his political views. I wasn't against civilian's rights to bear arms, but illegal gun runs, and cutting deals in the black market...I couldn't comprehend how Theodore thought it was all on the up and up.

While I waited for the bathtub to fill, I sat on a brass stool with a towel wrapped around me. I had tucked music buds in my ears and listened to Immortal.

A new journal rested on my lap. I scribbled my thoughts as they appeared.

An exhale travels a lonely path, leaving its director one less breath.
The weariness remains.
The pains don't digress.
The mind knows how thought flows.
Promiscuity doesn't abide here.
Love of fellow man might be my doom.

I reviewed what I had written and in a flash I knew what those words meant. Even though I was tired and lonely, I needed to be strong for Mikey.

I must learn from my mistakes and how to forgive myself, my attacker, and Cassius. Yes, forgive.

The bath was ready. I snapped the journal shut and put it on the towel rack. I dropped the towel to the floor. The bubbles moved in to blanket me as I slipped into the sudsy liquid.

Hmm, this is divine. I should take baths more often.

Time offered me the luxury to think of Cassius, a dangerous direction to follow, since he and I couldn't be together. Why torture my heart thinking of him?

One thing was certain. I couldn't allow Theodore to ever know about Cassius. I loved Cassius and feared his acquaintance with me could lead to his demise.

Two and half hours remain before I have to dine amongst drug lords, hitmen, and arms dealers. At least one bright light hovers above the murky swamp. Allison will be sitting next to me.

I relaxed against the tub's headrest. My ear buds were securely in place. Lyrics swirled in my head drowning all other sound. I closed my eyes and allowed the music's rhythm to fill my mind.

"Mariana, your forgiveness makes you who you are."

What? I sat up in the tub. I scanned the bath suite. There was no one, but me.

Sitting in the warm water, I felt an arctic chill web around my heart. The music played on as I stared at my robe hanging on the towel bar. Then the robe vanished and Cassius's image took its place.

"Mariana." Cassius called out.

Blood trickled from his mouth streaking his neck. Who had done this to him? His lips moved, but I couldn't hear his voice. I stretched out my hand to touch him. He was an icicle. Why am I seeing this?

I squeezed my eyes shut and shook my head. On opening them again, he was gone. The robe reappeared mocking me. I settled back in the water and I breathed in deeply.

I need to convince Cassius I don't love him. What I saw can't be true.

"Let it go, Mariana. It was just a daydream. Let go." I spoke out loud. Fear played on my erratic thoughts. I twisted my hair into a bun and took hold of the razor.

I better get ready for dinner.

I leaned back, hung my lathered leg on the tub's edge and I lifted the razor when…

The door swung open, smashing into the wall. Wood splinters showered the tiled floor. Stunned, I held the razor in the air as Drake barged into the bathroom. I pulled the buds out of my ears.

"Mariana, no!" He took hold of my wrist.

"What the hell! Get out of here."

"I won't let you do it."

"Are you drunk? You won't let me shave?"

Drake assessed the scene. His eyes followed the line of my leg with my foot dangling over the tub's edge. I dunked it back into the water and wrenched my hand from his hold.

"Get out!"

"I'm sorry. After our talk earlier today, Allison knocked on your bedroom door, you did not answer, and then I knocked on this door, still no answer—"

"Hold on. You're telling me you thought I was going to off myself."

"Well…yeah."

"Did you not see my lathered leg? I was going to shave. You do know that women shave their legs, right?"

"I uh, I mean…I'm sorry. I was worried you might have been depressed and…" Drake stared at his feet, perspiring.

Serves him right.

I laughed.

"You think this is funny? Allison called me. She thought something had happened to you and when you didn't answer—"

I held up high the ear buds that dangled from my fingers and said, "Music, daydreaming, I was in my own little world until you played Tarzan and came in swinging your arms. That was funny by the way. Drake, I'm not suicidal. Now, if you've had your eyeful, I'd like to get out of this tub. I'm shriveling."

"Yeah, sure go ahead."

"Right, as soon as you turn around." I twirled my finger

"Right. I'll…be waiting in the bedroom."

"Good idea, Tarzan." I held back a laugh. "And make sure no one else comes in, since the door doesn't lock, compliments of Mr. Drake."

He grabbed the doorknob and closed it. In five minutes, I shaved my legs and dried off. I put on my robe and stepped into the bedroom.

I noticed Theodore standing by the bay window in his Tribeca tuxedo. He caught sight of me. What a contrast, him in a suit and I in a satin robe.

Theo is pleasant to the eye. If only…

"Mariana, do not be angry with Drake. He was doing his job."

Drake stood near the door. He lowered his eyes as I glanced at him.

"Mariana, I know you've been sad. How can I make it go away?" Theodore faced me expecting an answer.

When I didn't say a word, Drake stepped forward. "Mr. Marino, I believe it was my misunderstanding. Mariana had her ear buds on and didn't hear me knocking."

Theodore kept his eyes fixed on me. "Thank you, Drake. Will you please tell Allison, Mariana is well and soon she'll be down for dinner?"

"Yes, sir." Drake said as he exited the room.

Theodore sighed and walked past me with his hands clasped behind his back. He then turned and ran his hands down my robe sleeves. I clenched my jaw, hoping he would continue to be the gentleman he had been up 'til now.

His lips brushed my earlobe as he whispered, "Mariana, allow me to make you happy. All you have to say is 'yes' and you become the center of my reality."

I leaned my head against his shoulder.

He helped me when I needed someone. Can I love a man who lives two realities?

Theodore's breathing quickened. His warm breath traveled down my neck. "Mariana, you are the *only* woman that matters. You are—"

I turned to face him as he straightened his posture.

"Theo, please. *Please* don't fantasize about us."

"How can love be a fantasy?" He held out his hands.

I stepped back and shook my head. "When you decide to leave this mansion, then we'll talk."

I left him standing in the middle of my bedroom as I escaped to the walk-in closet.

"Mariana, can you read minds on command?"

Theodore's question penetrated my frigid façade. I paused near the closet door with my back to him. "No, I can't tell you what you're thinking. But certain words come to mind."

He approached me and took hold of my hand. I drew in a sharp inhale and the knot of air pressed against my throat.

"What is it, Mariana?"

I turned and stared beyond him in the direction of the bay window. The curtains fluttered, but the window was not open.

"I sense the words, little boy, rifle, father, dark overcoat. They're part of a puzzle." I uttered in a hushed voice.

Theodore rubbed my frozen fingers. "Mari, let me help you shuffle through the pieces of the puzzle. You're the woman I love."

"I'm just one of many that you hope to bed."

"Mariana, we've talked about this, since you don't want to be my partner, I distract myself in other ways."

I withdrew my hands from his and stepped out of his space. "Partner, in what? Love and life are not part of a game board, Theo."

"You're wrong, Mariana. Life filled with love is a game. Think about it. Who will finish first and love the sensation? Who will make the most money and love bathing in it? Who... will gain what they desire." Theo stared with hungry eyes.

"So, I'm a prize? A conquest?"

"No, you're the rarest jewel. The other jewels shine, but are superficial. They don't know me as you do."

Tears filled my eyes. "Theodore, life's scale can unbalance. Please, leave this way of life and I'll help you and Allison find safety."

His cell phone dinged. He released a heavy, tired breath, and read the message.

"Mari, I'm sorry. Our first guests have arrived, but we will continue this conversation tonight after they leave. Don't be long." The bedroom door clicked as he left.

I dropped onto the French settee and gained my composure.
They're not my guests. I'm a pawn.

Theodore and I did talk a day later about leaving this place, but not before Randolph sought me out and added his two cents.

* * *

Dressed in a red, strapless evening gown, I descended the stairs. Guards stood near the front door. Their eyes scanned me from head to toe as I reached the bottom step. They nodded and I smiled, pretending to care. The laughter from the dining room rattled my nerves. I turned to my right and entered the room filled of piranhas.

Breathe in, breathe out. Breathe in, breathe out. You're doing this for Allison.

Dinner was served promptly. To my relief, shortly after dinner, Allison left the dining room. I hated her being exposed to such people. I, on the other hand, was expected to make my presence known a while longer.

"Mr. Marino, I do not recall meeting this lovely lady." The Russian guest, sitting across from me made a gesture with his head.

The other men along with their wives quieted and eyed us.

"This, Sir Anton…" Theodore linked his hand with mine and made it visible to all, "…is my lovely Mariana. The last time you visited she was away visiting family."

"Ahh, I see. It is a pleasure meeting you, Mrs. Marino."

"We are—" I was about to say we were not married, but Theodore stopped me with a gentle squeeze on my hand. Not far from our seating arrangements, Drake gave a slight nod of his head. I understood I had to play along.

"It is wonderful to see young couples in love and married. Marriage has become obsolete when so many just choose to cohabitate."

A scene appeared before my eyes. I saw Anton laughing and whispering promises into another woman's ear. She giggled and they kissed. It was not his wife, at least not the one that dined with us that night.

I felt my cheeks redden and heat shot out from my ears. The righteous old goat sat across from me preaching about the sanctity of marriage, when he dealt in guns and was known to have mistresses in all corners of the world.

"My wife and I have been married over forty years." He ran his hand down his beard. "What is good should always remain as such. You are of accord, Mrs. Marino?"

Keep cool Mariana. Don't tell him how you truly feel.

I didn't dare look at Anton or anyone else for that matter. Instead, I focused on Theodore's family portrait and said, "Yes, family is most important."

Anton gave a satisfied grunt and continued with his boorish conversation. This Thanksgiving dinner was a night for pleasantries with the who's who of the underworld business. After dinner, the liquor and cigars were presented. Soon a veil of smoke hovered above our heads. My throat constricted. I stood. The men did the same.

"Mariana?" Theodore spoke in a hushed voice near my ear. "What's wrong?"

"Theodore, I need a little fresh air." I patted his hand. "Please, continue with your conversation. It was a pleasure meeting everyone here tonight." I gave a slight nod and excused myself. The men sat back down around the dining table.

Randolph spied me near the opened glass doors, facing the garden. He joined me from the other end of the room. He'd been near the fireplace, eyeing the guests as he always did. I moved to the side to allow him to pass, but instead he came closer to me and said, "Darlin' it's time you have a history lesson. Let's take a walk." He clamped a hand on my elbow and directed me outside.

I peeked over my shoulder. Theodore was engrossed in a conversation with the Russian ambassador. He was too far into his realm to notice me. Sara was off for the evening so Drake had left the room to check up on Allison who earlier had one of her anxiety attacks. She had grown fond of Drake.

I allowed Randolph to navigate our walk. As we rounded the fountain at a turtle pace, I secured my wrap around my shoulders. Randolph paused, snuffed out his cigar, and dropped it in an empty bird bath while keeping a firm grip on my arm.

"It's a grand night for a walk." He turned his head to study me.

"Really, we're going to talk about the weather?" I tightened my hold on the shawl.

He sniggered. "No, I suppose we're not. You're a beauty, but cold." He waited for my response. When I said nothing, he laughed again and continued. "My grandfather knew your great, great-grandfather James Standford. I assume you know your heritage?"

"Oh, my God, where do the secrets end?"

I nodded. I would not give him the satisfaction of knowing I was surprised.

"Good. James was an exceptional man, but he decided he didn't want to play ball with the big boys any longer. He thought he could just walk away. Look at what that earned him, a one way ticket for his wife and him six feet underground." Randolph paused. He watched my eyes grow bigger. "Yes, darlin', now you're beginning to see the color on the canvas."

"He was gifted too?" I said.

211

"Exactly. And the man had made a good life for his family until he decided he wanted nothing more to do with Theodore's grandfather. Do you see the whole picture? You darlin' are like your father, your grandmother, and ancestors before them. The only thing is they didn't play the game like you do."

I shook my head in disbelief.

How could this be true? Generations entangled in a web woven by deceit.

"Now don't go thinkin' like James. He had the notion he could side with the feds and get the goods on us. Just like your father siding with the feds." Randolph paused for effect. He chuckled as he saw my eyes widen even more. "But we know, don't we, Mariana? Life has too many snares." Randolph laid his pudgy hand on my shoulder. "Best you keep to your business of protecting Theodore and do away with the notion of saving him. He needs no savin'. He and Allison are where they belong. His father and I built this empire and it now belongs to him and my daughter."

Daughter! Is Randolph saying Allison is his daughter? But—

"That's right, my daughter." He grinned, knowing he had caught me off guard. "You see, Theodore's mother, believed she could convince her husband to leave the business he had built. She almost did, until I convinced her I was in love with her. Women love that sappy stuff." He let out a hardy laugh. "But you are different, aren't you darlin'? And Theodore is too respectful."

"You're not even in his league." I sneered.

"That might be so, but Theodore's love is his one weakness, just like his mother. Telling Annely I loved her was enough to hook her and keep her chained to this mansion."

We paused beside the fountain. I yanked my arm from his grasp. The water trickling from the flower petals did nothing for my tattered nerves.

"Sit, darlin' you're lookin' a bit yella'." I sat. Randolph continued his story. "Annely was no fool. She had a mind like no other woman I had ever met. Beauty and brains is a hard mixture to tame. A man will fall just by lookin' at her and not know what hit him until she has done the damage." Randolph winked.

I held my composure stone-faced.

"Annely battled with her humanity for a year, but then she decided the truth needed to be told. She lost it and couldn't go on livin' as she had been. She told me she was goin' to tell Ignacio about our affair. On Thanksgiving evenin' after the guests left, hey just like tonight, how about that?" Randolph clicked his tongue. "Annely went lookin' for Ignacio. She found him in the guest house sittin' in his favorite armchair like a king, in a drunken stupor. I followed her. She ran to him and knelt at his feet, held his hands, and begged him to listen to her. 'Ignacio,' she said, 'We must leave this place. Randolph raped me and I'm now with child.' Ignacio, a passive man, held the devil's fire in his eyes that night. He stood and shook her until she fell to the floor. He shouted, 'You whore! You'll never speak of this to anyone, do you understand? Randolph saved my life more than once and if anythin', it was you who allowed him to bed you.'" With tongue in cheek, Randolph said. "Well now, did I say I convinced Annely I loved her? I did, but not on our first night. Annely might not have been a willin' party, but in the end she enjoyed it."

I rose and lifted my hand to slap him, but he took hold of my wrist. "Now, now, darlin' let's not repeat Annely's mistakes. You're smarter than that. Turns out Annely forgot to take her birth control pills. Can't say I'm sorry. Allison is a beauty, even though she doesn't have her mother's smarts."

Ugh! This wretched, disgusting man!

I trembled. I wanted to gouge his eyes out, but the grounds were littered with bodyguards due to the diplomatic dinner.

Randolph laughed from the gut. "You do have spirit darlin.' And a body."

"You ever touch me like that I'll make you holier than Swiss cheese." I sneered.

"Darlin', no need for such hostility, now where was I? Ahh, yes. Spirit broken, Annely left the guest house and never spoke of the incident again. After Allison was born, she fell into a deep depression. Ignacio had the best doctors examine her, but it was not her mind that was broken. It was her will to live and the fact of not bein' able to take her son and daughter away from here. That's what drove her to nothin'." Randolph leaned in close to my ear. "You see, she understood as you do that family comes first."

"Get away from me." I hissed. "You were the cause of her death. Does Theo know this? No. He couldn't or else he would've killed you by now." I needed to gain distance from him. My patience was wearing thin and my Berretta tucked in my leg garter reminded me of how much I wanted to use it.

Randolph grabbed my arm. I was about to retaliate when I noticed a guard coming our way.

"Remember this darlin', Annely fell asleep and never woke up. The fire chief declared she somehow knocked the scented candle from the night table onto her bed. She was too drugged up to feel anythin'. The fire was quick." Randolph gave me a sickening smile. "I know how much Theodore loves you. Let's keep it that way, shall we?"

"Theo told me his parents died in a plane crash." I spat.

"Half true. Theo's father had left on a business trip that mornin'. Supposedly his wife was with him." Randolph displayed a wicked smirk.

One of the men on watch approached us. "Sir, a man has come onto the grounds uninvited. He's in the den waiting to speak to you. Said something about a small package?"

"All right, I'll be there in a few minutes."

The guard eyed me, but then bowed his head and left.

Randolph faced me again. "Mariana, whatever it is you're thinkin' of doin', think twice or even three times about not doin' it. Annely had a beautiful mind, but in the end her morals finished her off. She believed she could fix her family's problem. But you see, good and evil counterbalance one another. "

"You're demented. How can you justify selling arms to the Cartel or any other parties and believe there's nothing wrong with this picture?"

"Mariana, you sound just like her. Let me tell you this, when I leave this hell hole, another will take my place. These types only see dollar signs, and if that's what makes the world rotate and sift out the weak from the strong then I'm the man for the job. You see, man has always plundered, destroyed, killed and loved all in the name of progress. Who are you, to say this way of life should be changed?" Randolph made a clicking sound with the corner of his mouth and sighed. "Sweet Mariana, when Theo brought you to this house, it was not by chance. You were chosen. Your father was destroyin' all our contacts by talkin' to the feds and I needed leverage. The bonus was that you could see the future at times too. Ain't that the cherry on top of the cupcake. Hmm?" Randolph stroked his beard. "Be a good girl. I have business to attend to. Enjoy the evenin'."

He left me standing next to the fountain as if we had been chatting about the beautiful countryside. I stared into space, attempting to digest all the information.

"Mariana, you okay?" Drake laid a hand on my shoulder.

I nearly jumped out of my shoes as I felt his touch. "Yes, just one of my migraines coming on. Drake, please give Theo my apologies. I'm heading to bed early. He should be fine with all the extra manpower tonight."

Drake wrinkled his brow. "Mariana, I've got your back. This will end soon."

Yes, it will.

"Excuse me. I need to lie down." I left Drake standing alone. I felt his sincerity, but the info Randolph had shared changed the game.

I will protect the family. My little boy will be safe, and I'll get Allison away from these vultures.

CHAPTER 17

PROTECTIVE LIE

As a kid, holidays were never special to me. When my father left us, there was no room for emotion or sentimentality. Even though Mom and Bianca were there for me, I could not let go of the fact that *my hero* had abandoned us. The way I saw it, love didn't conquer any obstacles, and I'd be damned if I would allow it to control me.

Turkey day brought a reality never to be categorized as a happy day, but this year had me thinking. My father sat next to my mother for the first time in over twenty years. I should've been grateful, and I guess I was to an extent, but I wouldn't rest until Mariana was with her family.

Mikey running around, making everyone laugh, completed the Thanksgiving scene. I realized then that family goes deeper than DNA. Family sticks around even when you try to push them away.

The past week in the Outskirts, I had kept to myself, but Mikey made certain I wasn't alone too long. He'd come to see me just long enough to make me smile, then Frank would carry him away over his shoulder.

I slouched back in the office chair, chewing on a pencil. On idled time my thoughts kept running back to Mariana.

This is friggin' messed up. Mariana should be here with her son. And I need to suffocate these memories of her scent, her lips, and—Cassius, get off this train to nowhere.

I threw the pencil onto the newspaper. The article stared back at me—Feds Investigating Marino Mansion.

Dang, this Marino crap is going to hit the fan soon. I need to get the game play in action. If Mariana is in the middle of the storm so be it. She made her decision loud and clear.

216

I sat upright and grabbed my cell off the desk. I hit the contacts button. Two rings sounded.

"Hello, Cassius. How's the family?"

"Everyone's fine. Listen, how do I keep her from knowing the truth?"

"My friend, she's an amazing woman, and you can't hide the truth from her. When the truth wants to be known it'll push its way in."

"Shoot, she's like some kind of witch."

"I told you old friend, she's like no other woman, but not a witch."

"Theo, I'm losin' it. When I'm around her—shit I need to keep my head in the game. I need to follow through on my orders and then disappear. She's back with you. My debt is paid."

"Cassius, you owe me nothing."

"I know it was you who sent me the info on my father's whereabouts."

"Cassius, I know all too well what it's like to grow up without a father even when he lives under the same roof. I did not choose this life. It's too late for me, but not for Mariana and Allison. The plan is set. The legal papers have been drawn out. The mansion will be converted to an assisted living autism home. Now, it's up to you, Cassius. You take my sister and Mariana out of here. I will be the one to vanish."

"And then what? You know as well as I do she wants nothin' to do with me, and this can't be pulled off. Mariana will see right through me and you."

"Always the pessimist, Cassius. Mariana doesn't want me. She loves another named Cassius Russo." Theodore cleared his throat.

"I'm not going to sit around like a hound dog in heat." I grabbed the pencil off the desk and snapped it between my fingers.

Theodore held back a laugh. "Cassius, she's blind for one man. And she believes she's doing what needs to be done for the family. She even thinks she's protecting you. I asked who had her heart. She flat-out lied. I'm not at the top of her list." Theodore exhaled a frustrated breath.

I could feel his resentment riding the cellular waves.

"How do you know, Theo? You've told me before her love has no limits. She'll come around."

"No. Whatever you two talked about has her stuck on you."

"If Mariana ever finds out the truth, the real truth, it'll be worse than me leaving." I swallowed in an attempt to rid the bitter taste of words that lingered. I hated how she made me feel as if I was not the captain of my own feelings.

"Cassius, I love Mariana. But undoubtedly she loves you. I've heard her cry out *your name* in her sleep."

"You watch her sleep?"

"It's all I can do."

"Theo, this was not supposed to go down like this. I was assigned to this mission. Then her father asked for my help. The man has some kind of power of his own that makes it hard to say no."

Theodore chuckled, "Yes, just like his daughter."

"This was a job like hundreds of others before this one. Why now?"

"Huh, the great Cassius Russo is human after all. My old friend, there's no why or how to explain love. As Mariana would say, 'the truth liberates'." Theodore paused. He drew in a heavy breath before speaking again. "She *is* one of a kind. Don't turn your back on this one, Cassius."

I had no psychic abilities, but even I could hear the pain in Theo's voice. "Theo, I'd rather run than see the hate in her eyes." I leaned into the desk and massaged my forehead.

"You don't understand who she truly is. Mariana's capacity to forgive is almost godlike. You made it possible for her to come back to me, and I am grateful, but I can't take much more of the heartache that's devouring her. She needs to see you, Cassius."

"I don't know about that. After all, she did leave me. But... rest assured. I'll find the low life that attacked her. That's a promise."

"Somehow, I know you will."

"Theo, can we talk?" Mariana's voice shot out through the cell. *Oh, man. Miles away and her voice…Cassius get it together.*

"Yes, of course. Give me one minute." Theodore said to her.

Mariana said, "Fine," and then I heard a door close.

"You heard, the light of my life beckons me."

"Yeah, I'll be seeing you when I see you. Theo?"

"Yes?"

"Theo, I don't trust Randolph. Watch over her."

"I know my friend. I know. Cassius, do not divert. Remember the plan. My lawyers have drawn the legal papers and I have signed them. The tunnels need to be destroyed. All must go according to plan."

"I understand."

The call ended, and I sat holding the phone in the palm of my hand. I thought back to when I had met Professor Theodore Marino. It was his first year of teaching. When my superiors sent me on my stakeout and I found out who I would be going after, I cursed the day up and down a hundred times. Theodore was not all that bad even if he was on the opposite side of the fence. What twisted my gut was that he should've helped Mariana more. Love sure can hog-tie a man.

A muffled grunt escaped me. *I know. I have to do it.* I called Drake.

"Drake here."

"Bud, the dance is on. Get your dancing shoes." I shut my eyes to the thought that the truth soon was going to ignite the fireworks.

"Okay, I'll get them out of the closet, polished, and ready to go.

"Drake, this one truth is cutting me to pieces. How is it that I can have a multitude of other truths and lies in my head, and I don't give them the time of day?"

"Easy answer, Bro. This one truth is connected to Mariana. See you in a few days." Drake ended the call.

The call to Drake cleared my mind. I figured out what had to be done. It would be the one way to secure Mariana's safety along with Allison's. She'd probably damn me to hell, but she would be left in the dark, exactly where I wanted her. My initial plan had been to take Mariana as far as possible from this town. But it was detoured when Marino's note demanded she return to the wolf's den.

Once Mariana was told about the note, her robotic alter ego kicked in. The look in her eyes said she'd protect the family at all costs. That's when plan B came into effect. One of my own joined the Marino pack. Drake volunteered to be my eyes and ears. I thought of going myself, but I had run into Randolph more times than I cared for. I couldn't risk blowing a two year investigation.

* * *

My cell phone alarm blared just as the sun peeked over the hills. I clicked it off, and stuffed it in my jacket pocket. Still groggy, I rolled the chair away from the desk, stretched my legs, and grabbed my bag. I had spent all night deciding how to handle this. A wall of distance had to be erected between Mariana and me. It would be the hardest thing I'd ever done.

I headed to the kitchen for a cup of java. It never failed— my mother was already in there. She was always up before the rooster crowed, kneading dough or preparing the day's meals. She turned halfway and gave me her your-up-early smile.

"Hey, Mom." I kissed her cheek.

She stopped kneading and wiped her hands on the apron. "So, it's that time?" she said as she turned to face me.

"Yeah, it is."

She nodded. "Godspeed, and please, no heroics." She kept her eyes fixed on mine.

"I'll try."

"Mom?"

"Cassius, she loves you."

"But, I…"

"Son, what is it?"

"Nothin'. You're right she loves me and I love her." Had I told Mom my plan, she'd most likely convince me not to go through with it. She knew about the mission, but this one thing was all on me, and it had to be done.

Mom handed me a cup of coffee, but didn't bother to offer me breakfast. She knew me too well. When my mind was on a mission, there wasn't much thought for food. I set the empty cup in the sink, and we hugged.

Mom tugged on my jacket collar and said, "I'll let the others know you left early to avoid traffic, but we both know it's because you're too chicken to look into Mikey's eyes and say goodbye for now." She gave me a tight lip smile.

She was spot on. I didn't want to face Mikey, because he'd most likely see right through me, and tell the others what I was going to do.

"I can't say you're wrong, Mom." She gave me another bear hug and then I headed out to my Harley. It was time to clean house.

* * *

Come on, Drake. Wake up. Answer the phone.

"This better be good." A muffled voice answered, followed by a yawn.

"Drake, bud, be ready. I'll be knocking in ten minutes."

"Ten. Where the hell are you?"

"I'm in the woods. Sweetheart, I'm home."

Drake groaned. I heard the bed covers rustle as he pushed himself off the bed grumbling, "This guy is goin' to put me in the crazy house." He disconnected the call.

Drake opened the back door as I reached it.

"Hello Sunshine, glad we could meet up." I leaned against the door frame, arms crossed.

"Man, do you even know what time it is?"

"Sure, I do. It's some time after midnight."

Drake sniffed the air while shoving his hands in his jeans pockets. "Cas, it's not like you to hit the bottle when you're on the clock. What's up?"

"Hey now." I lifted a finger and swayed a little. Drake steadied me with a hand on my shoulder. "I didn't hit any bottle. I might…" I squinted. "…have caressed a few beer bottles. They taste mighty fine." I grinned.

Drake shook his head. "What's up with the beard and…you changed your eye color?"

"Yup. Might run into Randolph." I slurred.

"Run into him. How long do you plan on being here?"

"Not long, but when the plan kicks in I need to be ready and I need to get used to these dang contacts." My left eye winked. "Shoot."

"Yeah, you're cute, but not my type. Get in here, hurry. I delayed the cameras for a three minute interval. We can talk in my room." Drake pulled me by the arm. He frowned. "Chit, you smell like a brewery."

"Lovely to see you too, dear."

"C'mon and stay close." Drake huffed. "You owe me."

"That I do, maybe someday I'll come around to paying you back."

I knew as we entered the kitchen we were in the North wing of the Mansion. I bumped into him.

Drake whispered. "Dude, I said stay close, but personal space, okay?" He waved a hand between us.

"Yeah, no problem." I belched.

He couldn't help but laugh. "She's messed you up *good*."

Drake shook his head again and pushed me through the kitchen into the hallway. I followed him up the staircase. We were close to his room when I heard a familiar scream.

"No, wait." Drake reached for my arm seconds too late.

On instinct, I opened the door.

Drake's phone dinged three times. "Dammit, I need to report to Theo and tell him I triggered the alarm."

"Marino installed a silent alarm on this?" I pointed at the door.

"Yeah, since the day she returned, he had it set up, and it signals his phone and mine. I told you this before."

"You might've, but right now I see hula girls dancin'." I drew my head back, and howled silently. "How do you deactivate it?"

"I click a number sequence on my phone." Drake hit the buttons as he explained.

"What you doin' now?"

"Man, you're slow when you're bombed. I'm textin' Theo to inform him it was one of her dreams again."

I waited for Drake to finish the text.

"There that'll do it."

"Good." I said. I stumbled into her room, and I was taken in by the moonlight that streamed through the high wall windows. Mariana sat upright. The soft illumination made her look celestial. Her eyes reflected a lost child not knowing what to do, but when she realized it was me in the doorway, they got even bigger.

"Hey, Cas, what's your game?" Drake stood near the door. He glanced over his shoulder making certain no one else had joined us.

"Bro, give me fifteen minutes." I hiccupped.

"Man, you're givin' me an ulcer, fifteen, no more." Drake closed the door and waited in the hallway.

"Cassius, what are you doing here?" Mariana hissed.

"I had to see you, Bright Eyes." I moved further into the room.

"See me for what?"

"You have something of mine, and I don't know how to get it back."

"Leave, Cassius. If Theodore finds you here, he'll kill you."

"Not until you answer me." I was killing time, waiting on Theodore's entrance.

"Cassius, you gave me your love, freely." Mariana yawned and then said, "So, what's the real reason you're here?"

I plopped down on her bed and forced her to look at me.

"I couldn't sleep, so I thought I'd visit you." I gave her my best smile.

"Stop it. I know you're lying to me. You're here because—" Mariana crinkled her nose. "You're plastered?"

"No. Well, maybe, a little buzzed. But nothing I can't handle. Listen. You haunt me, Bright Eyes. I can't sleep, because when I do…you show up. Christo. Help me, Mariana." I leaned my forehead on hers.

Mariana gave a small shudder. She scooted off the bed and gained distance. I cornered her near the armoire. "Mariana, be straight with me."

Chin down she eyed me under a stern brow. We stood motionless staring at one another until she bowed her head.

"Mariana, *look* at me." My demand was met with a cold glare. I took hold of her chin, tilting her head up. She had no choice but to see me. She closed her eyes, tightening them to the point of squishing her eyelashes. "You're doing it again. I know you love me. But your stubborn robotic nature is controlling your thoughts right now. Shut. It. Off." I whispered in her ear. Her sharp exhale brushed against my neck. "Mariana, I could take you right here, right now."

Mariana's eyes snapped open. She leaned her head against the armoire.

"Cassius…as drunk as you are, I doubt that would ever happen. I…I don't love you." She turned her head away from me.

"Mariana, you're a horrible actress. Lies have never been your strong suit. Not with me anyhow. Look me in the eye and tell me you don't love me."

She jutted her chin out and held her mouth half open.

"That's right, you can't. And you know how I know you're lyin'? Your left eye twitches ever so slightly. Yep, I noticed."

"If Theo finds you here—"

"If he finds me here, I'll at least have had one more minute with you, before I meet my maker."

"No. Leave." She pressed her hands flat against my chest and shoved me away.

I lost my balance and staggered into the desk. I drew my hands behind me, resting them on the surface.

"Cassius, why are you really here?"

"You really want to know? In about six seconds, I'll have you across my knees. You make me so damn angry. Why did you run, Mariana?"

Mariana stiffened. Her surprised body language energized me. She scooted closer to the window. The look in her eyes told me if I decided to act on my promise, she would try to take me down and then run for it.

"You will *not* touch me in such a manner, ever." She spoke through her tightened jaw.

"Oh no?" In a blink of an eye I ran up to her. Her gasp indicated she hadn't expected an intoxicated guy to book it. I cuffed her delicate wrists with my fingers.

"Let go of me or—"

"Or what, Bright Eyes?"

"I'll scream bloody murder."

"And then what?" I smirked.

"You're enjoying *this*." She whispered.

"Ha! No doubt. Mariana, you leaving the apartment was childish, selfish and completely lacking any consideration for your lover."

"My lover?"

"Yes, that be me." I swayed just a tad, "Unless, you have more than one?" I snorted.

"God, you're infuriating. Only in your dreams have I slept with you, Cassius. And my lovers are none of your business." Mariana twisted her wrist and kicked out. Her foot missed me by few inches.

"Hmm, feisty today are we? I'll fix that." I sat on the bench beneath the window and with one quick tug, Mariana fell belly down over my knees. I lifted my hand in the air.

"Cassius! If, you do this, in twenty seconds you'll have at least ten guns pointed at your head."

"Ha! At least I'll have the best twenty seconds of my life."

She squirmed. "Cassius, I don't wish to hurt you."

"Now there's a conundrum, I wish to hurt you, and believe me, I'll enjoy it." I laughed making her even angrier.

It's now or never. This is too good to pass up.

I smothered her scream with my left hand as my right came down on her shapely ass. She sucked in air and her eyes grew bigger as she understood I'd been serious. I lifted my hand and thought one more love tap wouldn't hurt. Well it wouldn't hurt me, anyhow. Instead, I rested my hand on her rump imagining what could be. She wriggled.

"There now, that spank should've come ages ago, Bright Eyes."

I released my grip and she jumped cheetah like straight for the door, but as an afterthought she spun around and glared. Tears lingered in her eyes, not from pain or humiliation, but from unbridled anger. I could definitely see the fire in them.

"You. Ever. Touch me like that again, I'll feed you to the sharks myself."

"Tut. Tut. Tut. Maybe one spank was not enough. You're still too wild." I stood.

"Cassius!" She pointed her index finger at me. "Don't you dare come any closer. This time, I won't let you take me. Drunk or not drunk. You will hurt." She trembled from pure adrenaline.

I couldn't help myself. I tilted my head back and hooted. "You promise, baby?"

"You fool! Leave, Cassius."

I thought I saw fear in her eyes. "Hey, you're really afraid for me?"

"If Theodore or Randolph finds you here they won't hesitate to kill you."

"Mariana, don't worry about me. No one is going to take me down."

Drake opened the door.

Mariana turned and said, "Drake, help me get this idiot out of here. Please."

I dragged a hand across my brow. The stifling air in the room plastered my hair to my forehead. I shook my head and then pulled Mariana's journal from my jacket pocket.

"I know the truth." I waved the book in the air. "I understand now that his mother really loves him."

Mariana's disheveled hair curtained her shoulders. Until now, I hadn't really noticed her white simple nightgown, going down to her knees. She bit her lip.

Hell, wish it were me biting her lip.

Mariana's intake of breath interrupted my thought when one more person entered her room.

"And what truth would that be?" Theodore's voice boomed. A satisfied smile flashed across his face.

Mariana jumped in front of me as I shoved the journal back into my jacket.

"Theo, this man is obviously drunk. He must be one of Randolph's guests and got lost searching for the bathroom. Drake offered to take him back to his room." She moved to the side and grabbed her robe, hanging on the armoire's doorknob.

As Mariana turned back toward the three of us, I caught the recognition in her eyes. She completely transformed before me. I'd seen that look once before. The cold stare had appeared when she told me about her attacker. Her body stood rigid and the spark in her eyes vanished. I realized then that Mariana had brought the Tin-Man out to play.

This is it. I've got her exactly where I need her to be. Shoot! I'm going to hate myself even more.

I eyed Marino. "Eh, Theo, I think the jig's up. And the truth…the truth is that she's in a good place, and she should be grateful. How's it goin', Theo?" We shook hands.

Theodore's eyes registered surprise.

Mariana stood quiet, but the blush on her cheeks spread across her neck and ears. I thought she would erupt soon.

"Yes, our lovely Mariana is safe here." Theodore held a controlled grin, one I came to know too well.

"Cas, you've been drinking. Tsk, Tsk. That's why our lovely Mariana was talking about a drunken man." Theo walked over to the chairs and sat. He crossed his ankles as if he were waiting for the curtain to be pulled aside for the second act. "Cassius, you always were quick to nurture the bottle when you wanted to erase the obvious." Theo said, contentedly.

"Yeah, well, you know me, always ready for a reason to celebrate. The package is delivered, right?" One quick glance at Mariana confirmed my words had hit their mark.

Shit. How can I justify what has been said?

Theodore nodded.

Mariana let out a sound which was between a growl and a disgusted gurgle. Drake stepped forward. He stared at her.

"What the hell, Cassius?" Drake stood near her for moral support.

I couldn't tell him I had planned this all along—that this scene had to go down this way.

Instead, I grinned, lifting my brow as high as it would go.

I hate that I'm hurting her.

Movement caught my attention. I looked up at the woman I loved, knowing I had killed all possibility of ever holding her in my arms again. Theodore more than once said she was a forgiving soul, but no one could overcome a betrayal like this.

"Mariana, perhaps you should sit." Theodore held out a hand.

She didn't move. The corner of her mouth twitched as she balled her hands into fists.

Drake stepped forward and in a low voice, tried to bring her back from wherever she had gone. "Mariana, I don't know why Cas is acting like this. It must be the booze. Don't listen to him."

I took a step forward. Drake eyed me with a tiger's eye. I halted in mid-step.

"But, listen to me," he continued, "I know you love him. What we all need to do is sit down and talk. Then all of this will be cleared up."

Mariana shook her head side to side. "Damn all of you to hell. Get *out* of my room." She calmly backed up toward a nightstand and drew her hands behind herself. We heard a scraping sound and in a blink of an eye, Mariana had a Beretta pointed at Theodore's head and a Sig Sauer at mine. Drake stepped forward.

"Drake, take one more step and there'll be three less bodies sucking up the oxygen in this room. You know I'm the best shot here and before you think of pulling your piece, you'll all be on the floor wishing you had not come in here."

The Mariana I had come to know locked herself in a safe room in her mind and the robotic tin-man was unleashed.

228

God, I did this to her. Theo did this to her and every other person who steered her wrong. I'm no better than her rapist. I wish I could tell her why I did this.

Mariana's training kicked in. Her steel glare sent a shock-wave down my spine.

In a low monotone she said, "It's not his fault, Cassius. Theodore helped me. I know Theodore in his own way loves me, but...his business is more important. As for you...God, bile creeps up into my throat just thinking about how much you disgust me. The diner, the meadow, your apartment, it was all lies. Tell me. Did you collect your fifty pieces of gold?"

"Ouch, can't say you didn't deserve it, Bro." Drake backed off.

I held out my hands and shrugged. "What can I say? You're hard to resist."

The spark in Mariana's eyes flickered and then it was out. My Bright Eyes shut herself behind a mirrored glass door. She could peer out, but no one could see in.

I hope I get the chance to unlock that door later. God please help me connect with her again! And I'm not even a religious man.

Theodore opened his mouth to speak. Mariana lifted her gun an inch higher. He thought twice and kept quiet.

One look at me and Mariana's left eye twitched just enough for me to know the real Mariana was still with us. But then, she reverted back to the cold veil.

"Theo called you Cas. If I recall, only friends call you Cas." She sneered. "God, I'm the dumbest female on this planet."

"No, Mariana, you're not. Listen..." I was beginning to doubt my plan.

"Don't. Speak. Mr. Russo, leave now and don't come back. If you do, I *will* kill you myself." Mariana cocked the pistols. "Now."

Theodore nodded. Drake stepped out.

"Mariana, heart of my heart, together we be for eternity." I rammed a fist against my chest recalling Samantha's words. Mariana loved me, but darn my job and Marino for not helping her stay with the family. Having a six pack of beer in my system didn't help either.

Mariana's eyes welled up, but she held strong. "Those are empty words. Leave."

Man, I effed this meeting up. But...I never claimed to be Romeo.

I blew out an unsteady breath and walked out. Outside Mariana's room, I heard Theodore asking her to lower the guns. He then closed the door and stayed with her until she calmed down.

I followed Drake to his room. Just as I entered, he slammed the door shut and turned on me. He looked as if he wanted to pummel me into a ball of dough.

"What the hell was that? You just killed the best thing goin' for you." Drake stared down at me as I plopped onto the sofa.

"That was me gettin' plan B into a full run and keeping Mariana exactly where she should be, in the dark." I leaned back and closed my eyes.

"Sometimes, Bro, I think your Dad's disappearing act scrambled your brain." Drake shoved his hands in his jean pockets and paced.

"Maybe." I sunk deeper into the sofa as I explained to him why I did what I did and then I conked out, right where I sat.

CHAPTER 18

DAGGERS OF TRUTH

Cassius's visit plagued my mind for days.

I tossed and turned in bed. The dream pulled me under and drowned my conscience in a pool of voices. Theodore. Randolph. Cassius—especially Cassius. I lay transfixed helplessly watching the scene play out.

The sepia lighting filtered through a screen in my mind that lifted my senses into hyper-mode. A sensation of slogging through mud set in as the weight of fear bogged my progress.

A rumble shook the north side of the mansion. I sat up in bed bewildered. Theo ran into the room, his eyes blood shot with a look of intent to shoot first then ask questions.

"What are you doing, Theo?" I heard my voice speak out in the distance.

"Don't move, don't even blink, or he's fish food."

Randolph rushed in at the end of Theodore's sentence. I had no clue as to what Theodore was talking about, but then the mystery revealed itself.

"Bright Eyes. Oh, Bright Eyes! Let's ride. You game?"

I thought, my God what is that fool up to?

"Eh, Theo your guards are taking a nap with the dogs. Why not come out and play? Did you think I wouldn't find her?" He grunted. "Her radar pings loud and clear and she sings like a nightingale."

Cassius's guttural laugh jabbed my senses. I jumped out of bed and pulled on Theodore's arm.

"Don't, Theo, can't you see he's drunk?"

Theodore approached the window. He then turned on me, pointing the gun at my chest.

"You slept with him?" His voice cracked.

231

The hurt in his eyes for some reason pierced me deeply. Frozen in fear of what he might do to Cassius, I shook my head. "No. You know me Theodore. You know me."

He turned back to the window and pointed the gun down toward Cassius.

Randolph joined him. "Theodore, is she worth the heart-ache, maybe we should take care of them both?"

"No! Theodore, don't—"

They raised their guns—one towards the window the other at me.

The window shattered. Glass showered the air. A second shot blasted.

An electric charge shot through my body and I jerked awake. My heart hammered against my chest, chipping away at my sanity. Mouth open, I breathed convulsively.

A horrible dream. Not a vision. Just a dream.

"You stupid fool, Cassius. Why did you come here?" I cried into my hands.

Minutes passed while I slumped against the headboard.

Lies surrounded me. I couldn't escape them. Mikey said Cassius loved me. How could I have been so wrong about Cassius? I grabbed a shawl from the foot of the bed, draped it over my shoulders, and walked over to the window.

A new memory shoved itself next to the others, Cassius's smirk as he admitted that Theodore was his friend, replayed in my mind's eye. I had wanted to wipe the grin off his face with my bare hands. But in the end, I couldn't hurt him even though his words stabbed me.

The ice queen over-powered my emotions and I noted Cassius's 'oh man, I messed up big time', expression when the cold Mariana reappeared.

I'm grateful for my training. The ice queen has served me well.

When I first arrived at the mansion and started to learn self-defense, Theodore repeatedly said, "Mariana, focus, listen, and withdraw when pain comes to wound. Nothing in this world can hurt you if you shelter your emotions. Close your eyes, Mari.

Find the room in your mind where you can hide when necessary." Those words had benefited me when Cassius entered my room—when my faith in him had been shaken.

Theodore's pep talks were drilled into my survival instincts. It was what kept me going and fighting to keep my son and family safe. I learned to secure my emotions in the dark gorges of my mind.

I believe that's why I never considered terminating my pregnancy. Determination to bury the pain that haunted my sleep guided me to the crossroads where morality and fear intersect. Fear clung to my essence and I questioned what would become of this child that grew within me? But then, common sense kicked in and revealed to me that it was not the child's fault that I had been raped. I was to blame for not listening to my elders and it was my duty to protect the young life growing in my womb.

The one thought that did follow me constantly was how to keep my child a secret from the underground world. There was no doubt in my mind the baby would be born with the gift. I had dreamt of this child more than once, only the fickle dreams didn't reveal how conception would occur.

Over the years, I dodged more snide remarks by recoiling into the empty emotions room. The price for keeping my family safe was to become the fake Mariana, the one person many men called the "Soulless Witch". This frigid woman protected Theodore on more than one occasion and did not blink an eye.

How much can my psyche bear? It feels as if it's being erased and soon all I will see is a white empty room.

Cassius wanted to save me, and I allowed myself to believe, to feel, to hope, that maybe, he could take me away from this life I now faced, *again.*

A knock sounded on my bedroom door.

"Mariana, it's me, Theodore. May I come in?"

I did not answer him. Instead I focused on the outdoors. The morning sunlight broken into brilliant strings by the clouds, streaked the front yard as the dogs played catch with Theodore's men.

He knocked again. "Mariana, I'm coming in."

The doorknob clicked. His footsteps were in sync to the metronome in my head. Tick-tock, nothing matters, tick-tock I'll protect the family. Tick-tock *this* is my world now.

A faint sound caught my attention. I twisted in my seat and saw Theodore place my journal on the nightstand.

My God, Cassius has gone insane! He gave Theo my journal. Did he read it?

Theo sat next to me. "Cassius thought you might like to have it back. He left it in my office the day he decided to… to surprise you in your room." He cleared his throat. "Mari, he loves you very much. But…so do I." Theodore rested his hands on my shoulders. He gently kneaded my tight muscles. "Don't worry. I didn't read a word."

I closed my eyes and laughed. "Cassius gave the journal to you or to Drake?"

He stopped the massage. "All right you got me. I saw him hand the book to Drake. I later took it from Drake's desk. I know it was a rotten thing to do. Drake's probably wondering what happened to it, but I'm serious, Mari, I didn't read it. I wouldn't do that to you. God knows I wanted to, but when you're ready, you'll talk to me."

"Okay." I mumbled.

Wish I could believe you.

Theo let out a heavy sigh. He continued running his fingers over my shoulders.

"Theo, I'm not one to hide my gift even though it can imprison me. I know certain truths about you and Randolph, but who would believe me? And even if someone did listen, they probably wouldn't live long enough to prove my truth. You say you love me. Shouldn't your love be enough for you to be honest with me?"

"Not if the truth will endanger another. You of all people know that."

I swallowed a gasp and nodded.

Does he know of my son?

Theodore stooped close to my ear. "Dear, Mari, you are more special than you realize."

I stiffened as his breath tickled the small hairs on the nape of my neck. I shifted in my seat to face him.

"Theo, I'm not special. I'm no one and no one is me. The existence of one person is the non-existence of another. Don't you see? My mother died in place of my dad. And…it was my fault, *my fault*." I curled my fingers into the palms of my hands, digging deeply.

Theodore unfolded them and rubbed the marks in my palms. Looking down he said, "Mari, you told me you were five. How could it have been your fault?"

Theodore's image faded from my sight as I relived that terrible day in my mind. The day…my mother died.

"The red balloon slipped off my wrist."

"Clearly, that doesn't make it your fault. You didn't pull the trigger."

"I…should've held on tighter."

"Mariana." Theodore rubbed my shoulders. "Listen to me, Mari, *please*." Our eyes met. "Do you know whose gun killed your mother?"

"No. And I don't want to know."

"Why not?"

"Because…I don't trust myself to not retaliate. I've thought of what I'd do if I knew who my mother's killer was, and I'm afraid of what I see, that dark part of me, wanting vengeance."

"Mariana, you're not vengeful." Theodore held me close. I kept my arms glued to my sides.

Theodore had never been one to hold back on affection, but his priorities weren't in agreement with mine. How was I to live with a man who believed violence could be tolerated for a good cause?

Still holding me, he rested his chin on the top of my head.

"Theodore, when I was a little girl my aunt Samantha told me life on Earth carries many lessons. But…"

"Yes, but?" His hands trailed up and down my back.

"But, if we learn, why do we continue to blunder? Mortal actions, inhumane occurrences drown this world in darkness. Human greed, illusion of power leads man to believe that total dominance is what matters. What have they learned, how to kill one another?"

I felt as if my thoughts were filtered through a sieve and the smallest of details escaped my mind. A headache ran from my temples to the middle of my forehead.

Theodore released me and stood. Hands drawn behind him, he paced the length of the room. His brow shadowed his eyes as he said, "Mariana, come here. Sit next to me, please." He patted the bed.

I did as he asked. He studied my profile while I brooded.

"Mariana, the day you left this house—left *me*, my world turned dark again. You are the light in my life—you and Allison."

Our unfinished conversation came to mind and I said, "Who was the man in the cellar, Theo? Why was he being tortured?"

"Mariana, it was Leroy."

My eyes widened. "Leroy?" I recalled the night I saw him in the cellar.

"Yes, Mari, the happy man who seemed to make every day special. Yes, the man who was ready and willing to do everything Randolph demanded of him. I wanted to fire Leroy, but Randolph refused. He once said to me, 'Theodore, you know this man does his work meticulously and leaves no traces. We need a man like him.' The glower in Randolph's eyes told me not to go against his decision and so Randolph kept him as his right hand man."

One more mistake to carve in Theodore's wall of regrets.

"But, months later I found him making advances towards Allison. She's a child in her own world of music and wonder and *that* animal tried to seduce her." Theodore curled his lips inward.

"So, you and Randolph were the judge and jury?"

"Don't go righteous on me, Mariana. We warned him to stop following Allison. I placed a tail on him. He was seen following other young girls, girls still in junior high. A friend of mine dug into his past. He wasn't just into child pornography. He's also a pedophile."

"Does your friend go by the name of Russo?"

"No. I ran into Cassius in a town meeting."

"Huh, you, my dad, and Cassius are big on town meetings. So why did you talk to Cassius?"

"I needed you back home, Mari."

"So, Cassius meeting me in the diner was planned? All lies." My voice faltered. I felt an invisible weight pressing down on my chest.

"Mariana, your father called Cassius. I was informed later he had brought you back to the farm. I needed you home, Mari."

"You and my dad are too much alike."

"Mariana, I would wager your father thinks as I do in one aspect. We don't have many true friends, but the ones we have are kept close to our hearts."

"No, argument there, but…going back to Leroy, why not turn him in to the authorities? He was obviously mentally disturbed and—"

"I had Leroy committed to a facility that specializes in mental disorders. With some convincing the doctor allowed me to read his records. The information was clearly stated. The man had no remorse and during every session, he laughed and said, 'I will do it again, again, and then again.' This wasn't the first time he'd been taken into custody, but Randolph didn't run a background check on him. Hours before you left me, I walked into Allison's room to wish her a goodnight and I found him in her room. His hand was over her mouth." Theodore swallowed and balled his hands into fists. His eyes darkened.

I gasped.

"Nothing happened and nothing ever will." He said.

"Theodore did you…?"

"Kill him, no I didn't. Although a bullet to the head would've been more humane. When you entered the cellar, and saw Leroy, you ran out, I went after you to explain. I followed you to your room. But, you had already made up your mind and would not listen to me. Do you remember?"

"Yes." I crossed my legs on the bed.

"Well, Randolph took it upon himself to deal out justice. The man lost his manhood and bled out."

"Oh, Theodore!" I leaned my head back.

"I was too late to save him." Theodore's voice trailed off.

I massaged my temples and said, "Theodore we need to leave this house. Randolph is lost. He's too far gone in this dark world of his. The other day I went to the storage room and saw crates of illegal arms and ammunition. Those can't all be for the men who work for you. Government or no government, it's just not right."

"Mari, many things in life are not right. I did *not* choose this life, it chose me."

"But, we can leave. We can, Theo—the three of us."

"Someday, we will, but right now—" Theo clapped his hands together. His dark blue irises lightened as if someone had flipped a light switch. "What you need Mariana, is a distraction—time to be carefree." He took hold of my hand. "Mari, let's go for a drive."

I raised my head and stared back. "A drive to where?"

Theodore chuckled. "To everywhere and anywhere, right?" He squeezed my fingers gently. "Remember when we first met and we'd go on long drives and picnics?"

I lowered my head, remembering Cassius. The urge to cry was not easy to control. "Yeah, sure why not? I'll be ready in fifteen."

"Excellent. I'll have the chef fix us a picnic basket. I'll meet you out front." His stride had changed from the business suit man to the carefree professor.

"But...Theo?"

"Yes?" He stopped, giving me the widest smile I had seen in months.

"How are you going to manage this? I thought you had a high power meeting today?"

"Randolph can handle this one. I have more important matters to attend to. And...Mariana?"

"Yes?"

"Time will help you heal. I'm here to help you forget the lies." Theodore whistled a lively tune as he left the room.

I caught a fleeting glimpse of Professor Marino when the world was his classroom and his love for teaching and seeing others enjoy the lessons made his eyes sparkle. I missed him. When and why did it change? The Theodore of now was at times heartless. This scared me because the kind Theodore was still alive, but the world of power was smothering his existence.

I jumped to my feet and picked up the journal. I turned to the page I had written about my son. Someone had taken the time to tear it out neatly. It was gone. On the next page the words, 'heart of my heart, together we be for eternity' blared out at me. I hoped Cassius had taken the page.

CHAPTER 19

NEVER DRAMA FREE PICNIC

I slipped on my well worn blue jeans, a blouse, and hiking boots. Then I shoved the Beretta into its holster and concealed it with an army green windbreaker tied around my waist. If I guessed correctly, Theodore would drive us up into the hills where the pine trees shaded the side of the mountain.

A girl can never be too prepared.

I descended the mansion's moon shaped steps and spied Theodore in his relaxed jeans and polo shirt, leaning against a new, black Maserati. The yard's post-card garden curtained the backdrop for his childish grin. He waved a hand and bowed.

"My lovely, Mariana, your journey awaits."

"A new toy, Theo?"

"Yes, it arrived yesterday. Do you approve?"

"There's no need for my approval. Where's the viper?"

"It's tucked away nicely in the auto museum. And yes, your approval is important." The Theodore I had met three years ago stood before me. He had a passion for exotic cars.

When Theodore lost interest in one of his vehicles he would auction it off, and the proceeds would go to St. Jude's Children's Hospital. He did have a heart, but many times it was snared by this world's distractions. The kind of traps that make one forget who they really are.

I rested a hand on his cheek. "I've missed you, Professor."

"I've been here the whole time."

"No, you haven't." I shook my head and entered the sleek car.

He hunched over and kissed me on the cheek. "I love how you wear your hair in a pony-tail. It reveals the curve of your neck."

Feeling my temperature rise, I gave him a playful push and closed the door. Theodore's loveable carefree spirit was the kind of character a woman could easily fall for. He walked around the front of the car, eyeing me all the while.

I rested my head against the cool leather, thinking how I wanted Theodore to care more about me than the family business.

Don't allow yourself to be fooled, Mariana.

Even though Theodore was willing to come out and play, I knew all too well how his dark nature could appear in a mere blink of an eye.

* * *

The sports car hugged the curves. We passed the hill sides in a blur as our bodies swayed with the momentum.

"Theo, are you trying to see if I scream like a little girl? Or, do you have a plan to plaster our bodies against the mountain?" I flattened my hands on the dashboard.

"Of course not, but you must admit it's exhilarating to take this baby for a spin. She handles the curves well, wouldn't you say?" He caressed my arm.

"Hands on the wheel, Theo." I dug my boot heels into the floor mat.

"Ha, the fearless Mariana is unsure of my driving."

Theodore shifted gears and glided through the turns as if he were a Formula One driver. I wanted to swat him, but this section of road demanded his full attention.

Eventually, the curves ended. Theodore pulled to the side of the road and parked near a row of pine trees. He retrieved the basket from the back seat while I took hold of the blanket. I felt a pang of sorrow creep up.

Maybe it was too soon to go out on a picnic.

Theodore looked my way. "Mariana, this will be good for the both of us. Let's go?"

"Sure, let's."

We strolled through the woods to a small clearing hidden from view.

I unfolded the blanket and set it on a patch of clover.

"This is a peaceful setting. How did you know it was here?" I crossed my legs and started to unpack our lunch.

"This property belongs to my family, well to Allison and me."

"Have you come here often?" I kept a straight face. Theo was not blind to my holding back a smirk.

"If you're asking have I brought other women here, no I haven't. I've gone through these woods with a hunting party, but no picnics. This is the first. Mariana—"

"Hunting? Human or other species?"

"Mari, don't do this. This is our time. I want you to trust me. I want you to look at me as I have seen you look at another." Theo lifted a finger as I opened my mouth to speak. "I'm not saying you must love me as you love him, but I love *you*, Mari. I know how you think, sleep, work, fight and cry." Theo's expression begged me to hear what he had to say.

I focused on the green landscape surrounding us. To my surprise, I found a four leaf clover and pulled it by the root. "Look, Theo." I twirled the lucky charm between my fingers. Theo scooted closer to me.

"Mari, listen to me. I'll *always* love you, no matter what you decide to do, but know that I—"

"That your love is real, but... Mr. Marino, the life you lead is not one you're willing to part with." The clover fell through my fingers and fluttered onto the blanket. I took hold of plates and napkins and placed them between us. Not once did his gaze leave me. I leaned my head to the side and said, "Theo, help me to not care about the life you follow. Show me how you can live both lives and not have them wreak havoc on your emotions or on your standards of morality. You can't, Theo. You can't live with me and continue the business with Randolph."

"I can. Give me the chance to prove it." He took hold of my hands.

I pulled away and jumped to my feet. "I'm trapped, Theo. There's only one way out for me and it's in a body bag. You see, I know too much of the business. Randolph will *never* allow me to leave."

He stood and held me. "No. I'll find a way. We'll leave with Allison. Now, let's eat. After we finish, I want to show you a very special place," he said as he released me.

I sat and eyed the food.

Always gourmet, never something simple for Theo.

"Is something wrong with the meal, Mari?"

"No. I'm just not very hungry."

Fresh turkey breast on a layer of cranberry and cream cheese, sandwiched between sourdough bread lay on my plate. Pastries and fresh fruit sat in bowls waiting to be devoured. The presentation was no less than what was expected from a world class chef, but at that moment I couldn't stomach food in any form.

"Mari, you've gained some of your weight back."

"Hum, just what a girl wants to hear."

"Ha. In your case it was a good thing. When I saw you the first day you returned home, I thought I might have to call the doctor. You were pale and the spark in your eyes was gone."

I studied Theodore's demeanor. He was truly concerned for me.

"At least try to eat half of the sandwich." He took a bite of his own.

I followed his lead and bit into mine, remembering the time I had shared with Cassius. I smiled to camouflage the sadness.

Theodore misinterpreted my action. "We can make this work, Mari." He crossed his ankles and continued to eat.

I told myself to pretend this was the norm—Theodore and I on a picnic, enjoying the day without a care. Soon our conversation traveled to a happy subject. Allison had been invited to perform a solo with the San Francisco Symphony. Thinking of Allison's angelic nature led me to my safety zone.

"So, you see, I thought when Allison goes to San Francisco it would be an excellent opportunity for the three of us to enjoy the sights and possibly go to Monterey or Carmel. What do you say, Mari?"

"It sounds like a dream, one I have hoped to come true, but that's not the life we lead. Do you believe Randolph will agree to this? He's become more territorial lately."

"Don't worry about Randolph. I'll take care of the arrangements." Theo waved his hand, dismissing my inquiry.

Concentrate, Mariana. Listen.

A voice murmured in my mind. I nearly choked on my last sandwich bite. After swallowing, I drew in a long breath.

The bird's songs were engulfed by a buzz in my ears. I twisted the napkin in my lap as an unbearable ring had me double over, flexing my fingers.

"Mariana?" Theo clamped his hands on my shoulders and straightened me. "What are you seeing?"

Tears blurred my vision. I stared at Theodore and heard my own voice as if I were a bystander.

"The world, Theo, is polluted. Politics smothers the air. Do you not smell the stench?"

Theo tightened his lips and lifted me to my feet. "Mari, listen to me."

I pushed away from him. "It's always about who's who and money." I felt my stomach twist at the thought that my life revolved around politicians, money launderers, hitmen and the innocent caught in the government's warfare. "Theo, gluttony exists in the absence of morality." I fell to my knees.

Mariana, breathe. Someday you'll find a tiny crack in the infra-structure and you'll escape. Or they'll finish my ongoing misery— "Maybe, sooner if I talk to the authorities." I heaved.

"What? Tell the authorities what? Mari, what have you seen?" Theodore knelt next to me. His hands cupped my cheeks. "Mari, trust me. I'll keep you safe."

"A few people want to keep me safe, and then there are those who want to manipulate my gift to their advantage. Theo, my hope is on a short rope. I'm alone. I need to find a way out."

"Stop! You have me and..." His jaw tightened. "You have Cassius. We'll get you out of here."

"We? You'll leave everything behind and start over?"

"I'm working on it. Trust me, Mari. Snap out of it. Let's go."

"Where?" My head still reeled from the dark vision I had seen of Theo amongst wolves that did not care who they hurt to climb the mountain of succession.

"There's something I want you to see." Theodore linked his hand with mine and led me further into the woods.

The distinct sound of rushing water greeted us as we stepped into another clearing at least two acres wide. Hidden from the modern world, a waterfall descended into a small lake. Deer scattered as we approached. Birds continued their melodic song. Foliage hanging from the rocky hills swung in a gentle breeze. I twirled where I stood, taking in the beauty before me. The sun's rays streamed through the clouds lighting nature's stage.

"This is the end of the property line." Theo glanced down at me and squeezed my hand gently.

"It's a poetic vision. I never dreamed of seeing such a place. But, where does the water come from and where does it go?"

"Snow melting from the mountains flows to this lake and then the water disappears underground."

"Thank you, Theo, for sharing this with me."

"You're welcome. Mariana, many other days can be like this one, if you agree—"

I lifted one finger to his lips, silencing him and signaled him to drop to the ground. Instead, he turned thinking he would see what I saw. In a rush I said, "Get down, Theo!" I bumped the back of his knees with my leg. He buckled, and I shoved him the rest of the way. Seconds later a bullet sliced through my earlobe. I grabbed the Beretta.

Theodore lay on his belly with me on top of him. I rolled off and fired a shot toward the woods. A shadow moved from the trees and ran. I jumped to my feet and the chase was on.

Theodore soon caught up to me. He dragged me to the ground.

"Mariana, there might be more than one."

"Well, I'm not staying here to find out. Let go of me. Whoever it was almost killed you. He's mine." I jumped deftly to my feet.

I felt the blood chilling in my veins. I was in hunt mode. I had hit my mark when I fired the first round. He had left a trail of blood to follow. It was not much, but enough. We reached the picnic blanket. No sign of him. It was as if he had disappeared into thin air.

The whine of a small jet engine sounded above the trees. A man strapped to a jet pack flew away. I took aim and fired, but he zigzagged and gained height.

I holstered my gun and turned toward Theodore. "I wonder how many people around here have one of those contraptions."

"Mariana, who's to say he's from around here?"

"Well, I figured he is, considering he had one of your firearms?"

"How can you be certain?"

"I got a good look at it right before he fired."

"You mean you saw the gun in a vision, Mari."

I lowered my head.

"Mari, don't hide from me."

"Theo, whoever it was, he left here limping. I know I hit him in the thigh. We should check out your men."

"I'll look into it, not you." He stared directly at me.

I grabbed his arm. "Theo. You were almost killed. I'm sick of this." I rested my head in the palm of my hand and blood trickled down my neck. "We need to follow his tracks. Maybe he left some kind of clue."

"Not now. I'm taking you home and calling Doctor Higgins to stitch you up." Theodore pulled the cell phone from his pocket.

"Theo, he can't have gone far. He's bleeding."

"I don't care about him. It's you who matters, Mari."

"But..." I squished my eyes shut. The more I tried to figure out who the assassin could be, the more my ear ached.

"I finished texting Drake. He'll do a run and count heads. If it was one of my men, he'll be found." Theodore guided me back to the car.

The last thing I thought and said was, "Good thing I found that four leaf clover."

"Mari, you're the lucky charm. Everything else falls short."

As we reached the car, I lost my balance. Theo kept me from falling and gently sat me in the passenger seat. I glanced up at him before darkness veiled my consciousness.

CHAPTER 20

MASKS AND LIES

Two weeks had passed since our picnic adventure. I slowly touched my tender earlobe and recalled the doctor's words, "The stitches will eventually fall out as the wound heals."

The doctor assured me there wouldn't be much of a scar. He told me this as if I cared. This wasn't the first wound I'd acquired. In my line of work it was bound to happen.

A hazy morning lit the room. I lay half-awake on my bed gazing at the ceiling.

Since the picnic, I hadn't had a private moment to talk to Theodore about going to San Francisco. How were we going to disappear with the hound dog sniffing around? Randolph had been acting suspicious ever since the near miss on Theodore's life.

I pushed myself up in bed, recalling the last few weeks.

Theodore had gone back to the waterfall clearing and found the round lodged in a rotted log. The thought of who'd done it hovered in mystery. Too many bodies wandered the grounds. Theo's men had all gone through the third degree. None of them had a bullet hole in their thigh.

It could've been anyone really. Theodore and Randolph had enough enemies all fighting for territorial dominance.

I should go see Allison. She's more clinging since my ear was nearly blown off.

When Theodore carried me into the kitchen and Allison saw the side of my face colored red, she went ballistic. The sight of blood set her off. She wailed and clung to my arm, crying, "Don't leave me, Mari! Don't leave me!" We sat with her over an hour until she calmed down. I sang a lullaby while she rocked herself to sleep. Poor Allison, her innocence kept her in her own world. At times, I envied her.

Once the doctor stitched me up, Theodore wrapped the gauze around my head.

The doctor stood off to the side. He peered down at me and said, "Young lady you were mighty fortunate. Had you not ducked when you did, well...let's say my expertise might not have been called upon?"

"Mariana, saved my life, *again*." Theodore's voice trailed into a whisper.

"She's fast, that's for sure, but... Mariana, you need to take care of yourself." The doctor gave me a stern stare.

I had talked to the doctor prior to this encounter. He knew of my angst and wishes to vanish from this place.

"Doc, if you hear anything on the grape vine about a male around six feet, shot in the thigh you'll inform me?" Theodore taped the end of the gauze and then eyed the doctor.

"Absolutely, Theodore." The doctor packed his medical bag as he spoke to me. "I don't have to tell you this, Missy, since this isn't your first time on the merry-go-round, but remember to keep the bandage dry and if you experience any sharp pains or the suture line swells, call me. Got that?" He leaned in closer and in a low tone said, "And even if you don't feel any discomfort and just need to talk, call." He then straightened his posture, bowed his head slightly, and left the bedroom.

I readjusted myself against the headboard and closed my eyes.

Theodore slid onto the bed and sandwiched my hand between his. "Mari, I'm sorry. I'll find a way to take you away from all this."

Eyes still closed, I patted his hand. "I know you will, Theo. If you don't mind I'll take a nap, now." I slid down. My head sunk onto the down pillow.

Theodore covered me with a throw blanket.

During the few hours of slumber, I dreamt of Michael crying out to me and Cassius staring down a gun barrel. I awoke again in a cold sweat, hands over my heart.

What if I never see Michael again? Will he hate me, or will he understand I did all this for him and the family? Michael loves Cassius. What if something happens to him?

249

My reverie was interrupted by a knock on the door. Theodore and Allison traipsed in. Allison hopped onto the bed and rested her head on my shoulder.

"Mari, you better? Your head doesn't hurt anymore?"

I caressed her sunshine hair. "I'm brand new, Allie. I'm ready to go frolic again." My eyes locked with Theodore's. We shared a silent laugh.

"Good." She did a little dance on the bed. "Tonight is my solo recital, before I go to San Francisco. I saved the front seats for you and Theo." Allison giggled. "Mari, Theodore loves you and I do too."

I gave Theodore a questioning glare.

He lifted his hands in the air. "Hey, I had nothing to do with this. I did *not* put her up to it."

"Okay, stop. You explain any more than you have to and I might believe you had her rehearse this." A care free laugh escaped me. It had been weeks since I felt happy. I guessed it had to do with the fact that Mikey was safe and as long as I played Theodore's dutiful bodyguard it would stay that way.

"What so funny, Mari?" Allison watched me quizzically.

"Life is funny, beautiful girl." I shuffled off the bed. She followed me. We linked hands and did a little slow dance around the bed. "I wouldn't miss your solo even if there was a tornado on the way."

Theo approached with arms spread open, may I have this dance.

Allison squealed and stepped aside. She jumped onto my bed and giggled. "Dance, dance, together forever," she sang.

"I didn't tell her to say that either." Theodore's eyes smiled, "Promise."

"Yeah, I just bet you two rehearsed this all week." I wrapped my hands around his neck while his arms went around my waist.

"Do you hear the music, Mari?"

"Uh-hem. I hear the song we danced to the first night I stayed here." We swayed, hip to hip. "But, Theo, the song is fading."

"I won't let it. That song will remain strong in your memories even if I die trying to keep it there." Theo held me tighter.

Good thing the pain killers had kicked in. The exhilaration of dancing and laughing had left me lightheaded, but I felt no pain.

Allison hopped off the bed and wrapped her arms around us. "I love you, both. Time for me to get ready, Mari, will you fix my hair?"

"You bet, honey. I'll be there in twenty minutes, okay?"

'"Yes." She skipped to the door.

"Allie?" I called out to her. She stopped and turned my way as I said, "I love you."

Allison's worry lines faded completely. "Love you, Mari." She waved goodbye and crossed the hallway to her room.

"You're the sister she never had, Mari. You're her hero and mine." Theo leaned his forehead against mine.

I sighed. "Theo, Allie's my sanity angel. It doesn't matter how sad I might feel, when she walks into a room, my whole perspective turns into a rainbow." I stopped dancing and slowly pushed away from him. "Theo, we must take her away from this place."

"I know. I know, Mariana. And we will." He rubbed his brow. "I better go now. I have a few calls to make before tonight's recital."

"Theo, it's magical when Allison takes hold of the violin. Have you noticed how all her anxiety disappears when she plays? The music takes her away from all the eyes on her."

"Yes, and you made it possible for her. You told Allie to follow the music. And that is what she does." Theodore planted a soft kiss on my lips and then left.

I remained in a euphoric state wondering if what Theodore had said would come true.

Will the three of us leave this place and be happy?

But...what about Mikey? At least he'll be safe.

I returned to bed and rested for another few hours.

The one good thing, the codeine the doctor had prescribed, swept my dreams under the subconscious carpet.

CHAPTER 21

MOVING TIME FORWARD

*I'm coming, Mariana. And you will leave
even if I have to carry you out.*

I waited hidden behind a century old redwood and watched the sun disappear beyond the horizon. Soon the moon would light the grounds. I sat with my back against the tree trunk, and waited for the grey light to guide me down the path to the mansion. I hated the thought of Mariana in that den full of conniving wolves with their fake smiles. But, I had no choice, but to wait another twenty minutes before I made my entrance.

As the last sign of daylight vanished, I pulled out my cell phone and speed dialed Drake's number.

Drake answered on the third ring. "The pack is in the grand room, sipping champagne and the flowers are upstairs," he said in a whisper.

"Excellent. Catering is covered and the rest of the team is in place. Drake, have you secured the perimeter on your side?" I wasn't one to sweat bullets, but this operation was personal.

"Yeah, all a go."

"Does she suspect anything?"

"From what I can see or hear, no."

"Good, if this plan goes south, Mariana needs to have no part in it. Randolph is not forgiving, but he wants Mariana. I know his men will not touch her, but they'll have no problem takin' us down."

"Cassius..."

"Just say it, man."

Drake cleared his throat. "Since your visit, she's gotten closer to Marino."

"Good, just as it should be. I want Mariana to be clueless." I rubbed my bearded chin. "How has Marino dealt with all this?"

"He's on board, for now, but if he thinks the women are in the slightest danger, he'll abort." Drake pulled in a rough breath. "Cas, if he reneges on this plan, you and your men need to be ready to run. There's enough hardware in the arsenal here to supply a full blown militia."

"Understood. Drake, make sure she's where she needs to be when the time is right."

"I'll do my best."

"Drake, there you are. We need to talk." Marino's voice boomed in my ear.

"All right, Theodore, let's step out near the fountain. The moon is bright..." those were the last words I heard, before Drake ended the conversation. I hung back while the men got in position.

I became the biggest scum bag on this planet when Mariana realized that Marino and I were acquaintances. The pain in her eyes was like a shank in my heart, but I deserved it. Knowing I did it for the better good didn't make the job any easier. Had there been a better solution, I would've taken it, but this way Mariana wouldn't have to pretend. Everyone knew she wasn't the best when it came to acting. What killed me inside was how she brought the tin-man to the surface. Her bright eyes grayed and she looked through me as if I wasn't there. A harsh yank brought me back to what needed to be done as I heard leaves crunch under foot.

I drew my gun and went around the tree. I had a clear shot when I saw it was one of my men.

"Is that you Sanders?"

"Yes, Sir." He swallowed once before he spoke again. "Sir, the explosives are in place."

"Good." I tucked my Glock back in place and slid a hand over my bald head. "Sanders, I want you to back me up tonight.

Your penguin suit is in the van. Go gear up and meet me near the kitchen's back door. Drake'll give you your orders."

"Yes, sir." Sanders nodded and headed for the van.

I shoved my arms into the tuxedo coat and pulled on the vest to make sure my holster was secure and then I marched to the kitchen's backdoor.

Theodore had put guards on the east side facing the main entrance of the mansion. The west was barricaded by mountains and rugged terrain. The north and south, outlined by thick woods were guarded by undercover agents.

The day prior to the recital, the unmarked FBI van was hidden in the woods, facing west. On Theodore's orders no one was to bother the men surveying the grounds from the van. He told Randolph it was an extra precaution because of the attempt on his life.

This better go down like clockwork, if not I could be signing Theodore's death warrant and maybe even my men's.

"Sir?" Sanders had returned and stood at my side near the back door.

"Sanders." I jerked, distracted by thought. "You ready?"

Sanders cleared his throat and then said, "I am, Sir." His reluctance to answer had nothing to do with him not being ready, but this was his first tunnel demolition. But given his exceptional track record, planting and disarming explosives, he was the best agent for the job.

We both drew in a lungful of air. Sanders straightened his shoulders and gave one quick nod. "Good. This has to go down tonight. Randolph is gettin' too suspicious." I turned the door knob and we stepped into the kitchen chaos. I scanned the area and nodded to a few of the catering staff. The team was set to go.

Drake had stepped into the kitchen at the same moment we entered and did a double take. He shook his head as he saw my new look and said, "Dude, it's smooth as a baby's bottom. For sure, Randolph won't recognize you. He rubbed my head." Drake then turned toward Sanders, "This is for you."

"A hearing aide, Sir?"

"Yeah, a super kick ass hearing aide. I heard your ears have been givin' you some trouble, so here you go, courtesy of Uncle Sam." Drake gave Sanders a crooked grin.

Sanders slipped the hearing apparatus around and behind his ear. His brow shot up. I knew he had instantly heard feedback from the van, where another of my men manned the computers.

Drake patted Sanders on the shoulder. "I bet you'll hear the sweet music better than ever now, even underground."

"Yes, sir." Sanders kept a straight face.

"Sanders, Brian's in the van. He'll give you the directions to the tunnels." I shook his hand. "We'll wait for your word."

"Yes, sir, thank you."

"Sanders, your position is next to the garden doors. The other guard has the same ear piece only his is not juiced up like yours." Drake shook his hand too. "See you on the other side."

My nerves kicked in. "Sanders, how will you get underground?"

"From my post, Sir, I'll have a full view of the room. Once the recital begins, I'll tell Randolph's guy that I thought I heard someone outside in the gardens, and I'll go check it out."

"Good man."

Sanders headed to his spot. I pulled on my shirt collar. The fancy duds didn't help my nerves. I eyed Drake. He gave me a quick nod and said, "Cas, it's such a beautiful night to play indoors. Let's get this party in gear. Follow me." Drake directed me along a spacious corridor all the while filling me in on the back drop to the Marino happenings. "The recital will begin in thirty minutes. All the big buyers, sellers, and traffickers under one roof—and Randolph's in his stride, puffed and stuffed like the pompous rooster he is." Drake grunted. "But, he's sharp as ever. The hit gone bad on Theodore left him wonderin' if the next one might be comin' his way. Randolph has doubled up on guards."

We entered a wide foyer. Drake handed me an invitation. "Bud, you're officially here as my plus one. And your prize is in the front row with Marino."

I took hold of the engraved metallic card and exhaled. "Drake, you're the man. I owe you."

"I'll say." Drake tugged on his bow tie. "I'm tired of these monkey suits. I want my good ol' boy jeans and shirt. Let's get this done today, and I can see my girl by tomorrow night."

"Uh, about your girl—"

"Hors d'oeuvres, Messieurs?"

"What da hell! Tracy?" Drake choked on her name as he pulled her aside.

A ten foot evergreen, garnished in gold streamers and lights hid them from the ball room.

"Oh, Monsieur, did you believe only you would have fun?" She winked and elegantly slid her arm from his grip. She held the platter professionally in the palm of her hand. "Tut, tut, Monsieur, I have no time to play." Tracy brushed by Randolph as he sauntered into the foyer. She disappeared toward the tables set at the other end of the grand room.

Randolph looked back over his shoulder and with a grin ran his tongue across his lower lip. "Hmm, nice specimen." He glanced our way. "Drake, you have a fine eye." He pulled out a cigar from his pocket and sniffed it. "Gentlemen, you care to join me?"

"Thank you, Sir, but we are actually looking forward to the quartet tonight. Miss Allison is a pleasure to hear." Randolph set his beady eyes on me. Jake introduced me. "Sir, this is a long-time friend of mine. We've worked together on unofficial business." Drake cocked his head to the side.

"Good to meet you, Mr…" Randolph offered his hand.

"Cosmos. Allen Cosmos." We shook hands.

"Ha! Now there's a name. Son you must've had a good time in school with a name like that? Your family scientists?"

"Just about."

Randolph snorted.

"Well, the lights are dimming. We better go in and find our seats." Drake intervened.

"A pleasure, Mr. Cosmos." Randolph's stomach jounced as he laughed.

"Same here." I nodded.

"I'll be with my Cuban friend." Randolph sniffed the cigar. "I don't follow much of the music scene, but the beauty you're goin' to meet is a mighty fine musician." Randolph held up his cigar and walked out the front door.

As soon as Randolph was out of earshot, Drake turned on me. "Who invited Tracy to the party?" His nostrils flared like a bull ready to charge.

"Man, you've been gone from the office too long. No one invites Tracy, she needs no invitation."

"Yeah, I know. She looks *good.*" He blew out loudly, releasing some tension from his shoulders.

"Hasn't she always?"

"Yup." Drake pulled on his bow tie again. "Dang, the man who invented this contraption should've been hit by a bus the day before. What we men do to please society."

I laughed under my breath and shook my head. "Come now, don't you enjoy being chic?"

"Chic my ass, there's nothing like a good kick-back on a tail gate downin' some beers and watchin' my girl dance for me. Oh yeah, and then doin' some dancin' of my own with her in my arms. Here, everyone is too stuffy. Sir, yes sir."

I draped an arm over Drake's shoulders. "My friend, you play your cards tonight like the shark you are and by tomorrow you'll be holding your girl tight and dancing in the moonlight."

"Now that's a supreme plan. Let's do this." Drake stepped forward.

He waited for me under the entryway. We entered the ball room side by side and found our seats just as the last of the lights faded. The backdrop exploded into hundreds of smaller lights as if the galaxy had been plastered on the wall.

CHAPTER 22

LOVE IS BORN FROM FATHER'S SIN

*I have to stop thinking of Cassius, but how? I smell his cologne.
How's that possible? Stop. Go to your empty room. Clear your
mind. His scent is so strong. No. I'm imagining things.*

I twisted in my seat to give the grand room a once over. A
dream of a man stared at me. Something familiar about
him held my attention longer than expected. He grinned as he
combed his fingers through his beard. I stole a better look and
he winked.

*My God! Can't be. His eyes aren't brown. And...he's bald.
Wait. Is there a scar on his nose?* My eyes got bigger. He bowed
his head slowly on seeing my recognition.

I squinted. *What's he doing here? He'll ruin everything!
Think. He's not your problem.*

Tonight was the night I would take Allison away from
this place. After her recital, we planned to escape through the
underground tunnels into the woods. With the grand room filled
with guests, I had at least thirty solid minutes before Theodore
or Randolph noticed our absence. But now, I had to deal with
Cassius. How he came on this significant night left me at a loss,
but it did not matter.

The previous night Theo and I had another heated discussion
about escaping this lifestyle, but he insisted I wait. His words
rang in my ears. "Mariana, trust me this one time. I have a plan,
but I can't share it with you just yet. Trust me." He then barged
out of my room as we heard footsteps in the hallway. Randolph

waited outside the door to speak to him. It was a strange occurrence since Randolph never came to this side of the mansion. I scurried to the door that had not been fully closed, but they had left before I caught the slightest clue of Randolph's mysterious visit. I was sure more was at foot than what I suspected.

Once Theo had left with Randolph, I crossed the corridor to Allison's room and we hatched our plan. Patience was not my forte and I didn't do well with being told what to do.

I'm my own navigator. Cassius and Theo do not own me.

I readjusted my lace shawl over my shoulders and faced forward. Allison opened with Samuel Barber's famous adagio—Naked Expression of Emotion, returning my attention to her. It was simply ethereal. The music calmed my nerves enough for me to go over my plan one last time. Escaping this place with Allison had to be today. My dreams told me that much. Later, I'd find a way to send word to Theodore of our whereabouts. I sat stiffly in my seat as Theodore eyed me. I refused to look at him and at Cassius. They would never know how unnerved I felt. Cassius's appearance turned out to be a thorn in my side.

No worries, I'll lose him in this crowd.

Allison and her accompanists, Samuel and Kara ended the adagio and waited for Sasha to join them at the piano. Days earlier she and Allison had met at a performance in San Francisco. The three violinists and pianist continued with Beethoven's allegretto in E flat major, releasing a lively hoard of emotion and capturing the audience's hearts. They shared a glimpse into their world of solemn and evocative music. I, like everyone else in the grand room, was moved by the musical energy, but my thoughts strayed to Cassius and why he could possibly be here. Fifteen minutes later, the last note brought the audience to their feet. A thunder of applause bounced off the walls and vaulted ceiling. Allison handed her violin to her fellow musician. She blushed and bowed slowly. Sasha, Kara, and Samuel resumed playing a rendition of Prokofiev's 3rd symphony—The Fiery Angel. Allison then quickly lowered her eyes and shuffled over to me.

Theodore stood at my side. "Allie, that was one of your best performances yet." He hugged her. In the same moment Theodore's phone buzzed and he glanced at the screen. "I apologize, but I must take this call. I'll be back shortly."

I watched Theodore's departure while Allison stood next to me rocking back and forth.

I took hold of her hands. "That was absolutely beautiful, Allie."

"Thank you, Mari." She focused on her pearl bracelet, twisting it around and around.

In haste, I leaned in closer to her and whispered, "Allie, go to your room and in fifteen minutes, I'll meet you in the cellar."

"Yes." She scurried out of the ball room.

I lowered my eyes, thinking of what needed to be done, and stepped forward to leave this prison, this world behind forever when a dark figure blocked my way.

"We need to talk." Cassius clamped his fingers around my wrist.

"What do you think you're doing? Let go of me." I pulled my wrist from his grip, but he clamped his fingers around my arm.

"I'm here to help." His eyes scoped the room.

"I'm not interested." I attempted to leave, but his hold tightened. I glanced at his hand.

His touch sent an electric charge up my arm. I bit the inside of my cheek to keep from gasping. He pulled me to a corner of the room where the chairs had been pushed aside. The trio played a slow hypnotic song.

"Dance with me." He commanded.

His deep voice nearly crumbled my barriers. I couldn't allow this man to take control of my heart again.

I jutted my chin and said, "I don't dance." I attempted to pull my arm from his grasp without making it noticeable.

Cassius wrapped an arm around my waist. "You know I don't either. But..." His cold leer lured me into his gaze. "I have the last dance ticket. So let's do this together." He kept a straight face as he pulled me to the middle of the dance floor. Guests followed our lead as if they'd been choreographed to do so. Randolph entered and eyed us. A bodyguard approached him and whispered something. Randolph straightened the lapel of his coat and disappeared. I scanned the room for Drake and Theodore, but they were nowhere to been seen.

"Where's everyone?" I asked in a hushed voice.

Something is not right. I need to get away from Cassius.

"They're dancing around us." Cassius grinned.

"Don't be coy. The ones that matter aren't here, namely Drake and Theo. Are you drunk again?" I knew he wasn't, but I couldn't pass up the opportunity of sticking it to him.

Cassius shut his eyes and inhaled deeply. "I wish I were, Bright Eyes, then being here with you wouldn't be torture. Your perfume drives me crazy." He closed the gap between us.

I could feel the pulse of his heart beat. "I'm not your Bright Eyes. Keep it in your pants. And let go of me." I stepped back, but Cassius kept a firm grip around my waist.

"Mariana, the day you left my apartment, I dreamt of pulling you over my knees and paddling you until your rump was redder than a tomato." His eyes danced over me, relishing the thought.

"Drake told me you had no recollection of being in my room. But, we know that's not true, is it?" I shot him a look of pure contempt.

Cassius released a guttural laugh, and twirled me around the dance floor. The more we danced, the more he glued his body to mine.

"Your wish did come true. And you were *not* drunk. Mr. Russo, keep the rest of your dreams to yourself. Now, take your hands off of me."

Cassius's lips brushed my ear. "What's the rush?" He then nipped it.

"Don't do this, Cassius. I need to go. Now." I stepped forward with the dance tune. Cassius anticipated and swayed to the left. My knee hit thin air.

"Huh, the cold Mariana wants to play? That's fine by me. You choose the Robotic Mariana or the Bright Eyes I love. Either way, you're coming with me." He licked his lips.

"No, I'm not. I want nothing to do with you."

"Are you sure about that?" He crushed our bodies together.

The music crescendoed as Cassius geared us away from the crowd.

"Yes, I'm positive. Let go! I promised Allison I'd spend the rest of the night with her. Too many people around makes her nervous."

"Allison's with Tracy."

"Tracy? Why is she here? Cassius, whatever your plans are, don't. I want nothing to do with you, or your friends."

We continued to dance. "Hmm, you're good at keeping a straight face, but I saw the little twitch beneath your eye. Mariana, the moon is blue."

"You have no right to use those words. Theodore and you can keep all your lies to yourselves." I stomped down on his foot, turned, and quickly shuffled through the crowd toward the double doors. I heard him hiss and curse under his breath. I knew he was close behind.

I'll lose him in the library.

I took a quick glance back and rammed into another's arms. "What da?"

"Good man, Sanders." Cassius gripped my arm like a steel vice.

"Sir, it's set. The music show will begin in forty minutes."

"That's my man. Gather the team and make certain the guests start to leave now."

"Yes sir." Sanders disappeared past the stair case. I followed his departure.

"Bright Eyes?" Cassius sounded tired.

I forced myself to not feel, or to even care he was here. Right then I needed to get away from him.

"Mariana, look at me." He took hold of my chin.

"What's going on, Cassius? Why are the guests leaving? If you think I'm leaving without Allison, you're mistaken." I twisted my arm to gain the upper hand, but Cassius grabbed my other arm.

"Listen, in less than an hour, the tunnels will be destroyed. I told you, Allison is with Tracy. Now, be a good girl." He opened his tux coat and exposed a syringe in the inside pocket. "Your choice, Mariana, sober, or cocktail?" He held me close.

"Allison is safe?"

"Yes."

"All right, but this changes nothing. Tell me where I can find Allison. And then we go our separate ways."

"Agreed, but only after I explain why I did what I did, at least give me that?"

"I owe you *nothing*. For all I know you'll just tell me more lies." I held my head up high, refusing to look at him.

"Yeah, I had that coming, but you will hear me out." Cassius pulled me along.

"Where are you taking me?" I kept my eyes straight ahead blocking the thought of his hand clamped around my arm.

"To the cellar." He tightened his grip.

I gave him a questioning glare.

"You know as well as I do, there's a hidden passage leading to the woods." He halted. Cassius listened to someone on his earpiece. I had not noticed it before. He pressed a small button on it and said, "The rose is with me. I'm in route."

I gawked, and wondered how Cassius knew of the mansion's floor plans. Instantly, Drake came to mind.

"I told you, Mariana, I'd find a way to help you leave this place."

"I don't want your favors."

"Mariana, right now it's not what you want or need it's what my job demands. And if you're thinking about giving me a hard time, I'll not hesitate to use the cocktail."

"Your job? I'm not on your payroll, so you can shove your demands—"

I was cut off by Cassius patting his pocket and the look in his eyes told me he was not bluffing. I thought of taking him down, but how far would I get with other agents in the near vicinity?

I guess I'll wait and see how this plays out.

I kept quiet and allowed him to lead us into the kitchen and down a narrow stairwell. As we descended the stairs a full blown conversation bounced off the concrete walls. We entered the dank cellar, and came face to face with Randolph and Theodore.

Randolph spat, "She's a manipulative witch and she's made you soft, Theodore. You'll never fill your father's shoes. Now, call off your dogs or Mariana and her love sick puppy will be the first to meet their maker." Randolph jutted his chin our way.

Theodore turned with his mouth open. It looked as if all the blood had drained from his body. Two other men stood at his side. They were new recruits that I had not met before that night.

"I'm sorry, Cassius. He was already here when I arrived."

Cassius said nothing, but his fingers tightened around my arm. He tried to pull me behind him. I refused.

"Did you think I wouldn't find out? I have ears in every corner of this state." Randolph laughed.

"Now, Miss Mariana…," Randolph drew his revolver, and aimed it at Theodore, "…will be leaving with me. The chopper is fueled and ready." Randolph scowled. He knew I would comply to save Theodore.

"Randolph, you really believe you'll walk out of here? I don't matter, and by the time you try to take her out of here, Mr. Russo will have pulled the trigger." Theodore suddenly took on a dark expression.

Theo's men drew their revolvers and pointed them at Randolph.

Randolph shared a sly smile with him. "Theodore, you'll stay here with your buddies, 'cause you'll never meet your father's expectations. You failed him."

"What makes you think it's I that will stay here? Randolph, you're outnumbered."

"Think again, little man." As Randolph spoke, two burly men came from behind the wine barrels. They too pointed their guns at Theo and his men.

This is crazy. Am I dreaming?

"Miss Mariana, our chopper waits." Randolph curled his lower lip inward and laughed. He then stepped forward and held out his hand for me to take it. "Ain't this rich, Darlin'? I get the pot of gold and rid the vermin all in one shot."

"Theo is more of a man than you'll ever be. His father lacked a conscience as you do, Randolph." Theodore's eyes told me to stay quiet, but I ignored him. "Theodore, Randolph raped your mother and had her killed. Allison is your half-sister. He's planned this all along, because he knew of my family's ability. My father's clairvoyance has been Randolph's thorn, but I was the ace card. He knew I couldn't allow you or anyone else to be hurt."

A slight flicker in Theodore's eyes indicated he knew. I stepped back shaking my head.

"Lovely, Mariana." Randolph snorted. "Since this is a sharing moment, let me tell you, your baby's father is in this cellar."

My chest constricted. And I staggered back two steps

"That's right, Darlin'. All these years the father of your baby has taken care of you. Now, do as I say. We be leavin' now." Randolph snickered, but then paused and glanced over his shoulder.

Cassius moved in, pointing his gun at Theodore.

"Cas, what are you doing!" I placed myself between both of them.

"Nothing yet." He growled. "But, soon Theo's brains will be plastered on the wall."

"Mariana, don't listen to Cassius. He's having one of his mental episodes. All will be fine." Theodore said calmly.

"Shut your pathetic trap." Cassius tightened his grip on the revolver. "All this time, you've been collaborating with us and you were her attacker?"

Collaborating? I didn't have time to ask with whom. Thought and words traveled faster than my ability to process the information.

I noticed the edge of danger in Theodore's eyes. He turned toward Randolph. "Randolph, you're a bastard." His hand instinctively went into his inside pocket.

"No, Theo." I drew my Beretta from under my gown. I pointed the gun at Randolph's head. "What's goin' on? This is insane. Theo, Randolph is not worth it."

"Darlin', you are his Bell' Angelo." Randolph jeered.

Reason dissipated. *Bell' Angelo!* I stood in an empty pool surrounded by four walls with no means for thought to emerge.

"Mariana, look at me." Theodore lowered his gun and squeezed my shoulders in an attempt to jar my senses. "It was either Randolph or me. Please, understand. I couldn't *bear* the thought of him touching you. I had to do something. He came onto the campus that evening with two of his thugs. He told me his plan. I tried to stop him. Mariana, I couldn't stand by and let him touch you. I...put on his sweatshirt, then...the gloves and mask. I'm sorry, Mari. Please listen to me. I had to do it."

"Had? How about warning me? Or calling the police?" I kept my gun aimed at Randolph's head.

Numb. So numb. God, Theo is Mikey's father?

"Randolph threatened to take Allison away and *you*. You know what kind of man he is. Please, Mariana, know that—"

"All this was orchestrated. I'm a pawn. You never loved me?" Bleary eyed, I focused on Randolph's smirk.

"Mariana, because I love you, I couldn't let him do it. His men were about to hold me down and make me watch." Theo slowly caressed my arm.

Randolph's words echoed in my head. *You're his Bell' Angelo.*

"It was you, Theo. But..." I remained immobile, listening to him, and fearing that one other person was in the cellar with us. "How can this be?"

Theo shook his head. "I was going to warn you, but his henchmen pointed a gun at my head. If I died...Mari, if I had been killed, he would've taken you. Mari, *please* understand."

"That's right, Darlin'. Theodore doesn't have his father's vision or tenacity to live the life he set up for him. And with you in the picture, I knew he was becomin' soft with all the idiocy you planted in his head. You've made it easy for me."

I slowly tilted my head to the left and stared into Randolph's eyes.

It was not the realization that Theodore was my attacker or the fact he was Mikey's father that kept me glued in place, but the reality of my little boy. Mikey was in the cellar!

"Mikey?" I whispered.

Cassius came up behind me and whispered in my ear. "Mariana, Mikey's not here. Concentrate and follow my lead."

"No, Cassius. He is here. If anything happens to him..." I stepped closer to Randolph.

"Who's Mikey?" Theodore followed my lead.

"He's my son. Who brought him here?"

"Your son?" Theo now held the same distant look I had earlier.

Mikey appeared from behind a wine barrel.

"He's a special little boy—bright like his Mama. I've been following his progress. You do recall our encounter, Sweet Thang. You look mighty fine as a blonde, Mariana." Randolph jeered.

"Mariana, I had no idea." Theodore's eyes held Mikey's gaze. "He has your eyes, Mari but..."

I felt Theodore's pain never knowing his son. I screamed inside my head.

Sometimes it's better to not know. Why did Theodore have to find out this way?

Mikey's presence triggered the Soulless Witch. "Mikey, come. Hide behind me." I summoned him with my free hand.

"Mommy, the man in black is here." He pointed at Theodore.

Mikey then hid, clinging onto my gown. I turned on Randolph. "I should've done this a long time ago." I curled my finger around the trigger.

"Mariana, you're not a killer." Cassius stood his ground beside me.

A showdown of who would get the first bullet played in my head.

Tracy and Drake ran in just as one of Randolph's men entered too. Drake drew his Glock on the guy as Tracy stood at my side shielding Mikey.

"Tracy, where's Allison?"

"She's safe."

I faced Theodore. "I had no clue you were his father..." I gulped.

"That was a good thing." Randolph chuckled. "It made my days a lot easier to plan out."

I cocked the gun, ready to put a bullet through Randolph's skull when another flash of thought came to me. "It was you, Randolph. You put out a contract on Theo. You sent the hitman after us in the woods."

Randolph beamed and nodded.

I fixed my aim a little higher making certain I wouldn't miss my target.

"Tracy, take him away." She didn't move. "Now, dammit!"

From my peripheral vision I caught her glancing at Cassius. He nodded. She picked up Mikey. I heard her turn and run toward the underground passage.

"Mommy! Fall down. Go down, Mommy. Mommy!"

I exhaled a gush of air and then breathed in deeply. My little boy was gone. As he left screaming, I kept my eyes on Randolph. But, I knew if I had glanced at my son, there was five more pair of eyes on Randolph. Drake remained quiet, but I heard his deep breaths behind me.

"If you recall, Mariana, I told you the next time you pointed a gun at me, you'd better use it. Your mistake, darlin'."

"Randolph one thing you're not is stupid. Drop your gun." Cassius's baritone voice reverberated against my eardrums.

"Yes, but I've always been a gambling man. I'll fire before you hit your mark." Randolph pointed the gun at my head. "What do you say my odds are, Mr. Russo?"

"Zero to none." Cassius's trigger finger twitched.

"Huh." Randolph grunted. "Perhaps, you're willing to gamble, Mr. Russo, if not, the beauty leaves with me."

"Not going to happen, Randolph. Your time has ended here." Cassius stretched his arm out further.

I stood steadfast, watching my dream in slow motion only this time it was real.

Open your mouth and scream, Mariana. Do something. Don't stand there like an idiot and watch it all over again.

"Theo! No!" I tried to move.

Theodore pushed me out of the way as Randolph fired his gun. Theo's eyes were the last I saw before my head met the concrete floor. Cassius and Drake fired a few rounds simultaneously. Theo's men hit the concrete dead as did Randolph's. I heard Cassius groan, as he fired his Glock once more.

Pain seared down the middle of my cranium, but adrenaline kept me alert. I flipped onto my back and pointed my gun toward Randolph, but was too late. He dropped next to my feet with a hole between his brows and another in his chest.

Theodore wavered with his gun in hand and then fell. I pushed myself up to my knees and cradled his head in my lap. Randolph's bullet had pierced Theodore's heart.

"I'm sorry, Mari." He gasped. "I believe my bill has been paid in full." Theodore coughed. His short, ragged breaths gurgled in his blood. I pressed my wrap over his chest.

"Please, Theo, hang on. Please!" *There's so much blood.* "Theo, do you hear me? Hang on."

Behind a curtain of disbelief, I watched Theodore's lips form the words, 'I love you'. He then closed his eyes.

Fate, you're so cruel? I'm find out he's Mikey's father and then you take him away.

"Mariana, he's gone. Let's go. We don't have much time before the tunnels blow like Mt. Saint Helens."

I lifted my head and gazed blankly into Cassius's eyes. I then saw blood dripping from his hand. Cassius had been hit in his left shoulder.

Had he not stopped me in the ball room this scenario might have played out differently?

I felt my body stiffen and my head lolled to the side.

"Damn it woman! Bury the Tin-Man. It's over. Randolph can't manipulate your life any longer and—"

"Cassius, he's dead. Mikey's father is gone."

"Yeah, he had it comin'. Mariana, can you walk?"

I stood, but stumbled. Cassius grabbed my arm and kept me steady.

"You hit your head harder than I thought." Cassius said as he winced.

Blood matted my hair and face. He took my wrap from my hands and wound it around my head.

Theo's blood is touching mine, ironically, too late.

"All this time, Mikey's father was near him. Could I have stopped this?" I spoke out loud not caring who heard.

Why must a child pay for his father's sins?

"Mariana, none of this is your fault. Snap out of it." Cassius took hold of my chin. "Did you hear me?"

"Sir, we must go now!" A man I had never met before ran into the cellar shouting. "Randolph, set his own bombs throughout the mansion. We have about five minutes!"

"Sanders, is everyone else out of range?"

"Yes Sir."

"All right then, get out of here."

"Cassius, there are tunnels under the mansion, that's how they smuggled the guns."

"I know. Look I'm sorry it went down like this, but there's no time to sit here and think about what could've been. We need to go."

"It's all over. Mikey is safe?" I felt my toes and fingers numbing.

"Yes, and so are you. Look at me. Mariana, can you walk?"

"Cassius, I saw you in my dreams and heard the gunshot, but I never saw who it hit."

I buckled under the weight of exhaustion and pain. Cassius drew me to my feet. I pushed away from him and started to pull Theodore's body towards the tunnel, leading to the woods. Cassius stopped me.

"Cassius, he saved my life."

"Mariana, he raped you." Deep grooves mapped Cassius's forehead.

"Cassius, I forgave my attacker a long time ago." I curled my fingers even tighter under Theodore's arms and pulled.

"Ah hell. Drake, get her out of here."

"Wait, where's Mikey and Allison?" My vision started to blur.

"They're with Tracy in the woods. Go, now!"

Drake without warning threw me over his shoulder. Cassius did the same to Theodore's body.

"Drake, I can walk." I squirmed.

Drake held me tighter and said, "Sorry, did you say something? No time to chat, I've got a dance to go to. My girl is waitin' for me in the woods and you're goin' that way too."

I could hear Cassius's and Drake's heavy breaths as they ran toward the tree line, but the pain had me close my eyes.

How did I not see Theodore was Mikey's father?

Drake propped me against a tree trunk and hovered near. Tracy sat next to us with Mikey and Allison in her embrace.

"Mommy!" Mikey's voice ripped into my thoughts. He scooted closer to me and buried his face in my lap. I doubled-over his little body.

I sensed Mikey had known for quite some time that I was his mother.

He's so young to have kept such a secret. I put this on him.

Mikey glanced up at me and said, "You needed my help, Mommy."

"I did, Mikey." I held him closer to me.

The Earth rumbled and the sky lit up as if it were the Fourth of July. The house I longed to escape from was gone. A new blank page was waiting to be written.

Freedom. Mikey is finally with me.

Cassius led us through the woods to vans waiting in a clearing. A man approached him. They shook hands.

"Good work, agent Russo. I want a full report in my hands by the end of the week."

"Yes, sir."

"Have all parties affiliated with this operation been terminated."

"Yes, Sir, and the laboratory, arms bunker, and the tunnels have been destroyed."

"Excellent. Is that Theodore Russo?"

"Yes, sir. He assisted us on this operation from the beginning."

I stood with Mikey at my side. I glared at Cassius, before the ache in my head took over and my equilibrium failed.

Cassius ran up to us and cradled me in his arms. "I gotcha, Bright Eyes. I promise I'll explain everything to you. Mariana, I love you." His eyes glistened.

"So many lies, *Agent* Russo?" I blacked out.

* * *

Two days later, after I was discharged from the hospital, Cassius came to the farm with his arm in a sling. It had been a clean shot, straight through the shoulder. He found me in the library and explained his mission and duty, but my new reality was too fresh to absorb the truth all at once and accept the outcome.

Cassius said to me, "Mariana, I'll give you some time to digest this info. A month should be ample time, don't you think?"

He believes a month is enough to erase so many lies?

I simply looked him in the eye. The man knew how to infuriate me, but I couldn't deny the fact that I loved him.

He smiled when he saw the fiery spark come alive within me and said, "My Bright Eyes is back."

"Your Bright Eyes? Think again, Cassius."

"Mariana, you were quick to forgive your attacker, but not me?"

"Hmm, it took me three years to forgive. Are you, Cassius, willing to wait that long."

He shook his head. "I'm a goner, Mariana. I have no choice, but to wait."

I had not expected his response, and instead just stared back at him. A smile spread across his lips and then he left me sitting in my lonely corner of the library near the French windows.

I wondered why I should allow Cassius into my life again. As if on cue, Mikey entered and sat in my lap. "Mommy, the moon is blue." He wrapped his chubby arms around my neck.

I thought of Mikey's drawing tucked away safely in my armoire drawer. I saw the stars and the moon and the words, "Cassius will love me only in a blue moon," resurfaced. I caressed my son's soft curls. How good it felt to finally have him in my arms and know that I would see him from now on.

He let go of me when I said, "Yes, the moon is blue, Mikey." We then sat in silence relishing the moment.

CHAPTER 23

A BUMPY ROAD LEADS TO FAMILY

The human mind has evolved, but one may argue the fact if it has been for the better? There is no denying technology has improved man's life. Humans who are paraplegic now walk, the deaf hear, the maimed have functioning robotic arms and legs, but...where there is good the bad follows.

Randolph was a vile man, but shrewd. The day he ran into Mikey and me in town, which now I know hadn't been a coincidence, he handed me his card. I took the three by two inch paper stock and tossed it into the jeep's cup holder and didn't give it another thought. Unknown to me, Mikey hid it in his pocket.

The simple act of a child's curiosity set the course of events. Randolph's calling card had a micro-chip imbedded in the paper's fibers. A tracking device that signaled my son's every step.

Mikey later told me Bianca had found it in his favorite sweatshirt pocket when she was doing the laundry. As fate would have it, Bianca thought it strange and handed the seemingly innocent piece of paper to my brother, Frank, who in turn didn't accept coincidences sent it to his tech friends.

The computer gurus were one day late in discovering the micro-chip. By then Randolph had found Mikey and abducted him in the middle of the night. My son had been under the same roof as me for several hours, before I knew he was near.

A clairvoyant child is still but a child. Mikey might or might not have known the peril he had placed himself in, but the evening I saw my son in the cellar, his eyes told the story— "I have arrived mother. I'm here to protect you."

274

Mikey, the child I chose not to abort, the child who is my life's light, was the key to Randolph's doom. His greed drove him to take my son because he believed he would have us both. Randolph would have used Mikey as a pawn, knowing I would do his bidding to protect him. Irony's steel fist took hold in the cold, dank cellar where sad memories of the past resided. It became Randolph's tomb.

One might think that Randolph would have disappeared with Mikey, but his ego controlled his common sense. I felt and saw the satisfaction in Randolph's eyes when I realized Mikey was ten feet away from me, hidden behind wine barrels.

I later realized that Mikey had known the outcome of our predicament in the cellar. Re-winding my memories and replaying them, I recalled the last words he said to me before Tracy ran out with him. He said, "Mommy, go down." Mikey was telling me to dodge the bullet.

Life's lines intertwine, leading humans to what we may perceive as a mistake or a coincidence, but are they really? Or, is fate leading us through life lessons?

A month later, salvation and forgiveness swathed me in a peaceful realization that my life had taken a turn for the better.

Bianca and Carla came by to visit me, and we had a heart to heart about Cassius. They explained how he battled against not telling me that he was an FBI agent. He feared my knowing would place me in more danger than I already was. What would have been the outcome can't be said, but what Carla told me is what stuck and lit the fire in my heart once again, and then I knew that Cassius was meant for me.

She said, "Mariana, when Cassius was ten, he was playing in the front yard with Buster our dog and without warning, he stopped, and dropped to his knees. I ran out of the kitchen and knelt next to him, thinking he'd somehow been hurt. I asked him, 'Son, what's wrong?' With tears in his eyes, he said, "Momma, she lost her red balloon."

Carla went on to say that her son never talked about that one incident ever again and he himself does not recall saying it, but I felt the strong connection between us. Cassius was my soul mate.

A week after their visit Cassius returned to the farm. I sat in the library near the French windows where so many of my ancestors had shared the view of the homestead.

He approached me slowly and knelt at my side. I knew before he even said anything. He wiped my tears and said, "Bright Eyes, will you marry me?"

"Yes, but only if you buy me that red balloon." I caressed his face.

"My mother told you." I nodded yes. Cassius laid his head in my lap and wept.

I believe the years of pain we shared, Cassius without his father, and I without my mother, was erased by our union.

We talked through the night in the library until the sun peeked above the horizon and the birds chirped their melancholy song. Happiness was but a finger tip away. Cassius explained why he hadn't told me he was an agent. I understood the mission was important, but I wished he had trusted me enough to tell me what was going on and save us both a lot of heartache. Cassius assured me, our love was real and that from that day forward I was a big part of his life where only truth existed. I looked into his eyes as he told me that and I laughed. I had to admit that had I known of the mission, I most likely would have tried to change the course of his plans because at the time I believed he was working for Theodore. However, there was one truth still hovering in his thoughts, wanting to be told. I could feel and see it in his eyes. I questioned him, but I knew asking wouldn't bring it forth. And so I played the waiting game, expecting, and knowing that in due time he would come to me.

Our wedding took place on The Outskirt's grounds. Mikey was our ring bearer, Allison my maid of honor and of course, Drake was Cassius's best man. After the wedding ceremony, Cassius handed me a red balloon with his name and mine on it. Together we released it into the air in memory of my mother, Amelia Castillo.

Should I have been wary of so much happiness? No, life was as it should be.

* * *

Nearly a year later, I stood near the oven as the bacon sizzled in the pan. Cassius dropped sliced bread in the toaster. Mikey hummed in the corner of the family room, pushing his truck and trailer filled with farm animals and Cassandra, our baby girl, cooed in her bassinet. The ninja Mariana was gone and if I had any control over my destiny, that part of my life would remain in the past.

This is how it should be, Cassius and I together in our own home with our children. I always dreamed of having my own place.

I flipped the bacon to crisp the other side when a small gasp escaped me. Cassius had kissed my neck and said, "Hmm, domesticity suits you."

I slipped away from his touch and poured orange juice into a sippy cup.

Cassius's eyes danced as he followed me around the kitchen island.

I then opened a cupboard and grabbed a bowl. I tilted my head his way as I cracked and dropped eggs into the bowl. "And what suits you, Mr. Russo."

"Watching you scramble those eggs suits me just fine, Mrs. Russo." He planted another kiss near my shoulder blade.

I still had on my nightgown. In this household everyone was an early riser, not taking the day for granted.

"So, are you saying you want me in submission— the pro-verbial barefoot and pregnant?"

"Uh, no, as if there were any chance of that." He chuckled.

Cassius skillfully skirted to the side as I tried to swat his butt with the whisk and said, "But, I do love the barefoot image and the act that might lead to pregnancy. That suits me just fine." He planted his soft lips on mine.

"Hmmph." I beat the eggs faster until they foamed.

"Are you going to cook those eggs or beat them to extinction?" He smirked.

"I plan to cook them, as soon as you stop distracting me." I swayed over to the stove-top, knowing that I was teasing him. I turned off the burner and scooped the bacon onto a plate.

He came around the island and wrapped his arms around me. I rested my head on his shoulder.

"Cassius it was you who tore the page from the journal?"

"Yes. Like you said, I was not drunk, just crazy in love with you." He kissed my neck again. "Why did you wait until now to ask?" He spread butterfly kisses behind my ears.

"I knew it was you, when I saw the shock in Theodore's eyes, but I thought I'd ask now. Cas, I still can't believe that Jacks is your father. All these years, and he's still alive."

"I'm sorry you had to go through the pain of your mom and then my dad. But seeing your face, when you saw him at The Outskirts helped me remember how happy I was to see him too, and that I do love him, even though he left us."

"But, Cas…" I turned to face him.

"Shh," He placed a finger over my lips. "I know. You and my father did what you thought was best for the family, and I'd be a liar if I said I wouldn't have done the same. I know sweetheart."

Cassius traced my lips, and moved in slowly to plant a kiss on them.

"Mr. Russo we have two little ones waiting on breakfast and then we have Aunt Samantha's birthday party to get to."

"Yes, but it's early. And we're only one hour away from the inn. How about after breakfast you show me how you sway those hips in my hands?" His soft lips trailed down my neck, giving me goose bumps.

"Uh, maybe?" I poured the eggs in the pan and started scrambling them.

"I'll take that as a yes." He set another trail of kisses on the back of my shoulders.

"You're guessing can leave you disappointed." I scrambled faster with every kiss.

"I suppose it can, but I'll wager that this time I'm right." He chuckled deeply in his throat.

I finished cooking the breakfast and then turned to face him. "Mr., you're always so full of guesses, but you never suspected that I was pregnant. You were clueless. Just goes to show you that you were wrong about me. I can keep a secret."

"Bright Eyes, when it comes to womanly things you have to spell it out for me."

"Uh-huh and then some." I smirked. He tickled me mercilessly.

Needless to say, Cassius scarfed his breakfast down eyeing me hungrily.

CHAPTER 24

EVENTUALLY TRUTH
IS REVEALED

"Mariana, what do you see in your dreams?" Aunt Samantha sat in an outdoor reclining chair in the Outskirts' backyard. Her eyes were half closed, but I sensed she was sharper than ever.

"I see a future with my family," I said. "This is such a peaceful place."

"Yes, it is." Aunt Samantha nodded. She had suggested we celebrate her birthday at the Outskirts, since traveling had become a chore for Jacks.

I sat on a blanket close to Aunt Samantha and placed my hands on her knees. I stared at the woman who knew the true definition of pain, adversity, and happiness.

Aunt Samantha peered down at me and said, "The moon hides tonight…"

"But the dreams remain bright." I finished the sentence and took hold of her hands in mine, giving them a little squeeze.

Wrinkles danced from the corners of her eyes as she smiled back. We glanced upward when my father approached.

"Momma Bear, your cub is hungry." My father laid my daughter in my arms. She squirmed, puckering her lips.

"Thanks, Dad."

He kissed my forehead. "I'm very proud of you, Mariana. You found your way back home."

The lump in my throat kept me from answering him.

"Mommy, watch!"

I twisted around in my seat to see *my son*. Those words made my heart feel as if it would burst from happiness.

Mikey held a yellow plastic bat. "Okay, Daddy, I'm ready."

"Keep your eye on the target, little man." Cassius tossed the ball.

I held my breath. Mikey swung the bat. A distinct *pop* was heard. Laughter and applause showered the air.

"Run, little man. Go." Cassius waved his hands while jogging toward first base.

"I'ma gonna get ya." Drake ran with the ball in hand after Mikey.

His young giggles traveled in the summer breeze while his little legs ran as fast as they could to the base. Drake trailed behind. Mikey dived onto the paper plate.

"Safe!" Frank shouted.

"Ah! Next time, Mikey. Next time." Drake threw the ball in the air.

"I did it, I did it!" Mikey jumped up and down. "Mommy, did you see me?"

I waved.

Cassius swooped him into his arms. "That's my little man." He and Mikey joined us.

"Mommy! Daddy can teach you how to hit the ball too." Mikey jumped up and down, wide eyed. His face was covered in a dust mask that made him look like a bandit.

They sat next to me. Cassius wrapped an arm over my shoulders and kissed me. Mikey sat in his lap. Unconsciously, Cassius twisted the gold band around his wedding finger. A wide smile spread across his face.

"I'd love to teach Mommy how to hit the ball. But I think she'll teach me first."

Mikey scooted closer and placed Cheerio-kisses on his sister's forehead.

"Mommy, Cassie smells good." His four year old hands cradled her head.

"Yes, she does." I kissed his cheek.

Bianca came out of the house holding a cake covered in candles. Allison followed. She was playing the 'Happy Birthday' melody on her violin. They started singing and the rest of the family gathered around Aunt Samantha.

Mikey ran up to Allison and wrapped his pudgy arms around her waistline. Sweet Allison had been freed from a corrupted life. She and Mikey were like twins. Many times they had their heads side by side working on a puzzle or coloring a favorite picture in a book. When Mikey was told that Allison was his biological aunt, he actually cried. We asked him why he was crying and he simply said, "I have an auntie and Mommy now." That was a good enough explanation for all of us.

There were times I found myself wishing Theodore's part in all this had played out differently, but 'Everything happens for a reason'. The happy birthday melody ended. Allison, set the violin on the table, lowered her eyes and joined me on the grass. She was content. The Outskirts had become her new home.

On hearing the last note, Aunt Samantha clasped her hands. "Well, if this isn't the best Cream Puff I've ever seen." That was Aunt Samantha's way of saying she was extremely happy. She pulled a handkerchief from her sweater pocket and blew into it, then said, "My family is united again." She eyed Allison. "Welcome, sweet Allison. You *are* home now."

Allison fixed her eyes on Aunt Samantha, an uncommon occurrence. She actually smiled and said, "Home. Yes, I'm home."

Fortunately, Aunt Samantha didn't say a word, or she would've had everyone sniffing and wiping their eyes.

"Auntie, blow the candles. Blow the candles." Mikey said as he hopped up and down.

"Mikey, Auntie Samantha needs to make a wish first." Bianca placed a hand on his head to keep him from toppling over on the cake.

"Oh, okay. Auntie Samantha, make a wish, then we eat cake." He dug a dusty finger in the icing.

"Hey now little man you know better than that." Cassius tickled him. "Let's go wash your hands."

Giggles came from my son—giggles which I had waited to hear for three years. His eyes smiled as he skipped beside Cassius to a hose in the front yard.

Hands washed, Mikey ran back. "You ready Auntie, Samantha?" He squirmed impatiently.

"Yes, I believe I am now." Aunt Samantha leaned forward, inhaled and exhaled as hard as she could. The flames flickered then faded.

Mikey ran up to me and whispered in my ear. "Mommy, Auntie Samantha's wish has come true."

"It has?"

"Uh, huh." He nodded vigorously. "She wished for the moon to be blue forever."

I eyed Aunt Samantha. She nodded yes and sat back in the chair.

Mikey then whispered in my ear again. "Mommy, Uncle Drake and Auntie Tracy ordered a baby too."

I felt my eyes widen. My head snapped to where Drake sat with Tracy in his lap.

"Mikey, what kind of secrets are you telling your Mom over there?" Drake wiggled his fingers, insinuating a tickling attack.

Mikey cupped his mouth and hid behind Cassius.

Tracy gave me the shhh sign.

I leaned my head back in sweet bliss and thought, if only I could bottle this moment and bring it out when gloomy days came around.

This is the life I've been seeking. I hope that I'll know how to listen and follow fate's direction.

Chuckles near the picnic table interrupted my inner monologue. I turned my head to see Frank helping Bianca place the full sheet of cake on the table. He stole a kiss, thinking no one had seen him. They cut the cake together when Frank sensed someone looking at him. He tilted his head and waved a finger at me. It was his sign, telling me to be good and not say anything yet. Secrets, my family and their secrets, it was amusing actually. Nothing ever changes—life just presents more colorful moments when it decides it's the right time.

Mikey crept up slowly towards me as he eyed his Uncle Frank. "Mommy, I have one more secret."

"Just one more, Mikey?" I laughed.

"Uh-huh."

"Okay, what is it?"

He brushed hair from my ear as his whispering breath tickled me. "Uncle Frankie, loves dancing with Auntie Bianca."

"Is that right?" I glanced back at the two of them. In a clear voice for all to hear I said, "So, Uncle Frank doesn't have two left feet anymore."

In three wide strides, Frank gathered Mikey into his arms. "You, little sneaky raccoon, need to keep our secrets between us. He tickled Mikey's stomach."

"Okay, okay, I promise." Mikey wiggled in Frank's arms.

"Pinky promise?" Frank held up his pinky. "Repeat what I say, Mikey."

"All right, Uncle Frankie."

"I, Michael Samuel Castillo, will guard Uncle Frank's secrets with my life."

Smirking, Mikey linked pinkies with Frank. "I, Michael, will protect Uncle Frankie and family forever."

"You rascal that's not what I said, but I like what *you* said better. You're off the hook." Frank set him on the ground and ruffled his hair.

"That's my boy." Cassius choked.

Mikey ran up to Cassius, wrapped his arms around his leg and looking up at him said, "I be like you, Daddy."

Cassius planted a kiss on Mikey's head. "Little Man, you're my hero."

The porch screen creaked. All heads turned to see Jacks, Carla and my dad descend the house veranda. They helped Jacks keep his step steady.

Jacks shuffled on and pointed a finger in my direction. He sat in a lawn chair near me and patted my hand. A grand smile spread across his face. "Hoo..me n.. noww...fam..ilyy... firrrst."

With each day, Jacks struggled more and more to speak, but the fact that he was able to hold his grandbaby and be with his family again was what he lived for.

"Yes, family first, Jacks." I kissed him on the cheek. Cassandra, sleeping in my arms, hiccupped.

Jacks, with a shaky finger, caressed her cheek. "Fammiily." He then glanced up at his son. Cassius crouched near me.

"How did we get here, Bright Eyes? I mean, I'm not dreaming, right?"

"I pinched him for good measure."

"Hey, I guess I'm not." He rubbed his bicep.

I laughed. "We arrived here eleven months ago, when you brought me home, proposed to me out of the blue and then we met up with your family and mine."

"A lot happens in eleven months." Cassius kissed our daughter's head.

"Definitely." We watched our baby girl pucker her lips.

"Mariana?" Cassius called me to attention. "I should've told you this a long time ago, but chalk it up to me being a coward."

"You? No. Not my Cassius."

"Sh, let me finish, please. Your mother—" His eyes filled with tears.

I squeezed his arm. "Cas, I know. My mother is watching over us right now."

"No. Listen."

"Cassius, I've been listening. I watch. I hear and follow. I know how she died, Cassius. And I know it was an accident." I gave Jacks a quick wink. "Family is where we belong. Right, Jacks?"

My father-in-law breathed a throaty yes and nodded.

"How long have you known?" Cassius said.

"When we came back to The Outskirts, Jacks and I talked." I caressed his cheek.

Cassius sought his father's confirmation. One look at his father and he knew I spoke the truth. His brow lifted high. I thought it might stay permanently that way.

"Dad, you let me sweat it all these months, knowing she already knew?"

Jacks laughed and everyone else joined in.

"Secrets are paybacks for secrets, right Agent Russo?"

He huffed, running a hand through his gorgeous thick wavy hair. "Yeah, right?"

"Cassius, I forgave my attacker. You must forgive and allow yourself to heal." I lay my free hand over his heart. "Cas, no more secrets. Heart of my heart, together we be for eternity."

Cassius leaned in slowly, "No more secrets, unless it's a birthday surprise," and even slower he kissed me.

I laughed heartily in silence, for I knew families hold on to secrets.

I stole a peek at Aunt Samantha while Cassius held me wrapped in his arms. She closed her eyes and nodded contentedly.

The ache when I awake is felt for humanity's sake. The burn in my gut, the want to forget that my son was given to me by rape will not dissipate, but... Mikey's love will coat the wound in my heart. And...family is the mortar of my sanity's foundation.

Review Requested:
If you loved this book, would you please provide a review at Amazon.com?

Printed in June 2019
by Rotomail Italia S.p.A., Vignate (MI) - Italy